Elusive Quarry

By R.W. Barton

"Elusive Quarry" is a work of fiction. Places, characters, events, incidents and capabilities are the product of the author's imagination or are used fictitiously.
Any resemblance to persons, living or dead, are purely coincidental.

ISBN – 13: 978-0-9903789-3-8

Elusive Quarry is Dedicated

To Laurie

Elusive Quarry

Chapter One

Saturday—September 10
Socotra Island—New Persia Compound

Khatib Al Daye was disturbed in his sleep by a loud knock on his door. A runner from the operations center was trying to wake him up, and he didn't like it. It was the middle of the night, or very early morning, and he had had an exhausting day. The relatively cool night air on tropical Socotra Island, just off the eastern horn of Africa in the Indian Ocean, was pleasant, and he did not like being disturbed. But the knocking was persistent. He grumbled as he got up and answered the door. The runner quickly told him that Abdul-Hakim, their defense minister, had ordered that he be awakened and that he was to come to the operations center immediately. There was an emergency that required his presence. He hurriedly got dressed, wondering what the problem could be in the middle of the night, and quickly walked the short distance down to the New Persia Operations Center. He looked around. There was a great deal of activity, and it was obvious that the security teams were busy sorting out what was going on.

He located Abdul-Hakim and got a quick briefing from him. The sensors were not accurate, the monitors were not displaying what was really happening, and it appeared that the infidel Americans had invaded the island compound. The rapid response team was out and there were intruders detected on the beach. The ayatollah was missing and it was assumed that the Americans had taken him away.

When he heard of the probable kidnapping of the ayatollah, Khatib Al Daye retreated to his small office, off the operations center, to think. He was stunned that this had come to pass, and, given the instructions he had received from the ayatollah several weeks before, was wrestling with his conscience. In addition to running the New Persia movement, he was now required to eliminate and replace the defense minister. The task before him was very difficult. He never thought it would come to pass. He looked out the window at the darkness of the early morning and slowly closed his eyes in concentrated thought. It would take all his reserves to accomplish

1

the second tasking to remove Abdul-Hakim, and it went against nearly all his internal instincts. He shook his head and went into the ayatollah's office, opened the drawer, and verified the gun was still there and loaded. Khatib, twenty-eight years old, tall, thin, and intense looking, with a wisp of a beard, took a deep breath and looked at the door. He walked out and down the corridor to the operations center. He had to complete the directions, but, he decided, not just now. They could wait a few days.

He walked into the operations center and located Abdul-Hakim near a console. Some form of calm and deliberate action needed to be established, and then the larger problem of continuing the movement could be addressed.

After determining that the sensors and other alarm systems were malfunctioning, maintenance personnel were dispatched to find the problems and fix them. Both Khatib and Abdul-Hakim were quite busy sorting priorities, sending out crews, and attending to the crisis.

Abdul-Hakim was trying to think of a way to retrieve the ayatollah from the Americans. The directions were crystal clear from Khatib: he needed to recover the ayatollah, and do it quickly. The implied threat was very real. Since he didn't know where the ayatollah had been taken, or how he was being transported, there simply was no solution for him.

Over the next few days, both Khatib and Abdul-Hakim worked issues and were able to see some of the shortfalls in the French-installed security systems. As the various issues came to the surface, Khatib was frequently glaring at Abdul-Hakim for his perceived carelessness, and Abdul-Hakim was frantically trying to find out what had happened to the ayatollah. There had been no news on his location or what might have happened to him.

Several of the guards that were on duty that night had been killed in the fighting near the beach, and funerals needed tending to. Always a distasteful but necessary task. Abdul-Hakim saw to the details.

Khatib was constantly mulling over the direction he knew he must follow. He was torn by the requirement and knew it was inevitable. But he did not want to face it until forced to do so.

Wednesday—September 14
Washington, D.C.

A press release was distributed to the U.S. media telling them of the capture and return of the ayatollah to the United States.

It included information that the ayatollah, an international terrorist criminal in the eyes of the U.S. Justice Department, would be held for a federal trial to be conducted in the near future. No other information was released, and there was little reaction around the world as other matters took center stage.

Wednesday—September 14
Socotra Island—New Persia Compound

However, there was a reaction in the Socotra New Persia Operations Center when the press release was read. It was quite obvious that Abdul-Hakim had failed to protect the ayatollah and that it would be very difficult to rescue him.

Khatib Al Daye, the ayatollah's principal assistant, after reading the brief press release, returned to his room for further thought. It was time.

Khatib stepped into the operations center and motioned for Abdul-Hakim to follow him to the ayatollah's office. Once in the office, Khatib shut the door, walked over to the ayatollah's desk, turned and faced Abdul-Hakim, and said, "You have failed us again. The ayatollah warned you before that there could be no more failures, and now he is in the hands of the infidels." He hesitated. This situation was very distasteful.

Khatib continued, "Do you remember what the ayatollah told you early last month? That failure again was not an option for you? That he expected you to make sure we were secure? That you were not to fail again?"

Abdul-Hakim looked at the ceiling and thought, *This is hardly the time for this.* But, as he returned Khatib's gaze, he said, "Yes. Of course I remember that conversation. What of it?"

"You have failed again. And this time really failed to the point we may have a problem holding this movement together. When you left this office after that conversation, the ayatollah gave me some additional instructions, and I intend to carry them out." As he spoke, he reached into the drawer in the desk and pulled out a Ruger model 306 .357 Magnum revolver. Continuing, he said, "The ayatollah said that if you failed again, you were to be terminated and a replacement head of security would be named."

Abdul-Hakim backed up as the pistol came into sight. His eyes got wide and he began to sweat. He looked at the gun then back to Khatib's eyes. He just barely whispered, "No."

"You have failed. Ramiz will be your replacement." And Khatib quickly raised the gun and fired two shots into Abdul-

Hakim's chest. Abdul-Hakim looked down at his chest, and the bloody blossoms, as he staggered backward, arms flailing to his sides from the bullet impacts, and collapsed to the floor. He died nearly instantly, as did his earlier vow to get back at the infidels.

Khatib slowly placed the weapon back in the desk drawer and looked sadly at Abdul-Hakim, lying dead on the floor of the office. He was regretful, and sad, as he quickly recalled several times in the past he and Abdul-Hakim had worked together on various projects within the New Persia movement. After a moment, he slowly shook his head and reached for the desk telephone.

Khatib, using the intercom system, called two guards in and told them to bury Abdul-Hakim's body in the cemetery within the hour. The two startled guards looked at the body of their supervisor, hesitated momentarily, and looked at each other and then back to Khatib. He motioned with his hands for them to get moving.

Finally one, then the other, picked up Abdul-Hakim's body and took it away. Khatib stood there for several moments contemplating what he had done. He had not directly killed anybody before, and it was troubling to him. It was ugly. But the ayatollah had told him to terminate Abdul-Hakim if there was another failure. He was just carrying out the ayatollah's wishes.

Khatib, after dealing with Abdul-Hakim and directing the immediate internment of his body, as called for in the Islam religion, called Ramiz Al Sahaf—tall, affable, American educated, and also intense in his beliefs—in to discuss the situation.

Ramiz arrived shortly with a quizzical look on his face. He didn't know what to expect and walked in hesitatingly. He now knew, as did most of the operations center personnel, that Abdul-Hakim was dead. Now he had been summoned to Khatib's presence. He was a bit nervous as he stepped into the ayatollah's office where Khatib waited.

Khatib began brusquely, "Ramiz, you are now the head of our security section. Abdul-Hakim has been dealt with, and we feel you are the most qualified person to take over his responsibilities. Even though the Americans have abducted the ayatollah, we still have very serious security concerns here. We also need to find out if there is any way to return the ayatollah to us. With your background, you should be able to find out how we might accomplish these tasks. In the meantime, I want you to make sure we are secure and that another infidel attack on us will fail."

Ramiz was amazed that he had been selected to run the security section of the Socotra Operations Center and the rest of the New Persia movement, but was also determined to ensure the security of the group. He responded, "I shall do as you request. May I assume that I can have the resources required to accomplish this tasking? And are we still planning on moving to another location?"

"Yes. Apply the resources you need. As for a move, that needs further discussion. The ayatollah did not want to leave here, but given the circumstances, we need to reconsider that decision."

"Can I also assume that you are in charge until we return the ayatollah to his proper position with us?"

"Yes. I am in charge, and will remain so for the immediate future."

Ramiz looked at Khatib. It was obvious to him that Khatib was being very aggressive and taking charge. At this early point, as far as he knew, it had not been decided by anyone other than Khatib. He was just assuming the power that had been the ayatollah's. But this was the way things were usually done in these organizations. And as long as Ramiz was in charge of security, and backed Khatib, there was little doubt that Khatib would be able to carry it off. After all, Khatib had the ear of the ayatollah, knew all of the New Persia plans well, was young and very knowledgeable, and had the forceful personality to direct the organization.

"We will be holding a council meeting later today so I can get things moving and continue with the rebuilding of our organization," Khatib said. "We will continue with our discussion in the small conference room at 2:00 p.m."

At 2:00 p.m., Khatib gathered all of the ministers together in the small conference room, directed that the door be closed, and began the meeting. Looking around the room, it was very apparent that a great deal of tension and uncertainty was present.

"As you are all now aware, the ayatollah has been kidnapped from our compound and taken away. According to the press release, he is somewhere in the U.S. now. And just to make sure you are all aware, Abdul-Hakim is no longer with us, and Ramiz"—he nodded at Ramiz—"will assume the security responsibilities. When events such as these occur, strong leadership is required in any organization. The ayatollah is gone for now and may not be back for quite some time. As his principal assistant, I am taking charge of the organization and continuing with our mission and goals. Here is a note from the ayatollah anticipating our current problem." He took a piece of paper, pointed at the ayatollah's signature, and handed it to the first person at the table. "As you can see, he has identified me as the successor should he run into the situation he is currently in."

He stopped and looked at each of the other ministers present, and each either looked right back at him with no emotion, or looked back at him and nodded their agreement. He continued, "I think you will all agree that, with my knowledge of the ayatollah's goals and methods, I am the best qualified to assume his position temporarily until we can return him to us."

Again, he interrupted himself and looked around. Ramiz shifted forward in his seat and leaned on the table looking around. No one met his gaze. He looked back at Khatib with a slight nod, then sat back in his chair.

After a moment of complete silence, Ghanim, the operations planner, spoke up. "And what of the ayatollah? What shall be done to rescue him and return him to us? Do we need to be planning an operation to accomplish that?"

"Yes," replied Khatib. "We do need to do that, but only after we find out where, specifically, he has been taken and where he is being held. Ramiz will head that effort, since he was educated in the U.S. and is very familiar with the country and its various ways." Looking at Ghanim, Khatib continued, "He will have to work with you after that information is available. Until then, we can do nothing about the situation. But we need to continue with our efforts to stop the oil imports and get the world to reduce their dependence on oil for energy. Our basic mission requirements have not changed, and your planned efforts for the future will go on as envisioned."

Ghanim then asked, "Why don't we negotiate this and get the western powers to accede to our needs that way? Why the need for violence?"

Khatib looked over at Ghanim and said with a great deal of disdain and impatience, "Ghanim, we have gone over this before. Because a negotiation, by definition, means reducing our demands through compromise, and that means we lose. The west will not reduce their oil requirements and usage unless they are forced to do so. I feel that way, the ayatollah feels that way, and that is why we are on the course we are on. No one in this world ever achieved a major change without forcing it on someone. Force is the answer, not compromise. By the time a compromise is actually reached, the resources will have been used up and the compromise is useless. It makes no sense. The huge use of oil must be slowed to a trickle and other sources of energy used more effectively. But, unfortunately, the only way to do that is to force the issue. The major oil companies and their support systems are entrenched financially and politically in the western governments. They continue to grow and become more powerful at the expense of the Middle East and its resources. They have to be forced to stop. The west won't do it voluntarily."

There was nodding and raised eyebrows around the room. Then Khatib said, "I will set up a series of meetings with each of you, and you can update me on your current status in your area of expertise. After I have completed those meetings, I will get all of you together again and we will determine a course of action and any changes that may need to be made to our current plans."

In the end, after the meeting and conversation was over, Khatib had taken charge of the New Persia organization and was moving forward with its mission goals. By pure guts and determination, he had taken over.

Later that day, Khatib began getting his reviews accomplished with each of his ministers. As part of the reviews, he was also watching each of the men for any hesitancy that might indicate some reluctance to accept him as the leader. Fortunately, he found none ... but that didn't mean there weren't any. Some may have hidden it well.

Thursday—September 15
Socotra Island—New Persia Compound

With his new responsibilities, Ramiz took quick action to resolve several issues he was aware of. After reviewing what had happened the previous Saturday night—the American commando kidnapping of the ayatollah—Ramiz immediately began increasing the number and frequency of patrols. He called the French electronic security team back in and, together, they figured out several immediate modifications to the security systems to increase effectiveness and to reduce the possibility of further sabotage. He was determined to make the compound as secure as possible. He also posted personnel at the airport and in the commercial harbor to be on the lookout for suspicious-looking people. Tourists were one thing; spies were another. The Taj Socotra hotel staff was also briefed on what to look for and what to expect should the Americans try to get back on the island.

Chapter Two

Friday—September 16
Socotra Island—New Persia Compound

Khatib, with a very busy schedule, managed to take some time to think through their current location and what, if anything, should be done about it. The Americans had kidnapped the ayatollah. They hadn't attempted to grab anyone else, and that was probably a mistake. The ayatollah did have, within New Persia, a succession identified in case of calamities that would require it. And this had come to pass.

With the ayatollah captured and hauled halfway around the world, it would require activation of the succession list in order to keep the mission going. Khatib realized all this, and had taken immediate action to implement the planning. Now he was considering the consequences. Had the Americans thought the movement would die without the ayatollah? Was that the reason they didn't grab him or some of the other senior leaders when they had a chance? If the Americans got what they came for, why would they come back? They wouldn't, until the next series of strikes by New Persia occurred. Then they might come back in force. If that happened, New Persia would have to be gone and located somewhere else. Somewhere it could still function but would be very difficult to attack.

And then there was the problem of rescuing the ayatollah. How could they do that? More than likely he would be held in a very secure facility with state-of-the-art security systems and well-trained guards. Once he was in the States, which was now the case from the press reports, and in their prison system, it would be very difficult to get him out. But they had to try. They couldn't let him rot in a U.S. prison for years. There had to be a way.

And, he thought, Ramiz was the key to that effort. While Ramiz might not be able to change the current situation of the ayatollah, he had enough understanding of the American mind to figure out how to interfere in the justice system and return the ayatollah to the New Persia movement.

Khatib called Ramiz to his office. He needed to better understand what they were facing in the American legal system. He wasn't sure how it might all unfold, and was uncomfortable with his lack of knowledge.

Ramiz arrived and said, "You called for me?"

"Yes, Ramiz. Would you please explain to me how the American court system is liable to handle the ayatollah? What are they going to do?"

Ramiz stood for a moment, thinking, then sat down. He looked at Khatib thoughtfully and said, "They will probably hold him in a prison with other, as they call them, terrorists. He will be tried in a U.S. federal court for terrorism, killing Americans on those planes, destruction of property—meaning the Gulf of Mexico oil wells—and probably a group of other, lesser charges. Assuming he is found guilty, he will be sent to an American prison. I would imagine he will end up in a supermax prison." He hesitated a moment then continued, "There will be other so-called terrorists in that prison, and I'm sure he would join them. He's not in the same situation as most terrorists. He has actually attacked the American government at high levels and caused damage to their oil industry on their own soil. And, even though he is protected by the Iranian and Yemini governments, he won't be freed to continue his activities. He has no diplomatic immunity."

Khatib looked at Ramiz with a puzzled expression.

"Supermax prison means he will be locked down in solitary and only allowed out an hour a day. No contact with other prisoners and in a super-secure area with several layers of security. Once in there, there's no way out."

"How long will all this take?"

"If I had to guess, it will be at least a year. With all the posturing, jurisdictional disputes and political maneuvering, and probable appeals, the trial itself will be sometime down the road. Then it will take some time also, maybe a few weeks, for immediate appeals to higher courts. I would estimate that it will be at least a year before he actually sees true prison time. In the meantime, he will be held in a federal facility somewhere near the trial location."

"So we are at least a year away from being able to possibly rescue him?"

Ramiz looked surprised. "I don't think we can rescue him at all. He will be under heavy guard and kept locked in secure facilities the whole time until he is moved to a supermax facility."

Khatib quickly stood up and paced the floor for a short distance. He turned back to Ramiz, smashed his hands together in a loud clap, and very angrily said, "You are the new defense minister. We need to get the ayatollah back. Even if it takes us months or years. We need him back to provide us with the leadership and respect our movement deserves. We won't give up on him. Is that understood?"

Ramiz, somewhat taken aback, said, "Of course. I was just explaining that it will not be an easy task. The Americans are tough and we cannot assume they will make any mistakes. And it will take time and planning to get ready. I think we may have just one chance at it, and we need to prepare thoroughly for it." Then he thoughtfully added, "And it has to be done before he is transferred to the supermax facility."

Khatib said with fervor, "I agree. This will take some time and significant preparation. I want you to make sure the goal is kept and that our training and skills are developed so we can accomplish this mission. He *must* be returned to us."

Ramiz momentarily looked at Khatib sharply and then said, "We also need to get some really excellent legal help on this. And it won't be cheap. He will need a defense team of some of the best lawyers in America to challenge whatever the U.S. government comes up with." Then he motioned with his open hand toward Khatib and continued, with emphasis, "That needs to be done immediately."

Khatib thought for a moment. Then he looked at Ramiz and said, "Okay. That does make sense." He hesitated then said, "How would you suggest we proceed?"

"Contact the Iranian government and see if they can help. He is an Iranian citizen and there may be something they can do. If not, perhaps they can suggest a legal team."

Khatib narrowed his eyes and said, "I will take that into consideration. Thank you for your time. You have a lot to do. Keep me informed as you progress in your planning."

Ramiz dipped his head once and bowed as he left the room. He had a major chore to accomplish and a lot of planning to be done. He knew he had to develop a core capability for a clandestine attack on foreign shores, but he needed more. He knew he needed a capability to attack the Americans in their homeland territory, grab the ayatollah, and get out without anyone being caught or compromised. It was a tall order. But he thought they could do it, given enough time. And a year was probably enough time. But first he had to make sure they were secure where they were in the operations center compound and that the Americans could not walk in again uninterrupted. He had a series of major tasks before him, and he knew it.

He also knew he needed help.

Khatib pondered the difference between the U.S. system and the short process he had been used to in Iran—weeks, not months or years. And with a lot of uncertainty.

In his planning Khatib realized he could not do much about the location of the ayatollah or the process he would be going through in the American justice system. The guards and special provisions put into place for the security of a terrorist were extreme. During the next several months, and possibly extending beyond a year, the ayatollah could not be rescued. It would be up to him, Khatib, to continue to lead the New Persia efforts until they could rescue the ayatollah. He looked out the window at the ocean beyond the beaches of Socotra, seeing the small waves breaking on the beach near the harbor, a few tourists walking along the beach, and resolved to keep the movement going.

Chapter Three

Monday—September 19
Socotra Island—New Persia Compound

Khatib, over the past several days, had reviewed the status of finances, logistics, training, operations, security, and facilities for the New Persia movement. He was familiar with the status, since he sat in on most of the meetings that the ayatollah held. But he needed to make sure of his knowledge and see if there would be any needed changes in their current planning. He found only minor changes. They would pursue their existing plans for convincing the western world to comply with their demands. The absence of the ayatollah would not change their basic mission requirements.

As he had promised in the middle of last week, he held a meeting of all the staff and laid out his desires for continuing with their current efforts. The general feeling was one of relief. No one wanted to take on any new, heavy workload during this time of stress and uncertainty. Most of the planning was already complete for the next few missions, and they did not want to alter those plans.

Khatib contacted the Iranian interior minister, Amad Essa, and asked for his advice on a good legal team to represent the ayatollah in the U.S. After several days of delay, Essa sent Khatib a note recommending the Washington, D.C.-based law firm of Whitson, Jackson, Johnson, and Taylor for New Persia's consideration. Iran had used them before in cases of possible terrorist activities and had found them to be quite helpful in navigating through the American legal system.

Within days of receiving the recommendation, Khatib had contacted the law firm and put them on retainer. It was expensive, but necessary. And within a week of being retained, the law firm had sent an attorney to Richmond, Virginia, and interviewed the ayatollah. Excellent legal expertise was on board, and the ayatollah was considerably relieved to know he had very capable help in his situation. It was obvious Khatib was coming through for him, and he was grateful.

Following the visit with the ayatollah, the firm sent an attorney up to Anchorage, where he visited with Kadar Al Sabah, the captain of the recently captured *Persian Desert,* and his men. The purpose was to determine their condition—good—and to give them encouragement. He informed them of the progress in both their case and the ayatollah's case. While the men were concerned, they were convinced that something would be done for them and they would not spend a lot of time in prison.

Tuesday—September 20
Socotra Island—New Persia Compound

Ramiz was determined to succeed. He did not have the knowledge to train his various guard force members in their duties, but needed to get the training accomplished. And they needed to get it done as soon as possible. The Americans could come back at any time, and he needed to have a force that could meet them and repel their efforts. He ordered several English-speaking magazines on self-defense and self-protection, thinking there may be some ads that might apply. He found very little that might be reliable.

He spent some time in his office thinking about the subject. After discussing it with some of his more reliable and capable guards, he decided to see if there was a way to contact a French company that specialized in security training. And the place to start, he felt, was with the company that was currently upgrading their electronic security systems.

He approached Khatib with the thought and they both agreed, given the recent abduction of the ayatollah by the infidels, that a good security and facilities review was required. Khatib agreed to let Ramiz perform the review, with French construction expert assistance, and then they would go over whatever recommendations resulted. Since the French firm had built the existing facilities, they both felt the company could provide effective recommendations for security improvements. Ramiz agreed and began to plan a course of action.

Ramiz called Paul Cherac, the local French security systems installation manager and the construction superintendent, and set up a meeting to discuss what might be done and how long it might take to perform the agreed-to improvements. Ramiz, with his engineering background from the University of Wisconsin, dug out the software files for the construction blueprints for the various buildings and support facilities. Projecting the files up on a large screen in the conference room, he started a personal review of all aspects of the construction. It didn't take him long to realize that there were several areas requiring improvements. It was obvious that security was not high in priority when the designs were initially developed. Camera locations, fencing structure, sensor and control locations, and basic building construction methodologies were all faulty. And the infidels had taken advantage of several of these deficiencies when they abducted the ayatollah. Corrections were needed, and needed quickly.

He made a list of the items he had discovered. It included moving several of the sensors, changing monitoring capabilities, adding fencing in several areas, and increasing the lighting in some sensitive locations. It also included a new facility down near the harbor that could handle up to four helicopters. Since the ayatollah was abducted and apparently spirited away by submarine, Ramiz decided that they needed some form of counter to the threat of another submarine incursion. A heliport with hangars would be very appropriate. There was no need for a runway, just helicopter capability. Helicopters, on routine patrol, would deter the infidels from approaching again, and he thought he might be able to get Chinese support in providing the aircraft and, at least at first, crews to man them while his personnel were being trained.

The combination of increases in both capabilities in security and patrolling for submarines, combined with some facilities upgrades, would significantly increase security. And once they had the ayatollah back, it would be a true deterrent to another kidnap attempt. He was satisfied with his analysis and would run it by Paul as soon as they could meet.

Thursday—September 22
Socotra Island—New Persia Compound

They met two days later, since Paul had to come in from another job site in Yemen and had to make arrangements for the flight. Meeting in the conference room, they reviewed the material Ramiz had developed.

Paul said, "You have developed several changes that we felt would have been appropriate at the time of construction. However, we were overruled. While we were not told the reason for not implementing the changes, we suspected that it was budgetary. It would have cost several hundred thousand euros to implement the needed improvements."

Ramiz responded, "Yes. And several recent events could have been avoided—and now we pay the price anyway."

Paul just nodded.

Ramiz continued, "I need to run these improvements by Khatib for his approval. Are there others that you know of that I have not identified?"

"No. You caught all the ones we had identified and added a few of your own to the list. We had not thought of the helicopter operational area, and adding some additional lighting to sensitive areas was not considered. Also, putting in powered gates at the entrance, controlled only from the operations center, was not something we had considered. You did a good job, and these enhancements will provide a much greater degree of security for your organization. Clear it with Khatib and I will begin the process of determining the details of how we would accomplish what you want done. I will also define the time and cost estimates for the work."

"Good." Ramiz paused for a moment, then said, "I have another question for you."

"Oui, monsieur?"

"I need to get some of my people trained in guard and special security processes and procedures. Since you are in the security business, I thought you might have some recommendations for me. Who might you recommend to provide training of that sort?"

Paul was not surprised at the request. He had certainly heard, from members of the local population, how the U.S. had invaded and kidnapped the ayatollah. He knew the current guard force and reaction teams were woefully underskilled and needed a lot of training.

Paul looked back at Ramiz and said, "You are fortunate. We install these new electronic systems for customers like you. It is a core business we have. But we also have another division that handles what we call physical security. That is, men who patrol, protect, and, where necessary, control situations. They have a training organization that assists customers in developing their own capabilities."

"They could train my men, then?"

"Oui, yes. I can contact them if you wish and have a representative come down here and discuss it at length with you. Gerard Beaulac is the manager of that division, and he would be pleased to discuss your requirements with you."

Ramiz nodded and then, using a motorized golf cart, took Paul to the main gate, where his rental car was parked. They shook hands and agreed to meet again in a week to discuss schedules, costs, and any further changes.

The next day, Khatib and Ramiz met, and they reviewed the proposed changes. Khatib was quite taken with several of the changes, and enthusiastically agreed. He called in Mansur, who took care of finances, and told him of their plans. They lined up some funding for the changes out of the budget, based on their own estimates, and set it aside, pending the meeting with Paul.

The financing the ayatollah had put into place was still functioning well, and Khatib had no worries there. Word had gotten around to the various governments and religious leaders supporting the movement and they had resolved to continue their support. Some had dropped out, but most stayed with them. The New Persia goals of forcing the west to reduce its overall use of oil and reduce, dramatically, its imports of Middle Eastern oil were still in place. They would not be dissuaded from their Allah-given mission.

Khatib would make sure of that.

Wednesday—September 28
Socotra Island—New Persia Compound

The following week, Paul returned to the operations center and they met in the conference room. He had laid out a schedule for making the changes and for building the helicopter operations area. Khatib and Ramiz met him in the conference room and they went over the schedule, making a few changes, since they had a slightly different set of priorities. Paul was able to make the slight changes, and they discussed the costs. The whole project would take close to a year to accomplish, but some aspects, such as changing the monitoring capabilities and building the helicopter facilities, could be done in the next several months. After two further days of detailed discussion, they were satisfied, and Paul said he could have the first workmen on site within a week. Khatib left Ramiz and Paul for other work. After some more minor changes, they signed the specification and financial documents and shook hands.

Wednesday—September 28
Washington, D.C.

The law firm, led by the senior partner Frederick J. Whitson, filed several motions and appeals before the trial was scheduled to begin. Mr. Whitson was very adamant, and had a strong negative fervor about governmental actions, and what he viewed as a seriously overstepping governmental authority. He had memories of the incident in Waco, Texas in the spring of 1993, and it colored his viewpoints during his long legal career. The motions and appeals were all based on the fact that the ayatollah, a citizen of Iran, had been kidnapped and brought back to the U.S., against his will, for trial. Thus the ayatollah's personal rights had been violated by the government. He should be set free and returned to his home, and, if the government insisted, extradition could be pursued.

As part of the preliminaries, the legal team made sure that groups sympathetic to the ayatollah and his movement were informed of the situation as it developed. Several demonstrations, primarily by extreme environmentalists from around the world supporting the ayatollah, were held in Virginia as the legal process moved along. In contrast, there were demonstrations in some of the western states by members of various right-wing groups praising the government for finally taking action against these "enemies of the state." Usually against the U.S. government, these groups were pleased with the covert nature of the capture of the ayatollah.

Friday—September 30
Washington, D.C.—The White House

Alberto Alvarez Martinez, the president of the United States, was in careful thought as he watched the demonstrations taking place on network television and was closely monitoring the legal proceedings. While not a lawyer, he wanted to make sure this particular terrorist, the Ayatollah Abdul Sarhardi, got what he deserved in the American justice system. President Martinez was a Mexican-American from Arizona, a former senator, former U.S. Navy engineer, and well respected by most Americans. A fit five feet eight and 175 pounds, he was quite active playing tennis and golf. With a quick mind and capacity for absorbing a lot of information quickly, he was a force to be reckoned with. While quite friendly in a social environment, he could also be very direct and short in a business or government meeting. Direction to his staff was not a problem, and he did not hesitate to provide guidance as needed.

The president continued to think and recall as he looked out the Oval Office windows at the outside world. The difficulties in dealing with the ayatollah arose from the ayatollah's insistence on having his list of demands met with no negotiation possible. And the list of demands was not something the west could tolerate. Complying with them would mean economic ruin throughout the western economies and a return to a lifestyle of the 1800s.

He turned and picked up the list of demands on his desk. He had practically memorized them over the months since they were announced by New Persia. He looked them over again as he read:

1. *Iraq/Iran and Saudi Arabia join politically to form a New Persia with a theocratic government*
   a. *Temporary head of the New Persia interim government will be Ayatollah Sarhardi*
   b. *All assets of previous regimes to become part of New Persia to include funds held in foreign bank accounts*
   c. *All international agreements to be in abeyance until New Persia government can review them for applicability/modification/elimination*
   d. *Over a period of 180 days, all current embassy personnel will be recalled and new assignments made based on internal judgments*
   e. *Internal elections for New Persia to be held within 90 days without any outside influence from western "democracies" ... no monitoring of election processes*
2. *Worldwide production of oil to be cut to 25% of 2015 quantities*
   a. *It is Allah's resource, and thus unbalanced use by western infidel powers must be stopped*
   b. *We need to extend life of oil reserves so Allah's people can share in the benefits*
   c. *The west needs to reduce its voracious use of oil and, if desired, develop alternative energy sources*
3. *Other sources of energy are available to world ... and to the world, I say, develop and use them*
4. *Oil funds in Arab countries are to be used for all Arabs and not for benefit of a few sheiks/leaders ... too much like infidel businesses in western world ... only the rich benefit; they will be impounded/confiscated*
5. *UN to sanction U.S. for excessive oil use and for not containing oil use to what the U.S. can produce internally*
6. *All foreign forces are to leave the New Persia territories within 30 days ... not even "advisors" allowed*
7. *All foreign forces are to leave the Middle East permanently within 90 days (Middle East defined as Turkey, Lebanon, Syria, Egypt, Jordan, Israel, Afghanistan, Pakistan, Iran, and Iraq*
8. *Western companies to train Arab personnel in oil well technical matters ... then out of the country ... within 1 year*
9. *All women/girls' schools to be shut down immediately; foreign teachers to leave within 15 days*

10. *All oil wells and associated equipment and pipelines will become the property of the New Persia government ... with no compensation to companies. They have already made enough profit over Allah's resources*
11. *All ports will be shut down for 60 days to allow time for production cuts to take effect*
12. *Any attempt to "freeze" New Persia funds will result in a total shutdown of oil production and stoppage of all shipping inbound or outbound*
13. *Other countries' oil production assets will be gradually disabled (as already demonstrated) if they refuse to cooperate*

The ayatollah had specified the list of demands during an Iranian-sponsored speech before the United Nations last year. Non-compliance with his list of demands by the west resulted in a series of attacks on western oil and political interests that were attributed to the New Persia organization. Unable to tolerate these attacks, and with no support from Iran (who was protecting the ayatollah) or most of the Mideast countries, the United States, under President Martinez's guidance, had taken matters into its own hands.

After an airborne attack in the southeastern Iranian desert by B-52s failed to kill the ayatollah and many of his staff, the ayatollah disappeared, but instances of terrorism continued to occur. It was only after a concerted effort to locate the New Persia organization that the U.S. finally found them on the island of Socotra in the Northern Indian Ocean. Through a series of events and close calls, a small team lead by Ryan McKenzie, a former colleague of the president and a retired U.S. Navy commander and SEAL, captured the ayatollah and returned him to U.S. soil for trial.

The president turned from the window and walked over to the ever-present coffee pot, refreshed his cup, and returned to his desk. Concerns over the ayatollah would have to wait. Water rights issues in the western United States and budgetary matters needed his attention.

Chapter Four

Thursday—October 6
Socotra Island—New Persia Compound

Paul called Ramiz and said, "If the schedule meets with your needs, I have talked with Gerard Beaulac, and he could meet with you next week here in Socotra."

Ramiz responded, "That would be fine. Friday would be best. I'll have more information and we can talk then."

Friday—October 14
Socotra Island—New Persia Compound

Ramiz met with Gerard Beaulac, the head of the training division for physical security. Gerald was a stereotypical physical security specialist. He looked the part. He was a bull of a man with buzzcut hair, very muscular chest and upper arms, and a stern, no-nonsense affect about him that could easily intimidate. You got the impression that he was ready to bite someone at any time. And then he would speak and it was a soft, easy-listening voice ... a contrast to his physical appearance. A soft voice, but firm and knowledgeable in his field.

They had a mutually respectful discussion, with Ramiz laying out his need for a combination of an upgraded guard force and a small force of commandos. Gerard said they could meet his needs, but wanted to see the facility they would train in. They agreed to meet at the stronghold in about three weeks

After the discussion with Gerard was complete and he had left, Ramiz sat down and began thinking about what the future held. Knowing the American legal system slightly, and much of that from reputation, along with information provided by the law firm, he suspected that the preparations for the trial, and the actual trial, could take several months. He felt that he needed to be ready in about eight to nine months. Ready with a force capable of rescuing the ayatollah and returning him to Socotra.

He realized that he did not have much spare time. Training a force capable of the rescue, and setting up the support for the rescue, was not a trivial task. It would entail both risk and a significant amount of work to prepare for a successful mission of this type. Training fifteen to twenty men in the ayatollah rescue plans, and getting the materials and supplies into position in the time available, would be difficult. But he was determined to get it done.

Monday—October 24
Socotra Island—New Persia Compound

Ramiz met with Paul Cherac again. Ramiz began, "How is the installation and modification of our systems coming along?"

Paul responded, "Quite well. We had recommended some of these upgrades when we installed the basic system. It is good that you are doing them now. The lasers across the fence line and the additional cameras, along with relocating the control cabinets to the operations center, will all add quite a bit of both capability and non-tamperable security."

"When do you think you will be finished?"

"We are still about seven months from finishing with the full upgrades. We have installed some temporary workarounds to give you the same capability, and those are fully functional now. But, as I said, to be fully complete with all of the facility modifications will take another seven months."

Monday—November 7
Southeastern Iran—New Persia Stronghold

Ramiz traveled to the stronghold and met with Gerard again. They reviewed the hardscrabble training facility and agreed on some minor, but necessary, improvements. Ramiz immediately set in motion the corrections and changes needed. Gerard said he could have a small training force at the stronghold the following week. Ramiz would have to select the trainees and get them prepared for the rigorous training activity. Knowing he had a large pool of trainees to select from, he readily agreed.

Ramiz met that afternoon with Abu Al Khayr, his training supervisor. He said, "We need forty to forty-five strong and capable volunteers to be trained as an elite commando force. Can you select them in the next two days?" Ramiz knew that there would be some that could not make it through the program, so he was asking for more than he really required.

"Yes, sir. With pleasure. How long will this training take?"

"About four to six months. And then they will prepare to rescue Kadar and crew in Alaska. That will be followed a few months later by a rescue of the ayatollah. Then they will deploy for another strike mission in America."

Abu's face took on a grim look. He looked across the stronghold wasteland and said, "A strike on the eagle! I shall have the volunteers named by tomorrow morning. I won't have a problem getting volunteers for this ... I will have a problem because there will be so many of them. And ... thank you, sir."

Ramiz nodded and headed back to talk with Gerard, who was still at the stronghold looking over capabilities.

"You shall have your list of volunteers tomorrow morning," he told Gerard. "A few days after that, you may start the training on your schedule. I am assuming a four- to six-month training effort for this."

Gerard looked surprised. He threw up his hands and partially turned around then back again. "What?" he exclaimed. "I take one to two *years* to do this ... not six months!"

Ramiz was surprised at the reaction. "But we have a mission to complete in six months, and it will require these men to be trained for it to succeed. And in nine months we have another mission of extreme importance that must be fulfilled."

"Can't be done. I won't even have the men in good physical condition by then, let alone skillful enough to perform this mission you refer to. What is the mission?"

"I can't tell you what we are going to do, but you need to have a force of twenty-five ready to go in six months. And another smaller group of fifteen ready to go in nine months. There will be a list of forty-five volunteers to start with." He paused for a moment and said, "And they are all very motivated, already in good condition, and willing to work hard. They are pumped up for this."

Ramiz finished and looked at Gerard. Gerard just looked back.

Gerard turned and paced about in frustration for several moments then finally said, "Oui, monsieur. All I can do is try. A lot will depend on the condition and smarts of the selected people. If they are strong and in good condition, and have some experience, it will help a lot. But it will be a real push, and I will have to task them both physically and mentally for the entire period of time. They will get very tired, but I will do what I can."

Ramiz smiled slightly and said, "Good. Let's proceed as fast as possible."

Both met their commitments, and the intense training of forty-five men began the following week. Gerard also sent an instructor to Socotra to train and instruct the guard force so they could increase their capabilities. The instructor looked over all of the security procedures and made several changes to make them more responsive and effective.

Wednesday—November 16
50th Space Wing, Schriever AFB, Colorado

The eye in the sky took it all in. The satellite cameras were focused on the stronghold, and had been since before the strike occurred. Since there was continuing activity in the stronghold, even after its destruction by a B-52, the satellite continued monitoring. Back at Schriever AFB in Colorado, Lieutenant Lucy Thompson was watching the activity with some degree of interest. She had noticed that activity had picked up and that there was a greater degree of intensity to the training. Just over the last few days or so, there was a small group of men not only conditioning themselves, but involved in hand-to-hand training, firing·different weapons in live training, and using building mock-ups. In her shift reports, she logged this activity, not really knowing what it meant.

Friday—November 18
50th Space Wing, Schriever AFB, Colorado

A few days later, Colonel George McMichaels, the 50th Space Wing commander, was reviewing the routine reports from the New Persia surveillance efforts. He went through a lot of the material and then came across Lieutenant Thompson's reports regarding the uptick in training activities at the stronghold. She had noted that a small cadre of men was undergoing some form of intensive training, and that it looked very much like commando training of some sort. Or what she took to be that type of training. He called her in to a meeting in his office. Captain Marcus Carver came with her as they met the following day.

"Lieutenant Thompson, you have noted this training activity and an increase in its intensity. What do you make of it?"

She responded, "I'm not sure, sir. But I would have to presume that they are training for some type of future clandestine mission. And, given their history, probably against us somewhere and sometime in the future."

23

Colonel McMichaels looked at Captain Carver and said, "Do you agree with that?"

"Yes, sir. I think they are planning some form of attack. I have no idea where or when, but think that is the purpose of the training."

The colonel looked at both of them and slightly nodded. "Do we have any way of determining how far along this training is or if there is any particular training emphasis going on? I mean, are they emphasizing ground operations, airborne stuff, or even water activities?"

Lieutenant Thompson responded, "No, sir. At this point I haven't seen any indication of water training. They have been live firing weapons up to small mortars, doing house-to-house types of exercises, and, of course, physical conditioning activities. Running long distances, calisthenics, hand-to-hand tactics, weight training, and those types of things. Of course, we can't see inside the buildings, and they may be doing other course work or even water stuff inside. We just don't know."

Colonel McMichaels, again, nodded at her comments. "But it certainly looks like they are not just the normal basic training activities we've seen in the past?" he said.

She nodded and looked over at Captain Carver. Carver said, "No, sir. It is definitely a change in pace and concentration."

Colonel McMichaels then stood and the meeting was over. Lieutenant Thompson and Captain Carver left.

Colonel McMichaels returned to his desk and wrote out a draft message for transmission to Air Force Space Command headquarters, just up Colorado Highway 94 at Peterson AFB. He was concerned, and wanted to make sure his superiors were aware of the training increase and the potential that it might have in the future.

Monday—November 21
Socotra Island—New Persia Compound

They needed to show the west that they had not been stopped by the abduction of the ayatollah. The resolve was still there and they would continue their activities. But they needed to modify their plans slightly and make sure the world knew they would not negotiate on the demands the ayatollah had put forth to the United Nations.

Again Khatib called Ramiz in to the main office. Ramiz arrived several minutes later.

24

"Ramiz. It has been a little over two months since our leader was kidnapped. You said it would take about a year for the American justice system to deal with the ayatollah."

"Yes, sir. That's correct. It could take even a little longer," responded Ramiz.

"And the chances of us rescuing him during that time are very remote?"

"Nearly impossible. He will be totally trussed up when they move him, and under guard all the time. Literally all the time. He won't be able to take a piss or a shit without someone there watching."

Khatib nodded in full understanding. He had seen similar things in Iran.

"So, basically, as I understand you, until they finish their legal charade with him in their system, we can't get him out."

"Right."

"But we can encourage him by using the law firm and by keeping up our activities showing the west that we have not been critically hurt by his capture."

Ramiz paused for a moment, thinking, and said slowly, "Yes. I suppose that is true."

"So, Ramiz, I think we need to revisit our various plans, begin to implement the ones we can, and plan for future ones. You have already begun the process of increasing our security here and at the stronghold. The French are training a cadre of our people for better guard protection and, with a small group, developing a commando capability." He looked questioningly at Ramiz.

Ramiz simply nodded as he looked back. He wasn't sure what was coming at this point in the conversation.

"Given the year that the Americans will take, that lines up nicely with the year that the French are saying it will take to develop a credible commando group."

"Yes, sir."

"I think we can do better and do some other things that will help our cause in the meantime."

"What do you have in mind?"

"I think six months would be adequate to get a group of commandos trained for a rescue of Kadar and crew, and then follow that a couple of months later with a rescue of the ayatollah and a strike on the U.S. oil industry in the Gulf of Mexico. Probably unopposed, since it would be a strike in secrecy. I am no expert in these matters, but I want you to go back to the French instructors and see what they think. So that would be three commando missions within the next nine months or so. I think that would surely get the western world's attention."

"We think in concert with each other. I have already given Gerard those time frames and he has begun the training. He wanted one to two years for the training, but I told him no. I too am no expert in these matters. They are getting very well paid for their efforts, and we are providing them with our best people. I shall check on Gerard's progress and get back to you soon."

Khatib smiled and nodded. Then he waved in dismissal and Ramiz departed the office. Khatib stood there for a moment and thought how good it was to have Ramiz on their team. Their combined talents, and plans for chaos in the west, should lead to western compliance to their demands.

Heading down the hallway, Ramiz knew he had been handed a major tasking. The strikes were not a worry to him, but trying to rescue the ayatollah from the U.S. Marshals service would be no small effort. It would take a lot of planning and advance work. It actually was a good thing that they had, perhaps, a year to set it up and execute it.

Thursday—November 24
Socotra Island—New Persia Compound

Several days later, Khatib again called Ramiz in for a discussion of an idea he had for bringing the concern for the oil demands to home in the U.S. After a few minutes, Ramiz showed up, bowed slightly, and sat down on a mat in the middle of the room.

Khatib began, "Ramiz, I think we need to bring this whole situation closer to home in the U.S. and strike at the eagle where it may do the most good. It's fairly minor in the whole scheme of things, but I think it will get the U.S. administration's attention and have the added benefit of encouraging the ayatollah. Here's what I have in mind." And he proceeded to explain to Ramiz what he wanted to accomplish.

Ramiz sat for a few moments and then said, "Well, if we do all this, strike at Ryan McKenzie, rescue Kadar, rescue the ayatollah, and hit the gulf and California refineries ... it will certainly get the attention of the U.S. president and some of his advisors. We will need to tie it back to our organization so there is no question about who is responsible for the action. And there will certainly be a reaction to us for it. Are you prepared for that occurrence?"

"Yes. I think we can handle anything they might throw at us, short of a full-blown invasion. And I don't think they will be that

26

foolish. Worldwide reaction to an invasion would be very top heavy against them, and the Yemeni army, weak as it is, would still be able to inflict some damage on them. And by then our facility upgrades will be complete. No. I think they might try something like they did a year ago at the stronghold, but that will have nowhere near the success they had then."

"I see. Then you want me to go ahead and carry out this first bit of sabotage against McKenzie ... our revenge for his role in capturing the ayatollah?"

"Yes. And let me know when you are about to launch it. It won't take long and will have an immediate effect on the Americans. I want to be ready with a news release at the time it happens. And then we will carry out the rescue of Kadar, rescue the ayatollah, and then a larger strike in the Gulf of Mexico, at Texas and Mississippi, in several months. That is what our men are being trained for."

Ramiz saw the intent that Khatib really wanted to carry out.

Ramiz said, "It will solve a desire I have to strike back. I will issue instructions right away. It will only take a few days to begin to implement the plan. Then we wait for the action to occur." He bowed slightly and left the office.

Chapter Five

Friday—November 25
Socotra Island—New Persia Compound

Ramiz called in his explosives expert, Zafir, and gave a series of instructions to him. He then went back to his office and thought the whole process through. It was a risky four-part strike plan, and it would be easy for it to go wrong, but it would certainly send a message to the U.S. president. While unsure of the advisability of the plan, he smiled at the thought of the anger it would generate in the president. And after several attempts on Ryan McKenzie, which failed, he would finally, personally, succeed against McKenzie.

The next day, Zafir arrived, as instructed, in Ramiz's office with information packets and several bottles and boxes of American home chemicals. After two hours of discussion, with cautions, Zafir gave a small demonstration using the chemicals. Ramiz repeated the demo, asking several questions as he proceeded. They then moved on to different simple triggering devices. Finally, after several hours and multiple successful demos, Ramiz felt confident he could carry out his mission against Ryan McKenzie.

Two days later, Ramiz met with Khatib. He said, "The first part of the plan is ready to execute. My knowledge of a homegrown explosive and triggering device is ready to go, and we have all the information we need to carry out the attack. It only requires your approval at this point."

Khatib looked out his office window. They were about to pull the eagle's tail feathers, and the eagle would not like that at all. But he wanted to do this in the worst way. And it might just lead to the release of the ayatollah. He looked at Ramiz and said, "Go ahead and execute the plan as we have laid it out. Take out McKenzie, then we shall see the results and move on from there"

Ramiz smiled, bowed, and left the office. He had several activities underway and needed to monitor them closely.

Monday—November 28
Houston, Texas

Elusive Quarry

Abdul-Salam Bitar was a student at the University of Texas, Houston, and had been there for two years. There had been no money for him to return to Iran and his family. He was a bit despondent and wanted to return, just for a little visit, and see his parents, sisters, and brothers again. But he had little money, certainly not enough to fly all that way and return. He was complaining about it during one of the weekly Pan-Arab university meetings, and Kamir overheard his comments.

Kamir had arrived a few months after Abdul. He was from a mountainous area of Iran and had sympathies to the New Persia movement near his home. Hearing the complaint, he began to wonder if there was something that Abdul could do to help the movement but not cause undue risk to them in the university, or to New Persia. It had taken him a long time and effort to get into the university, and he did not want to risk an incident. He contacted his brother, Shandi, in Iran, and explained the situation, and his brother said he would get back to him.

After Shandi brought the subject up in one of the New Persia support meetings at the stronghold, word was sent back to Ramiz that there might be a way to get additional information on the Houston Oil terminal. Since Ramiz was working on the plans for a strike in that area of the world, he was interested in getting any information he could ... especially firsthand information. He was intrigued and sent a note back to Shandi at the stronghold who, in turn, was able to contact Kamir again. They instructed Kamir to contact Abdul and feel him out to see if he was serious. Kamir readily agreed. He was pleased. He would be able to contribute to the movement without any risk.

Kamir approached Abdul after the next Pan-Arab meeting and asked, "Did I hear you say at the last meeting that you wanted to go back home for a visit but didn't have the money?"

Abdul said, "Yes. And I have no way of earning it, either. My scholarship does not allow me to work, so I have to make do on my monthly stipend."

"I think I have an answer to your trouble," said Kamir. And he proceeded to tell Abdul what he might be able to do to earn some additional money helping out the New Persia movement. Abdul considered it for a few moments and then said, "I'll have to think about it. If I were to get caught, I'm sure I would be sent back to Iran and not be able to finish my petroleum engineering degree."

Kamir nodded and responded, "Yes. That would be a risk, but I think it is very small. You would also be well paid to do this work they have asked about, and it's not very hard."

R.W. Barton

"I'll have to consider it and get back to you."

"I understand, but there is little time. I need to know within the next day or so."

"Okay. I'll let you know tomorrow."

Kamir looked out at the distant university buildings and nodded. He would wait until tomorrow.

Late the following afternoon, Abdul called Kamir and said he would do it. He needed more details on what was required, but would do it that coming weekend if all was well. Kamir was delighted, and he knew Ramiz would be too. There wasn't any connection between Abdul and the New Persia group. It would be a cold check of the Houston Crude Oil Terminal, with no apparent connection to New Persia.

They met that same evening and Kamir gave Abdul detailed instructions on the information needed. Abdul asked several questions to make sure he understood, and received assurances from Kamir that he did not have to cross the fence onto terminal property. He would remain on the outside of the fence to conduct his information gathering.

Friday—December 2
Houston, Texas

It was a Friday evening, calm and quiet. Abdul put on some dark clothes so he couldn't be easily seen that night. He had received his detailed tasking from Kamir, and, while he didn't like it, the money for doing it was good. He needed to get some equipment ready, and then he would leave for the fence surrounding part of the Houston Crude Oil Terminal.

He arrived just at Jacinto Port Road and walked to the terminal just past 1:00 a.m. He could see many lights and the mentally threatening, newly installed fence line with razor wire across the top. But he was not going to try and get in. That would be for others later, not now.

He stood in the small shrubs and grass, looking at the scene in front of him. Huge tanks were just on the other side of the perimeter. Circular ladders followed the sides of the tanks to the top. It would be quite intimidating to climb those ladders, but that was not his mission. The tanks were lit up by bright artificial sunlight from the light poles scattered throughout the tank farm. It was actually sort of pretty, in a mechanical sort of way.

Elusive Quarry

He stood in the dark, motionless, and nearly invisible with his dark clothing. He heard the all-terrain vehicles of the patrol before he saw them. They were running on an interior road that followed the fence all the way around the complex. With the darkness and the speed of the vehicles, along with the well-lit interior of the tank farm, he was certain they couldn't see him, but it made him nervous anyway, and he crouched down in the grass. After they passed by, without seeing him about fifty yards outside the fencing, he approached the fencing and took out what looked like a small pistol.

He decided he needed to move fairly quickly, and put the barrel of the pistol through one of the holes in the chain-link fence, resting the barrel on the wire. He sighted down the barrel at one of the lights nearby and fired. There was no sound except for a slight hum from the invisible laser. He waited for a moment while holding the trigger down. The light began to smoke slightly and then blew out. That area was plunged into darkness.

He took out a laser range finder and measured the distance from the fence to several of the tanks. He made a note of where it was on a map and left the grassy area. He repeated this process three times around the tank farm, avoiding the patrols each time. Then he left to go back to his apartment. No one had seen him. He had his measurements, and it was obvious that the laser pistol had severely damaged the lights.

The next night, Abdul came back to his positions outside the tank farm from the night before. He checked the lights that he had destroyed with the invisible laser. Two had been repaired and were on again. But two were not repaired. He made a note of it and then proceeded to repeat what he had done the night before, using the laser and taking measurements. There were four lights out when he left that night, and he was still undetected.

He came back again on Sunday evening, stayed off the grass so his footprints wouldn't register in the dew, and viewed his work from the road. Only one of the lights had been repaired. It was obvious that repairing the lights was not a major priority.

Abdul then went back to his car and drove around to the main entrance to the complex on Sheldon Road. He sat across from the large gate for a few moments, watched the guards as they checked documents of large inbound fuel tanker trucks, and noticed that it was all business as usual, even at that late hour. He took out a laser range finder and measured the distance to the guard facility, then wrote down the two-hundred-yard figure. He took a small camera and took a few pictures of the facility, then left the area.

31

He drove down Sheldon Road for a couple of miles, pulled over, and thought for a few moments. He had done all he could think of, and that was more than he had been asked to do. He had better get back to his apartment and get the information to Kamir. Then he would wait to see what happened from there. He was excited to have the chance to go home and see his family, and for such easy work. He smiled. It would be good. Allah was watching him and smiling.

He went back to his sparsely furnished apartment, booted up his laptop, and got on the internet. Going to a website, Stopplite.com, he found a form that had been described to him by Kamir, and filled it out. It asked for the results of his visits and what had happened to the lights. He described what he had done, and the information obtained, attached several digital photos, and closed out the site.

A few days later, Kamir approached him on the campus and told him, "You did an excellent job. Our future planning can now consider the lights, the guards, and the distances, and how to handle them." And with that comment he handed Abdul $1500 in small bills. Abdul was astounded. He could go home, and return, at the next school break!

Kamir continued, "I would hope that we could depend on you to do some similar things in the near future for us."

Abdul responded, "As long as no one gets hurt, I'll help where I can." He paused then, waving the money in front of himself, continued, "And thank you."

Kamir nodded and waved as he walked away. He had another one. His network was slowly growing.

Chapter Six

Friday—December 9
Socotra Island—New Persia Compound

Ramiz, after getting specific information required for his Gulf Coast strike planning efforts, sent a note back through to Kamir asking for some slight clarifications on tank locations. The map was not totally clear to him, and he wanted to make sure he had the correct facts. Kamir contacted Abdul and they worked out another map of the terminal and sent it back to Ramiz. Ramiz, satisfied, continued his strike planning. After drafting up the first aspects of the plan, he decided he needed to get moving on what he considered the favorite part of this series of strikes ... taking out McKenzie. The other planning could wait, since they wanted to time the strikes with the rescue of the ayatollah.

He had already received clearance from Khatib for the McKenzie strike and decided to fly to the United States and carry out the action.

Monday—December 12
Freeport, Texas

Ramiz flew to Houston's Hobby Airport and then drove down to Freeport, Texas, where he got a room in the Towne Place Suites in Lake Jackson/Clute. After getting the room, he had been able to get the materials for the homemade bomb at a local hardware supply house and other multiple domestic sources. He carefully reviewed the notes and instructions and slowly assembled the shoebox-sized bomb in his room. After close to an hour, he was satisfied, and finished the package. He then mailed it at the local Freeport post office with a false return address. Simple. And it would certainly get the president's, and his administration's, attention.

After placing the bomb in the mail, he drove over to Ryan's marina and checked it over. There had been multiple modifications to it since he had last seen it, but the office and apartment area were unchanged. He expected the bomb to be delivered the next day, and decided to watch the action from the nearby county roadway. He returned to the hotel and continued his future strike planning in the peace and quiet of his room.

Ryan was sitting on one of his piers waiting for Juan, his maintenance handyman, to return with a valve fitting. They were repairing a water line that would be needed for a new arrival to the marina. Ryan McKenzie was forty-two years old, a retired Navy commander and SEAL. At five feet nine and 175 pounds, he was not a big man, but maintained his conditioning through daily runs on the beach. As he sat there, his thoughts drifted to the past year and the capture of the ayatollah that he and his buddies, Jasper, Dave, and Corey, had accomplished. The ayatollah had been the source of several terrorists' activities, and President Martinez, a former colleague from the Navy, had asked for their assistance in covertly capturing the ayatollah. They had, after some adventures, managed to accomplish the mission, and the ayatollah now awaited trial in the federal justice system. Ryan looked out over the slow-moving, muddy Brazos River and enjoyed the quiet morning.

The next day, around noon, Ramiz stationed himself on the roadway and settled in for the wait. At a little after 2:00 p.m., he watched as a mail truck pulled up and left the mail in the box. The mailman also left the package leaning against the post box support. It had arrived. Ramiz smiled to himself. It was working. He watched as Ryan came out of the office and gathered the mail and the box and went back inside the marina office.

Ryan flipped the box over, looking at it with some curiosity. Ramiz watched the office, anticipating the explosion, but nothing happened. He prayed it wasn't a dud. He watched as Ryan headed out of the office, joined up with Juan, and went to one of the slips to begin working on the water lines.

Ryan was on one of the piers adjusting the water line for the incoming customer's boat. The new boat required a slightly larger shore fitting to mate with its water lines. Ryan looked around at the marina with a lot of satisfaction. All of the modifications he had planned were completed, and he now had a first-class, and up-to-date, marina. All the slips but two were occupied, and he was running with a couple of customers lined up waiting for permanent berths. His Wi-Fi was the envy of the area. He was making a good profit and was a respected owner/manager in the local area. With Jackie Conover, the U.S. president's primary activity scheduler, at his side a good part of the time, it was a good life.

Ryan had met Jackie while he was visiting the White House. Jackie, a 5' 3" petite brunette and former eight-year U.S. Marine military police member, was quite pretty. She was President Martinez's primary activity scheduler working in the Executive Office of the President. In the course of Ryan's visit, they had quickly become friends and then lovers.

Ryan was monitoring, as best he could though television coverage and message traffic being forwarded by Jack Harrison, the president's chief of staff, progress the justice system was making in getting the ayatollah behind bars permanently. It was obviously a struggle, because some of the best U.S. attorneys had been hired to defend him. The trial should begin in a few weeks, or months. Justice was making progress, but very slowly.

Betty, Ryan's admin assistant, was in the office working her normal schedule, and Jackie was in the apartment above the office working remotely on the president's schedule. It was a quiet day and they were all working at a relaxed pace. Betty had put up a small Christmas tree, and Juan had strung outdoor lights on the exterior of the office. Ryan had even ordered in some pizza for lunch, along with some soft drinks and beer. It would be an easy afternoon. Ryan had picked up the mail, looked it over briefly without opening anything, and turned it over to Betty for handling. Jackie was on the internet chatting with Maria, the president's secretary, in Washington. Things were smooth.

Betty picked up a small box in the incoming mail, looked it over, and wondered what it was. She took out her scissors and cut into the tape. Then she opened the box. It was the last thing she would ever do. The very large explosion tore her apart and ripped out part of the front wall of the marina, with part of the apartment collapsing into the office. Jackie landed on her back in the office, stunned, with a broken arm and several severe lacerations. Betty was only partially there, and in pieces elsewhere.

Ramiz heard the loud explosion and watched the marina office disappearing in smoke, flame, and falling debris. He'd been watching Ryan on the pier, and his head jerked over to view the office area. *I've missed him again!* But somebody triggered the bomb. He wondered who had done it, and decided to get out of the area. He would watch the news tonight, and perhaps they would identify whoever was killed. He slowly and quietly drove off.

Ryan, concentrating on the hose fitting, almost fell into the water as the concussion reached him. He looked up at the marina office and, in a near panic, saw pieces of it still coming down out of the sky. Some parts of the remains of the office were beginning to burn. With a lump in his throat, he raced for the office, afraid of what he might find. Juan was hustling right behind him.

Ryan reached the office complex. Amidst the dust and debris he found Jackie, covered in dust, wood pieces, and various office materials, and saw what looked like a fracture of her left forearm and multiple cuts and bruises. The bone was sticking out but there was, fortunately, little bleeding. He picked her up and ran down to one of the piers until he thought she would be safe. He gently placed her on the ground.

She looked at him and said, "Betty ... she's still in there."

He looked up at the damage and saw part of Betty's torso in the debris. He closed his eyes for a moment, tears beginning, and just shook his head. Jackie saw the motion and began weeping quietly. Gathering his wits, he quickly called 911 on his cell phone and got the fire department and police. They had already been called and were on the way.

He looked at Jackie's arm, placed his shirt around it as best he could, and formed a small sling. It would have to be set at the hospital. He wouldn't try to set it, knowing he might make it worse if he did.

Juan came back. He told Ryan there was nothing they could do for Betty. She had died instantly in the blast. He had turned off the electricity, gas, and water to the office. He sat down on the pier and just watched as the marina office burned fiercely. There was no more he could do.

After a few minutes, they could hear sirens in the distance, and the fire department arrived shortly afterward, along with the police. The police directed looky-loo traffic around the blaze, and the fire department finally got the fire under control after close to half an hour. A paramedic unit arrived and Jackie was taken to the local hospital for treatment. The coroner also arrived two hours later and, after taking many photos, finally took Betty's remains away.

Due to the circumstances, a state investigation began, and the marina office area was roped off as a possible crime scene while state fire and police investigators pored over the remains of the building. At first they thought it might have been a gas leak, but were gathering materials for testing. It made the late afternoon and evening news in the area. It was also picked up by CNN that evening, and everyone watching, including Jack Harrison, saw the rubble of the marina office and Ryan's apartment.

Ramiz, in the Towne Place Suites, was watching the news, and was a bit dismayed over the results. He had assumed that anything mailed to Ryan would be opened by Ryan. He was wrong. He had hoped to get rid of Ryan once and for all after his two previous failures. But it didn't happen that way. He thought about the situation for a minute and then sat down to write a short note. He placed it in a plain envelope that had a self-sealing adhesive, put a false return address on it, and took it to the post office. Again, after using a self-adhesive stamp and wiping off the envelope thoroughly, he dropped it into the outbound mail slot.

Ramiz was frustrated. They had tried three times to get to Ryan and had failed each time. This time he had decided to be in the area when the bomb was delivered so he could see the damage for himself. If he was lucky he might even see Ryan's dead body in the wreckage. Unfortunately, that didn't happen. Ryan was still alive and would be coming after him. But he had to send the note just to tweak Ryan and further upset him. He smiled grimly as he imagined how Ryan would react when he opened the letter.

Then he sat down and sent an encrypted note over the internet to Khatib in Socotra. They had failed again.

Wednesday—December 14
Freeport, Texas—Ryan's Marina

Jackie was still hospitalized, and Ryan had spent several hours with her. Once he got back to the marina, he had spent part of the night on his undamaged boat.

A day later the mail truck arrived, and Ryan went out to get the mail. Inside the mail was an unmarked letter. Puzzled, he opened it. His anger at what he read was difficult to control.

McKenzie,

You may remember me as "Ramiz." I visited last year looking for a slip. That was not the real reason for my visit. I wanted to meet you before I killed you. New Persia is going to win this little disagreement with the west. And people will be lost as a result of our winning. I'm sorry we missed you yesterday. But sometimes collateral damage occurs in these cases.

The next time will not be so lucky for you.

Tell the president that we are serious about the U.S. reducing their oil usage and will continue to emphasize our demand through any means necessary. Until we see a serious reduction in your oil usage, we will continue with these events.

And finally, we want the ayatollah released immediately. If he is not released, these activities will continue.

It was unsigned. Ryan could not believe what he was reading. Collateral damage! It was Betty's life they were talking about! Once again, he was faced with the New Persia organization, only now it was a more vicious and determined group, and he would now have to deal with it personally.

He set the note down on the small table in his cabin. Looking out over the piers, he couldn't believe he was involved in this mess. He had anticipated an easy and pleasant retirement, but this was far from that. And now this latest situation. The local police couldn't help. It was international in nature, and not even conventional at that. It was international criminal activity, and no one out there handled this kind of attack. The only thing he could think of was to appeal to the president for action. But he was afraid that might not work. It was too small an issue for the might of the United States to get directly involved again. Even with his friendship with the president, it just wasn't going to happen. But he thought he had to ask.

Looking back at the note on the table, he realized that he might have to take the issue into his own hands. And the situation worried him a little ... he would be going after a large organization with many resources. It wouldn't be easy. But first things first. Ask the president for help and then go from there.

After checking on Jackie by phone and finding that she was as good as could be expected and wanted to come back home, he made a run to the hospital and picked her up. Her arm was in a large cast that ran from her wrist up past her elbow. The bone had been pulled back in place, and the doctors said it would require the cast for six to eight weeks. She wasn't very comfortable with it but had little choice in the matter.

They arrived back at the marina and looked in dismay at the wreckage of the office. The police had established a perimeter with yellow crime scene tape. A patrolman guarded the scene. They watched for a few minutes as the various investigators went about their business of gathering samples and taking measurements, and then went back to the boat. Dave and Jasper were both sitting somberly on the stern having cold beers when they got there.

Elusive Quarry

Jack Charleston, or "Jasper" to his many friends, was a certified deep-sea diver who knew no fear. Standing six feet three and weighing in at over 250 pounds, Jasper was a little oversized for the work he did, but his quality of work and dependability kept him quite busy around the shipyards and docks.

Jasper worked for Ryan while they were in the Navy, and Dave did consulting work for Underwater Submersibles in Galveston, a company that built various underwater vehicles and structures supporting the oil industry. As required, Underwater Submersibles also supported certain unusual U.S. Navy requirements.

Dave Carlson reminded Ryan of a Woody Allen type—small and frail looking, but with degrees in both electrical and naval engineering, a nationally known expert in both fields. He only stood about five feet seven and probably didn't weigh more than 150 pounds. He had a comb-over that hid part of a balding top, and wore solid-frame glasses. But looks could be deceiving, because Dave was resilient and tough. On several occasions he had saved a mission due to his toughness and tendency to keep at a project no matter what.

Dave greeted them. "We got here as soon as we could. I'm so sorry about Betty. She was a very nice person and this should never have happened."

Jasper added, "Ditto for me. She was a neat gal and we're all going to miss her."

Jackie gave Dave and Jasper short hugs, and Ryan nodded as he helped Jackie awkwardly climb down into the cabin. He said, "Thanks, guys. It's going to take a few days to get everything sorted out and figure out what the next steps will be."

Jasper asked, "Do you know what happened? I doubt that it was some kind of gas leak. It seems more like some form of bomb."

Ryan looked back at him with tears in his eyes. "It was a bomb." He handed Jasper the letter he had received.

Jasper took the note, read it, and whispered, "Geesus. Here we go again."

Ryan nodded as Jasper handed the letter over to Dave.

Dave read it, read it again, and grimly said, "We need to find these guys and make sure they don't see the light of day again. This is going way beyond it. Betty's dead and they've certainly warned you. We need to find them before they can get any further along with their plans."

Ryan's cell phone rang. He answered it. "Ryan! What the hell's going on down there? I've been watching the news and it looks like you're in a small war zone."

"Yes, sir," Ryan responded to the president. "It is about that here. We're okay, but Jackie's got a broken arm and Betty, my assistant, is dead. I received a note from a person named Ramiz who is part of the New Persia effort, and they are trying to kill me, and also get you to cut back on our oil usage. I can fax it to you if you would like. But we need to get these guys and get them off the street permanently."

"I certainly have to agree with that. Send it to Maria and I'll take a look. And send Jackie back as soon as you can. I want her back here, where it might be safer."

"Can do. I'll have that fax to you in about an hour. I'll talk with Jackie and see what we can do. She may not want to come back just yet."

"Understood. Anything I can do to help?"

"Not right now. Once we get the results back from the investigation as to what caused the explosion, I'll be able to start rebuilding. But I have to wait for that. And, of course, I'll be helping with Betty's funeral."

Ryan hesitated a moment and then continued, "I'd like to come up and talk with you about this whole mess. It has gotten very personal for me now, and I can't let it continue. They will either get me in the future or they will do a lot more damage as they carry out their plans. I'd like to discuss it some more and see what we might come up with. Would that work for you?"

The president's voice softened as he replied, "Sure. Okay. We'll talk later. You be careful now." And the line was cut off.

Wednesday—December 14
Washington, D.C.—The White House

The president thought for a few minutes then called Maria in and told her to expect a fax from Ryan. He explained the situation to her. She was relieved to hear that Jackie was okay, and sadly shook her head over Betty's death. She went back to her desk.

The president then called Jerry Ocasio, the head of Homeland Security, and they met several hours later. The president gave Jerry a rundown on what had happened and showed him the fax Ryan had sent.

Jerry responded, "What can I do to help?"

"I think we need to expedite the search for explosive residue at Ryan's place. If the samples prove to be remnants of an explosive, we need to heighten our efforts to find this group and actually eliminate them. We can't have them going around trying to assassinate anyone they think is holding them up."

"I'll see what I can do with the Texas authorities. Maybe all it will take is a phone call to have them move this to the top of their list."

"Okay. Let's try that first, then we'll see."

Wednesday—December 14
Freeport, Texas

Ramiz realized that he needed to, somehow, get Ryan and remove him from their concerns. But so far, like a cat with nine lives, Ryan seemed to either be smart enough or lucky enough to avoid the traps. Looking around from the boat he had rented, he saw several other boats with news crews closing up and putting their equipment away. He had decided to briefly watch the scene as the investigation moved along and he fit in with the rest of the water-borne looky-loos. After returning the rented boat up the coast, he went back to the hotel, said his prayers, and sat down to think. There had to be a way.

As he sat in the room, frustration building, he realized that he needed to get on with the other phases of the overall attack planning. He had actually succeeded in getting the president's attention with this failed attack, and that was one of their primary goals ... to bring it home to the administration. Now he needed to move on and, perhaps, when time allowed, finish the task of killing Ryan McKenzie. But that would have to move back in priority, and the rest of the actions would need to be accomplished first. He still had the rescue of Kadar and crew, the planned attacks on the gulf oil facilities, and the rescue of the ayatollah to finish.

He settled into a troubled sleep.

Wednesday—December 14
Socotra Island—New Persia Compound

Khatib, after reading the cryptic note from Ramiz, and watching the CNN coverage of the explosion in Freeport, Texas, sat down to write a note to the U.S. president. He felt New Persia, in spite of the ayatollah's capture, might just have the administration's attention.

Dear President Martinez,

The demands of New Persia are not negotiable now, or in the future. As the leading nation in the west, you have the unique capability to lead to a new world of energy independence.

The recent incident that we caused in Freeport, Texas, should draw your attention to our purpose and create an understanding that we are not to be trifled with.

Mr. Ryan McKenzie has caused our organization many problems and can expect to see more of our initiatives shortly. Your administration's actions in trying to negate us will only lead to an escalation of our activities, and your illegal retention of our leader Ayatollah Sarhardi only moves us to a greater effort.

Comply with our demands and release the ayatollah ... otherwise there will be more activity in the near future.

The message was then sent out through several servers and computers to mask the source. It eventually found its way to the White House correspondence center, where it was quickly forwarded up to Jack Harrison.

Thursday—December 15
Freeport, Texas—Ryan's Marina

Ryan was looking over the ruins, since the police and investigation teams had left. It was obvious that he was going to have to start from scratch. The place was totaled between the explosion and the fire. He was scratching through the debris to see if there was anything he could save when he heard a car pull into the parking lot. He looked up and saw it was the Texas state fire marshal.

Jim Reynolds came over and introduced himself. They shook hands.

Ryan said, "What can I do for you? It's quite a mess, and your guys have gone over it pretty thoroughly."

Jim responded, "I wanted to come by and see what had happened for myself. These things just don't happen very often, fortunately. I also wanted to let you know that we expedited the lab testing on the samples from here. The bottom line is that explosive residue was found in several of the samples. It was a homemade bomb that caused all this and killed your assistant. It's now a murder investigation with the police." He looked at Ryan and continued, "I don't know what is going on, but you had better watch yourself. This is as serious as it gets, and there may be more attempts. That letter you turned over to the police sure wasn't a happy birthday note. Somebody out there is really working to take you out."

"Yes. I know. And I know who did this. And so do the police. But getting them first is going to be a real problem. It's international, and they are tough to find."

Jim shook his head and shrugged. He looked around for a few minutes, made a couple of notes, and shook hands again just before leaving. He said, "Well, all I can say is good luck. If we can help let us know."

Ryan smiled and said thanks.

After Jim left, Ryan went back to seeing if there was anything worth finding or saving. He didn't find much. At least upstairs, once they got the floor stabilized, there would probably be some things that could be salvaged.

He was very angry. He had just finished with the upgrades to the basic marina. Now he was going to have to rebuild the office and the apartment. And he would have to mourn Betty for a while. She had been a good, close friend, and she would be tough to replace.

Chapter Seven

Wednesday—December 21
Freeport, Texas—Ryan's Marina

Ryan was working on recovering from the attack on his marina and home. The office building and his apartment above it were totally destroyed and would have to be rebuilt. The closed-casket funeral for Betty on Tuesday had been difficult, with quite a few mourners. She would be sorely missed.

After the funeral, Jackie and Ryan sat down to figure out the near-term way forward. It was nearly Christmas, and Jackie did not want to go back to Washington just yet. She wanted to spend Christmas weekend with Ryan, even if the celebration and spirit would be a bit abbreviated. Ryan had insisted that Jackie get on the next plane for Washington, but relented to her request to stay. It was what he really wanted anyway.

In spite of her arm cast, Jackie went to the local Home Depot and bought a small Christmas tree and decorated the cabin of the boat for the holiday. It was a bit of a melancholy holiday so close to Betty's death, but they were determined to make the best of it.

Ryan's immediate task was to get the mess cleaned up and then get some form of temporary office set up for the marina. He had contacted USAA, his insurance company, the day after the explosion, and they responded quickly. On site the day after he called them, they began the claim process right away. It took over two weeks of effort to get the necessary demolition permits, removing what could be salvaged, and then get the buildings removed and the site cleared.

There was a short break in the work effort due to the three-day Christmas holiday weekend, and then back to work. Ryan was in the middle of all the action, making decisions and contacting contractors for potential work.

Wednesday—December 28
Freeport, Texas—Ryan's Marina

After the Christmas holiday, Ryan insisted that Jackie go back to Washington, and arranged a flight out of Hobby Airport. She resisted but understood his concern. And the president's concern. Flying back commercial, she really wondered how long this was all going to last. Months, probably. And that was not a comforting thought. But it was real and not pleasant.

When she got to Washington and into her apartment, she called Ryan to let him know she had made it safely. He was relieved and said he would come to Washington once he got things arranged at the marina.

Friday—December 30
Freeport, Texas—Ryan's Marina

Ryan was interrupted in his work by a visit from a Texas ranger. Trooper Wilson came back and told him they had definitely identified the dead Rafi as the attacker on Jackie during an attempted kidnapping this past July. They had been able to track his movements and confirmed that it was another attempt by New Persia and for Ryan to be very careful. As he received this piece of advice, Ryan looked around at his destroyed marina, looked at the ranger, and said, "Thanks."

The ranger, seeing the location and recalling his comment, blushed a bit and said, "I guess that was a bit of an obvious statement, wasn't it? And a bit late!"

"Yeah. But don't worry about it. I know what you meant." The ranger then left.

Friday—December 30
Freeport, Texas

It had been a long day, and would be even longer as Ryan drove to Hobby. He had decided to take a break from his problems, left the marina in Juan's capable hands, and decided to spend the long New Year's weekend with Jackie. As he drove north, he contemplated all that had happened in the past year, and wondered what was in store for the New Year. It had been truly a trying time, and he wished for better things in the near future.

Arriving at the airport, he parked, went inside through security, and eventually boarded his plane for Washington National. He spent a very enjoyable weekend with Jackie and was feeling much better when he flew back home on January 3.

Wednesday—January 4
Freeport, Texas—Ryan's Marina

Ryan went back to work, calling a couple of other contacts in the Freeport area. He had been working out of his boat as a temporary measure. He was able to arrange a temporary mobile office to be brought to his site and placed in part of the parking lot. After a couple of days, he was able to get an office back, phones and internet hooked up, and a minimal stock of marine supplies for his customers. It wasn't pretty, but it was functional. Several of the people permanently living in the slips came up and offered help if he could use it. No apartment, though. He would continue to live on his boat.

Jackie, in her efficient and loving way, did some research and sent Ryan some pictures of New England-style marina offices and apartment combinations. While his original building was New England in style, what she sent him was a larger version, with more space in the office area. Very attractive. He called her and they worked out what might be possible given the insurance money available. After agreeing on the style and general plans, Ryan obtained actual plans for the construction of the buildings, paying the architect's fee, and submitted copies to the local building department.

Judy Kendricks, an older woman who had known Betty quite well and had some bookkeeping experience, offered to help until Ryan could find a permanent replacement. She lived with her husband on a very nice powerboat in slip forty-one. Ryan accepted her offer and immediately set her up with a computer and the software to maintain his books. She was pleasant and easy to work with, and Ryan had her working part-time several days of the week.

All was beginning to come together again. He had a temporary office, and the permit process for the permanent marina administrative and apartment complex was moving slowly through the county building review process. He had been told that it would probably take about two weeks to get his permits and authorization to begin building. In the meantime, he got several bids from local contractors to do the construction once the permits were in place.

On Saturday, January 7, Jackie returned and joined him on the boat, her arm still in a sling. Even with the cool weather, they enjoyed an evening of gentle sailing and barbecue, with wine afterward. She nestled into his side in the rather narrow bunks of the boat's master "suite," and they both felt a sense of accomplishment as they continued to work through the recovery together.

Chapter Eight

Monday—February 14
London, England

Since the failure at killing Ryan four months before, and with the commando training well underway but not complete, both Khatib and Ramiz had been settling back and letting the western world worry about their next move. It would be a few more months before they would be ready to strike again. This time the target would be the rescue of Kadar and crew from the federal facility in Anchorage. Also, through their student networks, they now had information needed for the refinery strikes. In the meantime, they both agreed it would be a good use of the time to scope out the area around the supermax for a possible attempt at rescuing the ayatollah.

Ramiz, finishing his overnight stay in London, boarded his flight for Washington, D.C., and settled in for the eight-and-a-half-hour flight. After a long planning discussion over several days with Khatib, they had decided that they needed more detailed information on the location of the prison where the ayatollah would probably be taken after his trial. Khatib and Ramiz realized that they had to act soon to make sure the ayatollah never got to the supermax facility. They needed to make sure he was spirited away while being transported. Ramiz was, therefore, on a scouting trip to see what the territory around Florence, Colorado, was like and to figure out how to interrupt the transfer process.

After landing in Washington, Ramiz checked in to a Marriott hotel near Dulles Airport for the night. He had a flight out the next day for Chicago and then on to Colorado Springs, where he would stay for the duration of his investigations. Colorado Springs was only about fifty miles from the prison complex in Florence and would be a good center for his operations. After a good meal, he said his prayers and went to bed.

The next morning he made it to the airport using the Marriott shuttle and spent the better part of several hours flying across the U.S. heartland. After landing in Colorado Springs, he retrieved his luggage from the lower-level baggage carousels, got a Hertz rental car, and drove over to the Elegante Hotel at Circle Drive and

47

Interstate 25. After checking in, he got a late lunch and tracked down a Colorado state driving map at a nearby Target. Back in his room, he looked over the map, compared it to the internet driving instructions he had with him, and figured out his route to see the prison complex. The next morning he would drive down and look over the complex and general area around Florence.

In the morning, after prayers and a light breakfast of fruit and yogurt, he headed south on Colorado Highway 115, past the main entrance to Fort Carson, and on down to U.S. Highway 50. As he proceeded south, he got close to the small community of Penrose and observed several places in the road that were quite wide. It was a four-lane highway at this point, with very wide shoulders. Driving across the overpass over Highway 50, he noticed that the bridge had narrowed down to two lanes with smaller shoulders. He then followed Highway 115 into Florence. He was observant, gathering information they might need for their planned actions.

Coming into the town of Florence, he turned to the left at the first stoplight, which put him on State Highway 67. He crossed over a three-track railroad crossing and continued up a small hill and slight turn in the road. After a couple of miles, he saw the prison structures. On the left side of the road was a very impressive complex of prisons. The beige and red brick facilities were up on a slight rise, and perhaps a quarter mile off the highway. Some of the facilities were outside the fencing but most were inside. The fence was a double cyclone chain-link fence with razor-wire coils set between the fence lines. Even if you got over the inside fence, you would be right in the middle of the razor wire. Very intimidating.

He drove past the entrance gate twice to make sure he hadn't missed anything, and headed back in to Florence. He stayed on Highway 67 as he went through town, and spotted a post office on the left. He stopped and went inside. He wanted to see if he could get any information from the postmaster or clerk that might help. He was standing in a short line waiting for the single clerk. Two older gentlemen came in behind him and were conversing with each other.

He politely interrupted them and asked, "Can you tell me where I might find the supermax prison down here? I'm writing a book and would like to see it."

The two men looked at him and one, with a large package in his hands, smiled slightly and said, "Sure. Just follow 67 east and you'll go right past it. Not much to see, though. Just some heavy fencing, buildings, and, of course, guard facilities."

"Hmmm. Well, I think I'll drive by it just to see if there is something I can use. Thanks for your help." And Ramiz nodded as he left the post office. He sat in the car for a minute and thought, *No way can we ever get him out of there once he goes through those gates. We'll have to get him before he gets here.* He shook his head again and drove back to the overpass with 115 and Highway 50.

The overpass was located about five miles from Florence and probably seven miles from the prison. It was wide-open territory and, except for some scattered trees, you could see for several miles in every direction. The front range of the Rocky Mountains were off in the distance, and the roads were all good. He sat on the shoulder of the road watching the moderate amount of traffic and analyzed the overpass several times, studying it, thinking.

An idea began to form in his mind. He got back in the car, turned onto the on-ramp for westbound Highway 50, and drove for several miles. He passed the Fremont County airport, which he noted, and continued on until he hit the outskirts of Canon City. After doing another u-turn, he headed back east, past the overpass and on into the small community of Pueblo-West. He did another u-turn and went back to the overpass again. He pulled up the exit ramp onto Highway 115, crossed the overpass, and pulled off onto the shoulder. He got out of the car and walked back to the overpass, looking like he had lost something. He looked at the guardrails and the distance down to the Highway 50 pavement—probably around twenty-five feet. He noted that Highway 50 was a fairly straight divided asphalt highway with a grassy middle area for a few miles in both directions. The idea was firming up.

He took a last look around, then headed back north on Highway 115 into the little community of Penrose. Spotting the fire department, he realized it was totally volunteer, or at least it looked like it was. He couldn't be absolutely sure, but the town was very small, and it just made sense. They wouldn't have a very fast reaction time.

Back on the highway and heading north again for Colorado Springs, he continued to ponder his idea. It would be a bit radical and people could get killed, but it just might work to free the ayatollah. And that was his goal. Free the ayatollah before he got to the prison.

He arrived back at the Elegante, went into the restaurant, and ordered a salad and iced tea to drink. It would take a lot of planning to pull off his idea, and he felt they had no time to waste. Equipment had to be purchased and modified, and special weapons obtained and "imported." While the trial still hadn't started yet, once the ayatollah was sentenced in the court it would not take long for the Bureau of Prisons to transport him to Florence. They needed to be ready.

He went back into the hotel for several hours of planning and internet research. He then went back down to Highway 50, headed west, and stopped at the Fremont County airport. He looked briefly at the outdoor museum of aircraft from the Vietnam era and then drove around a bit, looking at the various small hangars and parked small aircraft. There was no tower, since it was such a small facility, and it had a six-thousand-foot east/west asphalt runway. It should work very nicely, and was only a couple of miles from the overpass. He was satisfied with his investigations.

Friday—February 18
Socotra Island—New Persia Compound

A few days later, and after a very tiring trip across the Atlantic Ocean, Europe, and the Middle East, Ramiz was back home in Socotra. He and Khatib had a lot to plan and think about. Khatib told him that, according to the law firm, they did not think the ayatollah would be tried and sentenced for another few months. And after that, there would be a series of appeals that might delay his transfer to the prison; however, he could also be sent directly to prison while the appeals were being processed. They just weren't sure what might happen. But they both agreed that they needed to be ready.

Meeting in the conference room, Khatib said, "Well, what did you find out on your trip? Can we break him out of the supermax?"

Ramiz responded, "No. Once he is in there, short of an army division of men, we can't get to him." Khatib reacted with both a slump of his shoulders and a severe frown. Ramiz continued, "I've looked at the situation very thoroughly and feel we need to get him out of the U.S. before they get him to prison. And I think I've figured out a way to do it. It will take a small amount of well-trained men and some equipment, but I think it can be done." Then he proceeded to tell Khatib his plans, what he had found out in Colorado, and how they could go about freeing the ayatollah.

Khatib listened very closely. "So you are saying that as they are transporting him to the prison, we capture him and get him out of there. That sounds very risky to me. Can we get the information we need to pull it off?"

"I think so. The infidels are very free about the information, and it could very well be in the news over there."

Khatib pursed his lips and looked at the table. He looked back at Ramiz and said, "I see. Well, we have to do something, and can't take the chance that he will make it to that prison. Continue with your planning and we need to continue monitoring what they are doing so we can be ready."

Ramiz nodded and left the room. There was a great deal of detail he needed to work out, and he had to get to it. He would be spending a lot of time planning in the next few weeks, but the end result would be worth it.

Chapter Nine

Monday—March 13
Freeport, Texas—Ryan's Marina

It was now March, and the construction of the new marina office and Ryan's apartment was finally well underway. It had taken Ryan close to a month to get the necessary permits and select a contractor. The local building department had insisted the complex be built on higher ground so the periodic hurricane flooding damage would be reduced. That had driven several changes to the planning, and required fill on the property to increase the ground height by nearly six feet. That changed the landscape and increased the costs for Ryan. But he had no choice in the matter. He signed off on the required architectural changes and finally got construction underway in late February.

Jackie came down for a visit and was also pleased with the progress. The larger facility would be much nicer and more comfortable for the two of them. She had finally been able to remove her cast a few weeks earlier and was relieved to know that the bone had healed well. Her arm was a little weak from the injury, but that would resolve with use and time. She was just glad to get rid of the itchy thing.

Jasper and Dave had stopped by several times and had enjoyed a meal or two with Ryan on the boat. They watched the progress and did the usual kibitzing over the construction as it was moving along. Corey also maintained contact via email from his post in Turkey.

Corey was a former Special Forces soldier and had a lot of smarts and courage in dangerous situations. Now retired and part of the State Department diplomatic corps, he was stationed at the U.S. embassy in Jordan. He had helped with both an escape from the ayatollah and then capturing the ayatollah a few weeks later. He was a real asset to have around. He stood just under six foot and had both a military bearing and somewhat muscular, burly build. At slightly over two hundred pounds, he was a real asset in a serious disagreement. His unruly blondish hair was a contrast in the Arabic countries, but his knowledge of customs and their internal politics and governmental processes was second to none. He was friendly to their mission and had been indispensable in capturing the ayatollah the previous year.

Ryan had been in touch with Jack Harrison several times over the past couple of months and was trying to keep up with both the ayatollah's pretrial proceedings and what they might know about New Persia's current activities. Jack had passed on some of the information and that several appeals had been hung up in the Justice Department, but they hoped to have them resolved soon.

He also passed on that they had not heard much otherwise from their tracking of New Persia. It appeared that New Persia was lying low and waiting out the trial results ... but the administration just wasn't sure. The satellite monitoring of the stronghold indicated heavy and continuous training activity, and that was making the Washington security folks a bit nervous. The CIA had pulsed several of their Iranian and Yemeni contacts, but none could provide any information on what might be coming.

While it had been over nine months since Kadar and his crew were captured in the Gulf of Alaska, the legal firm hired by New Persia to defend the ayatollah had also filed appeals in their case and delayed any trial proceedings for them. It was, to use the old military term, a real "goat rope." The American legal system really could be tied up in knots at times ... and this was one of those times. So Kadar and his men just sat up there at taxpayer expense while waiting for the snail-slow system to respond.

Chapter Ten

Monday—April 3
Colorado Springs, Colorado

Ramiz, continuing with his planning for the rescue of the ayatollah, arrived at the Colorado Springs airport, picked up his bags, and went to the Hertz counter for a rental car. He drove out of the airport, picked up the Milton Proby Road to Academy Boulevard, and then south down to Interstate 25. After picking up the interstate, he drove down to Pueblo. He drove out to the Pueblo airport and looked around briefly, noting the aircraft training activity that was being conducted for the U.S. Air Force Academy cadets, watched some of the general aviation activity from Flower Aviation, getting a feel for the Class D airport, and then took U.S. Highway 50 toward Canon City.

On the way to Canon City, on the western outskirts of Pueblo, he stopped at Steel City Trucking and looked over several used heavy semi-tractors for sale. After several hours he had made a deal on a well-used Peterbilt tractor, and said to the salesperson that he would call to tell them where and when to deliver it. Given the cash deal, the dealer readily agreed, as long as it was within a fifty-mile radius of the dealership. Ramiz also took out an option to buy a second tractor along with two well-used trailers if all worked out as he hoped.

Ramiz then continued over to Canon City for the next task.

Arriving in the small community, he pulled over to the right into a strip mall and looked at his notes. Continuing on, he turned left on Ninth Street, crossed the Royal Gorge railway tracks, and continued on for a short distance, looking for Cal's Automotive Welding and Body Shop. He found it and pulled into the small parking area for an oversized double garage with an office to the left of the garage bays that looked like it had survived, just barely, the 1930s. It had a big "Oldsmobile" sign on the front. A sign on a frame near the street read, "All types of welding done. If you broke it, we can fix it."

He got out of his car and went in to the old office that had seen better days half a century ago. A burgundy couch was on one wall, with several splits and cracks in the ancient vinyl. An old cash register, which looked like it belonged in an antique shop, was on a well-weathered counter with a heavily scratched glass display case below it. Inside the case were several boxes of cigars and miscellaneous pocketknives with decorated handles.

A very large man with gapped teeth, frizzy hair, and large, muscular arms turned around from an old desk in a broken, well-worn military swivel chair, looked him over, and said, "I'm Cal Ferguson. But just call me Pinky. Whatcha need?"

Ramiz said, "I have some major modifications I'd like to get done to a semi-tractor. Can you do that?" He hesitated a moment and then asked, "Why do people call you Pinky?"

"Because, since I was a little kid, I've used my little finger to point at things and people." Then he pointed at Ramiz with his little finger and asked, "What kind of modifications?"

Ramiz smiled and nodded, and then told him what he wanted done to the large Peterbilt. Pinky stood up, which really emphasized his size, and walked over to the counter. He laid a hand that looked like it had been broken several times over on the counter, looked at Ramiz in the eye, and asked when he wanted it done. As he waited for a response from Ramiz, he took the well-chewed cigar out of his mouth and placed it on a small tray behind him. Ramiz told him as soon as possible. Pinky said he could do it, but it would be expensive. Ramiz waved the comment off and said he would have the truck there in the morning. It would be a cash deal—half now and half when completed. Ramiz said he would be in contact, gave Pinky half the agreed-to amount, and left. A gleam appeared in Pinky's eye as he anticipated a very large profit.

Ramiz didn't care. He had a mission to perform and he was going to complete it … successfully.

Tuesday—April 4
Canon City, Colorado

The next morning, a tired and half-drunk trucker pulled in to Cal's driving a blue 2015 model 579 Peterbilt tractor. He parked it outside Pinky's garage, walked in, gave Pinky the keys, and then said, "Here it is. Have fun." He chuckled a little and left. He stopped at the truck, opened the door, reached in, and pulled out two bottles of some kind of alcohol. He put the bottles in a small carry case, turned and winked at Pinky, and walked off down the road. A clearly happy person.

Pinky pulled the semi-tractor into the bay and began to work. After two days of work, the inside of the tractor looked like a skeleton. The windshield was gone, all the upholstery was gone to include the headliner and the associated GPS and communication equipment, and the seats were removed.

He cut required holes in the driver's door and the inside of the overhead cab. Sparks flew as he took two more days to fabricate one-inch steel panels to specifications and fit them in place. A large amount of welding was required and, when that was finished, a unique exterior paint was applied. All dull black with absolutely no sheen. The modified seats, with steel side panels, were installed along with bulletproof windshield glass.

After finishing the work two weeks later, Pinky looked over the total result and wondered what his customer was going to do with such a monster. It reminded Pinky of a more current version of a vehicle from one of his favorite movies, *Mad Max*. But nothing about it was illegal that he could tell. He quietly mused about it as he chewed on his cigar. With a smile, he thought, *Up to no good.*

Wednesday—May 3
Canon City, Colorado

A month after he contracted for the work, Ramiz came in, looked over the tractor, and gave Pinky the remaining funds. He turned to Pinky and asked if he could do another one just like it, and also do some changes to a couple of semitrailers.

Pinky nodded briefly. Then he said, "You know, it's really none of my business, and I'm certainly glad to have the business, but I can't help but be curious about what these trucks are going to be used for. They are a curious mix of capabilities."

Ramiz smiled at the comment. He then said, "Yes, they are unusual. And I understand your query. While I can't go into the details due to confidentiality concerns, I work for a small company that has just won an Army contract to move some dangerous classified materials. We aren't taking any chances that someone out there might want to disrupt our required transportation of those materials."

Pinky pursed his lips and shook his head. "Makes sense. I was just wondering about all that armor." Then he added, "Okay. Let's go over what you need and get on with it. Again, I appreciate your business."

A deal was agreed to and, after another Peterbilt was delivered to Cal's several days later, along with two semitrailers, Pinky began work again. This time delivery wouldn't be for a few months, and Pinky agreed to store the modified vehicles until Ramiz called for them.

They had a deal. Ramiz was pleased and Pinky had a good profit.

It was win-win.

Chapter Eleven

Thursday—May 11
Socotra Island—New Persia Compound

The commando training had gone well, and thirty-eight men had completed the rigorous six months of training. Another fifty men were now beginning the French-led course at the stronghold. A select group of seven men, along with some aircraft support resources, were assigned a unique mission ... rescue the *Persian Desert's* Captain Kadar and his crew.

Kadar, along with his twenty-four-man crew, had been captured by the U.S. Coast Guard nearly a year before in the waters off the southern coast of Alaska. They had been sabotaging the Alaskan pipeline and were caught through a cooperative effort of the U.S. Air Force satellite systems and Coast Guard management in Washington.

The ayatollah, before his capture, had stated that they were to be rescued and returned to New Persia as soon as possible. Khatib and Ramiz had now made it a priority, and the first mission of the new commando force was to rescue the ship and its crew. It turned out that the ship had been partially disassembled by the Americans, in a reverse-engineering effort, and could not be recovered. Therefore, only the crew would be rescued.

The infiltration/commando team had been well trained by the French and had practiced executing their tasks for several months now. The plan was complicated and would be difficult to pull off. Khatib was doubtful, but Ramiz was convinced that they could do it, and finally convinced him to go ahead with the rescue mission. Each of the seven members of the team were skilled at their assigned tasks, and each was dedicated to the mission assigned to them by the leaders of the New Persia movement. There were no questions about their loyalties.

It had been over five months since he had made the attempt on Ryan McKenzie, and Ramiz was anxious to proceed with the next phase of their plan. His failure with Ryan was eating at him, and he needed a successful mission to save face internally. He was convinced that it would work, and, with the planning and resources completed, wanted to get underway. They were ready and the plan would be executed. Kadar and his crew would be back with New Persia soon.

Monday—May 15
Anchorage, Alaska

Qasim, the commando leader, still stinging from the defeat in the Indian Ocean the previous year at the hands of Ryan McKenzie and crew, was anxious to get started. Qasim, almost six feet, with a bull of a chest, very strong arms, and dark, penetrating eyes, was intimidating and hard-tempered. He was leading the effort and wanted to teach these infidels a lesson. His commandos had all infiltrated the Alaskan territory through different routes and methods. Most had simply come ashore in remote areas and joined up at a rendezvous in Anchorage. All spoke English reasonably well and all were in excellent physical condition. It was a team to contend with.

Through use of a small powerboat, transferring supplies from an offshore tramp oil transport, they were able to bring what they needed ashore. Their mission was simple—rescue Kadar and the rest of his crew. They would be going up against the Alaskan Corrections officers that maintained the correctional institution in Anchorage where federal prisoners were held. A force to deal with. But their plan should work and they would, after it was complete and the ship's crew was on their way back to the Socotra center, make their way out of the U.S. and back home on their own. This would complicate the search and capture plans of the Americans immensely. Each commando to his own methods. And there would be no leaks in that type of individual planning.

Tuesday—May 16
Anchorage, Alaska

The all-black Gulfstream G650 aircraft, tail number G-DNHE, registered in Yemen, landed at Ted Stevens International Airport near Anchorage without incident at 1:00 a.m. and taxied to the general aviation terminal, requesting fuel as they arrived. All appeared normal as they were marshaled into the Signature Flight Support Executive Terminal parking area and shut down their engines. Rod, the copilot, exited the aircraft and watched as the refueling truck pulled up and began servicing the aircraft. The flight crew requested a complete top-off of the tanks. They had a special mission to perform.

By 1:30 a.m., the refueling was completed and Rod returned to the cockpit and assisted Sam, the pilot, in preparing the aircraft for their next mission task. At 2:10 a.m., Sam started the right engine in preparation for the quick arrival of passengers and to minimize their takeoff response time. The airport personnel had no idea what was about to happen.

Qasim, looking over the team, was proud of what they had already accomplished in getting onto American soil. They had beaten the odds and avoided detection by the police. It was 2:00 a.m. and the plan was about to get underway. The aircraft was waiting and, through radio communications, he knew it had refueled and was ready. 2:00 a.m. had been chosen because it was both the middle of the night and the internal manning of the detention center was minimal at only six correction personnel. Surveillance verified this information.

He deployed his men. Two men took the small rental SUV and headed for the chief of police's home. They would have the task of delaying the chief as long as possible.

One technically trained commando, with an electronics background, headed for the local telephone company switch box, located on the side of the entrance road to the detention center. He also had the responsibility for taking out the local cell tower positioned just outside the center complex.

Two men, each carrying an RPG with a high-explosive head, moved into position outside the center. One also carried a small high-powered laser.

One man headed for the motor pool in the rear of the complex.

And finally, one man with three thermite grenades prepared to scale the wall of the detention center to access the roof.

Waiting for a confirmation call telling him the two men were in place at the chief's residence, Qasim was nervous. The call came through. By cutting off all four tire valves on all the vehicles, they had silently disabled both the official vehicles and the personal vehicles of the chief. The chief could not respond even if he knew something was going on.

The action then began at the detention center. Simultaneously the laser took out the front camera, the telephone switch box was destroyed with a thermite device, the cell tower cabling was cut at the base, and the two men with the RPGs walked into the lobby. They buzzed the deputy behind the glass enclosure, and when he showed up they threatened him. He ran back in to the interior and tried to talk over his two-way radio, to no avail. They blasted through the front desk area with a grenade and quickly followed him.

On the roof, the terrorist ran to the closest vent and dropped a grenade into it. It exploded with a tremendous blast and fire started burning fiercely. He moved on to two more vents and repeated the process. He lowered himself to the ground and joined Qasim in rounding up the guards.

The fire then set off an emergency evacuation process required by the local building codes and fire department. The fire suppression system, to avoid possible loss of life and sensing the heat, unlocked all the cellblocks. The entire crew, including Kadar, was released into the corridors. They headed out the back of the building while the six guards, with two of them wounded in the fray, now captured by Qasim and his men, watched. Sirens were going off, klaxons were sounding, but no one was responding. The captured guards couldn't let the few roving patrols out in the city know what was happening. The fire department would take at least ten minutes to respond to the remote alarms.

The New Persia crewmen ran out the back of the building to the detention center buses, where one of the buses was hot-wired and idling. Kadar and his crew piled into the bus and they were quickly driven out of the compound, heading for the airport. Qasim and the remaining men held the guards from moving, and finally, after the bus was gone, raced out to their vehicle and disappeared down the road. They would disperse across Alaska, blend in, and eventually make their way back to Socotra.

At the airport, the nearly invisible plane was waiting with one engine running. The two pilots saw a prison bus come barreling up an entrance ramp to the general aviation aircraft parking area. It smashed through the fenced barricade and raced for the Gulfstream. The bus screeched to a halt near the stairwell, and the men piled out and raced up the stairs, taking seats as fast as they could. Those that couldn't get seats on the eighteen-passenger jet sat on the floor. Having already received permission to taxi from ground control, Sam began moving the Gulfstream once the last man was through the door. Rod began spooling up the left engine as Abdul, the on-board steward, pulled up the stairway into the aircraft and secured it.

Taxiing down the taxiway to the end of runway 25R, Sam pulled up short of the runway, noting that a large cargo aircraft was on final a few miles out. The tower had told him to wait at the hold line until cleared for takeoff.

As they were anxiously waiting, Rod looked back at the general aviation terminal area and saw multiple emergency lights, with several of them headed for their position. He glanced over to Sam and said, "We'd better boogie out of here. It looks like the action at the terminal has picked up and several vehicles are coming after us."

As he said it, they were contacted by the tower: "Gulfstream November Hotel Echo, return to the terminal. There is a problem and you are not cleared for takeoff. Repeat, return to the terminal."

Sam glanced at Rod then out the window at the approaching aircraft. Noting that it was still some distance out, he keyed the mike and said, "Anchorage Tower, Gulfstream November Hotel Echo. Cannot comply. Direct approaching traffic to go around. We are taking the active."

From the tower came, "Negative. Do not enter the runway. Repeat, do not take the runway." But Sam had already increased power to the engines and was turning onto the runway as Rod continued to advance the throttles until they were fully open. The twin Rolls-Royce 725 engines responded with their full seventeen thousand pounds of thrust each, and the Gulfstream quickly accelerated. Sam told the tower, "On Runway 25 right and departing. Sorry 'bout that." He then heard the tower quickly telling the cargo aircraft to abort the landing and go around. As they rapidly accelerated down the runway, they could hear the engines of the approaching 747 cargo aircraft spooling up as the heavy UPS jet was breaking off to the right to avoid a collision.

Reaching rotation speed, Sam turned off the position and collision lights and pulled back the yoke, and they were off. At 2:20 a.m., only one person was in the tower, and he was stunned by the events. The other controller had gone to the restroom and missed all the action. Once the Gulfstream was airborne, the controller suddenly realized what had happened and finally sounded the emergency alarm ... too late. The black aircraft was gone into the darkness with no lights showing. Both the airport police and the fire department could do nothing about it.

They flew very low and unlit, staying under radar coverage as they headed south over the water of Cook Inlet, and finally, after fifteen minutes and close to one hundred miles out over the ocean, began climbing to a cruise altitude of forty-one thousand feet. The men in the cabin of the aircraft began to rearrange themselves so they could be more comfortable. They couldn't believe what had just happened. Several were praying, but most were thinking and grinning to themselves. Several high fives were exchanged.

Sam Drury, the senior pilot with over two thousand hours in Gulfstream jets, was relaxed and monitoring the flight instruments as they cruised. The jet was performing flawlessly at 510 miles per hour and, with a range of over eight thousand miles, would reach their destination in Hong Kong for refueling with no problems. A cup of steaming coffee was in its holder, compliments of Abdul, and he was comfortable. They were now nearly three hours out of Anchorage and over the northern Pacific Ocean. The autopilot was performing very minor changes, but they were hardly noticeable. All had gone according to plan, and he was confident they would have no further problems. While there was a slight overload of the aircraft limit of six thousand pounds, he wasn't worried about it. His twenty-six passengers from the New Persia group, squeezed into the spacious cabin built to hold eighteen passengers, were also relaxed, and most were sleeping after the flurry of excitement as they escaped. Abdul had provided all of them with some fruit snacks and water.

Colonel Joe Carson, commander of the 176th Air Defense Wing at Joint Base Elmendorf-Richardson in Anchorage, Alaska, was watching the action closely as two of his F-22 fighters closed in on the fleeing Gulfstream Jet. The Gulfstream was carrying the escaped prisoners from the detention center, and it had taken some time for the approval process to work through the federal bureaucracy in the middle of the night. After nearly two hours of waiting on the request from the Department of Justice to be approved by the Pentagon, he had finally been able to get his fighters in the air in pursuit of the Gulfstream.

Two of his best pilots were in the flight, led by Captain Steve Masters. The wingman was Lieutenant Curly Comoro. Both were experienced interceptor pilots and would do the job as required. After approval, both aircraft took off and were quickly in supersonic cruise mode to catch the fleeing aircraft.

He waited as the fighters closed in and slowed down to match the Gulfstream's speed. He listened as Captain Masters hailed the Gulfstream and they responded. Communications had been established. Now all they had to do was get the Gulfstream to turn around and return to Anchorage.

Sam's eyes went to the communications suite of equipment as he heard on guard channel, "Gulfstream, this is the U.S. Air Force F-22 off your right wing. My wingman is on your left. Please respond."

Sam said to Rod, "Damn. Thought we had gotten far enough away from those guys. What are they doing way out here? We're over twelve hundred miles from land."

Rod looked back and just shrugged. He adjusted the radio to guard channel and replied to the F-22 pilot, "Gulfstream to F-22. We read you loud and clear. What do you need?" He knew full well what they wanted, but was playing it cool.

"Gulfstream, we have intercepted you and are directing you to return to Anchorage. We will accompany you back there until you touch down. Do you read?"

Rod responded, "I read you loud and clear." He looked knowingly at Sam as he continued, "Sorry, but we cannot comply. We are not U.S. registered and are over international waters on our way to our intended destination. You have no authority to direct us to another course."

The F-22 on the right, with the flight commander on board, pulled slightly forward until he was even with the G650's cockpit. He looked over at the G650 crew, illuminated by the low lights in the cockpit, and motioned for them to turn around. Both Sam and Rod shook their heads. The F-22 then backed off slightly. They could see him adjusting something in the fighter's cockpit, and appeared to be talking with someone on a different frequency.

"176 CP, the Master, over," said Captain Masters on the command post frequency, using his call sign.

"Master, 176 CP, read you loud and clear. Status, please."

"176 CP, bogey refuses to turn. Request guidance."

Colonel Carson looked at the floor. Damn. It might not be that easy. Apparently the Gulfstream wasn't going to cooperate.

Colonel Carson pressed his mike button and said, "Colonel Carson, Master. Threaten them with any force necessary, but do nothing for now."

"Master. Roger that. Threaten but do nothing."

Captain Masters then eased forward and came up on guard channel again, and they heard, "I have just received approval to force you to return to Anchorage and by any means necessary. Do you read me?"

Sam and Rod both looked at the F-22 and then at each other. Looking back at the F-22, they could see missiles under both wings. The jet on their left also crept forward, and they could see the identical missiles under its wings.

Sam took the lead this time. "We read you loud and clear. However, we are not altering course, nor are we telling you where we are heading. You aren't going to splash an unarmed civilian aircraft with unknown personnel on board. The U.S. reputation would be severely harmed if you did, and proof would be in our black box recording this and all other communications. It is also being currently transmitted via satellite back to our home station and being recorded. It is a false threat. Since you do not have enough fuel to follow us to our destination and must shortly return to your home station, I bid you goodbye."

The lead F-22 stayed off their right wing for several minutes as the pilots relayed Sam's comments to their headquarters.

"176 CP, Masters. They are still refusing and calling my bluff. They say we wouldn't dare shoot down an unarmed civilian aircraft with unknown personnel aboard. Again, request guidance."

Colonel Carson thought for a few moments and realized he couldn't authorize the shooting down of an unarmed civilian aircraft, regardless of the circumstances. The U.S. Air Force just didn't do that. He briefly put his hands over his eyes, looked at his controller, keyed the mike, and said, "Master, 176 CP. Stand down and return to base."

He turned to the CP controller and said, "Continue to track the Gulfstream as long as you can." The controller nodded in acknowledgement and said, "Yes, sir."

Colonel Carson then went back to his office, composed a message of the circumstances, returned to the command post, and transmitted the "flash" precedence message up-channel. He knew it would cause all sorts of concern at the levels above him. But facts were facts, and he didn't want to fudge on it. Higher levels could do that if they needed to.

With a flurry of activity in the dark Pacific night, both fighters hit their afterburners, climbed out past the still-cruising Gulfstream jet, and reversed their heading back to Anchorage.

65

Sam looked at Rod and they gave each other high fives.

Sam's comments had hit the mark. He reached over and took a swallow of his now-cool coffee, looked out the window at the pale, starlit ocean far below, and breathed a sigh of relief.

Several hours later, they began their approach to Hong Kong's airport. Khatib had made previous arrangements, through their Chinese support representative, to support their arrival. They were able to refuel, get some additional supplies, and continue their journey south and west to Socotra.

Ramiz and Khatib, monitoring the rescue attempt, were ecstatic. They had received reports from Qasim via an internet connection from an Anchorage free Wi-Fi location. All had gone as planned, with no casualties to New Persia personnel. Kadar, while the aircraft was refueling in Hong Kong, had also sent in a report of the successful mission.

When the Gulfstream landed at the Socotra airport in Hadibo, both Ramiz and Khatib met Kadar and the crew. All were excited to be free and back home. Sam and Rod were thanked profusely and congratulated on the successful flight, and the stick-it-in-your-ear response to the U.S. fighters. The radio traffic had, indeed, been monitored and recorded in the New Persia Operations Center.

Ramiz and Khatib smiled as they realized that phase two of their planning had been successful.

The Gulfstream was then pulled into a hangar and modifications to the tail number designation made. It was readied for the flight out the following morning to its home base in Yemen.

Tuesday—May 16
Washington, D.C.—The White House

Reports of the situation, from the Department of Justice, the FAA, and the Pentagon, quickly filtered up to the White House. Jack Harrison briefed an incredulous president on the situation and what had been accomplished by the commandos. President Martinez was livid.

"Jack! What you're telling me is that they escaped from the detention center up there and left a flaming ruin of the facility. How could that happen? Where was the police chief? How could they get off the ground?"

Jack responded, "As I said, it was obviously a well-planned commando raid with the intent of getting their people back. They came in with a lot of firepower, disabled the radio net, disabled the chief's cars, all of them, and got off without permission from the tower. The tower was minimally manned, since it was the middle of the night. And then, when the fighters did finally catch up with them, they thumbed their noses and kept on going. It took a lot of guts, and they made it. We tracked them as far as we could and think they went to China somewhere. At least, that's what we think, since the Chinese, even though they won't admit it, have been helping them extensively. And we just found out the aircraft registration they used was bogus. No such number exists for a Gulfstream. They're gone."

The president nodded and said, "Well, I guess this proves the ayatollah's comment about them continuing with their movement without him." He looked out the window at the early morning, turned, and added, "This is getting to be too much. We have the ayatollah in custody and about to stand trial, and they pull this off. It sure will raise his cred in the terrorist community. The mighty U.S. could not hold his people. Quite a smear on our faces."

Jack stood mute. Not much else to say. The president was right.

The president gazed back out the window again, shook his head from side to side, turned around, and finished, "Well, draft up a letter from me to the two wounded guards."

Jack nodded and turned back to his office, dictated a short letter for the president's signature, and left it for the administrative staff. He was feeling very tired.

The escape could not be kept from the media. The damage to the facility and the difficulty the police chief had in getting to the prison all had the media's attention within minutes. The local news organizations all monitored the local law enforcement and fire department radio frequencies. They knew when an emergency was going down ... and they responded almost as fast as the emergency crews. The fire could be seen for some distance, and the fire department response was both quick and effective ... but not until the New Persia commandos had departed and were well on their way.

TV coverage on a national basis was complete, and several of the news organizations had observers and reporters on the scene within a very short time. When word got out that the prisoners had escaped, the airport was also well covered with news reports. The response from the Air Force was also covered but, for the most part, it was "no comment." The fact that their fighters had failed to turn the Gulfstream around was not released to the public.

Chapter Twelve

Monday—June 5
Washington, D.C.—The White House

The president was in conference with Jack Harrison and Mark Allison, his CIA director. They were in the Oval Office in the early evening hours, enjoying a small libation and informal discussion. The Anchorage raid had become old news and, after a few weeks, was not on their minds. However, the president was concerned over the progress being made, or not being made, on the prosecution of the ayatollah.

"Jack, you're kinda tracking this thing with the ayatollah. What's going on?"

"Well, between claims that we kidnapped an Iranian citizen, brought him here illegally and have kept him in prison illegally, and jurisdiction problems within the Justice Department, it's a real exercise in futility. I think now, after many months of wrangling, we aren't too far from getting him into federal court on terrorism charges."

"Where are we holding him?"

"Right now he's in Richmond."

"So, for the trial stuff, he would be brought back here?"

"No. The federal district court, the Fourth Circuit court in Richmond, will be the location for his trial."

"So he'll be transferred back and forth by the U.S. marshals?"

"Yes. And they are being real careful about his transport. They don't want any issues to occur."

After turning to Mark and sipping his drink, the president asked, "Do we have any indication of further problems from this group?"

"Yes and no."

The president looked puzzled. He looked at Mark, spreading his hands in front of himself in an unspoken question.

Mark continued, "We don't see any overt activity except for the continuing step up in training at the stronghold, which may not amount to much. But we have intercepted some message traffic that indicates they may be planning something in the near future. But we're not sure. And, of course, the breakout in Anchorage indicates they are getting much more sophisticated."

"What do you mean?"

"The attack in Anchorage was well planned, well timed, and took considerable commando expertise and effort. And now there has been an increase in some of their logistics requirements, including equipment and supplies that mean they may be trying to mount some form of other clandestine attack."

The president blankly looked at the far wall, took a sip of his martini, looked back at Mark, and asked, "Do we know where or when?"

"No. Not yet. But the satellite images we are monitoring show some of these supplies being unloaded in the New Persia harbor. There is a trimaran anchored there and the supplies and equipment are being loaded on board. They have also loaded a lot of food supplies, enough for a sizable force for several weeks. So there is activity ... we just don't know what they are doing right now."

"And all this is going on without the input of the ayatollah."

"Yes, sir. We have received word off the street that Khatib, his primary assistant, is running things there now. And if anything, he is more difficult to deal with than the ayatollah. And there has also been a change in their defense ministry. The rumor is that Abdul-Hakim is dead and Ramiz Al Sahaf has taken over. Several significant changes."

"So, even though it has been almost nine months since we captured him, they are still apparently preparing to continue their mischief?"

"Appears so." And Mark took a sip from his bourbon and ginger ale.

"I take it they are also monitoring what is happening in the legal area?" the president said to no one in particular.

Jack responded, "Since New Persia hired the crack legal team of Whitson, Jackson, Johnson, and Taylor, I would assume they are getting updates quite frequently."

The president shrugged. "Well, we can't do much about that. Mark, have we been able to get any information on the apparent Chinese support of this group?"

"What Chinese support?" Mark said sarcastically. "They deny anything to do with New Persia, even though we have two of the yachts and one of the trimarans they built. They claim they built the yachts and the trimaran for a wealthy Arab and he sold them to someone else. But they don't know who that might be." And as he finished, he smirked a bit. "Of course, they provide spare parts and technical support to this mysterious customer of the Arab." Then, in a more serious tone, he said, "Seriously. No. We haven't been able to crack the Chinese connection. We know it's there, but they totally deny it."

"And the trimaran that we captured in Alaska. Anything off that?"

"Again, yes and no. It is quite a ship and has capabilities unlike anything we have seen before. The propulsion system will drive it, if necessary, at over fifty knots. And it is more than capable of worldwide operations. There was nothing of note on the electronics, except they were certainly state of the art. And the little submarine that was the third hull was not as capable in terms of depth as the one we got in the gulf last year, but it could carry several more people. Ideal for a commando group. Otherwise, the trimaran was impressive in its size, and could certainly be used as a base of operations along our coastlines."

"Something to watch for?"

"Yes, sir. I think we need to alert the Coast Guard if we know it is in an area. It could be looking for trouble or planning on a raid in the future. And if we lose track of it, the Coast Guard should be put on alert. I'd suggest we send pictures of it to every Coast Guard station on our outer coasts."

"Sounds reasonable. Jack, talk with Bob Goldstein, our good treasury secretary, and make sure it happens."

"Yes, sir."

"Mark, is it possible that the ayatollah's friends could try to spring him?"

"Yes. It would really put egg on our face, and they want him back as soon as possible. That's one of the reasons the marshals are being so careful when transporting him. Given the protection he is getting, I don't think we need to worry too much at this point. And if we can get him into the supermax out in Colorado, he will be locked up permanently. That's assuming that our friendly courts find him guilty and he gets a good, long sentence. I say the supermax facility because he is definitely a flight risk."

The president nodded and pursed his lips as he said, "We really need to keep a close eye on that. If he were to escape ... well, I'd hate to think of the consequences. Not only our own people, but the world community would be astonished and outraged."

"Yes, sir. We need to keep our eyes and ears open to anything out there. I'd hate to see it happen, but you can never tell."

They all raised their glasses to that.

Chapter Thirteen

Monday—June 5
Oman—Salalah

Khatib stood at the ayatollah's office window in Salalah, looking at the deep blue of the Gulf of Oman, and pondering the kidnapping of the ayatollah over nine months before. He noted that several local fishing boats were moving around as they either went out or came back in. New Persia would eventually get the ayatollah back, but he had no idea when that might occur. The infidels in America were not complying with the New Persia demands, and the children of the future would be set back in their standard of living because of it. The president of the U.S., Al Martinez, was just not going along with their requirements, and the kidnapping of the ayatollah late last year added more problems to the pile.

He thought about the lack of response to their requirements, and it suddenly occurred to him that perhaps they were not putting pressure on the right place in American life. The president had a lot of influence over the American government, but he wasn't the only one. An idea began to form in Khatib's mind. He thought for several more minutes and then called Ramiz and asked him to meet in his office.

Several minutes later, Ramiz lightly knocked on the office doorframe. "You called for me?"

Khatib responded, "Yes, Ramiz. Please have a seat. I have some questions for you on how the American government functions."

Ramiz walked into the office and sat down in one of the softer chairs. He looked questioningly at Khatib.

Khatib continued to look out the window at the bright sunshine and deep blue waters. He gathered his thoughts. "I need to have a better understanding of how the American government works. It is very obvious that our efforts, so far, have failed with this infidel president. But aren't there other aspects of their government that have power and might be able to help us?"

Ramiz thought for just a moment and then looked back and responded, "Yes, there are. He is just one of many government

72

officials. The other main organization that would, or could, affect us is their Congress."

Khatib nodded. "Sort of like the British Parliament or the German Bundestag. As I understand it, it's a body of elected people that make the laws. And then the president has to sign them for them to take effect."

Ramiz nodded also. "Yes. They do that and they also have to ratify treaties and do other things to make sure the government runs well. They are the primary source of arranging funding for the government and set taxation laws for the people." He paused and then asked, "But why do you ask these questions? They have not been involved in our activities."

"Because, Ramiz, it has occurred to me that maybe we need some help with convincing the U.S. administration to reduce their oil usage. We have tried for some time now to get the president to lead the way to that kind of reduction, and that has not worked, even with the intimidations we have imposed. So, it occurs to me that we need to get the infidels' Congress to apply pressure also. They could do it through law changes or personal contact and convincing of the president. Either way, we would be ahead."

Ramiz sat there staring at Khatib. What he was proposing, at least what Ramiz interpreted, would be unheard of in the world up to this time. He knew Khatib's mind was thinking about "convincing" congressmen to support oil-use reductions. And that "convincing" would take the form of some type of coercion. Unheard of for terrorists. At least so far.

"If I understand what you are thinking, to basically threaten congressmen to pressure the president—that is a major step and it could really backfire at us."

"Oh, I'm not just thinking about it. I'm convinced it is a good idea and will work. Congressmen are just like any other people. They are concerned for their station in life and for their loved ones. They would listen to reason. We could approach the more influential ones and convince them that our cause is just and that the U.S. needs to help us win the world to our cause. That way we are sort of going around the president and his bullheaded ways. What do you think?"

Ramiz was listening. The idea was extremely audacious and probably had no chance in hell of succeeding. He found it difficult to accept. With 435 representatives and one hundred senators in Congress, there was more than enough choice ... but talk about pulling the eagle's tail feathers! Wow!

Ramiz looked past Khatib and out the window again. How did he answer this one? And he knew who would be tasked to carry out the required actions to convince the congressmen.

Khatib then added, "You looked unconvinced. Does this idea trouble you?"

Ramiz looked back at Khatib and said, "Yes. It does trouble me. I'm afraid it will not work and we will have many more problems to deal with. Many of those congressmen have a very high opinion of themselves, and they would be very upset if threatened. Especially if it was their families that were threatened. Some are quite powerful, and the backlash could be significant. And our cause could be lessened significantly."

"I see. So you feel we should just continue to accept the western world's waste and corruption? For us to not do anything to combat these entrenched enemies?"

"No, no, no, of course not. I just feel that we need to be more cautious. Especially since they now have the ayatollah in their grips."

"Hmmm. Now, that is a valid point. I think the rest of what you say is just not a consideration. People are people, regardless of their position. And they are going to be concerned about the welfare of their families."

Ramiz nodded. Khatib was running the effort and was the boss. He knew and respected that. But he didn't agree with what Khatib was suggesting. He was much more aware of the American mindset than Khatib, and he felt that Khatib might overstep and cause a major headache to their cause.

Khatib said, "I'm going to draft a message for all the congressmen. I will let you review it and comment on it. But we are going down this path, and I think it will ultimately be successful. Even if you don't."

Ramiz nodded, bowed, and left the office. Well, at least he had told him. Where it would all end up was anybody's guess.

Khatib sat down at the ayatollah's desk and began to draft a letter that he intended to send to every American congressman. It would be nice, but laced with threats should they decide to ignore him.

After several drafts, he finally wrote:

Dear American Congressman;

I am writing this note to you due to my frustration with your current administration in not complying with the requirements put forth by the ayatollah during his UN speech. As you are undoubtedly aware by now, we have taken several measures to convince your administration, and that of several other western nations, to comply with those requirements. Your President Martinez has decided to ignore our requirements. That is a mistake.

At this point in time you have, as a country, captured and kidnapped our leader, Ayatollah Abdul Sarhardi. He is to be released immediately. There is no valid reason for holding him in your antiquated penal system.

As mentioned above, we made demands some time back through the ayatollah's UN address and there has been no apparent attempt to comply with those demands. Not even a token effort. Therefore, as you well now know, we will begin another series of incursions on your soil to encourage you to comply. They will start soon and will have severe impacts to your economy. All of this can be avoided by the simple act on your part of complying with our requirements.

Should the above not be forthcoming—that is, compliance with our requirements and the release of our leader—we will take further steps to elicit your cooperation. Those steps will include selecting, at random, fifty of your colleagues for intense attention from our commando capabilities. There is no escaping this warning. We simply need your cooperation in convincing your administration of the need to meet our requirements.

I would hope you choose the right path and assist us in conserving our precious energy resources.

Tuesday—June 6
Washington, D.C.

The message was sent via email to every congressperson and selected organizations within the administration. The uproar was huge. It was obviously leaked to the press, and the reaction ran from total disbelief, to ridicule, to acceptance. Acceptance by some of the more radical environmental groups as they concurred with the goals of the New Persia movement. Tracing the message back, the source was a server in an unoccupied building in Yemen. A dead end.

The uproar created by the message from Khatib was unprecedented in U.S. history. While there had been individual threats on congress people in the past, there had not been one that potentially targeted every congressman or woman. The FBI and CIA had to work together once it was determined that the message originated in Yemen. But neither organization was able to gather any actionable intelligence on the source or the possible real location of the sender. New Persia had identified itself as the sender, and it was not located in Yemen ... but everyone, considering the attack on Ryan and the events in Alaska, took the message seriously. There wasn't any choice. Security was beefed up around the Capitol areas, and each congressman and woman was temporarily assigned a personal guard until the menace could be eliminated.

President Martinez walked into the Oval Office, where Mark, Jerry, and Andy Strasner, the FBI director, were present. The president sat down and looked at Mark.

"Mark. Have we got any information on the validity of this note?"

"Considering where it apparently came from, I'd have to say it's certainly valid." Mark looked over at Jerry and continued, "We need to consider it not only valid, but New Persia could be up to something as we sit here. It would appear that, between the raid in Alaska and this note, New Persia is coming out of hiding and making itself known again. And not in a good way." He looked back at the president. "Further actions to protect the congress people and their families are needed while we track this thing down."

The president looked back at Jerry and said, "Do we have the manpower to protect 535 congress people? It's a lot of manpower."

Jerry responded, "Yes, sir. We can do it, but I will have to bring people in from around the country. And the congress people would have to cooperate; not all of them will be willing to do that. It will be quite an intrusion on their privacy."

"Hmm. I think you are right. But what other choice do we have? Once we have taken out the head characters of New Persia, we won't have so much to worry about. But that will take some time, and resources too. We need to be seen taking quick action until that can be done."

"I have to agree with you," said Mark. "And we need to move fast. I would suggest we develop a quick plan and get with the leadership in Congress, explain it, and get their input. There may also be a plan for this type of thing already available and it just needs to be dusted off."

Jerry looked back, thought for a minute, and moved into a corner of the room, taking out his cell phone. A few moments later he came back and said, "You're right, Mark. There is a plan out there. I'll be reviewing it this afternoon, and then we can get back together and figure out what we want to do." Andy, who had been silent during the discussion, just nodded.

The president looked at the three of them and said, "Sounds good. Let's get together again tonight. Fortunately, I'm free this evening. We'll have some dinner about 6:00 p.m. and figure out a way forward. That sound okay to you?"

They looked back and nodded.

It was early evening and the dinner had been cleared from the table. After dinner, wine—a nice Pinot Noir—had been served, and the four of them were relaxing. It had been a long and exhausting day spent, at least in part, fending off congress people who were very anxious about their families. They all recognized the very immediate need of getting some additional protection out there—and doing it quickly.

Thursday—June 8
Washington, D.C.—White House Situation Room

Two days later, briefings were held in the White House Situation Room with the various leaders of the House of Representatives and the Senate. Tension was high, as they all felt the pressures of the threatening email. Members of the Capital Police and the Washington Metropolitan Police organizations were also present.

The president was there but let Jerry Ocasio lead the briefings as they reviewed the plans for protecting the 535 members of Congress. A herculean challenge in today's world of rapid travel and access to weapons. He took the stage and began:

"Ladies and gentlemen. The recent threats we have received from the New Persia organization are considered valid and of serious concern by the administration. We want to assure you that everything in our power is being done to track this down and, simultaneously, to protect you and your families. Each of you has already had either a police officer or a member of the FBI assigned to be with you twenty-four-seven to protect you. Your homes are all under constant watch and your transportation to and from your offices remains secure. In your various offices, the Capital Police have increased their presence to counter any potential problems. To assist in this effort and to help reinforce the protective presence, four companies of Army personnel are en route from Fort Bragg in North Carolina. Their function will be to provide relief for the current protective forces."

Jerry stopped for a moment and looked around. Then he continued, "We are doing all we can to try and track down the source of this threat. We know it came from New Persia but are not sure of the actual source location. And there is an enhanced effort underway at all entry points to the U.S. for travelers to make sure these so-called commandos don't get in to the U.S.

"I would suggest that, until we can get a resolution to this problem, you maintain vigilance. If you desire to, diluting the target base would be a good idea. By that I mean move some members of your families to another location. That will make it more difficult for these characters to find you. I don't mean to scare you, but this is a real situation we are facing, and we need to take all possible precautions."

Senator Jim McIlroy of Texas interrupted, saying, "Given what happened in Alaska, I think we all feel this is very credible. I, for one, have taken measures to protect my wife and kids. They are no longer in Washington. But I hate the feeling of giving in. When can we expect to see some further developments on tracking this threat to ground?"

"We are working it as hard as we can and in concert with several other nations in the west. But I won't pull your leg on this one. We aren't making much progress. The normally reliable Middle East sources have dried up and are not responding to our queries."

Senator McIlroy just looked back at Jerry. After a moment he said, "Well, we need to pull out all the stops on this. There is no way we can let anybody threaten this organization and the core of the U.S. government. I would suggest that we take on the locations of New Persia, if we know where they are, and remove them from consideration." He stopped and looked around at the approving gestures of the rest of the audience. Then he continued, "This needs to backfire on whoever sent it. We need to make sure they never have this opportunity again."

Jerry replied, "As soon as we can find these people, they will be taken care of. Unfortunately, since they are foreign subjects, we can't just go out and capture them. There are many issues that have to be addressed. The protections we have in place should provide some comfort and, if used properly and to the full extent of our capabilities, will block any further actions on New Persia's part. But it does require that you and the other people being protected maintain some vigilance and help us help you. I would encourage all of you to be very aware of your surroundings and take appropriate precautions."

78

The senator just nodded.

The meeting then broke up, with a lot of conversation and discussion as people left.

Chapter Fourteen

Monday—June 12
Richmond, Virginia—Federal Court

The court proceedings had finally started to move after months of delays due to procedural issues and appeals by the defense. The internationally known law firm of Whitson, Jackson, Johnson, and Taylor had managed to delay the proceedings until now. The appeals were all eventually dismissed by the presiding Judge Bernard Smyth, but they had caused a long delay in the trial proceedings. The U.S. Department of Justice was finally getting the trial underway.

A motion for bail by the defense team was submitted to an incredulous Judge Smyth and the prosecution team. In less than a few seconds it was denied, with the comment that this was a terrorist trial and the defendant was a serious flight risk.

Judge Smyth had made the decision, against the defense's objection, to allow live television coverage of the trial proceedings. In his decision he stated that since federal property, and its destruction, was one of the allegations for the trial, the American public was entitled to see the proceedings and results of the trial process. He was referring to the destruction of various aircraft belonging to the U.S. government. One of the more liberal judges on the federal bench, he strongly believed the public had a right to know what happened in courtrooms.

Friday—June 23
Richmond, Virginia—Federal Court

Jury selection took almost two weeks. The defense team was insisting on a total Muslim jury to satisfy the requirement of "trial by peers." Judge Smyth was irritated because the jury pool did not contain enough eligible Muslims, and the delays were getting more difficult to tolerate. He wanted to be more expeditious and move on. In addition, he did not feel that religion should play a role in the trial. The ayatollah was on trial as a terrorist and not because he was a Muslim. The final tally was nine people who professed to be Muslim. The other three, plus the two alternates, were noncommittal in their religious preference. The defense team felt it was the best they could do under the circumstances and did not wish to irritate the judge any more than necessary.

The ayatollah was a thin man, and some would call him very intense. He stood moderately tall at about six feet, but weighed only 160 pounds. He had a slight, dark beard that he kept trimmed fairly close. His eyes related his passion for his dream; they were piercing and captivated people close to him. He was well educated and spoke with both a knowledgeable background and fervent zeal for his beliefs. His distaste for the west and its wasteful ways was extreme. His voice fairly boomed when he wanted it to, and he was direct and to the point when he spoke.

The ayatollah, now sullen at his defendant position in the courtroom, had to be nearly dragged in and out as the proceedings progressed. He was totally uncooperative. While the option remained for the ayatollah to watch the proceedings via closed-circuit television, Judge Smyth insisted that he be in the courtroom to watch the drama unfold. It also permitted the courtroom spectators, and the jury, to see the man and observe his reactions as the trial progressed.

The federal-style home was located on a very pleasant tree-shaded street of prosperous attorneys, financial entrepreneurs, doctors, and other professionals. It sat back off the curbless asphalt road about one hundred feet, and had several mature trees in the front yard. The clapboard was painted white with dark green shutters, and the house had a small front portico with twin columns. It was obviously well maintained. The home of Judge Bernhard Smyth, it was well recognized in the upscale community as the source of many societal events.

It was also very vulnerable.

Ramiz drove by the home and made several notes to himself. He drove around to the street behind the house and saw that the attached garage was under what was probably a very large upstairs bedroom. There were no guards like he would have seen in his home country, and no apparent concerns for security. No fences or barricades of any sort. Just the trees and some hedges between properties. It was just open. You could walk right up to the front door and knock. The driveway was paved to the garage in the back and there was a basketball hoop in front of the garage. An ADT sign was at the front near the portico. Very American and very domestic.

And very easy.

Monday—June 26
Richmond, Virginia—Judge Smyth's Home

Ayatollah no guilty. For safety of family and you, the scrawled note read. Judge Smyth could not believe what he was reading. He was standing next to his Buick SUV and reading the folded note that had been taped to the driver's-side window. He was *inside* his garage and was about to start his commute to his office in the federal courthouse downtown. After his usual fast walk around the block and morning breakfast, he had gotten dressed, kissed his wife Jeraldine goodbye, and proceeded to the garage. He was stunned. Someone was threatening him ... and had come to his home to do it. Actually come into the garage. They were that close. He stood there for several moments; his eyes went to every corner of the three-car garage. He walked around to make sure no one was there.

After thinking about it for a few more minutes, he went back inside and called Maury "Moe" Chambers, the local head of the U.S. Marshals service for the area. Moe wasn't in yet, and the judge left a detailed message. Jeraldine was looking on with confused concern. Her husband didn't normally come back in to the house when he left for work. Overhearing the conversation, and the obvious threat, she became very nervous.

The judge put the phone back in its charger and came over to her.

With a lot of concern, she said, "What was that all about? Some kind of threat?"

He responded, "Yes. But I don't know if it is credible. I asked Moe to give me a call when he comes in. In the meantime, I think I'll stay home and make sure nothing comes of it. When he calls back I'll discuss it with him and see what he suggests we do."

Jeraldine gave a dubious look and a short nod. Not sure what to do, she said, "Okay. I'm going upstairs and getting dressed. Let me know what happens." And she turned, went through the center hall, and up the stairs to the bedroom.

Moe Chambers came in to his office, hung up his light coat, and went to his desk. He noticed that the phone light was on, indicating a message. He pushed the play button on the recording and listened to the message from Judge Smyth. His quiet morning evaporated. Threatening a federal judge in the U.S. was extremely serious and very uncommon. He called the judge and got a better rundown of the situation, and agreed to meet the judge in his home in an hour. He got his weapon out of the office safe and went back down to the garage. Driving out to the judge's residence, he thought over what might have to be done. A threat always had to be taken seriously.

He arrived at the judge's home, walked up to the front door, and rang the doorbell. The judge opened the door and invited him in. After moving from the center hall into the judge's private office, they settled in facing chairs. The judge reached over to his desk, grabbed a piece of paper, and handed it to Moe. Moe looked at it, read it, then turned it over and saw nothing on the back.

Moe looked back at the judge and said, "Well, I can call the forensic guys in, but there won't be much for them to look at. Whatever forensics might have been on the note will be gone since we handled it. They might be able to tell how they got into your garage, and maybe there is something there. I'd suggest we call them in. Don't touch anything else out there until they are finished."

The judge nodded and said, "Sure. I guess I shouldn't have taken the note off the car. But I just wasn't thinking, especially about something like this."

"Most of us would react that way. Don't worry about it. If I have to guess, there won't be anything for the forensics people and the note could have been clean."

Several hours later, the judge, in his office in the federal building, received a call from Moe. "Sorry, judge. The forensics guys, and one gal, just left. The outside door to your garage had been jimmied with some form of crowbar, but there wasn't anything left to collect. No prints, no nothing. The note had our prints on it but nothing else. They think that whoever did this was wearing gloves. Professional. Your alarm didn't go off?"

"Thanks, Moe. No. The garage isn't alarmed. Just the main part of the house."

"I'd suggest, given this kind of trial, and the threat implied, that you get your family out of town and have the marshal service give you some protection. At least until the trial is over."

"Good points, Moe. I'll have to think that one over. All of that can really be a pain."

"Yes. But better safe than sorry."

"Okay. If something else breaks in the judiciary, let me know. By that I mean if someone else is threatened."

"Will do."

Jeraldine came into his home office just as he arrived later that day. He said, "Don't be frightened, but you need to go visit your sister for a few weeks, and no one needs to know where you are."

83

Her eyes got bigger and she came to a sudden stop. "Why? What's happened?"

"We've had a threat and we need to consider it seriously. I need to know that you are safe and outside this environment."

She nodded, wrung her thin hands briefly, and went to pack. She was nervous and scared. This hadn't happened before.

The trial got underway after the various motions were presented and denied by Judge Smyth. The illegal oil well modifications to divert, or steal, oil as it was produced were reviewed, and the murky images of the mini-submarine, and eventual pictures of the mini-submarine after it was captured, were also shown. Several instances of sabotage to other wells and the deaths of several divers were presented. Evidence of the rockets used to shoot down the secretary of state's aircraft were shown to the jury, despite several objections by the defense attorneys. And perhaps as damaging as anything was the sworn testimony, though recanted, of Mujab, the lead crewman on the mini-submarine who had fired the ARPM, under the specific direction of the ayatollah, at the secretary of state's aircraft.

Ryan managed to attend some of the proceedings as he took time off from his management of his marina and the nearly complete construction of the office and apartment. He listened intently as the prosecution presented some of the draft future plans for western attacks that he and his friends had found in the ayatollah's office when they captured him. Ryan was pleased over the coverage and details the prosecution was able to bring out. It sure seemed like a slam dunk to him.

Unfortunately, he wasn't able to remain for the full time and had to get back to his marina. Work was being done and he needed to be there.

Chapter Fifteen

Monday—July 3
Socotra Island—New Persia Compound

Sitting in his small office in the Socotra New Persia Compound, Khatib couldn't believe it. The Americans were going ahead with the trial of the ayatollah in spite of the warnings and threats. The judge had been threatened but that had done no good. He was under constant surveillance by the U.S. Marshals and would be difficult to attack. The jurors were sequestered and couldn't be taken out. Congress had been threatened, but to no benefit. There had to be a way. Khatib called Ramiz into the quarters and said, "We have to get to this trial thing and see if there is some way to stop it. Our expensive legal help has not been able to do anything except slow the process down. Do you have any suggestions?"

Ramiz thought for several moments. He followed Khatib's thought process and conclusions. As he was considering the situation, another thought came to him. And it would take care of two problems at one time. He looked over at Khatib and said, "I think we can emphasize how serious we are and, at the same time, take out one of our more difficult adversaries."

Khatib looked back and motioned Ramiz to continue.

"We lost the ayatollah due to the invasion and kidnapping here in our compound. I think we should go after the lead of that effort and kill him ... kill Ryan McKenzie and make sure the court and the administration knows who did it and why it was done. It would take him out for the future and the courts would know we are serious. We need to finish that job."

Khatib never failed to admire the resourcefulness and intelligence of Ramiz. He realized that he had not been disappointed before and, once again, Ramiz had come through with an excellent suggestion. They had tried before but would succeed this time, and the message would be very plain for all to see. He said, "An excellent idea. How soon would you be able to execute such a plan?"

"There are some minor logistics issues that would have to be considered and planned out. But I would think a couple of weeks would be more than adequate, and then I, personally, will take care of it."

85

Khatib nodded. "That would fit very nicely with the start and continuation of the trial. Go ahead and carry it out."

Ramiz smiled at the thought as he was leaving. This time he would not fail.

Wednesday—July 5
Freeport, Texas—Ryan's Marina

Ryan slowly moved across the entrance to his marina, motoring along with all sails furled. He had been out in the gulf enjoying a short morning of sailing. He had only been able to get out for a few hours and was now back to overview some construction details with his contractor. They were getting the first-floor cabinets and display cases framed out, and there was some issue with one of the plan dimensions.

He pulled into his slip and tied up. After unloading some minor trash materials and leftover drinks, he went up to the small construction trailer in his parking lot. Orrin Hayes, his general contractor, was in the small office going over a few of the details when Ryan came walking in.

"Early afternoon, Orrin," said Ryan.

Orrin looked up, smiled, and nodded a return greeting. Then he said, "We have a slight problem with the display case you wanted in the office. It won't quite fit."

Ryan looked at the plans for a moment. He thought for a bit, turned, and bent over to get a planning paper that was on the floor next to the excessed military four-drawer safe filing cabinet. An explosion ripped through the small office. A barely visible trail of smoke went back to a small boat floating in the harbor. Orrin was killed immediately and the blast was heard throughout the marina complex.

Ramiz was standing in the back of the boat with an empty RPG launcher in his hands. A grim smile on his face. He had watched Ryan berth his boat and go into the construction office. He had him. He had fired the older, but just as effective, model RPG and it blew the office into small pieces. Some small pieces of the office were on fire, but not the whole building. The office pieces were too small to sustain a fire. A moment after he had fired, he turned, sat back down at the small boat's wheel, pushed the throttle forward on the 100 hp Evenrude outboard, and eased his way out of the marina. Turning toward the ocean he moved the throttles forward and quickly sped away. Mission accomplished after three tries. Persistence counted.

Several people in the marina didn't know what to do. Some started up the small hill off the pier toward the destroyed construction trailer and others watched as Ramiz sped away. None had a boat to pursue Ramiz, and they couldn't get the registration number because it was so small it couldn't be read at any distance. All they could do was watch in amazement, and some fear, as he sped off into the river.

John Shepard, one of the permanent residents of the marina, rushed up the small hill toward the construction trailer. Arriving at the twisted mess of smoking sheet metal and wood framing, he found the bloodied remains of Orrin, speared through with several pieces of the trailer's framing. Realizing that Orrin was dead, he looked around for anyone else. He saw an arm sticking up out of the wood behind the still intact remains of the heavy filing cabinet. The filing cabinet looked like a pincushion, with multiple pieces of wood sticking out of one side, and it was lying on its side over some debris next to the arm. John then pushed some of the debris aside and grabbed the arm and pulled slightly. It wouldn't move, so he began to clear the area around the arm. A shoulder showed up and then he was able to clear Ryan's head. Ryan was breathing but unconscious. As John was trying to free Ryan, he could hear sirens approaching. Other people arrived and helped him. Then a paramedic came running up, took a quick look at Orrin, and moved over to help with extricating Ryan. Two firefighters soon joined them and they freed Ryan, strapped him on a backboard, and carried him to a stretcher. He was still alive but unconscious. An IV was started and he was rushed to the hospital.

Ramiz abandoned his stolen boat, after wiping it down for fingerprints, in Surfside just north of Freeport, got into his parked car, and immediately headed for Hobby Airport. He had done what he had come there to do ... kill Ryan McKenzie. That headache would not stop them from their work now. At the airport he got a quick message off to Khatib of his success in killing Ryan McKenzie. He was pleased.

Jackie was at work when the call came in. Jasper was calling. Her thoughts were a combination of fear and puzzlement. Why would Jasper be calling her?

He said, "Very bad news Jackie. Orrin's dead and Ryan's in the hospital, unconscious and in critical condition. You might want to get down here as soon as you can. The doctors don't know if he'll make it. He was the target of a small rocket attack a couple of hours ago."

Jackie inhaled a quick breath as Jasper told her. She dropped the paper she was working on. "My God, Jasper." Then, tears forming, she took a deep breath and said, "I'll get there as soon as I can." And she hung up. She sat there thinking and crying for several moments and then quickly headed down the hall to Maria's desk.

With a shaky voice she said, "Maria, I have to leave."

Maria looked back at her questioningly.

Jackie continued, "Ryan's in the hospital and may not survive. His construction guy was killed and Ryan is in critical condition. Some kind of rocket attack at the marina. I've got to go."

As Jackie was explaining the situation, Maria quickly got up, came around her desk with tears in her eyes, hugged Jackie briefly, and pushed her toward the door. She said, "Go, girl, go. We can handle anything around here for a while. Just get going. I'll tell the president." And she continued to push her toward the door.

Jackie was half skipping backward, and said, "I'll call when I have news." Then she turned and ran out of the White House to her car. She headed for her apartment, made a quick call for airline reservations, and drove to Dulles.

Maria sat for a minute after Jackie left. She was still stunned and in tears. She, gathered herself, held back the tears, then stood up and walked over to the door to the Oval Office and opened it. She walked in, quietly closing the door behind her. The president looked up from his reading with a questioning look on his face. Maria had never walked in on him like this before. She looked back at him and the tears started again. He stood up, walked over to her, put his hand softly on her shoulder, and asked, "What's wrong?"

Maria then told him what Jackie had said and that Jackie was on her way to Freeport.

He stood there. Also stunned. He sadly nodded, walked around to his desk, and paged Jack Harrison. Jack showed up a moment later, saw the distress on both their faces, and walked on into the room. He too asked, "What's wrong?"

The president said, "Ryan's in critical condition after an attack at his marina. Please, look into it and see what details you can find out."

Jack said, "Yes, sir, will do." He hesitated as he turned to leave and said, "I'm sorry, boss. You too, Maria. I'll see what I can find out." And he left the Oval Office for his desk and phone.

On the way to Dulles, Jackie called Jasper back and gave him her flight reservation information and asked him to pick her up at Houston's Hobby Airport. They talked for a few minutes and he said he would be there.

A few hours later she arrived at Hobby, and Jasper gave her a brief hug and they headed out to the parking area. On the way south, Jasper told her that there were several witnesses in the marina who saw the attack. It had come from a boat, and they had seen the person but couldn't catch him. So it was a known RPG attack, not something else. He also said that he and Dave both thought it was probably New Persia again.

She nodded. It made sense. But her concern now was for Ryan, and she wanted to get to the hospital as fast as she could. Jasper understood and took her straight to the Brazosport Regional Health Center. They would worry about the who-did-it later.

Jack came back into the Oval Office an hour later and told the president, "It was an RPG attack. There were several witnesses in the marina that saw it. The attacker was in a stolen speedboat and no one was able to follow him. But the police recovered the boat in Surfside a few miles northeast of Freeport. No prints, though … it had been wiped clean and nobody apparently saw the attacker there. He got clean away. We don't know who it was. But, given that it was an RPG, I would strongly suspect New Persia. It has all their hallmarks, and Ryan was a known target for them."

The president said, "Another one, and this time awful close to home. The ayatollah is lashing out at us and we seem to be unable to get him. What has the world come to?"

Jack just stood there nodding. There was nothing more to say.

The president then said, "Okay. Please keep on top of it and let me know how he's doing. Jackie will probably be the best source."

Jack pursed his lips, nodded again, and left.

Hours later, Ryan was still unconscious in a hospital bed. He had suffered a serious concussion and a broken left leg in the explosion. The filing cabinet had taken the brunt of the explosive force and saved him. Jackie was standing by in his room, holding his hand and talking to him. His vital signs were changing every couple of hours, sometimes getting better and sometimes going the other way. She was encouraging him. Hoping, and praying, he'd pull out of it soon. Dave and Jasper came to the hospital to visit and give her encouragement.

Thursday—July 6
Socotra—New Persia Compound

Khatib concentrated on the note that had come in from Ramiz. This person, Ryan, was now dead. Perhaps it would be a lesson they could apply to the ayatollah's trial. A threat that could not be ignored. Perhaps when the judge saw the results of their actions, he would release the ayatollah and send him home.

Khatib thought for several minutes and finally wrote a short note.

Sunday—July 9
Virginia—U.S. Federal Court

Judge Smyth's clerk opened up his email and found a startling note from an organization called New Persia.

She read,

Judge Smyth. This short note is to let you know that we have killed Ryan McKenzie, one of the key leaders in capturing our esteemed leader the Ayatollah Sarhardi, whom you are illegally holding for trial. He is to be released immediately and returned to us unharmed. If he is not released, further actions will be taken by us to secure his release.

Monday—July 10
Brazosport Regional Health Center, Texas

It was white. Not a bright white, but dim and distant. He was somewhere he didn't recognize. The smells were different. The light was obscure and not defined. He was comfortable and warm, but not quite sure of where he was. It was as if he was in a dream and trying to get out. But at the same time he didn't want to get back out. He was fighting himself; it was a contented feeling, almost like being in a cocoon. Someone was there. He could hear a voice. Someone he knew. Someone he cared about. Someone very insistent. He opened his eyes just slightly and could see very little. It was not bright. He could make out some shapes and someone was moving around, but almost in slow motion, like a cloud moves slowly some days, barely noticeable. He didn't know. Didn't know where he was, what had happened, how long ago. No memory of how he got wherever he was. It was a dream and he was moving toward something, floating, almost flying. Surreal. Then there was nothing again. Blank. Out. Nothing.

Jackie was half-asleep in the chair. It had been five days now since the attack, and Ryan was still in a coma. No one knew when, or if, he would come out of it. She heard him moan a bit. He had done that yesterday but hadn't come around. She shook herself awake, stood up, and walked the few feet to his bed. His eyes were open! He was trying to focus. She grabbed his arm and bent over his face to look at him.

He stirred. Half-asleep and half-awake. Not sure where he was, but fighting to come back to something. He opened his eyes all the way this time. The room was still dim, but he could see equipment. A hand took his arm very suddenly and he was startled. A beautiful face looked down at him with tears in her eyes. He looked back. He blinked. She was crying. Another person came into the room suddenly. Another pretty face and cool hands. A bright light flashed across his face as the nurse checked his pupil responses. He flinched. It didn't hurt, but he was surprised by it. He turned his head slightly and realized he was in a hospital room, with all the monitoring equipment and hanging things. He tried to talk but something was in his mouth and he couldn't form words. He swallowed, and it was hard to do around a tube. The nurse left and the beautiful face appeared again. Someone very familiar. He thought hard and looked at her again, almost staring. She was still crying, but she seemed to be happy, tears of happiness. Then he remembered. It was Jackie, and she looked so lovely. He tried to raise his right hand and she stopped him with her hand in his. He squeezed her hand and mouthed "I love you" to her.

Ryan slowly recovered in the hospital. His left leg was in a cast and his concussion affected his hearing and balance a bit. He spent the next few days going through a series of balance exercises to regain some stability and learning to use crutches. His hearing also started to return to normal after another two weeks. But it was slow going. He was lucky, and he knew it, to be alive. The large filing cabinet had taken the brunt of the force of the RPG explosion. Had it not been there, he never would have made it.

91

Monday—July 17
Freeport, Texas—Ryan's Marina

Jackie stayed with him until he was checked out of the hospital a week after he woke up. She then stayed on in the new apartment for another week, working remotely with Maria, until she finally went back to Washington, D.C. By then Ryan was stable enough to get on by himself.

The police took a report from him once he came around, but were unable to get any firm leads on Ramiz. Some of the marina people did describe him, but it was such a quick action, they couldn't come up with a consensus. And since the boat had been stolen and wiped clean, it was a dead end also.

Monday—July 31
Freeport, Texas—Ryan's Marina

Ryan finally felt well enough, in spite of the crutches, to begin finishing his apartment/marina office complex. He had brought on another construction lead and, between the two of them, with some assistance from some of the construction crew, finished off the final parts of the construction.

Friday—August 11
Freeport, Texas—Ryan's Marina

The construction had been finished. Ryan invited all the marina residents and the other renters of slips in his marina, along with several friends and acquaintances, for a barbecue. Jackie flew down, Dave and Jasper came in, and it was a boisterous time for the evening.
The crutches were quite limiting, but he was determined to finally get back to "normal" again. He was very pleased, but with some melancholy over the loss of friends.
It was a mixed blessing.

Chapter Sixteen

Monday—August 21
Richmond, Virginia—Federal Court

After close to two months of trial processes, evidence presentation, discussions, accusations, challenges, and denials, the jury finally recessed to consider the results. All twelve members and the two alternates were sequestered in the federal building to determine the ayatollah's fate. The world watched and wondered. The evidence presented during the trial was pretty convincing to the average Joe on the street. But you never knew what the jury might decide.

A curious activity began occurring after the trial got underway. There was a good-sized gallery consisting of not only the press and media, but also members of environmental groups who were favorable to his cause, members of environmental groups who were only partially in favor, members of right-wing Aryan supremacists, and other members of various organizations both for and against the New Persia movement. After several days of court activity, the various factions began to recognize themselves and began sitting next to, or in the same area, as others who felt the same way. As a result, the courtroom became polarized with supporters in one area and detractors in another. Tension was high as the proceedings moved along. Outside the courthouse, the Richmond police had to break up several fights that broke out between the factions. It was not a pleasant scene, and the media was right on top of it.

Television commentators were busy recapping what had occurred during the trial and speculating on what the jury might do. During the period when the jury was sequestered, the various news agencies monitored the courtroom scene for some breaking news. While waiting, it was the usual speculating by the media that had become the norm.

But nobody was really certain.

Friday—August 25
Richmond, Virginia—Federal Court

Judge Smyth had basically ignored the threats, including the most recent one claiming to have killed Ryan McKenzie, and with a great deal of courage, continued with the judicial process. U.S. marshals were a constant presence in the courtroom and his life.

After five days of sequestered consideration, the jury indicated that it had reached a verdict and was prepared to announce its decision. They filed in after the court had been brought into session. Television stations around the country, and in selected places around the world, interrupted their programming to bring coverage of the event.

Judge Smyth slowly looked at each of the jurors and then back to the foreman. He then asked the jury foreman if they had reached a decision. The foreman looked back and said, "Yes, your honor, we have reached a decision." The bailiff took the decision paper from the foreman and handed it to the judge. Judge Smyth read the decision, quietly nodded in thoughtful approval, pursed his lips in thought, and, after a few moments, handed the paper back to the bailiff. The bailiff handed it back to the foreman, and Judge Smyth directed the foreman to read the decision to the court.

Judge Smyth turned to the ayatollah and said, "You will please rise for the reading of the jury's findings."

The ayatollah, nudged by his defense team, refused to rise. He looked back at the judge and from his seated position said, "I do not recognize this so-called court and will not respect your wishes. You have no right, as I have said many times before over the past several months, to try me this way." Then he looked off to a far corner of the courtroom.

Judge Smyth, after looking at his folded hands for several moments, looked back up at the ayatollah over his reading glasses and said, "You, or your organization, have threatened me personally. With great difficulty I have set that aside. I have tried, during these months, to respect your beliefs. We have avoided court proceedings during Muslim holidays and we have respected your right to pray as you desire." He stopped and then looked intensely at the ayatollah and continued, "I would expect the same back from you. That is, I would expect that you respect our processes and procedures as we have respected yours. Now, please rise to hear the verdict."

The ayatollah looked back at the judge, then over to the jury foreman, and then back to the judge. He looked at the tabletop in front of him, put his shackled hands on the table, and slowly pushed himself up. He looked over at the spectators, looked around for a minute, nodded to a few of the people in the seats, and back to the foreman. Khatib and Ramiz, innocuously dressed in western-style business suits, watched closely from several rows back. What was about to be said might trigger their actions over the next few days and weeks. Their planning would depend on what the results were.

The judge just nodded to the ayatollah. He then looked to the foreman.

The foreman took the piece of paper he was holding, cleared his throat, and said, "Rather than read these off for each count, I'll save everybody the time." Judge Smyth started for a moment then kept quiet. The foreman looked around the court in a theatrical moment and then continued, "We, the jury, find the defendant guilty on all counts." He looked up as the spectators gasped and then broke into a raucous combination of cheers, boos, catcalls, and shouts. A very mixed crowd.

The gavel slammed down on its pad several times with a fury and an urgency felt throughout the courtroom. Judge Bernard Smyth would not tolerate the outburst from the gallery that had just occurred.

The ayatollah quickly sat down amongst all the confusion. More of a slump down. Guilty! On all thirty-seven counts.

Judge Smyth hammered the gavel several more times to re-establish calm in his court. Finally the bailiff, aided by U.S. marshals, started to remove people and calm was quickly re-established. No one wanted to leave.

After a period of calm and thoughtful deliberation, Judge Smyth looked at the jury, thanked them for their participation, and excused them. After the jury had cleared the courtroom, Judge Smyth turned to the ayatollah and his small group of defense lawyers and said, "The jury has spoken. And their findings fit the circumstances. I agree with their conclusions and hereby set the sentencing for three weeks from today at 9:00 a.m. here in this courtroom." He reached over, hammered the gavel again, and said, "Court is dismissed." He then left the room as all rose in respect. Except the ayatollah, who was nudged several times by his legal team to rise. He didn't. He refused to stand.

There is a serenity that may wash over a person when a significant event occurs in their life. That moment occurred with the ayatollah. He was sad and thoughtful in his serenity as his belief in Allah was tested. He had faith. He was held, without any chance of escape, for his past deeds against the U.S. In his mind, this was just a kangaroo court and he would, somehow, get through it and survive. He would not perish until his mission was finished and the world's oil supply extended for centuries. The west would be forced to comply.

After the judge departed the room, two federal marshals reached over and nudged the ayatollah to stand and move toward the exit to the back corridor leading to the elevators and the basement garage holding area. The ayatollah refused to stand. He just looked at the marshals with disdain and then looked back at the far wall of the courtroom. They would have to force him.

Waiting until the court was cleared of all spectators, two more marshals joined the two already in the room. They bent over the ayatollah and quietly threatened him with a taser if he didn't cooperate. The room was empty except for the ayatollah and the four marshals. He cooperated. His mild protest was lost in the business of the court and none of the protestors saw it. Useless.

After the announcement of the findings of the jury, the media had a small field day in the hallways of the courthouse. As the jurors left the jury room after being excused, they were nearly accosted by various reporters and cameramen. Several of them just wanted to get out of the courthouse and return to their homes and normal lives. There were two men who hung back and talked with the reporters.

Said one of the jurors, "It took several discussions and thoughtful considerations over the large amount of evidence before we could come to the conclusions we reached. Shooting down the aircraft and, especially, the videos of the mini-submarine were pretty convincing. The prosecution just did a good job convincing us. And the recorded statements by Mujab when they were first captured, even though they deny it now, were critical. It actually took several votes before we could reach a consensus. There were a couple of the Muslim people who did not want to see him spend his whole life in prison, but considering that he killed without warning, and killed innocents on that aircraft, we just had no other choice."

The second juror added, "I'm Muslim, but I am also an American citizen, and it really got to several of us that he was being so high-handed about his movement. Islam does not need that kind of reputation, and he needed to be stopped. We are moderates, and we want the same thing he wants, but not at the cost he is willing to impose. It was the right decision."

There were multiple shouts for clarification, but both of the men declined and pushed on out of the courthouse. Khatib and Ramiz had been standing back listening. They looked at each other and moved on out of the building. They had work to do.

Judge Smyth had retired to his chambers and was relaxing after a very trying time in the court. The jury had found, as he expected, that the ayatollah had caused the deaths of several Americans and caused disruption and destruction of American oil facilities in the Gulf of Mexico. He had directed his people to shoot down the U.S. Air Force C-32 aircraft carrying the secretary of state, Sanford Billings, and his entire entourage. He had also tried to kill, in the same manner, the U.S. secretary of defense. He was simply guilty as charged. And in three weeks, Judge Smyth would have to pronounce judgment and sentence the ayatollah per the guidelines of the Judicial Sentencing Committee. He already knew that was life in prison without parole. The ayatollah would be turned over to the Federal Bureau of Prisons and sent to the supermax facility just outside of Florence, Colorado—the most secure facility in the U.S. and the current highly restrictive residence of other major crime and terrorism figures.

Khatib and Ramiz, departing after listening to the jurors' comments and under the watchful eyes of the marshals, looked at each other. They both knew that they would have to finalize the plans they had initiated several months before. Most of the work had been done and they only had the three weeks left before the formal sentencing occurred, and then maybe a few days after that before the ayatollah was moved to the assigned prison facility.

Ramiz and Khatib left the courtroom and went back to the Marriott Hotel on East Broad Street in Richmond. The ayatollah would be kept in Richmond until the sentencing occurred. They could do nothing more. They had hired the best legal team they could find, and that team was not able to stop the U.S. justice system. The evidence presented to the jury was just too convincing, even with the majority of jurors being believers. And even the personal threat to Judge Smyth had no effect; nor did the well-publicized attack on Ryan McKenzie.

They were going to have to implement their rescue and escape planning.

In the room, Khatib said, "Well, the worst has happened. He will be sentenced and then sent off to this Colorado place. We need to review our plans one more time and make sure there are no gaps or areas we might have missed."

Ramiz, very thoughtfully, added, "Yes. And with just three weeks, if there is something significant, we need to get right on it." He looked directly at Khatib and said, "But I think our plans are complete. You and I have been over them several times. The people are trained, the equipment is ready and in place in Canon City, and the escape route is well established. We even had a quiet practice simulation with our people at the intersection of Highway 50 and Highway 115 in Colorado. It worked.

"However, I agree with you. Let's spend the rest of the day and all of tomorrow reviewing the plan here in the hotel. Something may come out, and it would be good to be absolutely sure."

Khatib looked out the window at the distant, faintly visible, Appalachian Mountains to the west. He sat down in an armchair, put his hands on the table, and looked back at Ramiz. "We have gone over the plan several times and you have arranged to have the equipment available. Our small commando force has practiced many times and, as you said, even simulated the rescue. We'll go over it one more time after we have something to eat."

Ramiz walked over to the telephone and placed an order with room service. He was not in the mood, nor was Khatib, to go to a restaurant. There was a considerable amount of high risk in what they had to do, and he wanted peace and quiet, with no distractions, to concentrate on their review.

After a quiet meal in their room, they got to work. Ramiz brought their planning up on his laptop. Several hours later, they had worked their way through most of the logistics requirements to support their team. With some very minor exceptions, easily procured at a local Home Depot or Lowe's, they had everything lined up. They finished their efforts and went to bed for the night.

In the morning, after an in-room breakfast, they continued their review. The timing of the attack was closely reviewed to make sure potential problems were identified and plans adjusted to fit those situations. "What-ifs" were looked at, and they agreed on actions to solve them. However, there were only a few of them that had not been considered before. Ramiz's planning had been very thorough. At the end of the day they were convinced they could do it. The ayatollah would be returned home and the U.S. authorities would be stymied.

They would be ready. The ayatollah would not see the inside of a U.S. prison.

Chapter Seventeen

Sunday—August 27
Socotra Island Harbor

The New Persia trimaran *Persian Quest* left the harbor of Socotra, heading east across the Indian Ocean and the mid-Pacific for the Gulf of Mexico. Previously loaded with required equipment in anticipation of the mission, the commandos had boarded for the two-week voyage several days before. Khatib had directed the planning and implementation of a mission that would get the Americans' attention. It was the third, and biggest, mission since the ayatollah had been kidnapped. Khatib was going to make sure the trial was answered with one of his own actions.

The *Persian Quest* was actually a catamaran with a third hull that was a mini-submarine. It looked like a trimaran but did not function like one. It was also very large, at over two hundred feet. Equipped with two folding masts and twin turbine engines linked to synchronized prop shafts, one for each outboard hull or pontoon, under turbine power it was capable of greater than fifty knots. The masts could be raised and sails deployed using hydraulic hoist assists, since it would be too much for men to handle by themselves. Combined with a full suite of worldwide communications equipment, it was very capable, and provided the New Persia group with a concealed naval capability. With the trade-back of the previous oceangoing yachts to China, New Persia had more than equal capability without the west aware that the switch had been made.

Najid, the captain of the *Persian Quest,* was proud and happy with his assignment to the sailing vessel. It had taken close to three months of intensive training for the twenty-four-man crew to master the sailing qualities of the trimaran, and that was after he had already qualified as a master on other ships. Truly an excellent achievement.

They headed for the Gulf of Mexico, halfway around the world, on a new mission. This mission would put more emphasis on the need for the U.S. to accede to the New Persia demands, cut their use of oil significantly, and rescue the ayatollah from the U.S. criminal justice system.

They passed through the Panama Canal, moving under turbine power from the Pacific Ocean to the Atlantic, and then sailed up through part of the Caribbean Sea and the east coast of Mexico into the Gulf of Mexico.

Friday—September 8
Gulf of Mexico—Texas Coast

The *Persian Quest* cruised thirty miles off the coast of Texas in the languid Gulf of Mexico just off Galveston Bay. She was a remarkable feat of Chinese nautical engineering, and she was here on a mission of great importance to the New Persia movement.

It was midmorning, and two small powerboats approached the trimaran and slowed to a crawl as they tied up to the much larger oceangoing vessel. Material was transferred from the trimaran to the powerboats over about an hour. Mission requirements were reviewed once again, and the powerboats departed with their clandestine cargo. The powerboats headed in to the harbor near Galveston, Texas. With Texas registration on the hulls, there was nothing unusual about the boats. There were probably several thousand similar boats operating along the coastline.

However, these were different. They had picked up cargo at sea and brought it back to a marina. No checks by customs or the Coast Guard. If they had done a check, they would have been very surprised at the cargo. The boats also carried a contingent of men. Skilled men ... skilled in warfare and clandestine operations. Ramiz and his French advisors had done an excellent job of training this cadre of commandos.

Three large pick-up trucks backed down on to the pier and the material was moved from the boats to the trucks. The trucks departed to the west through Houston and beyond. They were headed for middle Colorado and the front range of the Rocky Mountains, where the various materials would be used for their mission needs. The remaining commando force loaded up in an expensive-looking RV and also departed to the west and the same area of Colorado.

Three weeks after leaving Socotra. That was what they assumed they would have, and now they were down to just one week. They had received word from Ramiz. They were to execute the planned ayatollah rescue and attack on the U.S. just a week from now. It was a daring plan, one full of risk. But the rewards were worth it.

Elusive Quarry

The decision of the U.S. court had been made, the ayatollah was guilty, and it would take another week for the sentencing to occur, as long as the federal court stayed on schedule. The semi-arid desert of the Front Range in Colorado was about to see another resident—a resident of the supermax prison located just outside of Florence. It was their intent, and mission, that he would not make it to the prison. He would be kidnapped from the U.S. federal authorities and returned to his own people.

After dropping off the commandos and their equipment in Galveston, the *Persian Quest* headed south. She was bound for the small port of Progreso on the Yucatan Peninsula of Mexico. Three days later she was at anchor in the small harbor. She was awaiting some additional personnel, equipment, and supplies for her next mission.

Thursday—September 14
Canon City, Colorado

It was a tense time. They had arrived two days before after making their way up from Galveston. They had been told it would be about ten days, after they arrived in Galveston, before the action would occur. A week to the sentencing and then a few days after that for the ayatollah to be moved to Colorado. Their equipment was with them and they needed to modify the trucks.

They located Cal's shop and Ramiz went in.

Ramiz said, "Pinky. Good to see you. We are here to pick up the modified trucks and the trailers you have in storage."

"Good to see you also," said Pinky. "The trucks are parked out back with a trailer hooked to each tractor. After you give me the funds you owe, I'll give you the keys and they are yours."

Qasim, the commando lead, and one other commando entered the shop behind Ramiz.

Ramiz nodded and reached in his pocket. He pulled out a large wad of money, counted out what he owed Pinky, and handed it over to him. There had been some discussion over keeping the money and killing Pinky, but Ramiz had won the argument. They still had a few days to go before they thought the ayatollah would be en route, and he didn't want anything to interfere with their primary mission. Especially a murder investigation. He paid and the keys were turned over to him. He turned and handed a set to each of the commandos standing behind him.

They then proceeded out to the back lot and located the trucks. After the men started them, Ramiz went back to his rental vehicle and led them to a garage he had rented on the outskirts of Penrose. After disconnecting the trailers, they pulled in to the two high bays and began to modify the tractors. Several hours later, they broke for the day, and Ramiz took them back to the motel in Canon City where the rest of the team was staying.

The next day, Qasim and three others returned to the rented garage, pulled the tractors out, and backed the two trailers into the two bays. Throughout that day and the next, they made the required modification to the trailers. They finished the modifications and, with everything complete, ran several test runs with the tractor-trailer combinations over the planned route. All was well. They parked the vehicles at the rented garage ... they looked, at first glance, close to normal, and when they put canvas covers over the tractors they looked completely normal. The trailers had no outward appearance that would draw any attention.

It was now late on Friday, September 15—sentencing day. They were now ready. Equipment and manpower ... set to go. They only had to wait for the final "execute" signal from Ramiz. They were anxious to get the mission underway.

Chapter Eighteen

Friday—September 15
Richmond, Virginia—Federal Court

Three weeks had passed since the jury had found the ayatollah guilty on all counts. Judge Bernard Smyth, well respected in all corners of the U.S. legal profession, had the unpleasant task of pronouncing sentence in this case. He reviewed the judicial guidelines several times and concluded that there was no real choice. He would follow them to the letter. He wanted to make sure any possible future appeals would be rejected.

He was in his chambers contemplating the actions he was about to take. Actions required of him by law and by the Constitution. He was protecting the country, and, given the recent circumstances, he was protecting himself and his family.

Court was about to convene. He rose from his large padded desk chair in his chambers, put on his black robes, and proceeded down the hall toward the back entrance to the courtroom. He looked at the closed-circuit television monitor sitting on the table next to his access door in to the courtroom, just behind his bench. The courtroom was full to capacity. People were in whispered conversations awaiting his arrival.

As the bailiff said, "All rise, the Honorable Judge Bernard Smyth presiding," he proceeded into the courtroom and, after arranging his robes in a fashion he preferred, sat down at the bench. He looked around and saw the defense, the prosecution, and the press with their many cameras and microphones. He looked and saw, at the defense table, the ayatollah in full shackles and in the orange coveralls of the jail, morosely staring back. As a protest, which the judge saw as useless, the ayatollah refused to wear anything else.

He looked down at the two teams, the prosecution and the defense. Both dressed to impress. But it didn't faze him one bit. He knew the theatre that frequently played out in these types of events. Especially with the TV cameras so evident.

He looked at the spectators and the rest of the large courtroom and said, "Please be seated. We are about to pass sentence on the defendant. He has been found guilty of all charges

103

by a panel of his peers." He stopped for a moment to let the solemnity of the occasion sink in. Then he looked at the ayatollah and said, "Before I pass sentence upon you, do you have anything to say?"

The ayatollah looked back at Judge Smyth and quietly stood up. He braced his shackled hands on the table and began to speak. "I will say it one more time. You have no right to do this. This so-called trial is nothing but a show, and not a good one at that. It is a small hindrance to my activities and will not stop my New Persia movement. I am concerned over the welfare of our children and their children to follow. You Americans continue to waste the world's resources, and I, and my movement, will eventually succeed at stopping you. You are the devil. I work for and am responsible only to Allah. You may imprison my body, but you will never succeed in imprisoning my mind. This is a farce and you will lose in the long run. Allah be praised." He then sat down and turned away from the judge and the bench.

Judge Smyth looked at him for a moment. Then he turned to the defense table and then over to the prosecution table. He looked back at the defense table and said to the recalcitrant ayatollah, "You and your organization have threatened my life and the lives of my family. You have murdered innocent civilians. And to what end? To what end? Your goals are admirable: the reduction of oil usage, the betterment of the environment, the extension of the life of our worldwide oil resources." He hesitated for a moment for effect, then continued, "But your methods of attaining your goals are despicable. In our modern world of interconnected economies, there is no room for your methods and attempts at intimidation. Your acts of destruction, murder, and non-tolerance for mankind are an abomination and must be stopped. You have been tried and found guilty of various crimes." He stopped again for effect. He looked down at the top of the bench, very aware that all cameras were on him. The world was watching. He looked back at the ayatollah and continued to speak in a very deliberate, solemn, and slow manner. "I hereby sentence you, under the guidelines of the U.S. Judicial Committee, for these crimes against the United States and humanity, to life in prison without possibility of parole. You will be remanded to the custody of the U.S. Marshal Service and transferred to the prison of choice by the Bureau of Prisons of the U.S. Department of Justice."

He then gaveled on the pad and said, "Case concluded."

Elusive Quarry

Khatib and Ramiz looked on in amazed disappointment. The threats had done no good. The ayatollah was on his way to prison and there was very little they could do about it. At least for now.

They looked at each other. The ayatollah looked around the courtroom and briefly caught their eye. There was no outward sign of recognition between them, but it was there. He knew he wasn't alone in his time of great stress. The unspoken message was not lost on him. He knew something would be done, but there was no way for him to know when or how it might happen. Allah would see to his needs.

Friday—September 15
Freeport, Texas—Ryan's Marina

Ryan, in his new marina office, was watching the proceedings with a great deal of interest. It would be good to see these criminals put where they belonged. He was concentrating on the coverage just before the jury came in when he got a call from Kathy Frome down in slip 48. Her electric had failed ... again. Ryan turned to Jackie, who was also watching with great interest, and asked her to record the coverage. He would have to watch it later. Then he went down to the slip with a spare circuit breaker from his maintenance locker.

For some reason, Kathy's particular slip had blown again, and he wasn't sure why. This was the fourth time in a week, and something was obviously not right. He got to the slip and opened up the panel next to the water's edge. The breaker had tripped but looked normal. He walked back up to his utility house, tripped the main for the series of slips so he could work safely on her fifty-amp breaker, went back down to the panel, and made the change in breakers. Then he reversed what he had done and restored power. He took the old breaker back to his workshop, and would take it in to Baker Electric tomorrow to see what might be the problem.

He went back up to the apartment and found Jackie just finishing up cleaning the kitchen. She had decided to let the recording run while doing some of the chores. They went back into the living room and turned on the TV. The news commentator was just finishing, "... and that's the final word, ladies and gentlemen. He will be spending the rest of his life in prison in our great state of Colorado. And now back to the studios."

Jackie rewound the recorder and they began watching as the recording began with the arrival in the courtroom of Judge Smyth. The video panned to the defense, then to the prosecution, and then

105

back to the judge. Ryan went to the kitchen to get a beer out of the refrigerator and came back in to the living room as the judge was pronouncing the sentence. The cameras were moving back and forth between the judge and the defense table. Ryan was smiling slightly as he saw the ayatollah nearly collapse at the life sentence without parole. The cameras backed off and showed some of the spectators and the frenzy of shouts and yelling.

Ryan started as he looked at the gallery. *My God*, he thought. He yelled excitedly at Jackie, who was looking out the window, "That's Khatib and Ramiz in that group toward the rear! They're there in the audience! In the courtroom. If they've been there the whole time, I must have missed them when I was there."

Jackie's head snapped back to the television. She glanced at the coverage and stopped the recording. She reversed until the two men were in view and froze the image. She said, "I thought they were on the lookout for those two! Somehow they slipped into the country and actually into the court." She, too, was amazed.

Ryan was staring at the image for several moments. He got up close to the ultra-high-definition TV and confirmed it was them. He walked over to the telephone and called the White House. After a short discussion with the White House operator, he was put through to Jack Harrison.

"Jack. Did you follow the sentencing a bit ago?"

Jack responded, "Yes. Both the president and I were watching and are pleased with the result. Of course, we couldn't see any other possible outcome."

"I agree, but there was something else in that coverage that really bothered me."

"What's that?" he said, with caution in his voice.

"Jack. In the background, in the gallery, we saw the ayatollah's two primary assistants! Khatib and Ramiz were both there ... here in the country and actually in the courtroom."

There was dead silence for a few moments as Jack digested the information. Neither he, nor the president, would have recognized the two men, since they had never met them. But Ryan did know them and was obviously alarmed.

"Hang on a minute, Ryan."

A few moments later, Ryan heard the president ask, "Ryan. Are you sure it was them?"

"Yes, sir. And Jackie saw them also. They were definitely there. Given their capabilities, we had better be ready for more action from them."

"Well, I have to agree with you on that one. Somebody, and it was probably them, did threaten Judge Smyth. Their presence kinda confirms that in my mind."

"I didn't know that."

"Well, yes. The U.S. Marshals service up-channeled a report several weeks ago, and the judge's wife was put into temporary hiding for her protection. The judge has been shadowed for several weeks now by a team to make sure he is protected also."

"Anything more that you can do? I mean, if they were in the courtroom, can we trace their location and at least follow them?"

"I doubt it. It has been several hours now since that all occurred, and I am sure they are well out of sight. They must have come in under false documents, because they are on our watch list."

"I see. Well, at least we know they are here."

"Given your background with these people, I'd be careful for a while. We'll talk about it here. Thanks for the call, Ryan, and take care." And the line went dead.

Ryan hung up, looked over at Jackie, and slowly shook his head. He didn't like the situation one bit. Watching over your shoulder for trouble was never pleasant.

Chapter Nineteen

Monday—September 18
Washington, D.C.—The White House

The president was relaxing in the Oval Office three days after watching the federal court proceedings in Virginia. The ayatollah had finally been handed his fate and would spend the rest of his life in a U.S. prison. After creating so many problems for his administration, the president was pleased with the results of the trial and sentencing.

After his conversation with Ryan on the presence of the two New Persia men in the courtroom, he had decided that there wasn't much that could be done. They had obviously come into the country illegally and would probably leave the same way. There simply wasn't any way to track them down.

He called Jack in and asked, "Jack. What happens now with the ayatollah?"

Jack responded, "He will be held in Richmond for maybe a few days or a week, and then transported to, I think, Florence, Colorado, and the supermax there."

"And how will he get there?"

"The Department of Justice has a program called JPATS. That's Justice Prisoner and Alien Transportation System. It's a program for moving prisoners and deporting aliens around the country. They use dedicated aircraft and, for security's sake, don't advertise when they move prisoners. I would imagine he will be put on one of those aircraft and taken to Pueblo, Colorado, then on to the prison nearby."

"So, once he gets there, he won't be coming back out and we can get on with our other government concerns?"

"Sure hope so. But I won't be happy until he is actually there and under lockdown for twenty-three hours every day."

The president nodded in agreement. Hopefully this thorn in his side would be gone.

Wednesday—September 20
Richmond, Virginia—Federal Detention Facility

The ayatollah was sitting in his cell in the Richmond federal detention facility. He wasn't sure what would happen next but was already pretty depressed about the situation he was in. One of the marshals came up to him and said, "Get ready to move. We will be taking you out to the airport in an hour and you will be flown to Colorado."

The ayatollah looked back at the marshal and said, "With no warning? I wasn't expecting this."

"Sorry about that," said the marshal. "We don't tell you when we will be moving you until just before. Saves us a lot of grief and, that way, you can't set up some kind of escape plan."

The U.S. marshals took control of the ayatollah and immediately began the process of transporting him to Colorado.

Farid had been watching for several days, ever since the trial sentencing had finished. He knew that JPATS never advertised when they were going to move a prisoner. It avoided, in theory, any chance of a potential breakout or problem with the transfer. So his only recourse was to watch at the Richmond International Airport general aviation terminal until the ayatollah was being moved. It was a waiting game, and he had to watch on a twenty-four-seven basis. Tiring and difficult. He and Jibril had spelled each other for several days, since neither could keep the twenty-four-hour watch.

He was parked in the general aviation parking lot and had his aircraft radio on, monitoring the tower frequency. It had just been routine traffic and fairly quiet, except for the occasional commercial or general aviation aircraft. Through the FAA aircraft registry database, he had been able to find the aircraft tail numbers registered to the JPATS and was listening for one of their aircraft to arrive. It was boring!

Finally he heard the Hawker aircraft contact the tower and knew the moment had arrived. He got out his binoculars and watched the terminal parking area as the Hawker pulled up and began to refuel. Checking the aircraft tail number against the FAA database ... it was a JPATS aircraft.

An hour later, the ayatollah, in chains and shackles, was placed in a secure van and driven to the airport where the Hawker 800 small jet was waiting. The ayatollah's history of problems, and the breakout of some of his people in Alaska, had caused the JPATS people to send a dedicated aircraft. He was considered too dangerous to use the usual 727.

An unmarked black Suburban pulled up next to the aircraft. Three people, two dressed in suits, and the third dressed, but in shackles, got out and began to board the aircraft. Through his binoculars, Farid could recognize the ayatollah in shackles, boarding the aircraft very slowly. The ayatollah was led into the aircraft and handcuffed to the seat. Two marshals, already on board, would accompany him on the aircraft during the flight to Pueblo.

After about ten minutes, two marshals came back off the aircraft, got in the Suburban, and drove off. The Hawker spooled up its twin Honeywell Aerospace TFE 731-5BR turbofan engines, obtained clearance, and taxied out to the end of the runway. After a few moments of final checks, the aircraft took the active runway and accelerated using the full 4660 pounds of thrust from each engine.

As they climbed into the sky over Richmond and headed west, the ayatollah looked out the windows and wondered what lay in store for him in this horrible land of corruption and waste. What had Allah intended when He delivered him into the hands of the infidels?

Farid started his car and pulled out of the parking lot. He pulled over and stopped just outside. He took out his cell phone and called the number. He got an immediate answer and told the deep voice on the other end that the aircraft was on the way. They disconnected and he went back home. He was done. And several thousand dollars richer.

Chapter Twenty

Wednesday—September 20
Southern Colorado

Two U.S. marshals escorted the ayatollah under guard as they flew west from Richmond, Virginia, in the dedicated JPATS Hawker 800 jet aircraft. After several hours of flying they approached runway eight left in Pueblo, Colorado. Landing softly around 1:00 p.m., they taxied up to the flight base services organization, where they met two armored federal prison Suburbans and a two-vehicle Colorado State Highway Patrol escort, for the final ride out to the prison complex. The complex was located about twenty miles to the west of Pueblo in the small community of Florence, Colorado. The small convoy left the airport and headed out U.S. Highway 50 to the west, a shackled ayatollah in the backseat of the second Suburban. Radio communications were established between all the convoy vehicles. They expected the ride out to Florence to be uneventful. With two CHP escorts, one in front and one in the back, four U.S. marshals in the Suburbans, and a DOJ helicopter overhead, they did not expect any problems.

They were very, very wrong.

Monitoring the highway patrol frequency, Qasim heard the convoy depart the Pueblo airport and head west on Highway 50. They were on the way. Using throwaway cell phones, he notified his two semi-drivers, the Humvee driver, the pilot, and several of the other commando personnel that the action was about to begin, and to be ready.

A dark four-passenger Cessna 182 was idling in a holding area at the west end of Fremont County airport's main east/west runway. Its registration numbers were intentionally difficult to read. Its fuel tanks were completely full, just in case they needed maximum range. The pilot looked for any approaching traffic and saw nothing in the pattern. He would have clear access to the runway when the time came.

Mike Powers was driving to work along U.S. Highway 50 from Canon City, as he always did on Wednesday morning. His job as a security guard at the supermax prison complex in Florence was something he did in order to do other things in his life. He loved the hiking, camping, hunting, and fishing in the local Front Range area of the Rocky Mountains, and this job allowed him to do that. Divorced with two kids, and a former wife who refused to work, he frequently was frustrated at the way life treated him. She just sucked on him and drained his financial resources dry every chance she got. It was the hunting and fishing that allowed him to maintain his sanity.

As he approached his turnoff at the Colorado Highway 115 overpass, in front of him and coming toward him from the east was a small convoy of Department of Justice hardened Suburbans. Two of them, along with a police escort, all to take just one prisoner from the airport in Pueblo to the prison compound just visible from U.S. Highway 50. But that prisoner was not a common man, and his incarceration was a big deal. Mike had read about it many times over the past months. Ayatollah Abdul Sarhardi was not a common criminal, and the world was watching. Mike watched as the parade of westbound vehicles slowed for the exit ramp leading up to Highway 115. Two more CHP vehicles were blocking oncoming traffic on 115. Security was tight.

Two odd-looking semi-tractors with heavy-looking trailers were approaching the 115 ramps as Mike slowed down to watch the action. One came from the east behind the prison convoy on Highway 50 and the other was coming from the west. Both looked the same, with heavier-than-usual steel cabs and very narrow windows, almost like the windows in earlier-model tanks that Mike had seen in WWII movies.

The DOJ convoy approached the exit ramp and began the climb to the top where it intersected with Highway 115. The front CHP vehicle, with full emergency lights blazing, made the left turn onto 115 and was followed by the two Suburbans and the rear CHP vehicle. As it began to cross the narrow bridge, the strange apparition of a semitruck pulled out of the eastbound ramp, ignoring the traffic stop, and into its path, completely blocking the road. The tractor looked more like an armored vehicle, with heavy steel windows with slits for viewing. Inside the tractor, Nizar notified the waiting pilot at Fremont County airport to take off and carry out the plan. With the trailer blocking both lanes, the state trooper did not know what to make of the situation. Nothing like this was supposed to happen. Glancing in his cruiser's rearview mirror, he saw that the Suburbans and the last CHP vehicle had turned on

Colorado 115 also, and they had likewise been blocked by another semi rig. The convoy was trapped on the bridge between the two semi-tractor trailers.

The lead CHP trooper looked back forward and saw the entire side of the trailer in front of him drop down, and he was suddenly facing two machine guns and a Bushmaster. It was the last thing he saw. Four men, dressed in camouflaged battle dress, dropped out of the semitrailer as the patrol vehicle was raked by fire. The CHP vehicle with the trooper was torn apart and completely destroyed. A very similar action was taking place in the back of the convoy. Behind the front semi, an armored Humvee pulled up and sat at idle. After destroying the front CHP vehicle, the Bushmaster operator trained his sights on the first Suburban and opened fire, taking out the entire front portion of the vehicle and instantly killing the two U.S. marshals inside. The battle-dressed men approached the rear Suburban with an RPG ready to fire, and motioned to the driver. The doors opened in the Suburban and the two U.S. marshals stepped out with hands held high. One of the battle-dressed commandos reached in, pulled the ayatollah out, and hustled him to the waiting Humvee.

The Department of Justice helicopter made several passes over the site as the action commenced. Unarmed, it could do nothing except observe. But it didn't last long. From the top of one of the trailers a panel opened up and a .50-caliber machine gun began firing at the helicopter. Struck several times with a pounding noise in the side and tail boom, the helicopter pilot saw the oil pressure begin to drop. He evaded more fire and headed west to the Fremont County airport, where he was able to make a safe landing on the concrete apron. He was out of the fight.

As soon as the first CHP vehicle was blocked, the highway patrol communication frequency exploded with traffic. Backup support was on the way but was not near enough to do any good. One of the locals in their own SUV stopped in the traffic and called 911, and the local police and fire department were called out. Again, to no avail.

The individual state highway policemen who had stopped traffic on Highway 115 for the convoy had recovered somewhat, and after making radio calls for assistance, began firing on the attackers with their twelve-gauge riot shotguns. They too, along with their patrol vehicles, were taken out of action by much heavier automated return fire. So far, nothing was stopping the attacking force from getting the ayatollah. The various police forces were just outgunned. And by now the ayatollah was inside the Humvee.

The Humvee, with the ayatollah in the backseat, headed down the eastbound entrance ramp to Highway 50 at high speed as the front semi pulled further over the bridge and against the guardrail right over the eastbound lanes of Highway 50. The men in the semi climbed out, headed for the nearest civilian SUV, and quickly left the scene. As they left, one of the men pulled out a remote detonator, turned to face the trailer, and triggered it. Four explosions occurred simultaneously under the left side of the parked semi-tractor and trailer. The entire vehicle lifted up and went over the guardrail in flames to the highway below. It completely blocked the eastbound lanes of Highway 50 right at the bridge. What little amount of traffic there was scattered and had to stop.

As the explosion occurred, the Humvee was well down the ramp and speeding onto the highway with the ayatollah, still shackled up, inside. The next phase of this spectacle began as the Cessna 182, whisper quiet with its engine at idle, slowly flew low over the bridge with full flaps down and landed on Highway 50. There was no eastbound traffic due to the burning semi at the bridge overpass. The 182 landed and stopped on the smooth highway. It waited a few moments as the Humvee caught up with it. The ayatollah, a commando, and the commando driver of the Humvee quickly got out and climbed into the small aircraft. The pilot gunned the powerful engine, gained speed, and accelerated down the highway and lifted off. He stayed very low, only a hundred feet or so to avoid any radar in the area, and banked sharply south with his precious cargo. Staying very low, barely over the trees, he flew over the Pueblo Reservoir and on down to the small Spanish Twin Peaks airport just off Interstate 25 near Walsenburg.

After less than fifteen minutes, they landed at the unattended landing strip. Using Uline 36 inch bolt cutters, they cut through the handcuffs and freed the ayatollah. They hangared the 182 so it was out of sight and hustled over to an idling Cessna Citation jet. The thirty-five hundred foot asphalt strip barely allowed the Citation jet to land and take off, but they made it.

Flying visual flight rules with no filed flight plan, the Citation, flying very low, went south and westbound through La Veta pass and did a touch-and-go in Alamosa. Climbing out of Alamosa, the pilot contacted Denver Center and, looking on radar like he had just taken off from Alamosa, filed a flight plan for Las Vegas. They were in the clear.

114

After landing at McCarran Airport in Las Vegas, Nevada, the three men were escorted to an awaiting limousine and left the area basically unobserved. A private civilian jet aircraft arrival, and limousine transport, was not an unusual event for the airport personnel in Las Vegas.

Except for the two surviving U.S. marshals, there wasn't much left of the convoy … and the ayatollah was long gone, leaving behind burning vehicles, two dead U.S. marshals in the first Suburban, two dead CHP patrolmen … and a stunned police and fire department in Penrose.

As soon as the ayatollah left the ambush site, the attacking force quickly withdrew using several of the civilian SUVs the police had stopped. For the civilians who were unlucky enough to be on the scene, it was hand over your keys or be shot. Three hesitated and were shot at close range and dumped out on the highway. Qasim was not happy over this problem, but shrugged it off as a necessary result. They had to move fast before reinforcements arrived. The attackers took off in five different SUVs and scattered across the Colorado countryside. Prearranged escape vehicles, with clothing changes and other supplies positioned in the thick wooded mountainsides, were then used by the attackers and they simply disappeared.

Mike, still in his prison guard uniform, rushed up to the scene and tried to help the state highway policemen. Two were dead and the other two were seriously wounded. Mike bound the chest wound on one officer to stop the bleeding and prevent air from getting into the lungs. As he was working, a medic unit arrived and took over from him. Looking over at the marshals who had been in the first Suburban, he realized that they were both gone. In some cases, major portions of their bodies were missing.

As the medics and volunteers worked to save those that could be saved, a timer in the remaining westbound semitrailer that had been left behind reached zero. A huge blast occurred, scattering pieces of the trailer across the highway and through the scene of bloody carnage. The medic unit was completely destroyed and the attending volunteer medics were both killed. A further distraction to the rescue crews that remained … a combination of fear and frustration … slowed down the rescue work. And in many cases it was a rescue of those who had been rescuers a few moments earlier.

Mike did not have to worry about his ex any more. He was torn in half by the explosion.

But the effect was what the attackers intended. A distraction from the escape of the ayatollah.

Very bad news.

CNN had an immediate story of the breakout. But there were no leads and no ideas on what they could do. The wounded police saw the 182 but, in all the excitement, did not see where it went. And the Citation jet, positioned at Twin Peaks airfield over twenty miles down Interstate 25, was a complete unknown. Within a few hours, the ayatollah had disappeared without a clue. The plan Ramiz had accomplished was quite remarkable and very effective.

The ayatollah's vehicle, out of McCarran Airport, headed for a high-end RV park on the west side of Las Vegas. He changed into Arab clothing while en route to the park. Once they arrived, the limousine from McCarran went back to its service location. The ayatollah was served some fresh fruit and bread and rested for an hour. Ramiz, joining the ayatollah during that hour, monitored the CNN broadcasts to see the effect of the raid. He was pleased with the results.

The driver of the specially outfitted RV waited until Ramiz told him to move. He then headed out for Reno and the airport there. Several hours of traveling brought them to the Reno-Tahoe airport southeast of Reno, where a private black Gulfstream 650 ER, with an eight-thousand-mile range, was waiting. After they cleared a casual customs check with false papers and filed a flight plan for Rio, the plane took off and, with center direction, came around on a heading for Rio de Janeiro.

They didn't go to Rio.

Chapter Twenty-One

Wednesday—September 20
Washington, D.C.—The White House

In Washington, disbelief was the best description of the scene in the White House, the administration, and Congress. The daylight attack on the convoy was incredible. Each of the major news networks had local representatives at the scene in very little time. The burning semis, the destroyed Suburbans, the abandoned Humvee, the casualties, and the totally destroyed CHP cruisers were all on video feeds. Newscasters were interviewing people who had witnessed the whole incident from their stopped cars. The Penrose Volunteer Fire Department was still cleaning up small brush fires around the vehicles and working to flush away some of the spilled fuel. Local hospitals in Canon City and Pueblo were overwhelmed by the casualties from the explosion.

After over an hour of watching, President Martinez and Jack Harrison were still glued to the television in the Oval Office. Neither was saying much as the scenes of carnage unfolded. The bottom line was that U.S. marshals and Colorado Highway Patrolmen were now dead, not to mention several unfortunate civilians, and the ayatollah had been grabbed and was gone. Where he had gone, they had no idea. The president stood with his hands on his hips and watched intently. He turned to Jack and said, "I don't believe it. We had him nearly at Florence and they pull this off!" He looked back at the TV.

Jack responded, "And I'll bet they get away with it. This was just too professional and well coordinated. If he's not out of the country already, I'll bet he is well on his way."

The president just nodded. He had to agree with what Jack had said ... but he sure didn't like it. They had spent a lot of time and effort to capture the ayatollah the last time. And the courts had found him guilty. It just didn't seem possible that this had occurred. And they were so close to putting him away permanently. He took in a deep breath, held it for a moment, and then released it.

Wednesday—September 20
Freeport, Texas—Ryan's Marina

117

Ryan, pretty well recovered from the attack several weeks ago, and with his leg cast removed a week ago, sat by the television, stunned, as the CNN news broadcast related the events near Florence. No one had a hint of the attack. It came completely out of nowhere and was spectacularly successful. The planning for it had to have been going on for months. Equipment modifications, weapons placement, personnel training, and very close timing all played a part in the attack. The sophistication that it required, he knew, did not exist in New Persia. Or at least it hadn't. It appeared that New Persia had developed a much more capable and determined offensive force. They had to have brought in some expertise from another country or organization. He considered that a serious development that wasn't good for the west. Things could get a lot more difficult.

Jasper, also stunned, said, "I don't believe it. When I was over there, I sure didn't see anything like this. It's been over a year, though, and they must have put together quite a training program for these commando types."

Ryan commented, "Well, when we were in there grabbing the ayatollah last year, we didn't see anything like it either. Someone has really improved their capabilities. This Abdul-Hakim character, their defense minister, must have had some form of help. He just isn't that sophisticated."

Jackie added, "I don't see how that group could get all that done in the year since we got the ayatollah out of Socotra. Whoever is running things over there now is doing a very capable job. I doubt whether it is the same group that the ayatollah had, or at the very least a few key players have changed."

Ryan looked thoughtfully at her and said, "You may be right. Abdul-Hakim had some skills with defensive setups, but he certainly didn't appear to be very capable of offensive operations, and this is certainly that. It's possible he has been replaced and another person brought in to run their so-called defense. Obviously, they have more than what we had to contend with last year."

It was worrisome to him. He still felt, on occasion, like he was a target of this group, and with the escape of its leader ... well, it worried him.

Ryan looked out over his marina and, as always, enjoyed the view over the upgrades that had been completed in the past year. Finally. He had a very popular and respected operation, with a small waiting list for his 102 slips. His private thirty-four-foot Hunter sailboat was his enjoyment, and he and Jackie spent a fair amount of time in the Gulf of Mexico leisurely moving along the offshore islands, picnicking and loving the warm waters.

But he was worried about New Persia ... and with good reason.

Chapter Twenty-Two

Thursday—September 21
U.S. Highway 50 and Colorado Highway 115—Colorado

George Rogers, a member of the Colorado State Highway Patrol, looked over the scene of the attack that led to the death of his colleagues. George was a private pilot and was thinking about the aircraft that apparently landed on Highway 50 and took off again heading south. They still had not located the plane. Putting himself in the pilot's position, needing to get away as fast as possible, where would he go? It went south. But it had not gone to Trinidad or Alamosa or on down to Albuquerque. The only thing he could think about was the small strip near Walsenburg. And then what would they have done?

George got back in his cruiser and headed south on Interstate 25. He got off at Exit 55 and headed over to the small strip. He pulled into the small hangar area of Spanish Twin Peaks Airfield, got out, and looked around for a few minutes. As he was looking around, he heard a wrench drop on the floor of an open hangar. Walking over to the hangar door, he looked inside and saw a person working on the brakes of a Cessna 172. He walked up and the person looked at him, got up off the floor, wiping his hands on a red maintenance rag. The man said, "Afternoon, officer. Can I help you?"

George responded, "Yes, you might be able to. I'm looking into an escape yesterday up near Florence. We're looking for a small aircraft similar to this one that would have come in around 1:30 to 1:45 yesterday afternoon. Did you see anything?"

The mechanic looked at the officer for just a moment and quietly exclaimed, "That's what it was all about! I never connected it to the news story last night."

George said, "What do you mean? Did you see something that might help us?"

"I can do more than that, I can show you the airplane. Follow me." And he headed across the aircraft parking ramp to another hangar. He walked up to the side door, unlocked it with his keys, and stepped in. George followed him closely. They stepped in to a moderate-sized hangar, and in one corner sat a Cessna 182 aircraft.

The mechanic said, "Yesterday, about the time you're talking about, I was working on my airplane when this airplane landed. ," and he nodded in the direction of the 182, then continued, "The pilot taxied up to this hangar and three people got out. They ran for a Cessna Citation jet that was sitting here waiting. The 182 pilot put the airplane in the hangar and then joined them in the Citation. The Citation then taxied out to the west end of the runway. I watched because I wasn't sure that small jet could make it out. But he went to full power before releasing the brakes, had partial flaps down, and made a run for it. I'll bet he wasn't more than fifty feet from the end of the runway when he finally got airborne. He had balls, that one. They headed north at a very low altitude and I lost sight of them."

George looked at the mechanic and pleasantly said, "Did they see you?"

"I doubt it. I was back in my hangar sitting on the floor when all this happened."

"What's your name?"

"Johnny-Mac Swain. I'm a mechanic here and do miscellaneous chores around the hangars."

"Well, Johnny-Mac, I'm going to need you to give me a statement of what you saw, and there may be some follow-on work needed. The people you saw take off killed several people in a prison break yesterday."

"Now that I think about it, I see what you mean. Sure. I'll help. Just let me know what you need."

George said, "Okay. Don't touch the 182. We'll have some people here soon to really go over it thoroughly for evidence."

George then filled out several forms and had Johnny-Mac fill out a statement of what he saw. They might just have the break they needed in the case.

Thursday—September 21
Washington, D.C.—The White House

The day following the ayatollah's escape effort, President Martinez was still stunned at the news. The ayatollah had been found guilty of terrorism, murder, destruction of U.S. property, and several other related charges. He was considered a serious flight risk, as events proved to be true, and thus had been heavily guarded. Obviously not heavily guarded enough. Rumor had it that he might be back in Socotra, or close to it, but there had been no proof of that. He was lying low and nobody knew where.

121

Ten people were killed and several wounded in the breakout of the ayatollah outside of Florence. The terrorist commando raid, and that was what the press called it, was well executed and successful. New Persia got the ayatollah back and he had disappeared to who-knows-where. There was no trace of him at this point. The commando force had just melted away, and no trace of them had been found either.

The president was absolutely livid. When word got back to him an hour after the raid occurred, he couldn't believe it. A prison convoy destroyed and the prisoner escaped, with no sign of his destination. After several hours, and a couple of unrelated meetings later, the president got back to his office and read a short synopsis, written by Jack Harrison, of what had happened.

"Jack, please come in here," demanded the president.

Jack Harrison came into the Oval Office.

"Yes, sir?"

"Sit down for a moment."

Jack sat.

The president turned his gaze from the windows on the office and looked at Jack. "How could this happen? We are a civilized nation and have all the capability to transfer a prisoner in safety and with assurance that he will end up where we want him. But this one escaped us. How?"

Jack squirmed a bit, because he felt the same way. It was obvious that the security measures taken in transporting the ayatollah were not adequate. "I don't know. And we haven't made any progress on how or where he escaped to. We suspect he is on his way back to Socotra, but we aren't sure. The few questions we have been able to ask in Socotra have been stonewalled by the locals, and they may be more or less telling the truth. They claim they know nothing about his location. He may, for all we know, still be in this country being hidden by sympathizers. DOT hasn't been able to locate any sign of him. Air traffic control has no record of any flights he might have been on out of Colorado, and an airplane would be the most probable way for him to quickly get out of the country. They're stumped too. I just don't know at this point. We are trying to track him down and are just as frustrated as you are over these events."

"Okay. Do we have any idea how the so-called commandos got into the country? Especially with all that equipment?"

"Well, we have some ideas but no evidence or proof. We did locate some of the vehicles they abandoned on the back roads of

Colorado. Of course, they were stolen at the scene from some of the innocent bystanders, so they weren't much help. And if they had some prepositioned beat-up old pick-ups parked on the side of those mountain roads, no one would have noticed them. We did get some equipment that they left behind, and most was made in China, but again, that isn't much help. Things like gas masks, Kevlar vests, and some ammunition are available all over the black market. No way to trace them.

"And the semis they used were heavily modified. Or at least what was left of them. Both were Peterbilts and both pretty well burned up. One on the highway and the other up on the overpass. The weapons, a couple of Bushmasters and the .50-caliber machine guns, are also readily available on the black market. They probably brought them in, somehow, from outside the country. And the airplane hasn't been located yet. We do know it headed south but don't know where it went. Perhaps in a few days we can locate it. But I'll bet it will be a while. It sure won't be obvious. All in all, it was quite an operation. Lots of planning and guts to pull it off."

"How'd they get in the country?"

"Not sure on that one either. Keep in mind that we have over ninety-five thousand miles of ocean and gulf coastline. We can't police all of it even if we knew something like this was going to happen. If I had to guess, they probably came in on a small boat outside our territorial waters, possibly supported by a larger boat. It wouldn't take much too just come in to a small marina and unload materials and men, or use several marinas to avoid suspicion. They could have been disguised as men fishing. Who knows?"

The president turned away, picked up a pen, and drummed it on the desk. After a few moments, he turned back.

"If you were the ayatollah, what would you do now?"

Jack thought for a moment, moved in his chair a little to be more comfortable, and teepeed his fingers in front of his face. After a long half-minute, he said, "For the moment, I would lay low and lick my wounds. If I'm out of this country and somewhere else in friendly territory, I would quietly convene a very small conference of associates and plan a way forward. Very small, so there is less chance of leaking my location and the fact that I made it out. If I'm still in the U.S., I wait it out with help from sympathizers until things calm down and then figure a way to get out. Possibly the same way the commandos came in."

The president had stopped drumming when Jack started talking. When Jack stopped talking, he started drumming again.

"So. Until we can determine his actual location, we can't do much. Wait and see what he does. And that could be months away."

Jack nodded. He got up, hesitated for a moment, went to the small bar refrigerator, thinking, and got a caffeine-free Pepsi. He set the odd-colored can down on the coffee table, popped it open, and sat down again, casually crossing his legs. The sun was shining in through the windows and his mind went to how nice a day it really was. Then back to the subject.

"I think we may be able to do some things. The ayatollah has an organization of roughly two to three thousand people, and still growing. The fact that it is still growing, and that there have been incidents since he was captured, tells me that someone else is running things in his absence. We're pretty sure it's this guy Khatib. The ayatollah may feel quite comfortable in staying out of the limelight for a while and letting the organization do its thing under the temporary leader. Or he may decide to renew his leadership in a clandestine way. Running it from a distance through communication links." He hesitated for a moment, taking a drink of the Pepsi, and then continued. "With an organization of that size, and growing, there has to be some information channels that we can access. Somewhere out there, someone knows something about his whereabouts, and, given the size of the organization, we should be able to find that someone. CIA or State should have some street contacts. We have already tried the Socotrans, and that didn't work. Maybe Yemen or Iran would have some information. Even some elements of the Saudis could know."

"I think you are right. I'll contact Kenton over at State and Mark at the CIA and see what they can find out. Knowing those two, they probably already have feelers out and working, but I'll ask anyway. Another subject. Was there any breakdown in the transfer process for the ayatollah? Did someone screw up and miss a sign of the pending attack?"

"Well, it's a bit early to tell. I mean, this just happened yesterday. But at this point, I don't think so. We used the normal protocols for transferring a supermax prisoner. All was done according to plan and there was no hint of a problem until they actually hit us."

"Where did they get those trucks, those overgrown tanklike things?"

"According to the FBI and the highway patrol, they were modified in a truck repair facility in Canon City. The guys doing the modifications thought they were a bit strange, but a customer is a customer and they didn't question the changes. They put in additional room for personnel in the driver's bed area, but they never saw the high-powered guns in the trailers. They saw some mounts for them but not the actual guns. And they also said that when the trucks were turned over to the customer, they had bulletproof windshields in them. Someone else modified the windshields into the armored slit formation."

"Pretty impressive."

"Yes, sir. Oh, and one other item."

The president motioned for him to continue.

"The Humvee that took the ayatollah away from the scene headed east on Highway 50. The Colorado State Patrol found it in a ditch on Highway 50. No attempt to hide it. There was a resident who saw a small airplane land on Highway 50, pick up three passengers from the Humvee, and take off again. He said the aircraft stayed real low, like one or two hundred feet above ground level, and headed south. We tried to locate the airplane, but, as I said earlier, without a tail number, haven't had any success."

"So that's how he initially got away from the scene?"

"Apparently. If the aircraft stayed real low to the ground, our radars in the area airports wouldn't pick him up. He could have gone anywhere."

"Smart."

"Yes, sir."

"Smart enough to not be the ayatollah's thinking. He wouldn't know all those details. Someone familiar with our way of doing things, and maybe our way of air traffic control, thought this out. Also someone with some knowledge or experience in commando operations. We're dealing with someone who is very familiar with the U.S."

Jack nodded. "Yes, sir. We are."

The president thought for just a bit then said, "And it's a bit unnerving to know we have a bunch of terrorist commandos running around the country."

Jack looked back, took a sip of his drink, nodded, and left.

The president thought for a few minutes and then remembered the comment about checking with the CIA and State. He picked up the phone and called Mark Allison at the CIA.

"Mark, have you guys picked up any vibes on the ayatollah's whereabouts? I know you have been looking. I'm wondering if there has been any result yet."

Mark responded, "No, sir. We have been out beating the bushes, but to no avail. There doesn't seem to be much out there right now. It's quite possible that New Persia has a very tight lid on it. If it were me, I sure would."

"Yeah. I guess I'd have to agree. Keep me informed if you get anything."

"Will do." And they hung up.

Next the president called over to the State Department and was put through to Kenton.

"Kenton, I know you guys are watching the ayatollah thing pretty closely. Have you had anything turn up?"

Kenton responded, "No, sir. Nothing yet, but we are keeping on top of it. It's just very quiet out there. And he does have some friends that we think may be helping him. But nothing solid yet. I'll let you know if anything develops."

"Okay. Thanks. Talk with you later." They both cut the line.

The president sat for a few moments, shook his head in disgust, and turned to some paperwork on his desk. It would be a long day.

Chapter Twenty-Three

Thursday—September 21
Mexico—Yucatan Peninsula

After several days of waiting in the port of Progreso, Captain Najid received word to send a vehicle to Rejon Airport in Merida and pick up the ayatollah and Ramiz. When he received the request, his eyebrows went up in a pleased expression. The escape had obviously worked. He complied immediately. The car arrived at the airport and met the ayatollah and Ramiz at a hotel just off the airport. The ayatollah, somewhat rested from his adventure, and Ramiz got in the car and shortly arrived at the port. Najid had already picked up the additional commandos that were going to be a critical part of his next mission. He prepared two of the staterooms on the *Persian Quest* so the ayatollah and Ramiz would be comfortable.

Najid welcomed them aboard, and *Persian Quest* quickly departed the harbor quietly and efficiently. They began their journey to the north and to the Gulf Coast of the United States, where their next mission assignment would be executed.

On board, they had a commando force of twenty trained men. Twenty men who would cause havoc and severe damage to parts of the U.S. oil industry. Twenty men who would bring the U.S. around to complying with the demands. Twenty men who had arrived through Mexico and were well trained in their mission. And they also had the ayatollah on board to observe the actions and mission accomplishment. He had not gone to Rio or Socotra. The U.S. had no idea where he was.

Monday—September 25
Gulf of Mexico—Galveston Bay

They approached the international waters just outside of Galveston Bay, contacted their "friends" on shore via satellite telephone, and arranged an at-sea meeting. Two hours later, a medium-sized powerboat approached the *Persian Quest* and was tied up alongside. Hashim, from Houston, came aboard and was escorted into the small main conference room. Captain Najid and Qasim met him, and they sat down to begin the detailed planning to complete the mission. After conferring for several hours, getting the mission requirements straight, the time schedules lined up, and the support necessary to accomplish the mission agreed to, Hashim left the *Persian Quest* and headed back into the port at Houston. The mission would be an interesting challenge.

The oil storage facilities in Houston and the surrounding area were constructed, for emergency purposes, to contain the oil in the tanks within bermed holding areas around each tank. In theory, the bermed area could hold all of the oil in the tank should the tank fail for any reason. The facilities also had chain-link fencing all the way around them. Razor wire topped the fencing, and additional security patrols helped ensure that no one got into the facilities.

They were basically protected from vandals and the casual troublemaker. Not from a dedicated group of commandos who were determined to destroy American oil facilities and interrupt the oil supply chain out to the U.S. population. Commandos ... like those on board the *Persian Quest* off the coast of Galveston Bay.

Galveston Bay is the main harbor for the entire Houston area. The oil shipments through this harbor complex carry a tremendous amount of the oil import traffic for the U.S. The Houston Fuel Oil Terminal Company is the biggest oil terminal in the gulf region, with over twenty-two million barrels of storage capacity. It became a major target for the New Persia group.

It was a quiet early evening, and the *Persian Quest* was at anchor outside the territorial limits of U.S. waters but within sight of the Galveston Bay complex. It was a busy time on board the trimaran as the recently trained commandos prepared for their night of adventure and mayhem. The air was light with a slight breeze and very comfortable in the early evening twilight. The stars were poking out from behind small clouds and the moon was well hidden on the other side of the earth. It was a dark night that was just made for invasion, damage, and withdrawal by a well-trained group. There was some nervousness in the air as the members prepared for their departure and arrival on U.S. soil. None of the commando force had been in the U.S. before, and anxiety was very apparent. While the trimaran was obvious, its mission was not, and they meant to keep it that way until all was completed.

The recently rescued ayatollah, along with Ramiz, was on the main deck in seaman's clothes looking at the coastline. They were there to watch the action that he and Khatib directed. If all went according to their plan, they were going to destroy a significant part of the U.S. oil refinery and storage capacity. The ayatollah was both anxious and content in his Allah-given mission.

Ramiz looked over the rail at the coastline. The escape he had planned for the ayatollah, and the strikes that were about to take place, had consumed him for months. And now he would be able to see the results. He was very satisfied at the moment, but kept his emotions in check. It was a solemn moment for him. A culmination.

Qasim, well versed in explosives and the layout of the oil terminal, was determined, and also nervous, about this assignment. He had led other, smaller raids, but this would be, by far, the largest. His men were nearly finished with their preparations and ready to board the powerboats due to meet them shortly. The excellent French training of the commando group was apparent in the preparations the group made for the strike. The briefings were over, equipment prepared, and the timing agreed upon. Each team of two men had their assigned targets and associated equipment for destroying those targets. They checked and re-checked their equipment more out of nervous energy than necessity.

Two medium-sized powerboats, little more than water-skiing boats, pulled up to the trimaran at 10:30 p.m., and six men got in each along with their equipment and weapons. Eight men would be held in reserve, to have their opportunity later. The water was fairly calm, with just a slight roll to it as they boarded. In the nighttime darkness, nervous tension showed on all their camouflaged, or balaclava-covered, faces. Eyes narrowed and determined. Some jaws tight and others loose. Some with butterflies in the stomach and others not. Once on board the powerboats, they began moving slowly for the U.S. shore and then picked up the pace. The lead boat, with Qasim aboard, headed toward a predetermined marina in Galveston Bay.

They arrived at midnight and tied up to a pier, where three dark quad-cab trucks awaited. Quietly and quickly they moved off the boats and into the preassigned trucks for transport to their targets. Four to a truck. The trucks moved out to several locations around the outside of the Houston Crude Oil Terminal storage tank farm.

At assigned locations, each two-man team was dropped off, then they got equipment and supplies out of the truck and moved toward the fence. Previous information gained from sympathetic spies told them when to expect the thirty-minute patrols to come by.

They waited until it was clear and approached the fencing. It was 12:30 a.m. on Tuesday, September 26.

After gathering the supplies at the base of the fence, one of the team took a laser gun, pointed it at the nearest light, and held it for a few moments until the light burned out. They knew the lights might not be fixed for some time. And they might not even exist after a few hours tonight. The information obtained through Ramiz appeared to be accurate. There was no reaction from the patrols.

The fence was normal chain-link fencing with razor wire along the top. The team lead glanced at the razor wire and then took small bolt cutters and cut a man-sized hole in the chain link. Both team members then hauled the supplies through the hole and headed for the nearest tank. The tanks were huge, holding thousands of barrels of crude in each one. Their assignment was to set three explosives each at three of the tanks, a total of nine placements, and then rejoin their group at the marina. Each team would do the same thing for a total of eighteen tanks destroyed, plus the interconnecting piping.

Each team approached the first assigned tank after they got inside the fencing. They set the charges, two for each location on the tank, one minor charge to put a hole in the outer shell of the tank, and then a much larger one to actually penetrate the interior tank wall. Two closely timed explosions. To the ear they would sound like one. But they're not; and they are very effective. They circled the tank and set two more locations with the same devices. Then they moved on to the next tank to do the same thing. And then once more as they finalized their efforts. If there was too much light, they burned it with the laser. All the explosives were set to go off simultaneously in one hour. They then headed back to the hole in the fence, patched it quickly with some baling wire, and waited for the truck to arrive. Once on board the truck, they headed back to the marina. They were nervous. They looked at their watches, waiting for the minute hand to crawl up to the hour point. It crawled. Slowly. They boarded the small powerboats and waited impatiently for the other teams to arrive.

Two specialized teams tackled the piers and on/offloading equipment. There were three tanker ships at the piers offloading their cargo of crude. This was an active process, and there were American terminal operators working in the area of the tankers, along with several tanker crewmen. Dressed as dock workers, and driving hot-wired forklifts carrying heavy loads of flexible pipe, they approached the offloading equipment. They stopped, looked at the terminal input plumbing as though they were inspecting it, and placed small timed charges in the small covered valve sheds. Then they moved on to the next shed. In all, they managed to place charges in six sheds, and moved back to the terminal maintenance buildings. They parked the forklift and departed through the gate they had entered. They boarded their truck and headed back to the marina. No one interrupted them and no one interfered.

Jim Madison was on patrol along with Pete Clarendon. They were patrolling the outer perimeter fencing around the tanks at the Houston Terminal. It took a full forty-five minutes to patrol the whole tank farm, and then they took a short break. Boredom was not the word for it. It was zombie-inducing. Around and around the fencing they went, driving their small ATVs. But it was a living, and with all the terrorist activities in the news, it was their responsibility to make sure the tank farm was safe.

They didn't know they had failed.

Charles "Chas" Mitchel, monitoring the terminal from the center where all the various plumbing, pumps, and valves were controlled, noticed that several of the lights had burned out in the tank farm. *Strange*, he thought. *They are usually much more reliable than that.* He called out to the patrol, "Patrol One, control."

Jim answered, "Go ahead, control."

"You guys seeing anything unusual out there?"

"No. Nothing at all. Pretty quiet. Why?"

"Oh. Probably nothing. Just checking. Control out."

Jim looked around for a minute, shrugged, and continued with the patrol.

One hour, at 1:30 a.m., after the commandos had set all the explosives, the night erupted in a fury of sound, light, and flames. It was a hell on earth as the explosions roared their death and destruction. Jim and Pete were in a part of the tank farm that was not directly affected by the explosives ... but they sure were. The blasts, and there were quite a few of them, hit them like a ton of bricks. The shock wave was strong enough to collapse several of the tanks in their immediate area, and the ruined tanks caught on fire almost from the beginning as the oil flooded into the holding berms. Jim and Pete headed as fast as they could to safety behind one of the berms, but they didn't make it. The flaming oil engulfed them and, with a final scream of agony, they died trying to escape the inferno. Nothing left. Just flames. And smoke. Twisted metal and two dead bodies, burned beyond recognition.

The ships at the berths were likewise engulfed in flames and destruction. The ship's cargo, and hoses attached to the piers, caught fire, and there was an immediate flash up to the cargo holds. All three ships were blazing infernos. The crewmen, trying to put out the fires, were just overwhelmed and had to retreat from the flames and heat.

Fire department response was quick, but they were overwhelmed by the size and heat of the fire. Plans had been in place to handle a potential of three tank fires, but not eighteen of them. And the ship fires were a lower priority until the tank fires could be controlled. By using smothering foam, they were able to snuff out some of the tank fires in the berm containment areas, but several others were beyond their capability. As the fire engulfed the bermed areas, the heat caused several other tanks to fail, which just added to the inferno.

From the marina, the explosions looked like a Fourth of July show. As the fireworks started, fist pumps and smiles were exchanged. And in some cases, individual commandos raised their eyes in silent prayer to Allah for their success. The commandos had accomplished their mission and were escaping without notice. They had struck the eagle and it was severely wounded.

They headed out to sea as the inferno blazed behind them. The *Persian Quest* crew was waiting for them in quiet wonder. Crewmen watched as the fireworks started, and were amazed at the result of the raid. It was obvious the Americans were caught with no idea they were about to be hit. That night, close to thirteen million barrels of storage were lost, along with the capability to offload future deliveries of crude from the Middle East. The three ships at berth would have to be towed to a repair yard, and it would be several months before they could continue their mission. Repairs would take close to nine months for the tank farm, and the pier and offloading capability would take close to a year to repair. It was a significant blow to the U.S. oil industry.

The ayatollah, Ramiz, and Najid, on board the *Persian Quest,* met Qasim and congratulated him on a job well done. They had succeeded in striking the U.S. oil industry, and it would show in the next few days as the news broke. There would be panic in the U.S. as the population, overcome by the news, reacted with lines at gas stations again.

Combined with the successful rescue of the ayatollah, it was quite a remarkable few days. They sent a message of success back

132

to the New Persia Operations Center. However, the operations center, with Khatib present, already knew of their success from watching CNN and other U.S. news channels. The raid results had been picked up quickly by the news media, and speculation was running rampant. It was obvious that this was an act of terrorism, but who had done it?

The ayatollah had been briefed on all of the planning, and merely stood by and watched as the detailed strikes were carried out. Since he had been incarcerated during the planning, he did not want to interfere. It was obvious that this series of strikes against the Americans would be breathtaking.

The commandos, after reaching the *Persian Quest*, had finally calmed down a bit, and were in quiet conversation with each other over what had gone right and what had gone wrong. They would correct any problems and apply those corrections on the next mission. There was a quiet jubilation in their ranks. They had succeeded where some others had not. And they weren't finished yet.

The *Persian Quest* monitored the U.S. news broadcasts and, after several hours through the dark night, Najid decided it was time to head for his next location further east in the gulf. They had another mission to perform just off the coast of Mississippi. He took his position in the captain's chair on the bridge and gave directions to the helmsman to make way. The ayatollah maintained his position on the bridge in the dark shadows, watching with wonder as his crew got underway. They were not finished yet. They had more work to do.

As the ship slowly got underway using its twin turbine engines, most of the commandos shed their gear and made their way to their cabins for a period of rest. It had been a long day and evening, and the next few days would test their stamina as they completed the total mission from Khatib, Ramiz, and the ayatollah. The ship moved out at a very slow pace. They did not want to draw any attention to themselves.

Chapter Twenty-Four

Tuesday—September 26
Houston, Texas—Houston Oil Terminal

In the main operating center for the Houston Crude Oil Terminal, pandemonium was the scene of the moment. They had obviously been attacked, but had no idea by whom, or where they had come from. It was a total surprise. Larry Schmidt, the operations center night supervisor, along with Chas Mitchel, had been trying to reach his roving patrols for the past fifteen minutes, with no success. The fire and police departments had their hands full trying to control both the fires and the crowds who had gathered to look. Larry had called all maintenance and operations personnel in for the emergency, and they were slowly showing up. As they did, he was assigning them to teams to help with containing the fire. Valves were being manually shut down to stop, where they could, flow of oil between tanks and to the piers. ATVs were being used to ferry people to the valve locations. A fire department battalion chief, George Patterson, had arrived to coordinate his activities with the operations and maintenance personnel. As usual, radio compatibility was a problem, and his arrival with fire department mobile radios solved that.

The fire was so intense that helicopters, hired by the media, could not get too close to the inferno. Updrafts and heavy smoke, along with darkness and flames, kept them from getting close. And there was always the danger of another explosion with the tremendous heat being generated. They were forced to film from a distance.

Tuesday—September 26
Washington, D.C.—The White House

Jack had been awoken at home by one of his staffers at 3:00 a.m.. Quickly informed of the situation in Houston, he got up and turned on the TV to CNN. Coverage was a bit chaotic, but as he watched he realized very quickly that this was a terrorist attack. Briefly thinking about it, it didn't take him long to connect the escape of the ayatollah with this attack on a U.S. refinery. He called the White House and was put through to the Secret Service detail. After explaining what was going on, the Secret Service quietly woke the president and he answered the phone.

"Sorry to disturb you, sir, but we have a situation in Houston. There has been a terrorist attack—at least, that's my take on it—on the storage facilities there. I'd suggest you take a look at CNN. It looks pretty rough."

"Dammit, Jack!" the president exclaimed. "I'll look and see what's going on. You think it's the ayatollah again?" And he turned to his TV to see what the coverage was. Pretty stark.

"Yep. That'd be my guess at this time. I'll get dressed and be in the office in a little while. Maybe there will be some more info available then. If it is New Persia, we'll need to make a statement to the press. I'll draft up something for you."

"Okay. Have to agree with you. See you in a bit." And the president turned around, got some clothes, and dressed. Then he went down to the Oval Office, where he started monitoring the news coverage. Not a good scene in Texas.

Later that morning, since the Houston fire was still not completely contained, investigators could not make a final determination of the cause. It could have been accidental, but the press was not buying that, given the fact that multiple tanks had gone up at the same time, along with the ship loading facilities. The press release Jack worked up with the president just stated that until a full determination of the cause was available, no further information would be issued. In the background, however, they called on API and all of the major refinery operators to increase their security in case this was of terrorist origin.

During the early morning discussions with Jack and several members of his staff, the president also directed that the Coast Guard increase their patrols near any of the coastal refineries. Perhaps they might find something of interest, or perhaps not, but it would be best to be as proactive as possible until they determined the cause of the fire.

Wednesday—September 27
Gulf of Mexico—Gulfport-Pascagoula, Mississippi

Late the next day, *Persian Quest* was outside Gulfport-Pascagoula, Mississippi, where there was another significant storage and refining facility. Chevron had a large refinery in

Pascagoula, and the commandos were determined to put it out of commission for a long time. Again, no warning. Just action.

The *Persian Quest* set her anchor some twenty miles from the coast. It was approaching nightfall, and the gulf was calm, with only slight ripples across the water. But it was far from calm below decks, where preparations were being made for the night's activities. Each of the commandos was preparing his own equipment, and his selection of weapons, for the night's attack. Additional packages of explosives and timers were prepared and placed in temporary storage, and the listings checked to make sure all the explosives were there. Small backpacks for carrying the explosives were also prepared. Each team member would be carrying his own explosive package to the intended target.

Several hours before the actual invasion effort was to begin, the internal ship lights were dimmed to help acclimate the commandos' eyes to the darkness. They gathered in the dim lights for the final briefings and the final review of each person's assigned target. The ayatollah, not wanting to interfere, stayed in the shadows of the group, but they were all aware of his presence. The individual reviews were conducted before all of them so they could see the total picture of the attack. Each would thus know what the other was doing, lessening the chance of accidental conflict. Each was excited. They had rested as the ship had moved along the Gulf Coast to their current location. Anticipation was high and they all wanted to get on with it. The success of the Houston strike was still in their minds, and they wanted another successful strike tonight.

In Houston, the remaining fires had been brought under control, but all of them had not been completely extinguished. Several firefighters had been injured in fighting the conflagration, and the bodies, burned beyond recognition, of Jim and Pete were found. Identification had to be made by the coroner using dental records.

A total of twenty-two tanks had been destroyed and another nine had been damaged. The piers had been destroyed, along with the three ships that had been tied up. They had extinguished the fires on the ships, but the hulks were just towed out into the bay and anchored, awaiting insurance inspection. They were considered a total loss. The piers were also a total loss and would have to be completely rebuilt.

The coordination between the operations center and the fire department had been good, but several areas were recognized as needing improvement. Communications and radio compatibility had been overcome by use of cell phones and mobile radios, but the problem needed to be resolved for future needs.

Security procedures were reviewed later that same day. There were only a limited number of cameras in use, and that was recognized as a problem. While the patrols had been doubled from once per hour to every half-hour after the warning from Homeland Security, it was obviously not enough. And the deaths of Jim and Pete pointed out the need for almost constant contact with the roving patrols. The location of the fence penetrations was finally discovered, although it took a little while, since the fence had been partially repaired using the bailing wire. There was no other evidence left behind for the investigators to find. No DNA, and no materials that could be traced. Investigators had nothing to use to figure out who was responsible for the attacks.

Khatib, watching the news coverage, was very pleased with the results he was seeing in Houston. The raiding party was successful. He began composing a letter for the U.S. administration demanding compliance with New Persia's goals, noting the escape of the ayatollah. He got most of the message composed and was rereading it when he changed his mind. It was too soon. He decided to wait until the next phase was complete. They were going to strike a second time within two days. The infidels would not have recovered from the Houston strike and would be still unaware of the danger they faced. The second strike would be quick and deadly. Then he would send his message.

Wednesday—September 27
Mobile, Alabama—API Headquarters

Jack Findley, the head of the American Petroleum Institute, was absolutely glued to the television screen in his office in Mobile, Alabama. The scenes from Houston were simply unbelievable. And he thought he knew what, or who, had caused the catastrophe. The ayatollah had just escaped ... and now this happened. The coincidence was just too great. New Persia was obviously getting very active, and in a very deadly manner.

Hundreds of thousands of barrels of storage and multiple lives were lost in the attack. The terrorists were brash in their attack and had caught the industry with its pants down. Obviously, there was nowhere near enough security, and what they had in place was woefully inadequate.

While watching the screen, he called in his primary assistant, Patrick Nelson, who had been watching in the cafeteria.

Jack said, "We need to get hold of the primary congressmen and get some action underway to foil this group. And foil them permanently. It's obvious the president isn't up to it. After the ayatollah escaped the other day, and the administration has no idea where he might be, I think it is time for others to act."

Pat said, "I'll get Senator McIlroy and Senator Sebastian of Mississippi on the phone and see if we can set up a meeting to discuss what can be done. What do you mean by 'others' to act?"

"We may have to go after these characters ourselves. They have obviously developed some kind of commando capability, as the new reports are saying, and that needs to be countered. I'm wondering about some form of mercenaries that we could put on the problem and solve it."

Pat recoiled a bit and said, "I think that is a bit over the top. That is what the government is supposed to do. I don't think the Congress guys will go along with it."

"Perhaps not, but we need to do something, and that would be a good start for the conversation. Then we can back off if they come up with anything that makes sense."

"So you're saying for us to put a plan out there that we know they won't go along with just to get them moving on their own."

"Exactly. Sometimes you have to be sneaky to get somewhere with this group of congressmen and women. And maybe, just maybe, this attack will spur them on to put some pressure on the administration to do something. They can't sit on their hands forever."

Pat thought for a moment then said, "Okay. I'll see what I can set up and we'll get on with it."

Jack absentmindedly shook his head as he continued to watch the TV screen.

Chapter Twenty-Five

Wednesday—September 27
Gulf of Mexico—Gulfport-Pascagoula, Mississippi

It was approaching 11:00 p.m. on Wednesday and the commandos gathered on the deck. The two nine-meter rigid-hulled inflatable boats had been tied up to the *Persian Quest* and were waiting to take the commandos in to the area of the refinery facility. It was located upriver slightly from the actual coast, in Bayou Casotte Harbor, and would have to be approached cautiously. With a refinery capacity of over four hundred thousand barrels per day and over two hundred large storage tanks, it was one of the largest refineries in the U.S., and a significant target for the commandos. This one would take a fair amount of time, since the intent was to take out over twenty tanks, the pier, a truck loading facility, and the main refinery towers.

The two RHIBs moving up the bayou had a space on the aft end that was open and, in normal use, was where people sat with chairs and fishing lines. In this case, that area had been modified. The floor was reinforced to handle the additional weight for a special aspect of the mission. With the briefings complete, the commandos loaded up, eight on one RHIB and seven on the other. They each had their weapons and the explosives necessary to accomplish their tasks. They had maps of the facility and knew exactly where they were going.

The RHIBs passed the refining facility and then eased into a small marshy area just to the north of the facility. The commandos offloaded in shallow water and quietly hurried inland. They made their way to the fence, cut through it, and were inside the facility perimeter within minutes. They spread out and headed for their specific targets. This time, the timers were all set for two hours into the night to give them enough time to accomplish all of their tasks. The darkness hid them except in areas lit up by overhead lights, which were primarily around the pier and some of the tanks. They took out some of the lights with lasers. But they moved with graceful and fast motion, avoiding patrols and the very few personnel who were out doing miscellaneous tasks. Two cameras were spotted, and lasers took care of them. The tanks were the easiest targets, and four teams of two each took care of all twenty targets within an hour and a half. The piers, with two ships berthed there, were handled by two more teams, and they were able to take care of them within the same hour and a half. The truck loading facilities, an easier target, since they were out in the open and very vulnerable, were targeted by one team. The temporary storage tanks and loading pipelines for the trucks were easy targets for the explosives.

As one team was finishing up on one of the pier explosives, a roving patrol came around the corner of a building and spotted them. All had been quiet up until this point. Aware of the situation at Houston, the patrol used a vehicle-mounted spotlight and found the team just straightening up from their task. The team members quickly hit the ground and swung their silenced AK-74 rifles around, taking careful aim at the patrol vehicle occupants. They fired several rounds, killing the completely surprised two-man patrol and taking out the spotlight. They hurried up to the Land Rover patrol vehicle, moved the vehicle into a shadow behind a building, and quickly left.

There was still a half-hour before the explosives were due to go off. All of the teams were finished and headed back to the rendezvous point. The team lead, Qasim, was quickly briefed on the fatal shootings and gritted his teeth in anger. Not over the killing, but over the fact that they might be discovered before the damage could proceed. But there was nothing to be done about it. They needed to get out in the bayou for the next stage of the mission.

They made their way back out the fence, made makeshift fence repairs, and boarded the RHIBs, which then, slowly and quietly, headed out toward the trimaran's position. They only had twenty minutes to go before everything went up.

Jennings Chapman was in security control for the Chevron facility. Nothing had shown up on the few cameras they had. Two of his cameras had gone down and he didn't know why. It wasn't the most reliable system, and he assumed it was another maintenance problem. But he was concerned. He had tried several times to reach the single two-man patrol in their Land Rover and had received no response. He had gotten his third cup of coffee and was trying again. Still no response. Probably out checking a building or something else they had seen. When they exited the vehicle they would usually call in, though, so he would know they weren't available for a little bit. But they hadn't done that this time. He tried again and still no response. He began to worry. He didn't know his world would come apart in less than ten minutes.

He called his supervisor in and notified him that he could not reach the patrol. He also said two cameras had gone down for some reason. Kyle Perkins, the security supervisor on duty, was immediately alarmed. He called out a secondary two-man response team and they mounted vehicles to begin a search of the tank farm.

Only three minutes to go. Kyle came into the security operations center and listened as the response team began to move. He glanced at the camera monitors and saw that two cameras were not functioning. It took the response team a few minutes to get to the first part of the tank farm.

Just enough time for all of the timers to reach zero.

The explosions did their job and caught the response team in the hail of fire and debris. They never had a chance as a significant part of the tank farm went up in explosions, smoke, and flames. The pier was also lost to the carnage. The two ships were stoved in at two locations, burning fiercely and spilling their load into the bayou, and the pier just disappeared in the flames and smoke of the explosions.

Chapter Twenty-Six

Thursday—September 28
Gulf of Mexico—Gulfport-Pascagoula, Mississippi—Very Early
Morning

Just off the shore, the RHIBs cruised out slowly toward the *Persian Quest* and the on-board commandos watched the scene of destruction. The commandos were in awe of their success, but they still had work to do. Opening up the aft reinforced floor of the RHIBs, they mounted, one on each RHIB, an M2 60mm mortar. Sighting in on the refinery towers about eight hundred yards away, they let loose a barrage of fire, both standard rounds and white phosphorus, that utterly destroyed the towers and their large piping complex. In the confusion and complete chaos that followed the tank and pier destruction, no one on shore initially realized this was a mortar attack. They thought it was more of the same onshore explosions.

However, three men who had stopped and were watching the fire from outside the fence line spotted the mortar fire and, since two of them were former U.S. Army veterans, realized what it was. One headed for his car and quickly brought back a small digital camera. He set it on "movie" and began filming. The other was busy calling the local TV station with news of the attack. A few moments later, one of the media helicopters that had arrived landed near them and a news team came out.

A roving reporter from a local TV station, Sheila Knowles, approached along with her camera technician. She interviewed all three men and they described the scene they had witnessed. She feigned shock when they mentioned the mortar attack. It was pretty obvious to her that the attack was well planned and complete. In the background of the taping could be seen the destroyed towers and an inferno in the tank farm. She said to the men, "So you feel this was an attack from the waters of the bayou?"

One of the men responded, "Yes, and whoever did it was well trained in commando techniques. Here's a bit of the attack." And he showed her a clip of the movie on his camera. He continued, "Those mortars were right on target. And the tank farm selection was designed to maximize the destruction. It will be quite a while before they can operate this refinery again."

But they could do nothing about the attack at the time. They could only watch in horror as the refinery was destroyed. As Sheila was conducting her interviews, the RHIBs slowly pulled away. The refinery burned and exploded, with more tanks and the ships completely destroyed.

Sheila then asked to borrow his camera, turned to the broadcast camera, and finished, "There you have it. Eyewitness accounts of the destruction here at the Chevron facility. Combined with the incident two days ago in Houston, it is obvious that someone out there is determined to attack and destroy our oil capabilities. And now, back to the studios." She had her cameraman copy the video and then returned the camera to the owner. She had quite a coup with that unique film. They wrapped up their equipment and headed for another location where they could film more of the destruction.

The RHIBs very quietly joined up with the *Persian Quest* and the commandos transferred over to the trimaran. Their mission now accomplished, they transferred the mortars back to *Persian Quest*, and then the RHIBs left. All aboard, except the engine crew, watched their work as the refinery burned, and they observed several secondary explosions. Again, helicopters from the media flew around but could not get close enough to directly film the carnage.

When the fires were finally brought under control and extinguished nearly a week later, all that was left of that part of the tank farm was twisted metal and a severe environmental contamination problem. Over twenty people died that night, and the refinery was out of commission for over a year.

After *Persian Quest* retrieved the commandos and stored the equipment, the commandos watched for several minutes at the railing as the harbor seemed ablaze with the inferno they had started. Each had his own reaction to the conflagration, but they were all pleased in getting the mission completed. After a half-hour or so they slowly, one by one, went below and to their cabins for prayer and rest. The eagle had been wounded.

Once the equipment was stored and the twin turbines, one in each sponson or pontoon, reached operating speed, they slowly moved out under cover of darkness. The *Persian Quest* had been cloaked in darkness with no lights for the entire mission. They did not want to give their position away. As they moved away quietly, Najid was very pleased with the results of the two missions they had carried out. Houston and the bayou were both outstanding successes. Now he directed his helmsman to take a course south and westward to the Panama Canal. They weren't finished.

Najid went to the bridge and drafted a message to be sent to the operations centers at both Socotra and the stronghold. He wasn't sure of the exact location of Khatib, and this would cover either location. After looking over the message several times, he had it encrypted and sent off. It had been a good few days.

Ramiz, standing on the bridge, had a very self-satisfied look on his face. The Great Satan was paying, and paying dearly.

The intent of the commando raids was not to destroy all the refining capacity, or even a significant portion of it, but rather to impress on the American people how vulnerable they were. And in the process to put pressure on the administration to comply with the New Persia demands.

Khatib, viewing the coverage of this latest attack, which included the small clip of the mortar attack, released the message he had composed.

The message was sent to all the congressmen and the administration in an email so there would be no question of the source of the attacks. The message became the subject of many news broadcasts.

Thursday—September 28
Washington, D.C.—The White House

The White House was lit up like a Christmas tree. Word of the attack had reached them quickly. The president was aghast. He had just finished watching news of the damage and destruction at the Chevron facility in Mississippi, still half-asleep in the early morning hours. The broadcast headed by Sheila Knowles had a couple of eyewitnesses who said they had seen mortars being used on the refinery, and the film clip was proof of it. He came across the report by Sheila. He stood there in stunned amazement as her report continued with the former U.S. Army members describing the scene they had witnessed of the destruction of the refinery by sea-based mortars. Combined with the drastic news about Houston two days earlier, there obviously were clandestine attacks occurring. Something needed to be done, and done quickly, to avoid any further damage.

The president had called a meeting of his staff and close advisors. They had just received a message from New Persia. He read it to all and then passed it around. It said:

144

Elusive Quarry

American congressmen and administration people. New Persia has struck you again, this time in the Gulf of Mexico and with no casualties on our part. This is just a continuing effort on our part to get you to see reason and reduce the use of oil resources. As you know by now, we have recovered our revered Ayatollah Sarhardi, and he is again with us carrying out his Allah-given mission. We are reluctant to continue with our course of intimidation, but your lack of cooperation gives us no real choice. Until we see progress by you in meeting our demands, these incidents will continue.

He looked around the room as he said, "Well, this clinches it. New Persia again. We don't have to wait until the investigation is complete. They did it." He turned to Bob Goldstein, the treasury secretary. "Do you have anything that might help?"

"Maybe. There was a very large sailing ship anchored out in international waters off the bayou area yesterday. We, the Coast Guard, didn't stop it because it was outside our jurisdiction, but it was suspicious. It has departed and is now heading southbound across the Gulf of Mexico. But we have no proof that it was involved. However, one of our cruisers out of Houston noticed it just before the Houston strike. Again, it was outside our jurisdiction. We put those two situations together and we think that ship might have been involved in these strikes."

The president nodded in grim anger. He turned to his aide, Admiral Watkins, and said, "See if there is any way we can intercept that ship, stop it, and see what we can see. I'll bet the ayatollah is there, or at least some of his people."

Jack interrupted, "That may cause some international heat. Depending on who they are and what they might be doing, we could have an international protest."

The president turned to Jack and said, "Tough. I'm not going to sit here and not do anything. We'll sort out a protest when we get it … if we get one."

Jack just looked back in response and smiled. He agreed with the action.

The admiral left and made several phone calls.

The ayatollah seemed to be everywhere and impossible to contain. Earlier at Ryan's, then in Colorado, and now in Texas and Mississippi. How could you fight a ghost?

Thursday—September 28
Mobile, Alabama

145

Jack Findley was, again, glued to his television screen as the news kept rolling in on the attacks in Texas and Mississippi. He was completely stunned over the events that had taken place. Calls had come in from both industry and political representatives wanting to know what API was doing about the strikes ... strikes that were done with impunity. And he didn't have any answers. His political contacts had been threatened and were very concerned over the possibility that some of them would be personally attacked. They were not even returning his phone calls, but were scattering their families all over the countryside. He was stymied.

Chapter Twenty-Seven

Saturday—September 30
Caribbean Sea

The *Persian Quest* continued, with full sails, south across the Gulf of Mexico toward the Panama Canal. She had completed the mission outside of Texas and Mississippi and was progressing nicely across the smooth and placid waters. The destruction and explosions left behind would announce to the United States, and to the world, that New Persia was still alive and capable. The oil storage facilities, and the offloading piers and docks, would no longer function in transferring the precious fluid from the Middle East to be wasted by the infidels.

The water was completely calm, and the horizon cut through the sky like a knife. The pale grey of the ocean contrasted with the sharp blue of the sky as they made progress toward the Panamanian coast.

They were a good two hundred and fifty miles from the coast of Honduras in international waters when the water next to their vessel began churning and a submarine broke the surface. It was nearly twice their length, imposing, and threatening in its appearance. In a medium grey tone and obviously nuclear powered, it effortlessly matched their sixteen-knot pace through the water. It moved over to within one hundred feet of *Persian Quest's* starboard side. The top hatch in the sail of the submarine opened up and, following an enlisted seaman, an officer appeared through the hatch.

Using a loud hailer, the officer said, "This is the United States submarine *Virginia* and I am directing you to heave to. We will be boarding you in a few minutes."

Najid, surprised and very unhappy over this intrusion, refused, waved in dismissal, and continued on his way. The submarine backed off slightly and paced them for several miles. The officer stayed on the sail and repeated his demand, and they continued to ignore it.

On board the submarine, Captain Marv Storie directed the submarine helm to match the speed of the trimaran and maintain position immediately aft of the starboard side.

147

Najid called on the intercom to his two primary passengers' cabins. Staying inside the ship to avoid being seen, the ayatollah and Ramiz immediately came up to the bridge to see what was going on. After getting a short brief from Najid, the ayatollah looked over at Ramiz and said, "This is piracy on the high seas. We will not tolerate it. Do we have any weapons on board that would help repel these infidels?"

Ramiz responded, "We have small arms and some RPGs. The small arms would do no good on the submarine, but the RPG might do some damage. For the most part, we would probably just anger them."

"So we have nothing that would truly stop them."

"No, sir. I would suggest we comply with their demands. They could certainly sink us if they wanted to."

The ayatollah replied brusquely, "But I cannot be found aboard this ship. I am already wanted by the U.S. authorities and I would be quite a find for them. In fact, I'm sure that's why they are trying to stop us. Somehow, they figured I might be aboard."

Ramiz thought for a few moments and then said, "We have the mini-sub on board. We could prepare the mini for launch with you aboard then slow down and come to a halt. Then we could immediately launch the mini. They would have the choice of staying with us or going after the mini. It's a bit of a gamble, but it would possibly give you an escape."

The ayatollah didn't think very long. He quickly said, "Do it. I will go on the mini and escape these infidels. After they have finished their business with you, we can meet again and continue on our way."

Ramiz bowed his head slightly and went to give directions to prepare the mini for the ayatollah's use.

The ayatollah, not used to being pressured like this, nervously went to the center "pontoon" and was directed by the crew into the mini's hatch. A senior crew member named Abdulla, qualified in operating the mini, then followed him aboard. Just before boarding the mini, Ramiz approached Abdulla and gave him a small suitcase with a small key to unlock it if the need arose. Abdulla, recognizing what it was, nodded and looked at Ramiz with some relief. After ensuring that the ayatollah was comfortably seated and strapped in to the copilot seat, Abdullah began powering up and doing the prelaunch checks. A few minutes later, after the checks were complete and all was ready, Abdulla notified the bridge of the *Persian Quest* that he was ready to go. The trimaran bridge crew checked the location of the American submarine, which was following them quite closely, and began to slow down. Sails were furled and they came to a halt in the water, moving around slightly in the slight chop. Moving quickly, Abdulla, coordinating with the bridge, began the launch sequence, and soon the mini was bobbing in the water. A moment later, the mini disappeared below the surface and under the *Persian Quest*.

As the *Persian Quest* began to slow down, Captain Storie began to breathe a little easier, thinking they were going to heave to and agree to be boarded. Then he saw, unbelieving, part of the center pontoon drop off the trimaran and rapidly disappear beneath the waves. He looked at the phenomenon and wondered what was going on. Either someone was escaping or they were ditching a part of the boat for some reason. He realized he had a decision to make—follow the trimaran or follow the "pontoon". The helm marked their exact location, and Captain Storie directed the helm to prepare for boarding the trimaran. His decision was made. He would find the "pontoon" later.

Abdulla dove the mini as fast as he could and headed off in the same course direction they had been following. He was also using an underwater speaker playing a biologic soundtrack to mask their departure. He briefed the ayatollah on what he was doing and what was coming next. The ayatollah nodded his understanding and continued to just watch what was happening. From earlier coordination with Najid, Abdullah reached an agreed-to depth of three hundred feet and leveled off. He shut down almost all the systems on the mini and let inertia slow him down to an eventual halt, with the biologics still being sent through the underwater speakers. He was maintaining buoyancy in the water and holding position. Absolute silence was what he was trying to attain. The ayatollah understood and kept quiet.

As the lead New Persia person on board, Ramiz directed the trimaran to comply with the American submarine demands. The trimaran, halted for the mini-submarine release, remained stationary in the water. The American submarine approached the *Persian Quest*, and shortly an armed boarding party launched off the submarine and approached the *Persian Quest*. Lines were thrown down to the boarding party, and Ramiz met the young U.S. Navy lieutenant heading up the party.

Ramiz said, "I must take extreme objection to your actions. We are on the high seas and you have no right to board us under these circumstances."

Lieutenant Colburn returned Ramiz's look and said, "Sir. I would appreciate it if you would let us go about our duties and search for a convicted criminal we think you have on board."

"There is no convicted criminal on board. Just our crew. I had no option, since we only have small arms on board for anti-pirate defense. Go about your business and then get off."

Abdulla reached nearly five hundred feet, near the limit for the mini. He knew the crush depth for the mini was just over seven hundred feet. By now the American submarine was well behind him, occupied by boarding the *Persian Quest*. Looking out at the dark waters beyond the viewport, the ayatollah was concerned at the depth but not overly worried. He felt that Allah would protect him.

Abdullah didn't have the same faith. He knew from school and experience that the laws of physics were tough to beat. He was monitoring his instruments to make sure they didn't go any deeper. It looked like he might have to use the suitcase Ramiz gave him.

It was dark and silent in the depths. Abdulla couldn't help but wonder what was going on back at the *Persian Quest*. He looked again at the small suitcase that Ramiz had given him. He and Ramiz had gone over its contents several times just in case it should be needed. And it might possibly be needed now. It made him a bit nervous, even though he was sure the maneuvers required would really work. Practice had indicated that it was not a trivial sequence, and, while he was sure he could do it, it still made him nervous.

Back on the *Persian Quest*, the boarding party searched the entire ship without finding any sign of the ayatollah. Even his room had been emptied as they were slowing down. The Americans were only slightly puzzled over the missing pontoon and the obvious connections for the mini-sub. Lieutenant Colburn radioed back to the submarine that it was an obvious mini-sub connection and that, while it was a large crew, there was nothing else on the trimaran.

Captain Storie directed that the boarding party return so they could get underway and locate the mini-sub. After about fifteen minutes, the boarding party was back on board and the submarine began to move out, slipping beneath the slight swells as it moved away. After just a few minutes of searching, the sonar operator found what she was looking for. The biologics were good, but not that good for the nuclear submarine's technologically advanced crew. Setting a course for an intercept with the mini, the submarine slowly closed in on its prey. Quiet and lethal, it moved through the water with an ease designed for this environment.

Sensing the stealthy approach of the American submarine, and "seeing" it on his own sonar, Abdulla's fears were realized and he knew he would have to use the suitcase contents. It would be risky but perhaps they might be able to pull it off.

Abdulla told the ayatollah that the American submarine was only a few thousand meters away ... closing in slowly. It was obvious that they were being pursued and would be contacted soon with a demand to surface. He couldn't wait much longer. He told the now worried ayatollah that they were going to go through a maneuver and, hopefully, it would be enough to fool the American submarine. The ayatollah nodded in understanding ... but he sure didn't like the idea.

Abdulla powered up the mini, since it was obvious the American sub was aware of their presence and was closing in. He began to move deeper, watching his depth very closely. He went through six hundred feet and continued on down.

The American submarine was slowly following the mini as it continued to go deeper. The exec said, to no one in particular in the control room, "He can't go too much deeper. That little can will crush if he does." There was a general muttering of agreement among the crew at his comment.

Abdulla took the key and opened the suitcase. In it he quickly read through the instructions to refresh his memory. He pulled out a small flash drive and a speaker system with a device to attach the speaker to the inside hull of the mini. After a moment spent hooking up the system, he powered it up with the mini-sub's electrical system and attached the speaker to the hull. He looked over at the ayatollah, who looked back at him with an air of worried confidence. He then put the mini in a rapid rise by over one hundred feet, powered up the speaker with the flash drive, and then dove the mini back down to the six-hundred-foot level. As he headed back down, the flash drive was engaged. A vocal and very muffled screaming "NO" sound was made, and a tremendous metallic ripping noise and horrendous crunching sound was emitted into the water. Then he stopped the mini totally and motioned for the ayatollah to be absolutely quiet. Burbles of sound continued from the flash drive system. Abdulla released one of the manipulating claws on the front of the boat and it dropped like a rock into the depths. Metal crushing sounds were made, along with the sound of bubbles of air floating to the surface. To enhance the illusion,

Abdulla released some air into the water that would also be picked up by the American sonar. The whine of their electric motors could be heard, which suddenly stopped as they faked their death throes. They continued to stay quiet and floated very slowly and silently upward.

On board the *Virginia*, sonar operators tracking the progress of the mini had to quickly turn down the input on their systems. They were recording the sounds. After a few minutes, the captain was beside them. He listened to the recording several times. It sounded like the mini had been crushed. Pieces of it were apparently going both down and up. Detritus could easily float to the surface, and at least one small piece was heading for the ocean floor. They put the sound sensor outputs on the speaker system. Nothing could be heard. Was their quarry dead? Or just playing possum?

They waited. Finally Captain Storie said, "Active ping."

The sonar tech sent out an active sonar ping and got a return roughly a thousand meters away. The return was sitting still in the water with just a slight movement upward. Was it still dead, or even really dead in the first place?

In the mini, Abdulla and the ayatollah heard the tremendous sound of the ping. They stayed still. They both knew that the American sub was looking for them and wondering what had happened. They needed to wait. It was very intense. Both men, even in the coolness of the mini-sub, were sweating and nervous.

A noise started to build in the water. Loud and mechanical. A ship coming near and thrashing the water pretty heavily. Making a lot of noise that continued to get louder. Twin turbines pumping water through a piping system for thrust, normally very quiet, but now, and intentionally, very noisy. And small explosions could be heard as the ship drew nearer. Grenades thrown into the water to contribute to the cacophony.

The American submarine's sonar and sound acoustic systems were overwhelmed by the noise. The techs couldn't hear anything over all the racket. Captain Storie swore softly. He thought he knew what was going on but had no way to prevent it. The trimaran was noise-polluting the water around them, effectively negating the sonar system's capability. It was dark and cold at four hundred feet. There was no way to "see" the object. His photonics system, with the noise generation and concussions, could not be used. Short of ramming the object in the water, he couldn't do

152

much. And ramming could damage his submarine, especially the anti-sonar acoustic coating on the hull. And, since they were not technically at war, he was stymied.

Abdulla heard the noise. He couldn't help but hear it. It was obvious that Ramiz knew he had used the suitcase and was trying to help them. Now what? How could he take advantage of what Ramiz, Najid, and the trimaran were trying to do? He could move slightly faster upward to the surface, but only if he engaged his drive system, and that might be heard by the American submarine. And, assuming he could reach the surface, then what? The Americans would just surface also. It was a real game of cat and mouse.

Sending out another ping, the American submarine saw that the object was still slowly moving toward the surface. In the control room the exec speculated that some air was trapped in the object and it was slowly floating to the surface.

Approaching two hundred feet down, Abdulla released the softball-sized communications antenna. It rose to the surface and he was able to talk with Ramiz directly. Ramiz was also able to pinpoint the mini's exact location. From his own sonar on the trimaran, he also knew the location of the American submarine, which was still about a thousand meters away. He saw only one way out of the situation. He hated the thought of losing another mini-sub but saw no other way out. They had already been searched by the Americans, and nothing of interest to the infidels had been found.

Coordinating with Abdulla, Ramiz positioned the trimaran between the mini and the submarine, continuing to make as much noise as possible. The mini surfaced rapidly after Abdulla released some ballast. Some more pieces for the American submarine to watch plunging to the depths. They surfaced just a few yards from the trimaran. The ayatollah and Abdulla both quickly transferred to the trimaran and they scuttled the mini. The mini then began to sink to the bottom. The ayatollah changed into clothing, like the rest of the crew, looking just like a regular seaman. Then Najid directed the helm to pick up speed and begin to depart the area.

On board the American submarine, which had been pinging more frequently, they saw the mini surface, disappear behind the hull of the trimaran, and then reappear sinking to the bottom. The thinking was that the mini must have broached the surface, filled with water, and sunk.

Captain Storie ordered the sub to surface and approached the trimaran on the surface. He would send a boarding party over to check out what had happened and see if there was anything unusual to be found. "*Persian Quest*, heave to and be prepared to be boarded again."

Ramiz listened for a moment. Then he directed the crew to continue moving away from the infidel submarine. Over the radio he responded to the American captain, "We will not heave to. We are continuing on to our destination without further delay. You have already checked our ship, illegally, I might add, and have no right to do it again. Two of our crewmen are dead on the mini-submarine that you, undoubtedly, saw sink. You have done enough damage and we are leaving."

"Heave to or you will be sunk."

"We have already notified our superiors of your actions. All of our communications with you are being recorded and simultaneously sent back to our home port. If we are attacked or sunk, there will be international repercussions. Leave us alone."

Captain Storie did not want to push it any further, but he could not leave it alone. He directed the helm to back off. He then directed a boarding party be organized and prepared to forcefully board the trimaran. Surfacing, they approached the trimaran from the starboard quarter. Over the radio, Captain Storie again requested the trimaran to heave to. Again the trimaran refused and continued on its way. The submarine stopped, then launched the boarding party, and they approached the accelerating trimaran.

Over the radio, Ramiz said, "We are not stopping in these international waters. What you are doing amounts to a form of piracy. We will defend ourselves if you continue to approach. I have given my men direction to fire on you and the boarding party if you continue. Now ... back off."

Captain Storie, incensed over this situation, stood there in the control room. Undecided. He suspected that they had done something they were hiding, but he wasn't sure. He looked at the floor and then at all the displays as he began thinking of the possible consequences. He took a deep breath, threw up his hands, and directed the exec to recall the boarding party. He couldn't afford to have possible damage to his sub and perhaps some of his crew killed.

Captain Storie had blinked.

Ramiz saw the boarding party skiff turn away and begin returning to the submarine. He, also, took a deep breath. They hadn't been bluffing, but he did not want to take on an American warship. They would have lost that battle. But they had won it, and he continued to push the trimaran to the west, picking up additional speed to get out of the area.

The submarine slowly backed away and began to submerge after the boarding party was back aboard.

The ayatollah, when told of the confrontation results, was both relieved and angry. Relieved that Ramiz's plan had worked and he was still free, and angry that they had to go through all this in the first place. And angry that a very expensive piece of equipment had to be lost. These infidels needed to be taught another lesson, and it needed to be a big one. They couldn't be permitted to trifle with him. Continuing with their planned mission on the U.S. West Coast would be that lesson. It was something big.

And he was really impressed with Ramiz. The man was a real asset in all sorts of situations.

Captain Storie sat down in his small quarters and developed a report of the actions he had taken, and the results of those actions. He mentioned the trimaran dropping a portion of its center pontoon and the suspected sinking of the mini-submarine by her own crew. They had merely been shadowing the action and did not cause the sinking to occur. He mentioned the first boarding party and that nothing of consequence had been found other than a very large crew on board. He mentioned the second boarding party and the threat to their safety and his action in recalling the boarding effort. He also mentioned his suspicions that they still had something to hide, but he was not able to identify what it might be. He finished the report and handed it to the exec for his review. After a few minor comments from the exec, he sent it to the comm techs for transmission back to COMSUBLANT at Norfolk Naval Station, Virginia.

Sunday—October 1
Washington, D.C.—The White House

Receiving the message forwarded from the *SSN Virginia*, the CNO, Admiral Jack Nelson, recognizing the possibility that they had missed the ayatollah, sent a copy of the Captain Storie's message to the White House, with a copy to General Newt Foley, the chairman of the Joint Chiefs. At the White House, Jack Harrison, working the weekend as usual, read it and passed it on to the president.

The president read the message. He looked off to the side, thinking, *They may have just missed the ayatollah.* So close yet so far. It wasn't the submarine captain's fault; what he had done made sense. It was just the luck of the draw, so to speak. He continued to think for a few moments, then called Maria in and asked her to get Mark Allison on the phone.

A few moments later, he was talking with Mark.

"Mark, are we still tracking the *Persian Quest*? I know it's in the southern Gulf of Mexico somewhere, but do we know exactly where it is?"

"Yes, sir. We are still tracking it. I'm not sure exactly where it is right now, but can find out for you very quickly."

"Please do, and let me know when you have the information."

"Yes, sir. I'll be in touch shortly."

With that, they broke the connection and Mark immediately made several phone calls and got the location of the *Persian Quest*. It was in the Caribbean just off the east coast of Panama, and moving rapidly to the south.

Mark called the president and informed him of the trimaran's location. The president then called in General Abe Fairchild, the Air Force chief of staff.

"Abe," said the president, "can you get a reconnaissance aircraft over that location and see what might be going on? While there might not be much happening, I think if we fly over and make ourselves known, they might get a bit more nervous."

"Yes, sir. We can do that. I'll look into it right away."

The president nodded. They shook hands and General Fairchild went to implement the request.

Monday—October 2
Caribbean Sea

On board the *Persian Quest,* en route to the entrance of the Panama Canal, Ramiz was on the bridge when an RC-130, a reconnaissance-equipped cargo aircraft with American markings, flew overhead at a very low altitude. The aircraft flew over, went on for a minute and banked to port, and did a return pass directly over the *Persian Quest*. Ramiz watched. The ayatollah, still in seaman's clothes, came out on the starboard bridge wing and watched also. What, if anything, were they doing? Ramiz saw the ayatollah step out on the open bridge wing, rushed over to him just as the aircraft flew over again, and pulled the ayatollah back into the enclosed bridge.

Elusive Quarry

As the RC-130 banked for another pass, the ayatollah looked questioningly at Ramiz. Ramiz said, "Sorry, sir. Even though you are in different clothing, they may still be able to spot you with the high-resolution cameras that I'm sure they were using. With this situation, you need to stay out of sight."

The ayatollah slowly nodded. He said, "You're right, of course. Can that aircraft do anything to us?"

"Probably not. It's a reconnaissance airplane, and they are usually unarmed."

The ayatollah, as the aircraft made another pass, said, "Do we have anything we can use against it?"

Ramiz thought for a moment, not wanting to encourage the ayatollah's thinking. He said, "We have some RPGs on board, but they would be very difficult to use against an aircraft like that one. I wouldn't recommend being aggressive with them. There's no telling what they might have just over the horizon."

The ayatollah stopped for a moment and thought. Then he shook his head once, watched the slow-moving aircraft making another turn in the *Persian Quest's* direction, and moved off the bridge and down to his quarters.

Ramiz breathed a sigh of relief. He really didn't want to engage the American aircraft. That would only cause additional problems and interfere with their current mission assignment. He too watched as the aircraft made another pass then began climbing and increasing speed. It then slowly disappeared off to the north.

On board the RC-130, high-speed digital cameras were rolling on each pass over the ship. The crew had no idea what they were looking for but had been instructed to film the passes to see what they could get. The digital recording was then sent back to Fort Meade in Maryland via satellite for analysis.

Analysts went through the digital images frame by frame. They caught the image of the "seaman" being hustled back into the main bridge area but did not immediately understand the significance of the move. They continued through the images and found very little of value. Part of the center pontoon was missing, and they could see some fittings that were unusual for a sailing vessel. They were not sure what they were for. They went through the images multiple times and selected fourteen images that might have some information. These images were then sent up to General Foley. Included was an image of the "seaman" who had been pulled back on the bridge.

Chapter Twenty-Eight

Monday—October 2
Washington, D.C.

General Foley, recognizing the image of the ayatollah, smiled to himself. He then sent the image over to the president with a short note. The note said, *Here's what they were hiding. He may have changed clothes, but that's the ayatollah on the bridge wing. And they yanked him back to try to avoid us finding him. He's on that ship.*

The president smiled as he read the note and looked at the image. Actionable intelligence, finally. But now he had to decide what to do with the information. Here was a criminal, but he was on the high seas and not subject to U.S. laws. He called Maria and they set up a discussion with several of his staff for the next day. General Foley, Miriam Blacock, Mark Allison, Jerry Ocasio, Admiral Watson, and Admiral Nelson were all invited to sit down and figure out a course of action. They couldn't let this opportunity slip by them.

Monday—October 2
Caribbean Sea—East Coast of Panama

Ramiz was concerned. He suspected the aircraft had cameras and they might have spotted the ayatollah. He needed to take some form of action and get the ayatollah off the ship and into safe hands. But they were just off the coast of Panama and had no nearby support to draw from. Slowly, in his cabin, he came to the conclusion that they needed to return to their base in Socotra, nearly halfway around the world.

Ramiz went to the ayatollah's room and respectfully knocked. The ayatollah called for him to enter and he did. "Sir. We need to head for home in Socotra."

The ayatollah's eyes brightened a little and he asked, "Why? I thought we were going to carry out our mission off the coast of California."

"I'm sorry, but we cannot perform the mission without the mini-submarine, and it is permanently lost to us. I am also concerned over your safety. If they spotted you on the bridge, the infidels may try to capture you again. We don't know for sure, but I don't want to take any chances."

"Hmm. I understand. I certainly do not want to return to the U.S. under any circumstances. What do you suggest we do?"

"I was considering going back on *Persian Quest* but have reconsidered. It would be too risky. We are off the coast of Panama. I would like to take you to Panama City, where we can arrange a plane flight for you and I back to Oman and on to Salalah. Then Najid and the others can return in the *Persian Quest*. It will take them close to three weeks to get back home, and I don't want you at sea for that long with the Americans trying to catch you."

The ayatollah took a deep breath and said, "Yes. I suppose that's quite right. I don't like it very much because I feel like I'm running away from the Americans. It's not a good feeling to be on the run. And I am. But it would be the prudent thing to do. Let's go ahead and implement your thoughts."

Ramiz bowed slightly and left the room.

Najid, after sending Ramiz's message to Socotra with the transportation requirements for the ayatollah, directed the helm to come about to a south-southwesterly course, taking them to the eastern entrance of the Panama Canal.

Wednesday—October 4
Panama—Panama City

A day later, they transited the Panama Canal and were in the Pacific Ocean. Due to the size of the ship, they drew some attention as they went through the Panama Canal locks over to the Pacific side. When they had come through the other direction on the way to the Gulf of Mexico, they had also drawn attention. There just weren't many sailing vessels of that size in the world.

After considering all aspects of their planned mission on the U.S. West Coast, and with Najid's convincing arguments for *Persian Quest's* capabilities, Ramiz and the ayatollah had decided to continue with the mission. There was a workaround for the loss of the mini-sub. After they departed for Socotra, *Persian Quest* would continue north for the final mission. It would resolve the ayatollah's earlier anger and need to teach the infidels another lesson.

They passed through without incident and, from there, a small boat transported Ramiz and the disguised ayatollah to Panama City and the airport. A waiting Gulfstream left Tocumen

International Airport outside Panama City for the west coast of Africa and on to the Omani capital.

In two days the ayatollah and Ramiz were in Salalah. Both were breathing easier. They had beaten the Americans and were back on familiar soil. The Americans were not aware of the ayatollah's location. There was no trace of his moves. Now they could get back to their mission and planning activities. They could also get status of some of their ongoing projects.

Wednesday—October 4
Pacific Ocean, Central American Coast

The commandos would have a much more difficult time now, since, they assumed, security would be significantly enhanced. They would have to be even stealthier and possibly have to kill more to accomplish their goals. Najid would proceed to his next destination for the continuation of their mission. The West Coast of the U.S.

Najid and crew were able to stop for fuel, food, and other supplies in Costa Rica, and slowly continued north. Several days later, they stopped in Ensenada, Mexico, and picked up multiple packages that had been sent from Socotra as part of the original mission planning and were waiting for them for their mission requirements. After spending two days in Ensenada, they continued north toward their target area. They remained twenty miles off the coast, well outside the twelve-mile international water boundary.

After receiving information on contacts in the U.S., Najid placed several international calls to those contacts and made arrangements for support. He also had the packages opened up and distributed to the commandos. The equipment in those packages was inspected and checked to make sure there were no operational problems.

Saturday—October 7
Washington, D.C.—The White House

The president called Mark Allison. "Mark, do we still know where that vessel is located?"

"Yes, sir. It is now off the western Panamanian coast and heading north. In our direction. We don't know where it is heading but are concerned." He paused with an air of expectation.

The president picked up on the pause and asked, "Is something wrong? You sound a bit unsure."

"Well, yes, sir. We think the ayatollah is no longer on the ship. He may have flown home, or wherever he went."

"How'd he do that? We've been watching him, haven't we?"

"Yes, sir. And because we were watching, we saw a small skiff leave the boat this past Wednesday and go into Panama City. It was probably after supplies, but could have been taking the ayatollah ashore. We aren't absolutely positive about it, but it makes sense for them to get him out of there as soon as possible, and a quick trip to Panama City's airport would be the fastest way to do that."

"Hmm. Good point. That certainly makes good logical sense. And with this new guy running things in their security systems, he probably is keeping the ayatollah moving around quite a bit to throw us off."

"Our thinking also. Ramiz is quite good and seems to have a sense of what's needed to keep ahead of us. So, under that assumption, I've ordered a resumption of the satellite coverage over Salalah. Maybe we can find him again. I'll keep you informed if we find anything." And with that, they hung up.

The president mulled over this new information. They might have missed him again. And he was nearly in our backyard in the Gulf of Mexico. He would be more difficult to find and apprehend in Oman. While the U.S. and Omani relations were reasonably good, he was still in an area that had sympathizers to his cause. And some of them were in the government. The president looked outside at the weather in the Washington fall, cold and rainy with low-hanging clouds scudding across the sky, and wondered what the next step or issue would be.

Chapter Twenty-Nine

Saturday—October 7
Oman—Salalah

The ayatollah looked off in the distance from his small office in Salalah. The waters of the Gulf of Oman were a welcome relief from his long months in U.S. prisons. He was neither in Socotra nor at the remains of the stronghold. Khatib had decided that he could not risk either location until they figured out what the United States might do. The ayatollah's health was not the best after his prison time, and, while it raised his spirits to see the Gulf of Mexico strikes, it would take several months for him to completely recover.

The ayatollah could not believe what he had been through with the threat of a lifetime in prison. Especially the supermax system in the United States. With the tight security and lack of any contact with the outside world, he had not been able to figure out any way to contact his organization and give directions. Even the lawyers had been cautioned against passing on any messages or information. They had refused his requests to contact Khatib and his group of followers. But that was all in the past now.

He had arrived in Salalah just a few days after his escape in Colorado. From Muscat, where the Gulfstream aircraft had taken him, he left by van the same day for Salalah and joined a small group of his advisors, led by Khatib.

Ramiz had done a wondrous job in organizing his escape. Before the raid the ayatollah wasn't aware of the planning, and was completely surprised when the New Persia commando force struck. Probably a good thing. He had been informed that the entire group of commandos had made it back to the stronghold through various means with no losses and just a few minor injuries.

After spending the morning in thought and prayer, he called Khatib in to the office.

"Khatib, I want you to continue to do the daily running of our whole operation here until I can recover. I also need, with Allah's help, to plan for the future. You have done a marvelous job for the past year since my kidnapping, and I think it best to continue that. Would you agree?"

162

"Yes, I would agree. I have set in motion several more actions to continue our efforts to get the west to reduce their dependence on oil, and I would like to see those efforts through to completion. In the meantime, your guidance to our followers will be invaluable to our cause. I believe the distractions of daily activities would be best handled by me, and you concentrate on our vision."

"Then we are in agreement on this. I would ask that we convene our advisors in a meeting and videoconference so they can be informed of our arrangement."

Khatib nodded and said, "I will see to it." He then departed the office.

The ayatollah turned his attention, again, to the window overlooking the gulf. The sun was brilliant, and the waters sparkled as a small fishing vessel sailed toward the distant horizon as he watched. Allah had, indeed, watched over him. He was free. His faith was stronger now ... and their mission was right.

After the meeting and videoconference was held a few days later, the ayatollah left Salalah. He was on the road east and north. He wasn't sure of his exact destination, but thought it might be the stronghold.

The ayatollah was concerned over the drop-off in support that occurred when he was kidnapped and taken to the U.S. After his trial and the guilty verdicts, several influential Muslim clerics had withdrawn support. He needed to contact them and renew his resolve with them. Since he had left Salalah for the stronghold, traveling overland in a small but well-furnished van, he had been thinking about how to convince the clerics of his mission in support of the Arab world of the future. Unfortunately, several of the clerics now considered him an outcast, and they were more concerned with the present, and its problems, than the future and the unknown. And that was understandable. The common Arabic people, poor and wanting for nearly everything, were not worried about the next generation ... they were concerned about today and tomorrow.

After praying while on the road, the ayatollah began composing a message to send to his various supporters. He wrote:

New Persia has come a long way in getting the attention of the western nations and in progressing with Allah's mission to reduce the world's oil usage. We must continue with our campaign, and I am asking for your renewed or continuing support for this important mission. I understand that today's needs are great, but we must look to the future and assure that our children and their children have the benefits of the Allah-given black fluid. I trust I can depend on you for your continued financial support. Allah be Praised.

The ayatollah then sent the message out at the next stop, where he was able to make satellite connectivity while on his journey north.

Monday—October 9
Pacific Ocean—U.S. West Coast

It was a beautiful day with some mist in the air over the water, but otherwise clear and warm. The *Persian Quest* slowly moved up the western coast of the U.S. after her stop for supplies in Ensenada, Mexico. Staying twenty miles off the coast, well outside the twelve-mile territorial limits, she cruised at a very leisurely pace of ten knots looking for her targets. Off the Long Beach coastline she weighed anchor. Najid and Qasim studied the coastline areas closely using high-powered telescopes and binoculars. The refineries were very obvious. And the security, they assumed, would be heightened but not impossible to penetrate.

This refinery location was one of the biggest in the U.S., and processed most of the crude oil into other petroleum products for the entire West Coast. Especially gasoline and diesel fuels ... fuels that made the California economy hum.

Najid looked at the refinery through his small telescope and shook his head. Such a symbol of American waste and excessive oil use. Steam and other smoke products were being released by the refinery as it conducted its operations. He watched. So unnecessary.

He continued his thought line. There was wind power, tidal movements, hydroelectric, and solar. These refineries did not need to even exist. Alternate forms of energy were available and needed to be used. The black fluid from the ground should not be depended upon, due to its atmospheric pollution and waste. And this was the so-called civilized devil on earth that used the most and wasted the most. While it was an Allah-given resource, it shouldn't be wasted this way. It should be preserved and used at a much-reduced rate so the generations to come could also benefit from it. It was an abomination of the infidels.

He continued looking and commented to Qasim about the need to take out as much of the facility as possible. Qasim just looked back at Najid. The planning had already been accomplished and they would carry out that planning. The supplies were ready, his men were ready, and the communications with their contacts on land were complete. All was ready for that evening and tomorrow's very early morning activities. They had been monitoring the Americans' reaction, through their news broadcasts, to the hits on Houston and Pascagoula, and saw no serious impacts to their current mission plans.

Qasim, as they were both looking at the refinery complex, said, "We will carry out our plans as we have established them. The refinery will be destroyed and the tank farms will all be burning by morning. The infidels in this part of the U.S. will really feel the impacts of our mission. The oil will be significantly reduced and their commuting will be much more expensive and difficult. Instant carpooling." And he smiled at the thought.

They were twenty miles off the coast of California and could see Catalina Island to the south and east of their location. Long Beach was directly east, with its large refinery complex. Through the telescopes they could see the *Queen Mary* at her permanent dock. Periodically they could see the high-speed hydrofoils coming out to Catalina and returning. That evening, after they had dropped anchor and had their evening prayer and meals, they could see the lights of the greater Los Angeles area completely overwhelm the northern and eastern view. Quite amazing, really. And almost all powered by oil-powered turbine electrical plants.

Monday—October 9
Iran—Desert of Southeastern Iran

They had crossed the Gulf of Oman from Muscat to Char Bahr in a small ferry and continued northbound. They were traveling north in relative comfort and were being as unassuming as possible, since they did not want to leave any indications of their location that could be picked up by the U.S. spy network. The roads were just moderately good, and in some locations were dirt. The main road north out of Zahedan was in pretty good shape and asphalt paved. Once they hit that portion of the highway they were able to make pretty good time. Short of Birjand, near Behabad, they turned off to the west on little more than a dirt track and spent several hours getting to the remains of the stronghold.

As they entered the small compound that had been built since the stronghold had been destroyed, the ayatollah looked around and saw many changes. Several new buildings had been constructed on the adjacent mesa for training and administration of the forces. A small electric power generator provided power for a portable satellite communications facility and for some of the administration buildings. There were some smaller outbuildings used for explosive training and there was an obstacle course for personnel conditioning. There were minimal shelters built for the constant influx of trainees and recruits. On the whole, it looked like a well-functioning training facility. He knew it was from here that the commandos had trained and departed to rescue him. And for that he was grateful.

Looking off to his right, he nearly wept as he saw the remains of the old stronghold. The steep dirt and rock slope from the collapse of the stronghold was very obvious. There were several markers haphazardly placed on parts of the rubble as grave markers. A physical reminder for the families who lost relatives and friends.

They pulled under a small overhang at the entrance to the administration building. He was not visible to the constant presence of the satellite miles above the stronghold. His van was surrounded by many of the fighters and family members, all anxious to see the ayatollah in person. Many had not seen him since he had been in the U.S. prisons for slightly over a year. It was not a carnival atmosphere, but it was close to it.

The ayatollah stepped out of the van and greeted his well-wishers with a wave and blessing motion with his hands. He was escorted through the crowd by Omar Al Habash, who had been the training facility manager since Marid left for Socotra several months earlier. They entered one of the newly constructed buildings and he was shown to an office with sleeping and study quarters attached. Some cool water and fruit was brought in and he sat down on one of the floor carpets to eat and rest. He felt he really needed both.

Waiting for him were multiple messages from various clerics and mosques. Most had responded with pledges of renewed or continuous support. Only a few had rejected his plea, and they did not have a severe financial impact. New Persia would continue.

Tuesday—October 10
Pacific Ocean—U.S. West Coast

Off in the distance to the west, north, and south, Najid could see three of the large cruise ships that regularly traveled up and down the West Coast of the U.S. They were all out beyond the twelve-mile international limits. He thought of the ungodly activities these heathens were doing on the ships. Gambling, drinking, and many other activities. And all of it powered by the fuel of Allah ... oil. It was further evidence of the need to reduce or eliminate the oil imports from the Mideast. These godless people were truly wasting the precious resource on their mindless activities.

Elusive Quarry

They waited through the night and into the next day. Several of the commandos needed a little more rest and recovery due to motion sickness. Plus, there wasn't any particular hurry anyway. They would strike that night.

Coordination with their contacts on shore was completed, and at 11:00 p.m. two medium-sized powerboats bumped alongside the *Persian Quest*. They had their lights extinguished and could not be seen in the low light of night. Equipment was loaded and the commandos transferred to the powerboats. The entry into the harbor complex was uneventful and, with their scuba gear, they were able to slip into the water in the harbor without notice. Each was equipped with their assigned explosives and, through the darkness of the water, made it to the assigned piers. Several crude carrier ships were in the water, berthed at the piers, and they were the first targets of the commandos. Simply using magnetic charges, they attached several explosives to the three ships' exterior hulls just below the waterline where they could not be seen. With the dark coloration of their scuba gear and suits, the commandos were very difficult to see in the water, and there was nobody really looking. There were a few guards patrolling in a pretty casual manner, but nothing really serious that might impact their mission.

There were several refineries in the Long Beach area. They found the tank farms and, in a duplicate maneuver to the efforts in Houston, cut through the fences, lasered the cameras and lights as needed, found the tanks, and placed the explosives. The "won't happen here" attitude was quite evident in the lack of security. Texas and Mississippi news must have been known, but there was no apparent resistance to the commando activities. After they rendezvoused back in the water and waited to be picked up by the small boats, Qasim looked back at the complex and wondered about the management of the complex. They should have very attentive guards out all over the place looking for intruders.

A few minutes later, and right on time, the powerboats began picking up the commando force. Unfortunately, at this same time, a Long Beach Police patrol boat came near, saw they were retrieving what appeared to be divers out of the water, and decided to check them out. The commandos were hailed by the police patrol and the powerboats decided to initially comply. The patrol boat came close to them with a spotlight and told them to prepare for boarding. There was no warning. The commandos, staying below the gunwale, opened fire on the police boat, shattering the cabin and killing all three aboard. They fired more into the hull of the boat and it began to sink. That was how they left it. Dead and sinking.

167

When the last commando was finally on board, they headed out for the *Persian Quest*. After they reached the trimaran, the commandos relaxed a bit and then came up to the railing to watch the action. Even from the distance off the coast, the action was very hard to miss.

The refinery was suddenly consumed in fire, with explosions occurring in several areas. They could see it, but it was so far away that they didn't hear it right away. It took several seconds for the sound to reach them, and then, due to the distance, it was quite muffled. After the two previous efforts, they were a much more subdued group of commandos now. They watched with satisfaction, but most of the cheering was gone. They had done their job well.

Qasim then retrieved a small remote control from the bridge station. A low-light telescopic video scanner was turned on from the remote, and he could see the coastline and the burning refinery. But the refinery itself was not ablaze, just some of the tanks in the tank farm adjacent to it. They needed to finish the tasking. Manipulating the remote and the channel assignments, he turned a small remote-controlled attack boat, about twenty feet long and painted all black, toward the shoreline. A second small identical attack boat was also turned toward the shoreline about a half-mile further east. Through the remote he identified the exact GPS coordinates of each attack boat, adjusted the range of the 60mm mortars to the refinery towers, and, when the small boats were in range, sent the fire message. The internal fire control of the mortars had the exact GPS coordinates of the refinery towers already loaded. A series of minor automatic corrections were made by the electronics, and the mortars fired a sequence of twenty shells at the refinery in a broad, sweeping curve that took out the primary towers and distillation equipment. Then the attack boats completely self-destructed and sank out of sight. There was no evidence they had ever been there.

It was a sight to behold, and Qasim was pleased with the results. Picked up during their stop in Ensenada, the remote controlled boats, advanced mortars with automatic firing capability, and the electronic controls he held were a product of India and did an excellent job. They had proven their worth and could possibly be used again. He was impressed.

Again, Najid sent in a report to the stronghold and the operations center in Socotra, detailing the attack and the apparent results. Then he returned to the bridge and his captain's chair for the course south and west. It was a long cruise across the South Pacific, and they might as well get started now. The mission had been an unqualified success. Without lights for the first thirty miles, they moved slowly in the darkness and finally put on the minimum lighting for safety, and continued their westerly course for home.

Long Beach Police dispatch could not reach their patrol boat. It had called in that it was stopping two powerboats to check out what they were doing. It looked like they had divers in the water. It was dark and that looked suspicious to them. Since that call, there had been no further contact with the patrol boat. That got the dispatch supervisor worried, and she decided to send another patrol boat to assist. But that would take about thirty minutes. There was nothing else close by that would help.

When the backup patrol boat arrived at the location, there was nothing much there. The darkness was almost absolute, and they had to search with their spotlights. Some bits and pieces of the sunken patrol boat, some oil and fuel, and several uniformed bodies were floating in the water. But no sign of the patrol boat itself. As they reached the last known position of the missing patrol boat, the shoreline erupted in a series of deafening explosions and fire. Startled, the backup police crew turned to watch the huge fireballs that consumed so much and lit up the entire area.

Dispatch couldn't believe it.

As the backup patrol was tending to the recovery, they heard the distinct muffled *whumping* sound of mortars being fired. Looking in the direction of the sound, they could barely make out two boats, dark and low in the water. Small, slight flashes of light were coming from the boats as the mortars were firing on the refinery. After just thirty or so seconds, the firing stopped. Then there was a smaller explosion on each of the boats and they quickly sank out of sight. The harbor police patrol could not believe what they were seeing. First their partner boat had disappeared and now this ... the shoreline ablaze and mortar fire from boats that no longer existed.

The Coast Guard was notified that the police patrol boat had apparently been sunk. They sent out a patrol boat and assisted in the recovery of the bodies. Since there wasn't much they could do at that point, they headed back to their headquarters and met with police supervision. The Coast Guard looked back at their radar recordings of traffic in that area earlier that evening and saw nothing of note. There was a large sailing vessel anchored well out off the coast, but, other than normal ship traffic, nothing else was unusual. But the police had three people dead and no idea of what had happened.

When the Coast Guard looked at their current radar, they saw that the large sailing vessel was moving further out to sea and was well beyond the territorial limits of the U.S. ... and beyond their jurisdiction.

Chapter Thirty

Thursday—October 12
Washington, D.C.

The president, when briefed of the attack on the Long Beach refinery facilities, could not believe the details. Multiple tanks destroyed, refineries out of commission for months, several people killed, and no sign of the attackers. How could he possibly protect all the remaining refinery systems in the U.S.? There were over fifteen hundred of them operating. After the briefing, he went back to his office, puzzled and angry.

"Jack. Get in here."

Jack Harrison came in quickly. He watched as the president worked the remote controls on CNN and muted the sound.

"Yes, sir?"

The president motioned toward the muted coverage that showed the fires still blazing in Long Beach. "Any suggestions on how we stop this?"

Jack looked at the muted TV and then at the ceiling of the Oval Office. He responded, "Yes, sir. I have some thoughts."

The president, in an irritable tone of voice, said, "Okay. Out with it, man. What do you suggest?"

"Three things. One. Call API and get them to make sure their members know about this and increase their internal and external security significantly. I don't mean just increase patrols, I mean electronic watches with alarms, a more alert force to any problems that show up, and hire some truly capable security people. Two. Notify the Coast Guard to patrol closer to shore and more frequently in areas where refineries are near shorelines. If a ship of any sort comes within a mile or so, stop and question them. And three, get Ryan in here to capture these guys. Just the ayatollah is obviously not enough. We need to take out the entire leadership of this group. And given what happened to Ryan, and his background, I'll bet he'd be anxious to go."

The president nodded as he was pacing back and forth. "We don't really know where they are, and they seem to strike with impunity. How do we locate them and take them out?"

"I'd suggest a full-court press. Put a small team together and have them track this group down. And, by the way, they could be in several locations at one time. I mean, it is a group of people and they may be spread out. Tough one to solve."

The president didn't stop his pacing. He talked as he walked. "Okay. Let's assume we find this group, even if it is in several locations. What do we do about them? We can't just have American commandos of some sort going around killing people."

"Not unless we can prove they are at fault and taking these criminal actions," said Jack. "If we can locate them, we do have the option of taking them out with Hellfire missiles mounted on drones."

The president stopped and looked surprised at this suggestion.

"Yeah. I know. It's been outlawed for a few years now. But so are their actions. They have killed our people and downed some of our aircraft. And now these refinery attacks. We need to respond in kind and take them out without warning, and, even though it's outlawed by international treaty, we still have the capability. Tough decision, but I think the situation warrants it. Boots on the ground may not work. These guys are pretty mobile."

The president nodded and shut off the TV. He turned to Jack and said, "Let's get our staff together and discuss this a bit more in a less heated environment."

"Will do. I'll see what your schedule looks like for tomorrow and we'll set something up."

The president nodded and said, "Okay. Do that and we'll see what comes out of it."

Jack left the office and made arrangements through Jackie and Maria to get an hour on the president's calendar late tomorrow afternoon. It would be a tense session but needed to be done. He gave them instructions to make sure that Mike Detirro, Mark Allison, Miriam Blacock, Jerry Ocasio, Kenton Marshal, and Bob Goldstein were all present.

Friday—October 13
Washington, D.C.—The White House Situation Room

The next day, all of the invited attendees met in the Oval Office with President Martinez. They all understood what the meeting was about and had their positions and ideas ready to go.

The president began, "You all know about the multiple strikes on our oil refineries in the past few days. People have been killed and our refining capacity has been reduced. Fortunately, we have a fair amount of excess capacity and can handle these outages without impacting the general population. But the general population doesn't know that, and that's why we're seeing runs for gasoline in some parts of the country. The purpose of this meeting is to figure out what we need to do to stop the raids and also reassure our people that there is little to worry about."

He turned and spoke to his national security advisor.

"Miriam, what do you make of this situation, and how do we get it resolved?"

"Well, my expertise is usually in foreign government troubles and threats. Not terrorist problems, which I think this is. But that comment aside, I think we need to do several things to counter this threat. One. We, as government officials, cannot possibly protect all the refineries that could be targets. The companies that are owners and operators of these plants need to provide their own enhanced security. If we haven't already done it, we need to get the word out to the companies and get them off their collective butts. Two. We need to understand where these attacks are coming from. We know who is responsible, New Persia, and need to figure out an appropriate response. And three. We need to hammer them out of existence. And this time do it for sure. If we can't hammer them, then we need to decapitate their organization. By that I mean we need to capture or kill their entire leadership. Not just one or two people."

The president looked around the room and shook his head. "Well, are you sure you don't have an opinion on this?" And smiled at his sarcasm. "However, I can't say I disagree with what you say."

The president turned to Mike Detirro and asked, "Your thoughts, Mike?"

"Miriam hit the nail on the head. We, at least my advisors and I, think this is more work of the New Persia group. They have gotten more aggressive since we captured the ayatollah, and we think they are behind this latest series of strikes. While they recovered the ayatollah, the planning for those strikes had to have taken months. The pattern fits, and, of course, their email after Mississippi pretty well clinches it."

"My thoughts also. Bob, the Coast Guard is part of your Treasury organization. Do they have any ideas on who might be doing this?"

Bob responded, "Yes and no. They are going through their radar databases to see if they can find anything at Houston, Pascagoula, or Long Beach. They are looking for anything that might stand out as common between the three attacks. It will take a few days, but hopefully we can find something. Other than that, there isn't much out there. The explosives used in all three of the cases are the same and are readily available on the black market. We can't trace them."

"How about the eyewitness reports on the mortar attacks?"

"Yes, we can confirm that they were 60mm mortars that hit the refineries. It wasn't part of the explosions destroying the tank farms. And, from those witnesses in Mississippi, we have found out that the rounds were fired from some relatively small boats in the harbor. Their video on the news confirms that story. The initial mortar attack was thought to be part of the other explosions. Then when the witnesses showed up, we were able to analyze the ruins in the refineries and identify the mortar remains. And while there apparently weren't any witnesses in Long Beach, we think the same thing happened there. It is a new wrinkle they are now using."

"How do we protect ourselves from this type of attack?"

"The only answer to that is to catch them. With the small boat mortar capability, they could hit us anywhere on the coastline, and we simply can't watch it all."

The president nodded and teepeed his fingers in front of his face. He looked at all six of his advisors in the room. "Okay. So how do we catch them? We know from their message that this is New Persia again. No question."

A moment of silence. "Well, I can have the Coast Guard expedite their review. I'm sure they are moving along with it, but perhaps I can get faster results," said Bob.

"They had to come ashore somewhere. And that's assuming they came ashore at all. This could have been a land attack and we just don't know it," said the. "Is it possible this was a land attack with some mortars in boats and we're on the wrong track?"

Mike spoke up: "I don't think so. Where they penetrated the fences, and the fact of the boat launched mortars, tells me they came in from the water. Don't forget, the situation in Long Beach was in the water. The police just happened to come across these guys doing something. At least, that's what we think happened."

"Yeah. That's true," said Mark. "I'd suggest we check with some of the marinas in the areas where they struck and see if the managements might have something of value. That's right down the FBI's charter."

The president nodded. He looked out the window. The weather had turned stormy again, and he could hear the thunder in the distance. Rain was falling and hitting the windows with a shallow pattering sound. It fit his mood.

174

Kenton then spoke up. The president turned as Kenton began speaking. "I know this comment may go against the grain of this meeting, but one option we haven't tried in all this time and mess is to begin to comply with what they want."

The president said, "I think I misunderstood you. What did you just say?"

With some testiness, Kenton said, "I think you heard me. I said perhaps we should look at complying with at least some of their demands. To reduce our use of oil makes a lot of sense to me. It would help out the environment, reduce our foreign energy costs, and stop all these terrorist activities. We haven't tried any of it, and I just think it might help if we started."

Mike Detirro looked over in amazement. He almost shouted, "I don't think you know what you are saying. We can't do that! There are multiple reasons for not giving in to this bunch of crazies. If we did that, every nutcase out there with a cause would be targeting us."

Kenton responded, "Mike, that's what you say every time there is even a slight challenge to our capabilities. 'Let's stand up and fight.' Well, I don't buy that solution. Sometimes we are better off working with these people instead of creating this adversarial environment."

Miriam looked over at Kenton and just rolled her eyes. He was unbelievable.

The president then took over again. "Kenton, I appreciate your views and pacifist ways. But we simply cannot do that." He leaned forward on the table and put his fingers up in front of himself. He touched one finger and said, "One. They are using force and violence to try and get their way. We simply cannot permit that to succeed." He touched another finger and said, "Two. Our economy could not stand the reduction in energy that they are trying to impose. To reduce to twenty-five percent of the 2015 use is ridiculous and simply cannot be done. Three. Caving in to their demands, with absolutely no negotiation—and remember, they won't negotiate those demands—would be an invitation, as Mike just said, for every other wild-assed organization to hold us hostage to whatever their agenda might be. The short answer is no. We are not going to do that." The president then looked around the room and watched the positive nodding going on to his comments. He also noticed that Kenton was staring at some point on the opposite wall.

After a few moments he said, "Okay. Let's see what the Coast Guard can come up with and have the FBI canvass the areas around the refineries to see what they can find. And Jerry, notify all the refineries and ask them to step up their security. Seems like we've been here before. Let's get together in a few days and see where we are."

With that comment, the meeting broke up. The president asked Maria to set up a follow-up meeting in two days so they could review their progress.

Notification to the three chief executive officers on the three strikes was fast and complete. With over one and a half billion dollars in damage to the three refineries, and the reduction in refining capacity for the individual companies, it was an enormous blow. For Chevron and the Long Beach facility, other facilities could be either brought back online or their production increased to a point closer to their capacity. They did have significant reserve capacity and it could be used.

However, as each CEO was briefed on the way forward by his staff, each was dismayed to find out that the repair costs would have to be taken out of current income. Insurance would not be a factor in the repair costs. Each of the insurance programs were very close to the same. The policies covered natural disasters, accidents, manufacturing incidents, employee work stoppages, and even riots, but they all discounted terrorists and their activities. The industry giants would have to fork over a lot of funding to get the repairs done to their own facilities. It wasn't a pretty picture.

And in each congressional district, the congresspeople heard about this problem long and loud. Multiple meetings were being held in the congressional districts, with the CEOs insisting that the government do something to help them out. After all, the financial industry and some parts of the auto industry had been rescued in the early part of the century. Why shouldn't the petroleum industry receive the same treatment?

Friday—October 13
Southeastern Iranian Desert—New Persia Stronghold

The ayatollah was mulling over an idea he had come up with while crossing the desert to the stronghold. He had been thinking about all their efforts in getting the west to comply with their demands, and about the west's complete refusal to meet those demands. He needed to try another tactic.

Over a secure communication link with Socotra, he called Khatib and Ramiz. After a few preliminary greetings, he said, "I have decided that we need to be more forthcoming in our dealings with the infidels." Ramiz and Khatib looked at each other in the New Persia Operations Center conference room. They wondered what was coming next. The ayatollah continued, "Khatib, I want you to send a message to Martinez. I want you to suggest that we meet in a neutral area so we can work out a solution to our mutual problems. That means I want to talk and convince them to begin to reduce their need for our oil." Both Khatib and Ramiz sat back for a moment ... in surprise. The ayatollah continued, "Send it out today and we can work through our Iranian friends to set it up."

Khatib leaned forward and said into the telephone, "That could put you right back into their hands. Are you sure you want to do this?"

"Yes. I understand the potential risk, and that is why it has to be in a neutral area like Bahrain. Let me know when you send it so I can coordinate with Iranian authorities."

"I'll get it out this afternoon, sir."

Chapter Thirty-One

Friday—October 13
Washington, D.C.

In Washington there was an air of both frustration and despair. From satellite photos and the email message, they knew that New Persia was responsible for the two attacks in the Gulf of Mexico and the attack on Long Beach, and that the attacks had been successful. People had been killed and they were basically powerless to stop it. Both had been total surprises, and the security forces were caught completely unawares. The companies involved, Houston Oil and Chevron, were at a loss to explain the lack of effective security. And they were paying dearly for it.

The president made sure all the other oil companies and their facilities were informed of the details of the attacks so they could develop, and field, effective security measures. While several had already increased security at their facilities, they enhanced their procedures and capabilities even more. The cost was significant, but a destroyed refinery or storage tank farm was far more expensive to replace than enhancing security.

They had a massive problem in trying to ensure their security. The U.S. has a coastline exceeding ninety-five thousand miles, and trying to protect all of that would be nearly impossible. And much of that coastline involves estuaries and coastal islands, which, since the days of the pirates, had been a haven for smuggling operations. Organizations like New Persia were out to take advantage of this weakness.

While *Persian Quest* was in transit across the Pacific Ocean, there was a considerable effort on the part of several congresspeople to try and determine both what was going on with the attacks in Texas, Mississippi, and California and what the administration might be doing about it. Led by Senator Jim McIlroy, with help from the Mississippi Senator Charles Sebastian, they contacted Jack Harrison.

"Jack," said Senator McIlroy on the phone, "what the hell is going on? The strikes on these refineries and storage facilities have been devastating, and I have a constituent problem of large proportion because of them. So does Chuck Sebastian. And this is all on top of the personal threats. What are we doing about these guys?"

"Hello, Jim. Good to hear from you too," Jack said sarcastically, since there had been no preliminary salutations. "To answer your question, we are tracking their movements to try and find out where they might strike next, if at all. And since New Persia sent that message out to the entire world, we know who is doing it and can guess why. They are trying to force us to buckle under to their demands."

"Jack, you know we can't do that. The economic impacts would be huge. And my state of Texas would be one of the worst hit."

"That's right. And we aren't going to buckle. We are trying to find them so we can stop them. But they are very good at remaining hidden and are being helped, we think, by some people inside the U.S., and that includes some of our environmental extremists. We are trying to find out where their base of operations for these attacks is coming from. It is obvious that they are using some form of ship to mount the attacks and they are very good at their commando-style attacks.

"We are going to locate them and take them out. How, I don't know yet, but we will do it."

Jim sat there for a minute in thought. He was in the conference room of his offices and looked out the window at the foul weather. He didn't say anything.

Jack said, "You still there, senator? It has gotten pretty quiet."

McIlroy stared for a moment then said, "Yeah, I'm still here. I was just thinking." He paused for just a moment then said, "So, given what you say, what is the president actually doing about stopping these renegades?"

"Rather than answer you over this unsecured line, why don't I set up a short meeting with you, and a few others in Congress, with the president, and you can tell us your concerns, and we can tell you what we are either doing or plan to do. I think we certainly already know what your concerns are, but it would be best for you to articulate them to us so we are sure we are all in the same ballpark."

"Sounds like a plan to me. I'll wait for your call … perhaps by tomorrow?"

"Yeah. Sure. I'll see what I can get set up. But in the meantime, be assured that we are very actively trying to track these guys down. It may take a while, and we may have another incident before we can get to them, but we will get them."

"Not good. But understandable," the senator said with a resigned and glum-sounding voice.

"No. Talk with you later." And the connection was broken.

Jack sat there and pondered what to do. A meeting would help bring all of it out in the open and they could reassure the congresspeople. But they still really didn't have a good idea where the bad guys actually were and what they might do next. They needed to get some additional information so they had something concrete to tell the congresspeople when they met. And he wasn't sure how to do that.

Friday—October 13
Freeport, Texas—Ryan's Marina

Ryan went out onto the new deck and enjoyed the sight of the slips and people busy at their fall leisure. He sat down on one of the deck chairs and began to think. The attacks on Houston and Pascagoula and now Long Beach, along with the personal attacks he had endured, made him wonder what might be coming next. The president and his administration couldn't seem to get a handle on where and when the New Persia group might strike next. Even if they knew exactly where New Persia, and the ayatollah's men, were located, they couldn't just walk in and take them the way they had before. "Forewarned is forearmed," as the old saying went, and the ayatollah had certainly been forewarned.

He moved his leg a bit, since it still bothered him a little after the fracture had healed. As he sat there, Jackie came out with two frosty drinks and joined him. She had also wondered what might be coming next. The world at large didn't seem to care too much about the attacks. There were enough problems and strife to go around, and most nations were dealing with their own situations.

Jackie asked, "Ryan, what are you thinking? You are being a bit quiet."

He looked back at her, patted her hand, and said, "I'm kind of pensive right now. It just seems that this situation with New Persia is taking all the enjoyment out of life. I'm worried that they may try something again. Actually, I'm sure they will. It's like waiting for the next shoe to drop."

She just nodded and looked off in the distance.

He continued, "I don't understand why outfits like New Persia seem to feel that they have the right to dictate their views to the rest of mankind. That kind of thinking has been the source of trouble for all of human history. You'd think we would have learned by now."

She just nodded again. Then she added, "Yes, and while it isn't a pleasant thought, we probably aren't going to change it. There are just too many people out there with radical ideas that feel they are right, and are willing to pick a fight to impose themselves on others."

He nodded and looked off in the distance. Not much else to say.

Chapter Thirty-Two

Sunday—October 15
Washington, D.C.—The White House Situation Room

Two days later the staff met again. Looking at Bob Goldstein, the president asked, "Well, what do we have? Coast Guard come up with anything?"

"Yes, sir. They have. At each of the refinery attacks, apparently the same large sailing vessel was present. And at each of the attacks, the sailing boat was gone within a few hours."

"Do we have a picture of this vessel? What does it look like?"

"Thought you might ask that. Yes, sir, we do. But it's not an official photo. One of our Coast Guard enlisted guys took a personal picture because of the size of the sailing vessel. He hadn't seen one like it before. Here it is." Bob turned on the projector and an image of *Persian Quest* showed up.

The president had a startled look. "Son of a ...!" exclaimed the president. "Just like the one in Alaska. That confirms it. It's New Persia again. Damn it all."

"Sir, this picture was taken in the Gulf of Mexico. We sent it to the Coast Guard folks in Long Beach, and they confirmed that there was one like it anchored outside our territorial waters just before the Long Beach hit. Then we contacted our people in Panama and they confirmed that a vessel just like this one passed through the canal a few days ago ... between the Pascagoula and Long Beach attacks. We think it was the same vessel. By now, it is probably halfway across the Pacific." He hesitated a few moments then added, "Or somewhere else on our coastline. We think this is the source of the commando attacks."

The president nodded. Mike Detirro had moved forward in his seat and was leaning his elbows on the table. With concentration he studied the image and said, "I think we need to notify all the Coast Guard stations to be on the lookout for this ship."

Mark interjected, "That's the same vessel we've been tracking for several days now. It left Long Beach heading west and, somehow, we lost it. We're trying to find it again, but it's a big ocean."

"Just an update," said Jerry Ocasio. "The FBI hasn't located any witnesses as yet in Long Beach. It's early in their efforts, though."

The president nodded and the meeting broke up.

Monday—October 16
Washington, D.C.—The White House

The next day Mark asked to see the president for just a few moments, and Maria arranged for him to get ten minutes.

The president asked, "Whatcha got?"

"We've reacquired the mystery sailing ship. It's well across the Pacific, on its way, we think, back to Socotra. It's currently located about three hundred miles west of Hawaii on a southwesterly course."

"Good. I think we should track it back to wherever it's going and then figure out what needs to be done. If it's going back to Socotra, we may want to consider another strike of some form, combined with a capture-or-kill mission for the New Persia leadership. We're slowly convincing some of the rest of the world that these guys are just uncommon criminals and need to be apprehended." He paused, pleased with the results, and said, "Thanks for the update."

Mark left the office.

Jack Harrison interrupted the president for a moment. "We've just received, through the Iranians, a request for a meeting with the ayatollah. Apparently the Iranians are functioning as a go-between and the ayatollah wants to meet with you in Bahrain in a few weeks."

The president took the request note that had come through the State Department. He quickly read through it, looked back at Jack, and said, "This is bullshit. There's no way I'm going to meet with that criminal terrorist. Tell State to tell the Iranians to shove it … diplomatically, of course."

Jack smiled. "I thought that might be the reaction. I'll pass on your view to Kenton."

Monday—October 16
Pacific Ocean

Najid was making good time across the southern Pacific Ocean. The weather was pleasant and the winds quite favorable to

183

their crossing. The *Persian Quest,* with all sails deployed, was doing about fourteen knots. They were southwest of Hawaii and anticipated being back in Socotra within the following two weeks. The commandos maintained their fitness through two exercise sessions each day, but otherwise just relaxed and enjoyed the ride. They had received a short congratulatory note from Khatib and were basking in their success. They were unaware that they were being tracked across the ocean by one of the U.S. military satellites.

Tuesday—October 17
Washington, D.C.—The White House

"We're tracking them," Mark said. "They're making good time. And the FBI found where it looks like they came ashore in Pascagoula. There were some small marks in the dirt and footprints across some of the marshland. In Houston, they found a marina that had been used to unload supplies. The management there said they didn't see anything unusual, but that's to be expected, since everything was covered up. The bottom line is that we don't have much to go on. We haven't discovered where the boats with the mortars are located, and we may not. There's a lot of coastline out there, and the mortar boats could be anywhere by now."

The president shook his head. "Well, tracking them out on the open ocean tells us that at least we shouldn't have to worry about them for a while. Unless they left some 'presents' behind somewhere."

Mark nodded with a worried look. "That's a possibility." And then slowly shook his head.

The president had now been briefed on the location and progress of the *Persian Quest* as it made its way across the southern Pacific Ocean. He was anxious to see where it went. Satellite coverage could be relentless, and the CIA was following the ship's progress very closely. Communications intelligence was small, but they were able to get some information off the data stream as the *Persian Quest* reported her progress to both Socotra and the stronghold. Even though the signals were processed through a Chinese communications satellite, the fact that they broadcast the information to the satellite meant that anyone, with correct equipment, could pick up the broadcast signal. Encryption experts at Fort Meade in Maryland were able to decipher the signals and obtain some minor intelligence. They also thought the terminal at

Salalah would forward the information to the old stronghold ... and they were right.

They were able to determine that the *Persian Quest* was headed for Socotra, and that she had been tasked for a future mission. But they did not know what that mission was.

Chapter Thirty-Three

Wednesday—October 18
Washington, D.C.—The White House

The president met with Mark Allison again to review what the CIA had discovered regarding the ayatollah's whereabouts. The president had become almost obsessed with locating and eliminating the ayatollah and his immediate staff.

Mark came into the Oval Office, shook hands with the president, and sat down on a couch. He inserted a flash drive into the projector and the system, recognizing the inputs, booted up and projected an image on the wall. The image was somewhat blurred due to distance, but was obviously of the stronghold in southeastern Iran. Mark focused the image and zoomed in on an individual.

"We think this is the ayatollah. His size matches, and, even though protected by the umbrella, the deference paid to him leads us to believe it's him."

"So, he's back at the stronghold, then?"

"Yes, sir. Seems so. At least when this was taken about a week ago. This person was escorted into one of the main buildings. There was a small throng of people around him, and that kind of attention just leads us to believe it's him. Our guess is that he came overland over several days."

"Back in the middle of it."

"Well, it does sort of make sense. It is a protected area, and, even though we know where it is, it is still very difficult to get to. And now it can be defended more easily, simply because they have more people. And better-trained people and perhaps better weapons."

"So we're back where we started."

"Not entirely. We now know that the trimarans are something to watch closely and we know he is back in home territory. He won't be easy to get to ... but at least we know where he is for now."

"Mark, we need to keep a close eye on this. See what else you can find out and keep me informed."

"Yes, sir."

Elusive Quarry

The *Persian Quest* had made it back to Socotra after sailing from the U.S. West Coast. She eased into the Socotra New Persia Operations Center harbor under engine power and tied up to the pier. Her crew and the commando force were glad to be on firm land again after their adventure.

Najid was pleased with the results of their mission. He spent some time briefing Khatib on the details of the mission in all three locations. Ramiz was also present for the briefings and discussion. Since he had been responsible for the training of the commandos, he was quite interested in how they performed. He was relieved to hear that they had done quite well.

Khatib and Ramiz were quite familiar with the mission results, since Ramiz had seen the Mississippi strike and they both had been watching the CNN coverage of the refineries. Najid was able to fill them in on the details of the final results of the attacks. They were, of course, familiar with the detailed plans, but there were some aspects of the mission accomplishment that had to vary from their planning. Some of the information on locations of facilities were not quite accurate, and they had found it necessary to kill several people in the attacks. An unfortunate necessity that might only draw more negative attention to their movement.

The ayatollah read through the various reports that had been emailed to him. It was a very good and successful effort. He sent a note back from the stronghold thanking all the people who had participated. Then he left the stronghold for Char Bahar.

The *Persian Quest* was being resupplied and restocked for another mission. The logistics people were going through a routine restocking to save time, since they did not know what the next detailed mission would entail. Najid spent time each day monitoring the restocking to ensure he knew exactly what was on board. He didn't know what the next effort would be, but he would be ready to support it.

Khatib looked at the response to the suggested meeting they had received back through the Iranians. In nice terms, it said no. The president was not available anytime in the near future for a meeting. Nothing elaborate … just "no."

Khatib went to the intercom and called Ramiz.

Friday—October 20

Washington, D.C.—The White House

Two days later, meeting with the president, Mark Allison walked slowly into the Oval Office after Maria opened the door for him. The president walked around his desk and sat down at the center coffee table with Mark.

"Were you able to get anything more?" asked the president.

"Yes and no," responded Mark. "We were able to get photos of the Socotra compound through our national assets—in this case it was one of our MilSats, with Project VII capability. We can get a color resolution of several inches through the clouds with this technology." He inserted a flash drive into the built-in computer projector in the table. On the screen an image appeared of the entire island of Socotra. Using zoom controls, Mark moved in on the compound, and the resolution immediately adjusted on a series of obviously military-style vehicles parallel parked next to each other in precise formation.

Mark continued, "These are Chinese-made personnel carriers and are capable of transporting twelve men with their equipment. They were not there, that we are aware of, six months ago. We think they are beefing up a response force to repel any invasion, or at least slow one down. They are capable of littoral water operations, meaning shallow coastal water operations, or full land capabilities. They can be used for defensive or offensive operations and carry a full suite of comm gear. This is a significant upgrade from New Persia's earlier capabilities. Whoever is running this show now, or was before the ayatollah escaped from us, has done one hell of a job."

"And while we sit here, fat, dumb, and happy, they are building up."

Mark looked away from the screen and over at the president. He sat back for a moment and then said, "Yes, sir. They are. And without causing an international incident, we can't do anything about it." He stopped for a moment and worked the zoom controls again.

Leaning forward over the projector, he said, "And here is another surprise. This is located down near the harbor area that they constructed."

The president looked at the screen and said with concern, "Are those hangars?"

"Yes, sir. They are newly constructed hangars with small aprons out in front of them. Given what happened to the ayatollah, meaning his kidnapping, we think they are developing, or may

188

already have developed, helicopter capability to look for submarines."

"My God. Who is doing all this? It can't be just the ayatollah's doing. He was here for the past year."

"Agreed. As we previously guessed, we have had some information coming off the street that his principal assistant, Khatib Al Daye, is running things. His defense minister Abdul-Hakim was executed, and a person called Ramiz is now running the defense program. And this Ramiz person is very familiar with the U.S., having studied at the University of Wisconsin in Madison."

"And the two of them are doing all this build-up?"

"It appears that way. But they are getting a lot of help in this. In addition to the Chinese providing some of the weaponry, the French are providing training in commando techniques and expertise in explosives."

"Well, that explains a lot. The Chinese have been involved for some time, but not the French."

"Yes, sir. We know the Chinese built the mini-submarine we captured in the Gulf of Mexico last year, along with its large yacht tender, and they built the trimaran we recently captured in Alaskan waters. But the French involvement is new. And they are good. Close to the equivalent of our Black Water response group."

The president's eyebrows went up at that statement. "That good?"

"Afraid so. The French are good. That's why the incident in Colorado was so successful. Not only because we didn't know it was coming, but also because we didn't know the capability for that type of operation even existed with New Persia. Total surprise for us. We, in the CIA, are playing catch-up on this. We missed it entirely. The FBI missed it too. And the refinery attacks are even more convincing."

"So anything we attempt in Socotra now will be met with a lot more"—he hesitated, searching for a word—"problems."

"Yes, sir. But, and it is a big 'but,' we don't think the ayatollah is there. As I said the other day, we think he is, or was, at the stronghold. He may not still be there. If I were him, I'd be moving around a lot. His center on Socotra is still there and they have beefed everything up, and we think he was there for a short period of time, but there is no sign that he is still there. Watching the island, there doesn't seem to be the same deference being paid to the compound we saw last year before we got him. And we haven't seen him walking around the way we did then."

"Okay. Given all this information, what would you suggest we do?"

"Nothing."

The president looked back expectantly.

"I don't think, given our current circumstances, that there is much we can do. Perhaps the FBI can find out a bit more about how they pulled the refinery attacks off, but we don't have any, to use that overworn saying, actionable intel. We know he is out there somewhere and being protected by his own organization ... again, somewhere. But we don't know exactly where. If we did we'd be after him. I think we just need to keep our ears to the ground and wait to see what develops. That's a hard pill to swallow, but I think that's all we can do."

The president put his hands up to his face and leaned forward in the chair. He was frustrated, and it showed. They had gone through so much to get this guy, tried him, and were putting him in prison when he pulled off the escape of the century. So close yet so far. And then the refinery attacks in the gulf and at Long Beach.

"You're right, of course. We can't invent information. Keep an eye on the island and the stronghold and let's see if anything develops. Anything else?"

"Only one thing. The yacht that was in the harbor has departed, stopped off in Salalah, and now appears to be heading back to China. There is a trimaran in the harbor. It's the one we've tracked from the West Coast. They made good time. It looks like a duplicate of the one we captured in the Bay of Alaska. What its next mission is, we have no idea."

The president was thoughtful and then asked, "When did the yacht leave?"

"We're not sure. Why?"

"Because if it left since the ayatollah escaped, could he have been on board?"

Mark looked startled. "It's possible. We'll have to look at some past video and see if we can determine when it left. And following your thought, he might have gotten off in Salalah and then possibly gone on to the stronghold."

The president winked and said, "Follow it up." And smiled slightly. Maybe, just maybe.

Mark left the office and the president went over to the windows. Another bright day with billowing clouds, and the world appearing in a false peace. The Washington scene was too quiet and too serene. Things were about to change.

Elusive Quarry

In was very late at night at the complex at Schriever AFB in Colorado. The 750th Operations Squadron was performing its twenty-four-hour monitoring mission as usual, monitoring the activities at the stronghold. The joint military satellite was staring down at the stronghold coordinates, constantly watching for any activity that might be out of the ordinary. They had observed much of the training activities and routinely sent reports up-channel.

But nothing came of the reports. The training activity was old news.

Chapter Thirty-Four

Monday—October 23
Washington, D.C.—The White House

The president called in his closest advisors. They met in the Oval Office.

The president smiled around the room. He said, "Just so everyone is aware of what is going on, I have turned down a request from the ayatollah for a meeting. I find it hard to believe that a terrorist, one who has shot down our aircraft and killed our people, would believe that I would meet with him." People around the room just looked back, and agreement was quite apparent.

He continued, "Through some of our communication intercepts and satellite coverage, we now know that the *Persian Quest* has arrived at Socotra Island. We also know, or at least suspect with a high degree of confidence, that the ayatollah is at the stronghold. He may move at any time, though, so we can't depend on his location being stagnant. We need to get him and make sure he is captured and put away for a long time. But this time, we need to get his top lieutenants also. We know about Khatib. We need to define who the other top people are so we can target them for either capture or elimination." He stopped for a moment and looked around the room. Everyone was listening and silent.

"Miriam," he said. "You suggested we locate him and then figure out how to handle the situation. Well, we've located him, and it won't be easy. He's apparently back where all this started. Any suggestions?"

"Yes, sir. I think we need to take some action instead of just talking about it."

The president was a bit surprised at this quite blunt comment, and he looked at her in a questioning way.

"By that I mean we need to put pressure where it will do the most good. Economic pressure on all the people or organizations that support him. All those that we can identify. We also need to begin finding out, as you just alluded to, who his top advisors are, and get to them one way or another."

"Those are good words you speak. How do we implement them?" he responded.

"We can't do too much with the Iranians because some of their top-level people support him. And economic measures probably won't work. Unless ..." She looked at the table and then out the window, thinking, and then back to the group. "We take some drastic action on our part and cut off all supplies of oil out of Iran. In other words, we not only cut off all imports from them, but convince our friends to do so also. Then cut off all supplies and materials necessary to keep the oil infrastructure in that country operating. That will effectively, after a few months, cut off the rest of the world from the Iranian oil source. And in the process, it will starve the Iranians of their income."

Kenton was aghast. "We can't do that! It would impact the entire world's supply, and our 'friends,' as you call them, wouldn't be our friends much longer. To take out a major source of oil for the western world, which is what you are suggesting, would cause an economic collapse of major proportions." Then he emphatically said, "No! We can't do that."

"Kenton, settle down," exclaimed the president. "I want to hear all the ideas and then we can sort through them for viability. Thank you for your comments, Miriam. Mike, what do you think?"

Kenton felt and looked chastised. He didn't like what was being suggested, but was stymied by the president. He wasn't comfortable, especially in front of some of the other cabinet members.

Mike Detirro said, "In many respects I like what Miriam just said. If we basically starve them out—the Iranians, that is—maybe they won't be so willing to host this parasite. However, I'm afraid it may not work. Yes, we could embargo the supplies and equipment and stop importing the oil from Iran, but I'm afraid they would just turn to India or China for help. At least, that is what I would do under similar circumstances. Our equipment would be slowly replaced and we would force the Iranians to deal with these two energy powerhouses. And both are hungry for the oil resources Iran possesses." He stopped for a moment and looked at his hands on the table. Then he looked up again and continued, "I think we need to positively locate all his henchmen and take them out. That aspect of Miriam's comments I totally agree with. It has now been proven to us that just grabbing the ayatollah was not enough. We need to do more. We need to get him again and the other top leaders." He looked at Miriam and said, "You mentioned Khatib. We now know about this American-educated fellow, Ramiz. The two of them are apparently the ayatollah's top guys."

The president interrupted at this point. "Yes, Mike. I think we are all in agreement. But what specifically should we do to get them? We can't start a war with these countries protecting them, and we have already been unsuccessful in shutting them down. We even lost the ayatollah to his own people during the raid in Colorado. What do we specifically do?" The president's frustration was clearly showing. Everything they had tried to do had either failed outright or had been compromised in some fashion.

"Okay," Mike responded. "You want to know what I think? I think we need to wipe out the viper nest on Socotra, capture his top advisors there, put at least some pressure on Iran, as Miriam said, and then we need to go after the stronghold again with a combination of air and ground strikes that cannot miss."

The president spread his hands out in front of himself and said, "We tried that, and—"

"And we succeeded," interrupted Mike. "We succeeded. They have rebuilt on essentially the same site and they can be taken out again. But this time we need to make sure we decapitate—Lord I hate that term, but it is appropriate now … decapitate their organization so the phoenix cannot rise from the ashes. Break it up until it cannot be a viable threat ever again."

The room was quiet. The air conditioning was running, and you could just barely hear the air coming out of the vents. You could almost hear the wheels turning as the president's top advisors and their staff were thinking over what had just been said. The group was very quiet. If the U.S. tried again and failed, it would be a severe diplomatic embarrassment and last for a very long time. And the press … what a mockery they would make of any failed effort. Whatever they decided to do would *have* to succeed. No questions.

Mark, the CIA chief, spoke up. "I'm not sure an embargo of Iran would have much effect. I have to agree with Mike. They would just find other sources. And don't forget, in today's world, the black market is very active and could probably provide necessary parts for the oil infrastructure. Third-party support and so forth. So, no, I don't think an embargo of those materials would have much effect, except possibly to piss everyone off in the Middle East that would be affected by it. It would appear to me that, since this is a criminal element we are trying to eliminate, we bring in some of the so-called dirty-tricks guys to handle it. They can get in, do their work, decapitate the organization, and get out. If it were timed correctly, it could all be accomplished in a few hours and the job would be done. Then we could get on with life again."

"Guys"—the president turned to Miriam—"and gals. You still haven't told me *how* to do this. You have expounded at length on what needs to be done, but no specifics so far. *How* do we do this?"

Mike looked around at the group of advisors, sat back in his chair, and scratched his head. He sat forward again and said to the president, "You want to know the 'how' of it. We need to all agree on the 'what' and then we can figure out the how. We have batted several ideas around here in the past half-hour or so, and still, I don't think, have a consensus of *what* needs to be done. The goal is pretty obvious ... eliminate the New Persia movement. I've heard economic strangulation, hit them with an air and ground strike, track them down with a clandestine effort and take them out, and ... not do anything." He looked at Kenton, the eternal pacifist, as he made his last comment.

The president nodded at these comments. He looked around the room as the secretary's comments sank in to the advisors. "Okay. So what I think I just heard was a call for direction. Mike, you do have a way of expressing yourself that is unique." He smiled slightly at this comment. "Does anyone have anything else to add?" He looked around the room again. Nobody said anything.

"Okay. I have to agree that cutting off some of the supplies and equipment is probably an exercise in futility. Won't work. Might at first, but not in the long run. But I do think it might be helpful for our embassy in Baghdad to have a conversation with the oil interests there and let them know of our concerns and that we are discussing embargo options. And Jerry, I think notifying our local U.S. major oil companies that have dealings with Iran is a good idea. They need to be aware of our concerns."

Jerry just nodded and looked over his shoulder at one of his aides. The aide nodded and wrote down a note on his tablet.

The president continued, "Mark, have your resources beefed up. I want all three locations monitored constantly. The stronghold, Socotra, and Salalah. We need to get a better handle on who is where. And keep track of that sailing ship. I don't want it lost again." Mark nodded.

"Kenton, have each of the embassies work with our friendly allies, and I mean our true friends, and see if they can come up with any off-the-street information. Nothing overt. Just pulse them.

"Miriam, I want you to keep track of all this activity. It is of prime importance to our overall national security. If you see anything going haywire, let me know immediately." Miriam just nodded.

"Jerry, work with Bob at Treasury and get the Coast Guard to come up with some analysis of what has already happened and what our vulnerabilities might be for future attacks. I know we are already discussing this with the oil companies. I need to know how serious this could get.

"Mike. Do some initial work on how we might strike back at these guys in their own backyard. We have some better intel now after we hit them the last time, and we know what's at Socotra, so we should be able to come up with some good initial planning ideas."

The president then looked around the table and said, "Does anybody have anything else to add, and are these instructions clear?"

The various people in the room all looked back, but nobody said anything. It was quiet.

"Okay. I appreciate all of your help in this matter. We have an adversary that is just very difficult to deal with, especially given the international political climate. He is protected, but still an international criminal, at least in our minds. And he needs to be stopped. I think that if we can get a good handle on where he is and have some assets nearby that can be applied, we can eliminate this problem. I know it is taking way too much of all of our time, but that can't be helped. We need to deal with it. We need to finish it."

He then turned to Miriam and said, "Work with Kenton, Mike, Jerry, and Mark and keep up with it and keep me informed."

She nodded but kept quiet.

Then the meeting broke up with a silent nod around the room from the president.

Chapter Thirty-Five

Monday—October 23
Southeastern Iranian Desert—New Persia Stronghold

The ayatollah talked with Khatib, who had joined him at the stronghold from Salalah several days before. "Khatib, I'm getting nervous. The Americans are being very quiet about the attacks we did on their oil systems in the Gulf of Mexico and California. Other than some news broadcasts, there has been virtually nothing. The outrage expressed by President Martinez shortly after the attacks has resulted in no apparent action on their part. I'm afraid they are up to something, and I'm not sure what it might be. They may try to catch me again, and I need to keep moving to avoid that. So I want to go back down to Salalah again with absolutely no fanfare. I'll take a supply truck to remain completely invisible."

"Agreed, sir," said Khatib. "I will arrange for it in the morning. I too am concerned over their apparent lack of concern or action. Something has to be going on. They aren't going to simply ignore our rescue of you and the strikes on their refineries. We need to keep our wits about us and keep our people in Washington on the alert for any activity."

Monday—October 23
Washington, D.C.

Jackie was getting anxious. It had been too quiet and she wanted to visit Ryan. There was a big international conference coming up, and she was very busy setting up meetings and arranging visitors for the president. She was completely conflicted. She loved her job in Washington as the primary scheduler for the president, but she also loved Ryan, who had his marina in Texas. How long could she expect to put up with the forced separations? She wondered, but didn't know the answer to her own question.

Monday—October 23
Freeport, Texas—Ryan's Marina

Ryan, Jasper, and Dave were all watching the periodic coverage of the catastrophes in Mississippi, Texas, and California. The refineries had been seriously damaged, and the media was in a frenzy. From the days the events happened, and the message from Khatib claiming responsibility for those attacks, there was a nonstop windstorm of coverage in the media. And, of course, the talking heads and "experts" were discussing details and remarking on unreasonable speculations.

Dave said, as he nursed his gin and tonic, "Sure looks to me like the work of someone we know pretty well."

Jasper, a committed beer drinker and having a cold Coors, said, "I think so too. It is certainly well organized, and they obviously have developed a pretty good capability for mayhem."

Ryan responded, "Well, I certainly have a bone to pick with them. Just look around at the mess here." He winced a little as he moved his head too quickly. Then he added, "And I need to get back at them for killing Betty and Orrin and seriously injuring Jackie. Not sure where to start, though. I'll bet President Martinez has some actions up his sleeve right now. He simply can't ignore all this."

"I wouldn't doubt that for a minute," said Dave. "I wonder if there's anything we could do to help out. He hasn't called us, but maybe we could offer."

"What do you have in mind?" asked Ryan.

Jasper gave Dave an expectant look.

"Well, I'm not sure. But since we know the island pretty well, and have dealt with the ayatollah before, perhaps there's something we could contribute. Nothing specific in mind, just a general idea."

Ryan called Maria's private line. She was glad to hear from him. "Hi, Ryan. How are you doing?"

"Pretty good now that we've got the construction finished."

"With your recent upgrades and a new office and apartment complex, you'll just about have a whole new marina there."

"Yes. But I'd rather not have had to go through all this, Maria. I called because I'd like to talk to the president if I could. Does he have some time available?"

"Not right now. But I'll ask him and see when he could be available. What's the subject?"

"Same, same. New Persia again. I'd like to touch base with him and see where we are, and if I and my guys could help out in any way. Maybe we could go back there, or to Salalah and snoop around a bit. See what we might find."

"Okay. I'll let him know and get back to you as soon as I can."

"Thanks, Maria. Appreciate it."

After the call, Ryan thought for a few minutes. He wasn't sure how they might be able to help, but felt there might be something they could do. They would just have to wait and see.

Chapter Thirty-Six

Tuesday—October 24
Southeastern Iran

In the morning, a supply truck moved slowly across the Iranian desert on the dirt road toward the highway connecting Birjand and Zahedan. It wasn't a comfortable ride, but it was progress. The ayatollah had entered the truck in a warehouse connected to the administration building so the satellite could not see him. He was taking all precautions. He did not want to go back to prison in the U.S. He looked out the windshield at the barren desert as they slowly made their way to the main highway. It was stifling hot and the wind was totally absent except for the movement of the truck. It was just barely comfortable in his white dishdasha, his white robe-like attire. He wondered, as they moved, how long he would have to live like this, always on the run and looking over his shoulder for the infidels. It was not the life he had planned when he founded the New Persia movement.

They reached the main highway and turned south.

The paved asphalt highway stretched into the distance with some rolling hills on the horizon. Rippling waves of heat radiated off the pavement and they could see it on the sands well out in front of them. The driver, specifically selected for this trip and impressed with the importance of his passenger, concentrated on the road, and they were able to make reasonable time on the southward journey. After reaching Zahedan, they refueled and rested for the evening. They continued their journey the next morning. They would go to Char Bahar, where the ayatollah would board a rented boat for the trip across the Gulf of Oman and then down the coast of Oman to Salalah. There he would stay in a small compound near the satellite receiving and transmission site. A compound that the infidels did not know existed. He would continue to be in contact with Khatib, Ramiz, and his other advisors via encrypted Chinese satellite communications and undersea cable.

However, for the first week, to conceal his whereabouts, he would not send any communications himself. There were a few routine logistics matters and some security issues that he would deal with, and he could communicate through the stronghold via landlines or the undersea cable systems.

For the next day, Khatib continued from the stronghold to direct the ongoing missions that *Persian Quest* would be a significant part of, and then moved to Socotra. Ramiz continued to support from Socotra and functioned as the lead at that location. He was preparing some new missions for his people and liked the seclusion that the Socotra compound provided. He didn't need to concern himself with Ryan McKenzie this time. He knew Ryan was dead.

Wednesday—October 25
Oman—Salalah

After two full days of travel, the ayatollah reached his small office complex in Salalah and tried to relax. It was exhausting to be constantly looking for your adversary. But he had no real choice. He felt that if he kept moving around he could avoid being found and captured again. Salalah was an almost ideal city for him. While it was a fair size, and thus he could get lost in it, it was not so large that he felt intimidated by it. And his followers would find it accepting and reasonable to visit and conduct business.

After spending the evening in prayer and contemplation in his simple quarters, he finally got a good night's rest. He began his day, after morning prayers and a small breakfast, planning a trip to visit some of his supporters. He wanted to regain support from those he had lost, and perhaps get the ones who stayed with him to increase their financial help. It would take a fair amount of effort, and a pretty convincing story, for them to come back on board.

He sent a message via the secure underwater cable to Socotra. While the ayatollah was moving to Salalah, Khatib had moved from the stronghold over to Socotra to work with Ramiz on their security systems in the compound and to plan for their next action against the west. They felt that the west still needed a lot of prodding to meet the New Persia demands.

They met in a small conference room. Ramiz had finalized some plans for a strike in the United States and he went over them with Khatib. "I think we have planned significant strikes against the U.S. and will carry them out in the near future. But I also think we need to begin thinking about the rest of the western world. They are also wasting much of this precious resource and need to reduce their needs. I recognize that they have a better transportation utilization than the U.S. simply because of their geography. Their rail lines and roads are all much closer than those in the U.S., and they use smaller cars and vehicles. So their oil use is reduced. But they still need to reduce further. I think a planned effort in their area would be beneficial."

Ramiz just nodded. He had thought the same thing, but only had so much time for his planning. "I will begin planning a series of efforts in the other western nations of Europe. I agree, they too must submit to our requirements."

Thursday—October 26
Oman—Salalah

Ramiz was more comfortable now that the ayatollah was safe and moving around between the New Persia locations. Ryan McKenzie, he discovered from news broadcasts, had, miraculously, barely survived the attack on the construction trailer. Ramiz was taken by complete surprise when one of the staff passed on that news. But the information had come from a Houston-based TV station making a follow-up on the bombing story. He couldn't believe it, but it was apparently true.

Ramiz was in his small office on Salalah and thinking about the next moves that might be taken against the U.S. They had succeeded marvelously so far with the recovery of the ayatollah and the strikes against the refineries in the Gulf of Mexico and California. But there had been no real reaction by the U.S. government, at least so far.

They needed to get to the president. The protections the FBI and the Capital Police were giving to the members of Congress were very good, and he was afraid to test them with an attack. Just let them wear themselves out "protecting" those 535 people; it was a good diversion, and one that took a lot of assets to continue. He sat for several minutes thinking and finally, in an Allah-inspired moment, came up with it. The president's staff was not being protected as far as he knew. If New Persia could capture a staff member or two, it would be a real attention-getter. And it would be righteous payback for the kidnapping of the ayatollah. An eye for an eye!

He sat for several hours planning out what they needed to do ... and he had a target in mind that would be perfect. Ms. Conover would be the ideal pawn in this oversized and deadly chess game. Her relationship with McKenzie was an additional plus. After working out the details, he called Khatib and told him of the plan. Khatib was surprised, but pleasantly so. The plan would fit in nicely with other plans they had for the president ... plans for a meeting and discussion.

Ramiz looked at the internet information available for the refineries in Europe. There was a significant amount of information, and he took several hours reviewing and deciding on his course of action. He finally made his decision and began work. Then, after several hours, he had a draft plan that he explained to Khatib.

Ramiz never failed to amaze Khatib. They put the plans in motion.

Friday—October 27
Oman—Salalah

Ramiz had finalized his plans for striking back at the United States for their latest attempt on the ayatollah. The infidels had missed capturing the ayatollah while he was returning to the safe house in Salalah, but only by a hair. Had it not been for some extraordinary effort in the Caribbean off Panama with the mini-sub, the events could have turned out quite differently. Fortunately, he had escaped their near-clutches and was, again, back in Salalah after a short time at the stronghold.

While he was a little nervous about all three of them being in one place together, Ramiz felt they needed a face-to-face discussion over plans. He and Khatib moved from Socotra to Salalah for a meeting.

Ramiz went down a narrow hallway to the ayatollah's office and quarters. He approached Khatib and asked him if he could see the ayatollah. Khatib nodded and went in front of Ramiz as they approached the door to the office area. Rapping softly on the door, Khatib stuck his head in and was told to enter by the ayatollah. Both Khatib and Ramiz approached the ayatollah, bowing their heads in greeting.

"Sir," said Ramiz. "I have completed some plans for an adventure against the U.S. and strikes in Europe, and would like to get your approval to proceed."

The ayatollah responded with a nod and waved his hand at the projector. "Go ahead, Ramiz. I will be interested to see what you have devised." He smiled as he gave his approval for the brief. "And since the president has rebuffed my request for a meeting, I think we need to respond with something that will get him to change his mind."

Ramiz nodded, and with a gleam in his eye said, "I think what I have devised will be a good answer to the president ... and in line with your desires."

Khatib watched carefully as the director of security for the New Persia movement inserted a flash drive into the projector. The projector, sensing the input, started up on its own and projected a title slide for the New Persia movement. Thirty minutes later, Ramiz finished with his very professional presentation. The ayatollah and Khatib looked at each other with both shocked and knowing looks.

The ayatollah looked at Ramiz and said, "What you have proposed will certainly really get their attention ... and then some. Along with Europe and the rest of the world. It is very bold and thoroughly thought out. Are you sure it can be done that easily?"

"Yes, sir. I think it can be done, and, until it takes place, the U.S. and Europe will have no idea what is coming. This will garner the world's attention."

The ayatollah looked at Khatib and asked, "What do you think? Should we proceed with these proposed projects?"

Khatib looked at Ramiz and then back to the ayatollah. "Yes, sir. I think we need to bring the situation a little closer to the American people. So far our actions have pretty much been against the U.S. and British oil industry, which have not responded to our demands, and some of the political officials in Washington and London. It appears to me that this project will put very heavy pressure on the president to accede to our demands. I think we should proceed as Ramiz has laid it out."

The ayatollah stood, turned around, and looked out the window at the calm blue sea. It was a peaceful and very pretty view. He turned back to the table and sat down again. He looked up at Ramiz and said, "You know executing this plan may very well bring the weight of the American forces down on our heads."

"Yes, sir. But they tried once before, when they eliminated the stronghold, and did not achieve their goal of eliminating us. This move will, in my mind, bring a lot of support from the anti-American countries in the Middle East. We will have taken an action that will be the envy of al Qaeda, Hamas, and Hezbollah."

"You make a good case, Ramiz."

Khatib folded his robe over his arms and nodded. He could tell what the decision was before the ayatollah said it.

The ayatollah looked at Ramiz and said, "Proceed with your detailed planning."

Ramiz smiled. It was a go. The American president would pay for his conceit and ignoring of the New Persia demands.

Elusive Quarry

Friday—October 27
Washington, D.C.—The White House

President Martinez came back in to his office in the early afternoon. It was stormy out and the rain was beating on the windows of the office. It had been raining all day and was interfering with his golf match. But he couldn't control the weather, so he had decided to go back to the office and catch up on some of his reading. On his desk, in among many point papers and files, he reviewed a note from Maria from last Monday with an explanation of what Ryan had suggested. He read through the note and sat down to think.

He stared out the window at the rain as he thought. Even if he didn't have Ryan and friends involved directly, they could be a good group to bounce ideas off. After all, they had captured the ayatollah and might have some insights he hadn't thought of. And they could help counter the DOD, who were obviously champing at the bit to take this mission on. Even Jack had recommended using Ryan and his buddies. Perhaps it would be good for Ryan's group to come to Washington and sit in on some meetings.

He read through the short note again. The satellite monitoring was going along pretty well. They were keeping an eye on the three locations that might support the ayatollah. So far they had been able to follow what they thought was him, from the stronghold to Salalah, the third possible location. Once in Salalah, they had lost him in some of the warrens and small roads. Perhaps some eyes on the scene would help out. But that could be better done by the embassy people in Muscat, the Omani capital, as they had done before. At least some of them spoke Arabic and would blend in better than a couple of Americans. So the idea was good, but implementing it would be the State Department embassy staff.

And the satellite coverage over Socotra continued as they tracked the sailing vessel. It had entered the New Persia operations center harbor. It was still there but had been restocked and readied for its next sailing. Where it was going was anybody's guess. They thought that Ramiz and Khatib were on Socotra and the ayatollah was in Salalah. But that could change momentarily. And there was no way to predict when a move might occur.

He thought about it some more and decided to get Ryan involved, at least from an advice standpoint. Then he smiled to himself. Ryan could see Jackie again. Quite a pair.

He called Maria. She came right in with her note tablet. "See if we can set up a meeting with Ryan and his friends here in the

White House in a few days. I want to see what he has to think firsthand. Ask them to stick around for a few days and, after I talk with them, perhaps we can get some other folks together and figure out what we can do."

Maria took a few notes on her tablet, nodded, and left. She called Jackie and told her what the president had asked for. Maria could just about see the look on Jackie's face as she passed on the request. Several minutes later, Jackie came over to Maria's desk and they laid out a plan for an hour's discussion with the president in another week. Then Maria called Ryan.

"Ryan," she said after he answered the phone. "Good news. The president wants to talk with you, as he put it, 'firsthand.' Can you, Jasper, and Dave come up here for a meeting week after next on the seventh?"

She continued to explain that the president wasn't available for the next several days. But his message was to see if they could think up anything they might be able to do to help. And there was some indication that the ayatollah was moving back and forth between the old stronghold and Socotra. Perhaps that would help in their brainstorming.

Ryan looked out of the small window in his office as she was talking. Pleasant day. He responded, "I'll check with Dave and Jasper, but I'm sure they can break loose for that kind of meeting. I'll get back to you later today."

"That'll be fine. We're looking forward to your visit." And she hung up.

Ryan smiled to himself. He thought, *Maybe we can get a piece of this action after all.*

Ryan, after getting the message from Maria, along with some additional information passed on by fax from the president's office, sat down for several minutes to think. What they had done before, capturing the ayatollah in his own quarters on Socotra, would obviously not work again. He was sure they had beefed up the security and it would not be so easy this time. So they had to figure out another answer. And they needed to figure out how to capture some of the other people in leadership positions. Just getting the ayatollah would not be enough.

Ryan called Dave and Jasper to see if they could come over for a few hours and help figure out a solution. Neither was immediately available, but agreed to meet in a week at Ryan's.

Ryan called Maria back and they confirmed an appointment with the president for Tuesday, November 7. Ryan then called Jackie and told her he would be visiting. They could get together again.

Elusive Quarry

Chapter Thirty-Seven

Thursday—November 2
Washington, D.C.—Evening

Jackie was low on food and wine, and a few other essentials, in her apartment, and decided to get some supplies at the local supermarket. With Ryan planning to come up and visit the president, she didn't want to be short. She took the elevator to the parking garage, fished around in her purse for her keys, and approached her car. As she reached her car she beeped the lock, opened the door, and started to get in. Two men, medium build and armed, quickly and silently ran up from the next car over behind her. They reached out and grabbed her arm, and one of them swept her feet out from under her. Before she could react, down she went, hitting her head on the bottom doorframe and nearly knocking herself out.

She went all the way down to the garage floor. Her car door slammed shut. She could feel herself being lifted and carried to a van parked nearby. While still very woozy, she felt plastic ties being used to bind her hands behind her and her feet together, then a gag over her mouth and she was roughly thrown into the back of the van. The van then moved out of the parking garage and onto the streets of Washington.

They hadn't blindfolded her, and she looked around as her head cleared a little. She had a real sore area around her right temple from the impact with the car. One of the men was seated in the back with her on the floor. The other one was driving, and doing a good job of it. Driving slowly so he wouldn't attract attention. She thought they were headed out of the city, but she couldn't tell what direction they were going.

Then the man in back realized she could see and was regaining consciousness. He reached over and put a blindfold on her head. A moment later he reached down and caressed her breasts, moving his hand from one side to the other. She could hear his breathing picking up, and feared the worse. What was going on? Who were they and what did they want with her? She strained at the plastic ties and realized she wasn't going to break them, or even move them. His hands pulled back and she felt him undoing the

207

buttons on her shirt. His hands then went under her shirt and under her bra. He felt her breasts, directly touching her nipples, and following the curve to her chest. His breathing increased even more. She could smell his rancid breath, and his sour body odor washed over her. It was obvious he hadn't had a bath or shower recently.

Oh God, she thought. *'Would she survive this and where are they taking me?* She twisted to get away from his hands, but he followed her and finally kicked her viciously in the side.

"Stay still," he said with a strong Mideastern accent.

Her ribs hurt from the kick and his hands roamed freely on her chest. She knew what was coming next and was fearful that they would get too rough and hurt her. But that didn't happen. The van took a sudden turn to the right and pulled to a stop.

"Knock that off," said the driver in Arabic. "We aren't here for that and she is not to be touched. You know that. Ramiz was very specific in his instructions, and you are to leave her alone."

Her assailant said something unintelligible, but pulled his hands out of her shirt and was muttering to himself. He sat back in his seat, scratched at his crotch, and looked out the van windows.

Jackie could not understand what they had said, but was relieved when he stopped feeling her. She was sweating a bit under the restraints and beginning to understand who they might be. The driver had used the name "Ramiz," and she knew who he was. This was a New Persia thing.

She lay on the floor and didn't move. It wouldn't help if she did move, since she was trussed up and couldn't see. She listened. Trying to figure out where they might be. No good. It was quiet in the van, except for the vehicle's own sounds, and she couldn't pick up any clues. She had no idea where they were, but from the sound of the tires, they were moving pretty fast. Maybe an interstate?

They traveled for some time without a break. Without some form of reference, she couldn't tell where they were. Finally they pulled off the main highway and entered a secondary road that was not as smooth. For another hour they traveled, and, after a couple more turns, they pulled into a driveway somewhere. She could hear gravel under the van. A moment later the van stopped and the driver shut down the engine. He came around to the back and opened up the doors. It was cold and she could smell pine trees and grass. She felt hands on her legs and was pulled roughly out the back of the van. Then she was carried into a house and pushed on to a couch. Her blindfold was then removed, along with the gag on her mouth.

She looked around at her surroundings. She was in a decrepit old 1950s-style living room that had seen much better days—shag carpeting on the floor that looked like it hadn't been cleaned in decades and awful paint on the walls that defied description. The couch she was resting on was dark brown, lumpy, and filthy. The two men were watching her as she looked around.

The driver said, "I am called Kasim." And, pointing at the other man, he said, "This is Carlos." She looked questioningly. "Yes," he continued, "his father was Spanish and his mother Iranian. You will be here for several days. We are out in the middle of the country and a long way from anything. You cannot escape, and if you do, you will perish in the woods. We are going to remove your leg restraints but are leaving the hand restraints in place." With that comment, he came over and cut the plastic leg restraints off.

She looked at him. He was of medium build, Middle Eastern looks, and slightly dark skin, dressed casually in jeans and a red pocket t-shirt. She looked over at Carlos, the one who had been in the back with her. He also was of medium build, but was rougher looking, with a scar on his forearm that went from his hand to the elbow. He was also in jeans but had a sport shirt hanging out and unbuttoned. A dirty t-shirt underneath it. Very unclean. His dark, thick hair was mussed and unkempt.

She said to Kasim, "Who are you and what do you want? And could I have some water?"

Kasim responded, "Who we are is of no consequence to you. Our boss will be here in the morning and you will be able to talk with him at that time." He motioned to Carlos to get Jackie some water.

After Carlos brought her a bottle, she drank it quickly. While drinking, she continued to look around the room. Pretty ugly. And she could get no sense of direction. All the well-worn curtains were closed. No way to look outside. No way to even guess where she was. It was cool and she could smell, faintly, propane. They were out in the country. Propane for heat.

Kasim asked, "Are you hungry? We have a few sandwiches in the kitchen, and some drinks."

Knowing she had to maintain her strength, but still hesitant to eat anything these goons would provide, she finally said, "Yes."

Carlos then went in to the kitchen and brought back a ham and cheese sandwich that apparently had come from a 7-Eleven. It was sealed in its triangular package and was cold to the touch. That was at least some assurance to her that it would be all right to eat.

"I can't eat with these restraints on. Please take them off."

Kasim said, "Not so fast. We'll remove the plastic restraints, but only after we put on some handcuffs and cuff you to the chair.

They will give you more motion to work with." He placed handcuffs on her, placed another set of handcuffs on her ankle and the chair, and then cut the plastic ties.

She rubbed her arms where the ties had been. There were marks on her wrists, and they would take a few days to disappear. She reached out for the sandwich, undid the plastic wrap, and slowly began to eat. She couldn't move without moving the chair. It was a good anchor. Kasim knew what he was doing.

The two men, satisfied that she couldn't go anywhere, left the room, and she could hear them talking in the yard. Arabic. Other than an occasional use of a name, she couldn't understand any of it. Could have been a bit of an argument, because the voices rose in volume at times, but she wasn't sure.

She started to assess her situation. She had no idea why they had kidnapped her. They wouldn't discuss it and the "boss" would be in tomorrow to talk to her. She didn't know where she was, but guessed out in the country somewhere, as Kasim had said. It was too quiet—no traffic noises and no sounds of neighbors. And the house was in such disrepair that it might have been abandoned at one time. But they had electric power and heat, so it had to be somewhat occupied. Couldn't tell for sure. They had driven for some time on the interstate, she thought, but she was not sure how far or which way. Virginia, North Carolina, Maryland, Delaware, New Jersey? No idea. The handcuffs did give her some more capability to move her hands, but she was chained to the chair. No way out of that without a key, and she didn't have one handy.

She finished the sandwich and a Coke they had brought her. Tired from the exertion and fear of the trip, she eased back onto the couch and relaxed as best she could still handcuffed to the metal kitchen chair. Just a few hours ago she was fine, coming home from work at the White House and expecting a non-event for an evening. Now this. By now it was very early morning and the darkness was oppressive in her mental state. And if it was New Persia, they knew who she was and what she did. Could she end up as some form of pawn in an international game? Or worse, ... dead?

And when she didn't show up for work. What would happen then? They would have no clue as to where she was or what had happened to her. She could just disappear and no one would find her.

Stop it! Just stop it! she thought. *Shit! All you're doing is scaring yourself. Perhaps, after tomorrow's discussion with the "boss," something will turn my way. In the meantime, try and relax and begin to figure a way to escape. Because, since there were no clues on my disappearance, it is up to me to get out.*

Friday—November 3
Over the Atlantic Ocean—Morning

Ramiz was flying into Washington from London, and anticipated a successful day. The weather was nice and warm, and he had been informed that Jackie had been captured by his men and was being held in their safe house in the hills and forest outside of Greensboro, North Carolina. He was anticipating talking with her and then he would make sure that Ryan would be outraged, with a short note, at their actions. The president too. But he had them over a barrel because, at this point, they didn't know she had been kidnapped. He held all the cards.

He looked out the window, watching the countryside slowly go by at thirty-three thousand feet. It was such a large country, with so many resources, that it didn't make sense to him why they weren't using all of the alternative energy capabilities available. He knew the answer, of course. Oil companies and their political pull. The oil industry had a very close-minded and myopic view of the world. While there was still time, much more effort should be put into alternatives, and the New Persia actions would ensure that happened. The western world certainly wasn't going to do it on their own.

Chapter Thirty-Eight

Friday—November 3
Freeport, Texas—Ryan's Marina

On Friday, Jasper and Dave came over for their meeting and discussion. They all met at Ryan's new office area. After some coffee and chitchat, they got down to it.

Ryan said, "Well, I heard from Maria last week, and the president isn't available until next week. He wants to meet with us next Tuesday in Washington and figure out how we might be able to help." Ryan then gave them a quick rundown on what the ayatollah and his group were apparently doing. Going back and forth to avoid capture. "So here we are. What do you think?"

They both sat there thinking. Finally Dave said, "I think we could help, but it won't be easy. One thought I've had: if the ayatollah and his henchmen are moving around a bit, going back and forth between these two or three locations, they are trying to protect themselves from us knowing where they are. But they are also exposing themselves as they travel. If there was some way to determine when they are traveling, perhaps we could get them when they're on the move."

Jasper nodded in thought. "Yes, that might work if we can get the information. I don't think an outright frontal assault on Socotra or the stronghold again would work, for both practical and political reasons. If they have any sense, they have some backup plans available to escape any attempt we make. We need to be real sneaky about this one."

Ryan warmed up his cup of coffee. He sipped on it for a moment, and then said, "Okay. I agree with both of you. But how do we contribute to it? Even if we can somehow determine when they are moving around, what would we actually do about it?"

Dave and Jasper both just looked at him. Jasper said, "Perhaps a meeting with the president and Homeland Security and DoD guys would help. There may be more to this than they are letting out. And we are kind of in the dark on the details."

Dave added, "Yes. There are some details that would come in handy. Like how frequently they are moving around, and how are they traveling? Boats, trucks, aircraft, motorcycles, camels, or something else? Since they have mini-submarines, they could be using those and we wouldn't see them. And, perhaps, we could flush them out with the appearance of a raid. It would force them to move and we might be able to snag them. Or at least one of them."

Ryan responded, "Hmmm. Hadn't thought of those ideas. If they had a sub in the area of Char-Bahar, they could make the crossing without us knowing about it. It would take a while, but it could be done. And vice-versa, they could go from Socotra to Char Bahar. By flushing them out, we could then be waiting to grab them. The only drawback is that we don't know for sure if they're using those mini-subs. They may have some other escape plan."

Dave said, "Yes. They could also be using small aircraft or even commercial aircraft back and forth. Given their clout in those governments, they could easily pull that off."

"Okay," Ryan said. "Those are some good thoughts. Can we think of some other ways to get to these guys? I sure want to get back at Ramiz for what he has done, and tried to do, to me. Betty and Orrin were good friends, and I'm still not completely up to speed."

Jasper added, "You know, I think we are onto something. If they are being so careful about being seen and trying to avoid us knowing where they are, maybe they are going overboard with the secrecy attempts."

"I don't follow. What do you mean?" asked Ryan.

"Well, if they are moving in trucks or vans from the stronghold down to Char-Bahar, supposedly as a supply run, and they are going in just one truck, that could be a tip-off. I would think that most supply runs would be to Zahedan and have several trucks involved. A single vehicle, truck, or van could be spotted with our satellites, and, if it goes beyond Zahedan, could be closely watched. If it goes to Char-Bahar and the docks, we know someone is moving around. We wouldn't necessarily know who, but it would tip us off to the possibility someone fairly important in the movement was shifting locations."

"Do you think we could pick up on that kind of detail from the satellites?" asked Ryan.

"Are you kidding?" exclaimed Dave. "The digital cameras on those satellites can read the bolt numbers on the head of the bolts holding license plates. And by the dye marks on the license plate metal, they can even tell you what prison or manufacturing facility made them ... and when and on what shift."

Jasper and Ryan both reacted with screwed-up faces and completely recognizable arm and hand motions.

Dave grinned and said, "Okay, maybe that's a bit of an exaggeration ... but not by much. They actually can read the bolt numbers. Back to the subject. Believe me, they can spot any movements at all three locations. I say all three, because if I were the ayatollah, I would have another hidden hole to retreat to, and that must be this place in Salalah. I think two locations are too vulnerable. Anyone thinking security in their organization, and this fellow Ramiz certainly is capable of that, will recognize the need for more locations. One suggestion for the president would be to ferret out possibly even a fourth location so we know the total problem."

Ryan shook his head. "You know, it amazes me to think how much energy and effort is going into this. The ayatollah could have accomplished a lot, maybe not all he wanted, but a lot, by following reasonable diplomatic processes. And a lot of lives would have been saved." He looked over to Jasper and then back to Dave. "I will forward these ideas, and any more we come up with today. But what can we, the three of us, do to help? There has to be some action we could take to help out."

"I see," said Jasper with a grin. "You want some of the action on this too! That old urge from SEAL days hasn't faded much, has it?"

"Nope," responded Ryan with a serious smile. "But, as I said a little bit ago, I want not only to get the ayatollah back where he belongs, in prison—I want to take out Ramiz for what he did to Jackie and me ... and Betty and Orrin. And since this fellow Khatib is obviously so dangerous, we need to get him too."

"Well," Dave said, interrupting, "I think we could offer to go over there again and see what we can find out. There may be something at Char-Bahar or at the satellite ground station in Salalah that would help us out. And a visit to Socotra, with some form of disguise, might be useful also. And another thought that just occurred to me. Why don't we get Corey Gaskins involved again? He sure helped us out in capturing the ayatollah the last time, and I'm sure he would like to get in on the action."

Ryan's eyebrows went up. "Of course! I don't know why I didn't think of that before. He really saved our bacon the last time and would probably like a break from his embassy staff position in Jordan." He turned to Dave and added, "And I told Maria that maybe we could go over there and snoop around a bit."

Dave and Jasper just nodded. It was a good idea. Corey was a former Special Forces solider and had a lot of smarts and courage in dangerous situations. Now retired from the U.S. Army and part of the State Department diplomatic corps, he was stationed at the

214

U.S. embassy in Jordan. He had helped with both an escape from the ayatollah and then capturing the ayatollah a few weeks later. He was a real asset to have around.

"Okay," said Ryan. "That was an excellent point, Dave. I'll see if the president will go along with having Corey join us on whatever it is that we do. And we still need to define that in better detail. Dave, you and I have suggested that we go over there and see what we can discover. I think we need to get more specific. The president isn't going to let us just wander around. We need a plan of action."

"I think we can come up with a pretty detailed one if we put our minds to it," said Jasper. "Dave has already kind of outlined one. We know the ayatollah is commuting back and forth, along with some of his staff doing the same thing. If, and it is admittedly a big *if*, our satellite guys can get a handle on when and where they are going, we could be the boots on the ground and get these guys. A small group; just the four of us. The big question is: can the satellite people find them and track them? If they can, and can watch them for a period of time, they should also be able to determine the frequency that these moves are taking place and what transport they're using."

Ryan nodded. It made sense. They had been able to get the ayatollah before with some naval support. Perhaps they could get the job done again, and this time capture Khatib and Ramiz and maybe a couple of other senior staff people.

Dave added, "I think we can come up with a generalized game plan and give it to the president. Then, depending on what the satellite people come up with, we can modify it and begin to take action."

"Okay. I agree," said Ryan. "I'll put together the general game plan and run it by you guys before sending it up the chain, meaning back directly to the president. At least he will know we are thinking about the problems and have some ideas. Then it will be up to him to decide what he wants to do. Time for lunch."

They walked down the beach to the Dolphin restaurant and had both some liquid lunch and a bit of the other kind—some food. It had been a productive morning, and Ryan would put it all together that evening, run the basic plan past them, and get it off to Maria.

Friday—November 3
Washington, D.C.

The president, as part of his normal early morning routine, pulled up his secure email. One item from Mark really got his attention. The trimaran that had been in the Socotra harbor had left, and appeared to be heading for the Suez Canal.

Chapter Thirty-Nine

Friday—November 3
Washington, D.C./North Carolina

The plane landed at Reagan National airport in Washington, D.C., and Ramiz proceeded to the Avis counter, where he got a car for the week. The weather was pleasant in the very late fall, and most of the leaves were now gone.

He anticipated doing business in Washington and, of course, in Greensboro. He headed out to the lot, picked up his car, and headed south on Interstate 95 toward Richmond, Virginia. From there, south of Richmond, he took I85 to U.S. 58 then to U.S. 29 and into Greensboro. He wanted to make sure Jackie was okay and to check up on that business first. Then back to Washington.

Locating the safe house, he pulled into the long gravel driveway, through a thick stand of trees and large shrubs, over a slight rise, then back down again, and came to the decrepit house. Perfect. No one ever bothered the old house, and it was far enough away from traffic and other houses that no one could hear a yell for help.

He got out of the car and met Kasim on the porch. Kasim had come out with a 9mm Glock in his hand, not knowing who was approaching. He quickly put the gun in his holster when he saw it was Ramiz. Kasim said, "Never know. Just being cautious."

"Careful, that thing could go off and then we'd have some problems," Ramiz said. "Where's the woman?"

"She's inside on the couch."

"Okay. Since I haven't been here before, take me to her."

Kasim nodded, turned around, and went through the front door. Immediately on entering, Ramiz wrinkled his nose at the smell of the place. A combination of mold, mildew, smelly furniture, and overripe food assailed his senses. The carpeting that was still remaining looked like a reject from a landfill, and the few curtains on the windows were torn and covered in bird droppings. He looked at Kasim and said, "Whew. How do you stand this place? It stinks, and is filthy."

"One of the attractions. Nobody wants to come here. Makes it safer for us. Yes, it stinks, but we get used to it. Here she is." And he pointed at Jackie, handcuffed and on the couch.

Ramiz walked over to the couch and looked down. Jackie was on her stomach and could tell he was there but not what he was doing. He was just watching her. Finally he bent down so she could see him. "Hello, Ms. Conover. My name is Ramiz. I hope my men have been attentive to your needs. You will be kept here for a while until we can complete some negotiations with your government."

Jackie's eyes were wide open. She rolled over and sat up as best she could. Ramiz! She recognized him from the courtroom video Ryan had been so excited about. So this was definitely a New Persia action and she was really caught in the middle of it. She had suspected so. Her thoughts from earlier had just been confirmed ... and she was obviously on her own.

Ramiz continued, "I expect that will take a few days or weeks. Who knows? But I do want to make sure you are comfortable here."

Ramiz turned and said in Arabic to Kasim, "Release her and give her some decent food. We need to make different arrangements for her. Do you have a room that could be used to hold her?"

Kasim responded, "Yes. One of the bedrooms could be used. We'd have to make arrangements to be able to lock her in, but that's a simple thing to do. The windows could be covered with plywood and a deadbolt put on the door."

Ramiz nodded. "Simple enough. See to it."

Jackie was watching this exchange but could not understand it. Kasim came over, unfastened her restraints, and helped her sit up. She thought that was a positive move. They couldn't possibly be ready to turn her loose. Ramiz had made that plain to her.

Ramiz said, "I've given instructions to Kasim to change your living conditions. You will no longer be placed in those restraints, but you will be confined to one of the bedrooms after we secure it. It will take several hours for them to make those changes. In the meantime, you and I will make ourselves as comfortable as we can under the circumstances."

"Why are you holding me?" she asked.

"Because you are close to the president and we needed a pawn, you, for our dealings with him. And, I might add, so we can lure Ryan into our net. A net he won't survive. Somehow, he survived my last attempt. He won't this time."

Her eyes grew very big over this statement. "What can Ryan do to you and why are you after him? He is not involved in this matter anymore."

"He will be soon. I'm sure the president will be calling on him again, since he was so successful the last time. After all, he is the one responsible for the capture and retention of our ayatollah. He has disrupted our plans, in one way or another, too many times. We cannot allow that to continue."

She recalled that the president had called Ryan and they would be meeting in a day or so. She didn't let on. "The president and Ryan will never fall for that. I'm not that important to either one."

Ramiz smiled broadly. "Oh. In that respect, I must strongly disagree. I think you are very wrong. When we have our little discussion with the president in a few days, we shall see what their reaction is. But I think you are much more valuable than you say. Especially to Mr. McKenzie. He will come looking for you with all guns blazing. And we will lead him to you."

With those comments, they lapsed into silence. Ramiz pulled out his laptop and, through a satellite connection, brought up the internet. He developed a report on their successful capture of Jackie for Khatib and the ayatollah and sent it off. He then started looking through some of the other information the ayatollah had sent him, including *Persian Quest's* progress toward Europe.

Jackie just sat there watching. While she had the training, and could probably overpower Ramiz, even though he outweighed her by forty or fifty pounds, she was reluctant to try until she better understood what they were going to do. Since they were planning on killing Ryan, she needed to act calm and collected until the right moment.

A little while later, Carlos came back with several sheets of plywood, a deadbolt, and other supplies necessary to lock the bedroom. He and Kasim went to work on the side of the house, and she could hear the battery-powered saw and screwdriver as he worked. He placed plywood over the windows and then installed the deadbolt on the hall side of the door. After he was finished, Kasim came into the living room and told Ramiz that they were finished. Ramiz left and a few minutes later came back.

"Okay, Ms. Conover. Your new quarters are ready for you. Please come with me," said Ramiz.

Jackie looked up from the couch and nodded as she got up. She followed Ramiz into a small room that had only a bed and one small light on a stand. It was as filthy as the rest of the house. With the closing up of the windows, it became more stifling and smelly. Air wasn't moving around at all. She briefly looked around and then asked, "And how do you feed me and how do I go to the bathroom?"

"Kasim and Carlos will see to your needs. I have instructed them, with a great deal of emphasis, that you are not to be harmed in any way."

"I see."

"Now I must go. You will be hearing from me in a few days."

With that, Ramiz backed out of the room and she heard the deadbolt latch. He headed for the front door and left the building. Turning to Kasim, he said, "No harm is to come to her. And get her some American food. Is all that clear?"

"Yes, sir."

"Good. I will be in touch with you by cell phone every day to make sure all is well. Do you have my cell number?"

"Yes, sir."

Ramiz looked at Kasim. Kasim could not hold the gaze, and turned away. Power of personalities. Then Ramiz headed for his car, started it, and pulled out of the gravel driveway. It had been a long day. He headed for the closest Courtyard Hotel, checked in, said his prayers, and went to bed.

Jackie was scared. It went against all her training, but ... she was both worried and scared. No denying it. She was locked in a room somewhere. The plywood was secure and the deadbolt was pretty final. She looked around the room but didn't see anything she could use to help her escape. And the odor was nearly overpowering. She went over to the bed and sat down. She had to adjust herself several times to find a comfortable position on the bed. She started to weep. She knew no one would be able to find her. Her car was still in the parking garage and there weren't any clues left behind. Her wrists and ankles were still sore from the plastic ties used on her. She rubbed them to make them feel better. After a few moments, she forced herself to stop crying and, despite her anxiety, lay down to rest a little.

Chapter Forty

Friday—November 3
Washington, D.C.—The White House

The president called Maria into the office. "Have you seen Jackie this morning?"

"No. Now that you mention it, I haven't. I'll go check her office and see if she's here," responded Maria.

Maria left and went over to Jackie's office. The white six-panel door was still shut. She knocked and got no response, so she cautiously opened it. The room was dark and Jackie was obviously not there. She turned on the lights and looked around for a moment in case there might be a note, but she found nothing. She went over to Jack Harrison's office, knocked lightly on the doorframe, and looked in. Jack looked up from editing a speech. "Yes, Maria. What can I do for you?"

"I'm looking for Jackie. Have you seen her this morning?"

"No," he said. "She didn't call and didn't ask for time off. If she's not here, we might check her apartment and see if she's ill or something."

"Okay. I'll give her a call. Thanks. Sorry to disturb you." He nodded in response and went back to his editing and morning staff review paperwork. She could feel the tenseness in him. He didn't like the fact that Maria was outside the normal "executive office of the president" organization structure. She had come along with the president, and he had insisted on having his own secretary and that it be Maria. While it really wasn't a big deal, it bothered him because, as a recognized control freak, it was outside of his control but within his normal organization.

Maria left. She went back to her desk and called Jackie's cell phone. She was immediately put through to voice mail. And then the voice mailbox said it was full. So that wouldn't work. She sat for a minute and called security. Carl, head of security, answered right away. "Yes, ma'am. What can I do for you?"

"Carl, would you check the parking garage and see if Jackie Conover's car is in her parking spot?"

"Sure. Be back with you in a few minutes."

221

A few minutes later, Maria's phone rang. "Maria, it's Carl. No, her car isn't there, and our security monitor at the garage entrance didn't remember seeing her come in this morning."

"Hmmm."

"Something wrong?"

"I don't know yet. It just isn't like her to not call." Maria hesitated for a moment then said, "Okay, Carl. Thanks for the info."

"Sure. Let me know if I can help with anything else. Bye."

Maria sat there. Jackie wasn't answering her phone and her car wasn't here. Maria began to get a bit worried. Maybe something happened to her at her apartment. She got up and went in to the president's office. "Can't find her, sir," she said to a slightly concerned president. She told him what she had done and the results. He furrowed his brow.

"Hmmm."

"That's what I thought too," said Maria.

"Ask Carl to send someone over to her apartment. It may be a bit of an overreaction on our part, but maybe not. I'd rather be sure."

She turned to leave and said, "Yes, sir."

She called Carl, explained their concern, and he agreed to send one of his men over to her apartment and see if she could be tracked down. Then Maria went back to her work reviewing some materials the correspondence section had sent over for the president's signature.

An hour and a half later, Carl called. "Maria, Carl here. My man has come back. Her car is there and her keys were under it. He contacted the manager and they went to her door. They knocked and there was no answer. So the manager opened the door. Nothing. Nothing was amiss from what they could tell. Everything was in its neat place and there was no sign of either a forced entry or a struggle. And she hadn't left any message with the manager. But I think something's wrong. Her keys were under her car, and that's not a good sign."

"Thanks, Carl. I'll take it from here," said a now very concerned Maria. She went into the president's office and relayed Carl's information.

The president listened to Maria and really got concerned for Jackie. He could think of several things that might have happened, and none were any good. Maria sat on the couch wringing her hands. She and Jackie were good friends now, and she was hoping it was something simple, but she was afraid it wasn't.

Elusive Quarry

Saturday—November 4
Greenville, North Carolina/Arlington, Virginia

Ramiz awoke at the Greenville Residence Inn on West Fifth Street at his usual 7:00 a.m., did some minor exercises to loosen up, said his morning prayers, got dressed, and went down to have some breakfast. There was much to do today, and he needed to get moving. After some coffee, fruit, toast, and yogurt, and reading *USA Today*, he went back to his room.

He stood there thinking. They were about to pull the tiger's tail, so to speak, and he wondered how it was going to go. They had Jackie in captivity and she was hidden well. He didn't think they'd left any clues as to her capture, but couldn't be sure. His discussion and review of the capture process with Kasim the previous evening at the safe house led him to think they had pulled it off. It would take a day or two for people to realize that Jackie was now missing. Phase two of the plan, a second kidnapping, would take place Monday and put him in a very good negotiating position.

He drove back to the safe house and talked briefly with Kasim then headed for Washington, D.C. While he was driving, using his cell phone, he contacted Alim and set up a meeting at a restaurant in Arlington, Virginia, just outside of Washington. They had several efforts that needed to be accomplished in the next few days if his plans were to work.

He approached the beltway and headed for Arlington. In addition to eating lunch, he and Alim would be discussing his next move. Alim had some of the resources he would require to make his next move, a move that would also be in secret, at least for now. He stopped at the restaurant and, after ordering just water to drink and a small fruit plate, he was seated, and waited for Alim to arrive.

Alim was a successful car sales manager and was about to open his own Mercedes dealership on the southern outskirts of Washington, where a lot of new housing construction was underway. Of Iranian heritage, he maintained many ties with his former countrymen. While he was taking advantage of U.S. capitalism, he had distinct connections to the Iranian government and their clandestine operations. He had expressed his New Persia sympathies to Ramiz on a couple of occasions, and was willing to help as long as he did not have to either leave the country or get his hands dirty.

Alim arrived, dressed as you might expect of a successful businessman. A beautifully tailored double-breasted dark grey suit, light blue open-collared shirt, and well-polished burgundy tassel loafers. He was not trim, but was not overly heavy and stood about five foot ten. He spotted Ramiz and came over to the table. Ramiz stood and, looking down from his slightly taller perspective, a little over six foot, reached out, and they did a manly hug and shook hands.

"It's good to see you, Ramiz. You are looking well and must be spending some time outdoors. You are dark," said Alim.

"Yes. I spend a good deal of time in the weather, one place or another. It is good to see you also, Alim. I see the Washington environment is good for you ... in more ways than one!" He smiled.

"Ahh, yes. I certainly like it better than our college days in Madison. The U.S. version of capitalism leads to a good life for those who wish to pursue it. And I am truly enjoying the life I have made here. But that is not why we are here, is it?" He was interrupted by a waiter. They ordered their food and began again.

"No," said Ramiz. "It isn't. I need your help. As I outlined to you in my email, I need some resources that I believe you have at your disposal, and I can pay them well for their efforts. And you also for your brokering the effort."

"Yes. I read your proposal and was quite startled by it. It is very audacious and quite possibly very dangerous. Kidnapping at that level?"

Ramiz merely nodded and focused on Alim's eyes.

Alim continued, "I can support your movement in many ways, but this one has me a bit concerned. The potential for failure is high, and the cost of failure is even higher."

"Yes it is. But it won't fail. And the benefits to our movement are enormous. We will be recognized by all the world governments for both our audacity and the truth of what we say. And, in the long run, the world will benefit from our initiative through longer-lasting oil reserves. Our children's children will bless us."

Their food arrived. Alim began eating his salad. He looked at a seared ocean bass with orange highlights in front of him. He said, "You do not need to convince me of the movement's overall goals; I understand and agree with them. It is the methodology, and especially this specific project you have brought to me, that gives me serious pause."

"But think of the impact! The president will be completely stymied and forced to give in to our goals."

"Yes. I agree. But if you fail ... well, you'll either be dead or in prison for a long time, and the movement will probably go into permanent hiding or dissolve."

Ramiz shook his head slowly, smiling slightly, and said, "But, as I've said, we won't fail."

Alim looked up from his fish, lifted his head high, looked down over his nose at Ramiz, and then took a long, very intentional breath. From there he shook his head. He set his silverware down and put his arms, with his hands flat on the table, in front of him. He looked at Ramiz with a hard look that Ramiz thought reminded him of his father when he was angry. *Perhaps I have played this too hard,* thought Ramiz.

Alim cleared his throat and pushed back a few inches from the table. He was having a hard time making up his mind over this daft proposal. But he was also intrigued about it. If it was successful …

He relaxed a bit and said, "All right. I will give you the resources, and at a fair price. Now give me the details." He began to finish his meal.

Ramiz smiled, delighted at this turn of events. After completing his meal and taking a glass of water, Alim also pulled himself forward so they were both leaning over the edge of the table. Ramiz pulled out a few papers from his pocket and they went over the details several times. Alim repeatedly shook his head as they proceeded, but did not object. He asked several questions until he fully understood the required actions. Resources were agreed to and timing arranged.

After all was arranged, they stood, shook hands, and departed the restaurant.

Saturday—November 4
Washington, D.C.—The White House

The president, after a troubled sleep, met with Maria in the morning. "After giving it some thought, there is one other possibility, and we need to check it out. She might have gone down to Ryan's in Texas on a quick trip. I doubt it, but she might have. Call Ryan and see if she's down there. If not, then we need to begin hunting for her in a serious manner."

Maria nodded and went out to make the phone call.

Ryan answered on the first ring. "Hello, Ryan's Marina."

"Ryan, it's Maria."

"Hi. How are you doing?"

"I'm fine. Is Jackie down there with you?"

"No, she's not. Why?" Some level of concern immediately appeared in his voice.

"Because we can't find her. She's not at work and not at home. She didn't tell anybody she was leaving and her car is at her home too. We thought she might have made a quick trip to see you."

"Haven't heard a thing, Maria. Was she at work yesterday?"

"No. She was here two days ago, but not yesterday. And there weren't any problems at all. She said nothing about leaving. We're getting very concerned here."

"I talked with her just two days ago and she was in good spirits then. I have no idea what might be going on. Let me think about it for a bit and I will call you back. Thanks for the call." He hung up, very concerned and not sure what, if anything, he should do.

Maria went back to the president and let him know the results of the conversation with Ryan. Her voice began to quake and she was nervous.

The president, very concerned, called Jerry Ocasio. A couple of hours later, Jerry appeared at Maria's desk. She escorted Jerry into the Oval Office and left the two men to discuss the situation.

The president gave Jerry a rundown on the missing Jackie. Jerry immediately said, "Let me put some guys on it. It may not be anything, but it would certainly be better to check it out. I'll get an FBI agent to check out her place and get back to you yet today."

"Appreciate it. And keep Maria informed. She's pretty shook up over it. Oh, and thanks for coming in on a Saturday, Jerry."

Jerry nodded and left.

Saturday—November 4
Freeport, Texas—Ryan's Marina

Ryan quickly called Dave and Jasper. He couldn't reach either one of them, and left messages that said he wanted to meet as soon as possible and that Jackie was missing. Dave called back several minutes later and agreed to come over right away. Jasper was out of touch.

Dave came over and, after Ryan explained the situation, they began talking about options. There weren't many. There wasn't much information to go on, just what Maria had passed on. Jasper finally showed up, but the three of them still couldn't figure out much.

Jasper said, "Seems like this might be the work of New Persia again. I don't know why, but it's just a feeling I have."

226

Dave said, "It certainly could be. It has been a little quiet for a while now since the refinery fires, and maybe they are starting something new."

Ryan thought about that. It was a possibility. And they couldn't come up with anything else at this point.

They all agreed to think about it some more. They would be going to Washington on Monday, and perhaps there would be some news by then.

Ryan called Maria and said, "Anything new?"

"No," she said. "The president has the FBI on it but there's nothing new, and no word from anyone yet. You guys think of anything?"

"No. We're stumped. We arrive on Monday, day after tomorrow, and maybe we can figure something out then, if she's still missing."

"Well, I'm going to spend the next couple of days very worried. This just isn't like her to take off like this. Something's happened, and I don't like it."

Ryan responded, "Yeah, me too. It isn't good." He hesitated a moment and then said, "I'll see you Monday. Bye for now."

Chapter Forty-One

Sunday—November 5
Washington, D.C.

The FBI sent an agent to Jackie's apartment complex, the last location where Jackie was known to have been. The manager showed the agent the apartment and the garage where her car was still located. It was a reasonable apartment in a mid-level economic section of Washington. Looking around, the agent saw nothing that might lead to what had happened to Jackie. He went out to the garage and looked at the car again. He looked at the pavement where it was parked and noted some minor-looking red spots he took to be blood. He opened the unlocked door, and, on the doorframe, he saw slightly more blood. The first sign of possible violence. He called for a lab team to come out and sweep the immediate area for anything they might find.

While waiting, he looked around with intensity born of past experience. There must be something he was missing. He turned to the manager and asked, "Do you have any security systems other than the secure locks on the apartment doors?"

"There are several security cameras in the garage at both the entrances and the exits. We also have a camera on each floor of the parking garage. They record anybody in the area." He hesitated for a moment then added, "I can have the flash drives to you in a few minutes, or we can see them in my office if you prefer."

The agent asked the manager to show him the last two days of recordings and to do it now in his office. This was possibly a critical find, and he wanted to verify it immediately. They headed to the manager's office. An hour later, they were interrupted when the lab team arrived. The team went out to the car while the agent continued his review.

After another fifteen minutes, the agent and manager struck pay dirt. Jackie was on video approaching her car as two men approached her, grabbed her, threw her in a nearby van, and pulled away. The manager was astounded. They stopped the drive and concentrated on the image of the van. After a few minutes of trying, they realized they couldn't make out much with the recording and playback equipment.

The agent, with the permission of the manager, took the flash drive, signed for it, and, after connecting with lab personnel, took the flash drive back to the FBI laboratory complex. The lab personnel who had been on site followed him in quickly. They were going to test the red spots for blood. The flash drive was taken to the electronics analysis center. After several minutes, the technicians had been able to verify part of the license number on the white Ford van. They got the last three digits, but the rest was blocked by dirt and could not be read. It was a Virginia plate. Continuing with the investigation, the FBI agent contacted the Virginia motor transportation department.

Ramiz met with the assigned resources from Alim. Three men, physically well built and fearless. All of Mideastern background and all ruthless. They knew their mission and were willing to carry it out. After giving them some additional background and directions, they left the coffee house. The following morning, they headed out to complete their tasking.

Monday—November 6
Washington, D.C.

The next morning, Maria headed out to her car and began the drive in to work. Her mind was on Jackie and where she might possibly be. She refused to accept that something bad had happened to her. This morning, like every morning, she pulled into a local donut shop and got a cup of coffee and a single glazed donut. Her daily treat for herself. Then she continued on her way to the White House garage. But this morning she didn't make it.

She pulled up to a stoplight, getting ready to turn right, when she heard a popping sound and the left side of the car tilted a little bit. Damn, she thought. A flat tire. Funny it would go like that, though. She pulled around the corner, the flat making a flapping sound as she moved, and pulled into a small parking lot. She got out and, sure enough, the left rear tire was completely flat. Fortunately, she had roadside assistance insurance, and got out her cell phone. She got in the passenger side of the car, leaving the door wide open, and looked in the glove compartment for the phone number.

When she looked up again, two large, intimidating men were standing next to her car. They did not look at all friendly. One of the men made a quick motion with his hand and she felt a slight brushing feeling on her arm. A moment later she passed out from the skin-permeable drug. The men lifted her up and out to their van and drove off. In the large amount of very busy traffic, no one noticed what was going on.

Maria woke up some time later with a small headache and realized she was tied up with plastic bindings and a gag. She didn't know how much time had passed. They were on a major highway and, judging from the sun's position, were headed south. After a couple of hours of traveling, they turned off the main road and headed onto secondary roads. Another hour or so and they turned into a gravel driveway. They stopped and she was hustled out of the van and into a filthy-smelling old house. She was unceremoniously tossed on a trashy old couch. Two other men were in the house, and her three captors and the two men had a short conversation in a language she didn't recognize but thought might be Arabic. Shortly, the three men who had captured her left.

After a few minutes, Kasim came over and talked with her. "You will be held here for several days. I am going to remove your restraints, but don't try to escape. It is miles to the nearest civilization, and you will not make it." Then he cut the plastic ties off her and removed the gag.

"Why are you doing this?" she asked.

"We have our reasons. You are a pawn in some negotiations with the president that will be held soon. In the meantime, we will make you as comfortable as we can, but you will be locked up."

"What do you want? I have no money and my family doesn't either. I'm just a working woman and don't have any savings."

"We aren't after money. We are after a much bigger prize, and it will have an effect on the entire world." He hesitated a moment and then continued, "I will show you to your room now and you will be locked in it. Food will arrive soon and you can eat then. Please follow me."

He took her to a back room, undid the deadbolt, and let her in.

Jackie, at the sound of the deadbolt, stood up next to the bed. Amazement covered her face when she saw Maria walk in to the room. Maria was, likewise, shocked. The door closed behind Maria and the deadbolt was thrown. The two women rushed into a close hug.

Jackie backed up a bit and said, "Oh geeez, Maria. Not you too! I thought I was the only one."

"You were until a little while ago. They grabbed me on my way to work. And no one will know what happened to me."

"What have they done with you? Are you okay?"

"Well, so far I'm all right. But I'm beginning to wonder what this is really all about. Now that you're here, I'm worried that this may be a quiet attack on the president. I mean, you and me together? That's our main connection. And they said something about being pawns in a negotiation with the president."

Ramiz was called by Kasim and given the word that this part of the plan had come together and that the two women were locked in the safe house. He smiled at the news. The plan was unfolding as he had envisioned it. They would succeed. From his hotel room in Greenville, he composed and sent a message back to Khatib and the ayatollah telling them of the success so far.

In both Socotra and Salalah, the news was greeted with pleasure. Their movement was making progress toward forcing the Great Satan to do their bidding. Khatib, looking at the calm waters of the western Indian Ocean, was pleased, and looked forward to the next message from Ramiz. Ramiz had been a good find for the movement. He was smart and resourceful, and had the background in American methods that they needed.

The ayatollah also received the message with a glad heart. Part of the plan was now going to be up to him, and he relished the thought. Meeting with the president would bring home the seriousness of their movement, but would also strike at the president in a personal way. He sent off a message to Aban Essa, the minister of interior in Iran, with a request. A few hours later, an answer was received. His request would be acted on soon, and they would tell him the results.

The president was really worried. Maria had not shown up for work. A few phone calls to the local police revealed that Maria's car had been found, doors open and with a flat tire, in a strip parking area. No sign of Maria, though. Now he had two people to worry about, and they were probably connected.

He brought his top advisors in, along with members of his immediate staff, and gave them a quick rundown of what had happened in the last few days. Many in the small crowd got quite worried that they could be next. People exchanged views and opinions. He finished up with the admonition that everyone be very careful. Someone out there was up to no good.

While he had no proof, he called Jerry Ocasio and asked him to come over with the FBI director again. Jerry arrived a short time later and was joined by Andy Strasner. The president gave them a rundown of what he knew, and asked for opinions.

"Well," began Andy, "after what we found at Jackie's apartment and, under the assumption that they have been kidnapped and maybe crossed state lines, it would fit into our mission. In other words, we would have the authority to pursue whoever is doing this."

Jerry nodded. He turned to the president and said, "So there is no indication of where or why they might have been taken?"

"None. We haven't heard ... yet, from anybody so far. Nada, nothing. And I am worried that this may not be the end of it. I think someone, for whatever reason, is targeting us."

"Okay. Let me get my guys together and we'll get on it. I'm sure we can find out what's going on. Give me a few days. Hopefully something will turn up."

Chapter Forty-Two

Monday—November 6
Washington, D.C.—The White House

Ryan, Dave, and Jasper got off the airplane two days after
Maria had called. They were at Andrews AFB just outside of
Washington. Ryan called Maria's number and, oddly, got a recorded
message. Strange, he thought. She didn't usually do that. It was the
direct line to her desk. He called an alternate number for Admiral
Watkins, the president's military aide. The admiral answered right
away.

"Admiral. It's Ryan McKenzie. I'm trying to reach Maria
about Jackie. I'm out at Andrews and need to find out what's going
on."

"Ryan. We'd all like to know that! Maria has disappeared
also."

"What!" exclaimed Ryan. "What do you mean? I just talked
with her day before yesterday about Jackie disappearing. She
seemed to be okay then. She was worried about Jackie but didn't
say anything about leaving."

The admiral said, "Well, she's not at work and the police have
located her car. Something's up."

"Thanks. We'll be over there shortly."

Ryan and friends went straight to the White House. Their
clearances were verified and the security personnel recognized
them. They were escorted up to the executive offices and met with
the head of administration, Marjorie Hansen, whom they had met
on several previous visits. She welcomed them in to her office and
offered coffee, which they politely refused. They were all too nervous
and upset.

"Ryan, I'm sorry you, Dave, and Jasper had to make this trip
for these reasons. Both Jackie and Maria have disappeared and we
have no idea where they might be."

"The president asked us to come up few days ago on another
matter. These disappearances just happened at the same time. Are
there any leads at all? Surely there must be something we can do."

"The president has the FBI on it and they are looking into possible leads. At this point we know that Jackie was kidnapped in her garage. The garage security cameras picked that up, and we got a partial license number on the van. They are checking with the Virginia vehicle people to see if they can trace the vehicle. We have absolutely nothing on Maria. Her car was found in a parking lot with the doors open but nothing else around. And no fingerprints on it other than hers. So, at this point all we can do is wait and see if the FBI can come up with anything."

Ryan sat there not sure what to do. Jasper and Dave were in the same quandary.

Ryan said, "There must be something we can do. Sitting around waiting for some word just won't hack it. I need to do something! I just don't know what."

Dave and Jasper both and agreed. They were stumped also. If the FBI and all of its resources were on it, well, there just wasn't much else they could think of to do.

They left Marjorie's office and went down to the situation room, found some empty seats, and sat down. Ryan thought for several minutes and decided to call Corey Gaskins. Ryan wanted his full team, the group who captured the ayatollah, together.

Through the White House operator, a call was placed to the American embassy in Turkey where Corey was assigned. After several minutes of delay, the staff at the embassy finally located Corey in an internal trade planning meeting. A call from the White House had a high priority.

Corey finally answered the phone.

"Corey, it's Ryan." He got straight to the point. "We have a real problem and need you back here in Washington ASAP."

Corey responded with some concern, "What is it, Ryan? I haven't heard anything."

"Both Jackie and Maria are missing. We have the FBI, and anybody else we can find, out looking for them. It appears from some information we have that they were both kidnapped." He stopped for a moment as he heard Corey take in a deep breath of surprise. "We don't know where they are and I think you need to get back here as soon as possible. Can you make it?"

"Sure. I'll make some fast arrangements and be there tomorrow. What can you tell me right now?"

"Not much. We're going to try and see the president, but, given your background on this, I'm sure he would welcome your presence and input. Because it is so sensitive, I don't want to talk much about it over the phone. We'll give you a rundown when you get here."

"Okay. But you sure have my attention. I'll let you know when I get there."

"Sounds good. See you tomorrow."

Monday—November 6
Arlington, Virginia

Ramiz left the safe house and headed up Interstate 95 toward Washington. He had no concerns about the prisoners. His two men were competent and he could get on with the next part of the plan. He had to make some deadlines in order to complete the notification to the White House. He arrived in Arlington and checked in to the Residence Inn, taking his small bag to the room. He showered and then sat down, powering up his laptop.

Calling up Microsoft Word, he began to compose the written message he had to send to the president. Timing was of the essence. He knew the written correspondence went first to the White House postal center to make sure it was safe before it was forwarded to the correspondence section in the executive office of the president. So it would take a while to get to its destination.

After it was sent, he had to catch a plane for the Mideast and the meeting they hope to schedule between the ayatollah and the president. Through the Iranians, an invitation would be sent in the next few days, through diplomatic channels, to request the president attend the meeting. His note would provide additional motivation to the president to attend.

He looked at the screen. It was always hard to work with a blank sheet. The first few words were difficult. Once started, however, it moved along fairly well. He worked and reworked the letter many times over the course of the next three hours. He composed. Then he stepped away for a few moments, then back to it. He repeated this process several times and finally had the missive the way he wanted it. After finalizing it, he went down to the lobby and grabbed an apple off the counter. He went over to a chair, sat down, and ate the apple, thinking. Not quite right. He felt he needed to be more specific and blunt. He went back up to his room and did some rewriting until he was, again, satisfied.

He moved the file to a flash drive and went downstairs. Inquiring at the desk, he was told where the business center was located. No one was in the center. He took out a pair of surgeon's gloves and put them on. He placed the flash drive in the hotel computer and pulled up the file. Then he printed it out. He took the printed version, took an envelope from the computer desk supplies, and placed the letter into it. He took a self-adhesive stamp and placed it on the envelope, still with gloved hands. Then he addressed it to the White House. In the return area of the envelope, he simply put "New Persia" and the comment "Open Immediately—President's Eyes Only." He knew that would not happen, but it made him feel better. He then went for a short walk, found a mailbox, and dropped it in. All the while wearing the gloves. Once he had dropped the letter in the mailbox, he took off the gloves and threw them in a nearby dumpster.

Smiling, he went back to the hotel, said his evening prayers, and went to bed for a night of rest. He had a plane to catch in the morning, and it would be a long flight to Bahrain.

Tuesday—November 7
Washington, D.C.—The White House

The next day, at the White House postal facility, Ramiz's note was scanned for any harmful substances and checked for potential bomb materials. Neither were found, and the letter was sent over to the president's correspondence center. It was opened by one of the clerks who worked in that center. After reading through it, the shocked clerk sent it through her supervisor, who, in turn, passed it on to the chief of staff's office. The staff there quickly passed it along to Jack Harrison. Curious about the front of the envelope, Jack read:

Dear Mr. President,

This note is to request your adherence to our request, which you will receive in a day or so, for a meeting to be held in Bahrain. The meeting will be between you and Ayatollah Sarhardi of the New Persia movement. We wish to re-emphasize our desire to reduce the world's consumption rate of oil and transfer the energy requirements to other environmentally sound methods.

As you know by now, the ayatollah has escaped your biased judicial system and is, once again, actively leading our movement. His whereabouts will remain a secret, since we are sure you will pursue him.

As an incentive for you to accede to this request, we are holding two of your immediate staff at an undisclosed location. Ms. Jackie Conover and Ms. Maria Aragon are fine and being treated well. They are, however, captives in your own country. Upon satisfactory

Elusive Quarry

completion of the meeting, they will be returned to their duties. Please do not attempt to locate them; it cannot be done.

To assure their release, simply attend the meeting and agree to the demands put forth by the ayatollah before the UN General Assembly some time back. We will be watching for your response and actions.

The letter was unsigned. Jack read through it several times to make sure he was reading it correctly. He had read it correctly the first time. Coercion and blackmail? They were holding these two people, with an implied threat, so the president would go along with their plans. He thought about it for a few moments and then got up, slowly walked the short distance to the Oval Office, and showed the letter to the president. He stood by quietly as the president read it several times. The president then set the letter gently down on his desk and got up. He went over to the window and looked out at the day.

He turned around. "Jack. What do you make of it?"

"I think it is pretty well self-explanatory. They've got Jackie and Maria and are threatening to do them harm if we don't give in to their demands. They don't come out and say that, but given the circumstances, it is certainly implied in the note."

The president nodded. He waved his hand in dismissal. "Jack. Two people. In the larger sense of the world, they really mean nothing. But this outfit has decided to strike home. And that's the reason for the note. They not only want me to attend this so-called meeting, but I have to agree to what they want. And I can't do that."

Jack stood there, arms across his chest, just listening to the president thinking out loud.

The president stopped. He looked at Jack for a moment. He turned, walked over to his desk, and slammed his fist down on it. "Damn it," he said. He hesitated for just a moment and the said to Jack, "Okay. I'll go to this meeting whenever we get the actual invite. But I'll be damned if I'll agree to their demands. Their methods are ridiculous. I think we need to put a full-court press on finding Jackie and Maria. We need to take the teeth out of their threat."

"Sir. We already have a full effort going by the FBI and the Virginia state police. There just isn't much out there. These guys weren't stupid. It won't be easy, but we do already have, as you put it, a full-court press on it."

"Okay, Jack. I'm just so pissed off I can't see straight. This pissant outfit is driving me nuts, and I really don't like it. We'll go. And then maybe we can figure out a way to finish this off permanently."

237

"Yes, sir. As soon as we get the invitation for the meeting, we'll set up the trip. Sorry about the bad news, but I thought you needed to know quickly."

"Thanks, Jack. Sorry I blew my stack."

Jack nodded then retreated and went back to work. The president just stood there for several moments muttering to himself. He walked over to his desk and called down to the situation room and asked for Vice President Swanson.

Milt Swanson got on the phone right away. He said, "Nothing yet, sir. We're still chasing that Virginia plate on Jackie and we checked for cameras where Maria's car was found. Nothing there either."

"Thanks, Milt. Appreciate the update." The president hesitated just a moment and then said, "Are Ryan McKenzie and friends down there?"

"Yes, sir. They're here."

"Ask them to come up. I want to talk to them."

"Yes, sir."

A few minutes later, Ryan, Dave, and Jasper were escorted by Jack into the Oval Office. Corey had just arrived from his overseas flight, and joined them.

Ryan, Jasper, Dave, Corey, and the president all shook hands around as they took places in the Oval Office. Jack Harrison joined them.

The president started, "Well, Ryan, this hasn't turned out to be quite the meeting I intended. We were going to discuss what you and your people might be able to do to help us find and remove the New Persia leadership. But now, we have a new wrinkle."

Ryan asked, "Do we have any progress at all in finding Jackie and Maria?"

The president shook his head and responded, "Not really. The FBI and the Virginia authorities have been able to narrow down the search for the white van that was used to kidnap Jackie. There are fifteen white vans with those same last digits in Virginia. They are very common. They have been able to rule out fourteen of them and are trying to find the last one. But without much luck. It turns out that the registration was falsified and there is no such address in Virginia. So they have an all-points bulletin out for it, but no luck so far. For all we know it is hidden back in the mountains somewhere, or junked. Other than that, there isn't really anything."

Ryan nodded.

The president continued, "The blood found at Jackie's parking spot matches her type, and the video footage pretty well clinches it. But where they took her is anybody's guess."

Corey asked, "I just found out about Maria disappearing when Ryan called. How about any progress on Maria?"

The president turned to Corey and just shook his head. "It's awfully early in this thing, but so far there's just nothing there. We're all stumped."

The president turned to Ryan and said, "We were going to meet to discuss what you might be able to do to help us eliminate the New Persia group. While we have these other concerns, I'd still like to hear what you think."

Ryan said, "We think, if we can get the information, that the ayatollah and his senior people are most vulnerable when they are moving around. If we can determine when and where they are moving, maybe we could intercept them. That is, capture them or, if necessary, kill them." He stopped as the president was absorbing the ideas. Then he continued, "We also think that, since we have some experience in that area, it might be worthwhile to go over there and snoop around a bit. There might be something we can pick up on as to where they are and what they are up to. Some of the people loading their supplies are locals, and they might be bribed or paid to provide some information."

"So you're suggesting that we determine when they are moving and intercept them on the ground? In theory that sounds good, but we would be in foreign territory, and the governments may look unkindly on us doing that."

"Yes, sir. That's true. And that's why three or four civilians would be involved"—he waved around at Jasper, Dave, and Corey— "so there wouldn't be any form of responsibility back to your administration. And there wouldn't be any military actions either. Just clandestine captures and return to the U.S."

The president thought for a moment and then said, "I'd have to think about this a bit. We have these kidnappings to consider, and they may use them as leverage to not only get us to reduce our oil usage, but also stop chasing them all over the world. They are already using them as leverage to get me to attend this meeting they want so badly, and it sure makes sense that they won't stop there."

Ryan said, "Sir. I need your help. This has become personal for me, and even more so now that Jackie and Maria have disappeared. They have destroyed my marina, killed two of my friends, and tried to kill me several times. They have to be stopped … permanently."

239

Everyone in the room was nodding at these comments ... including the president. He said, "I have another meeting in a few minutes and I need to prepare for it. Ryan, you make a lot of good sense, and I'll take your comments into consideration for now."

The president then stood up, they all shook hands, and Ryan's group left.

Jack remained in the office with the president. "What meeting do you have coming up? There's nothing for the next two hours ... it was reading catch-up time for you."

"Yeah. I know. I just had to break it off and get some thinking done. Ryan's suggestions do make some sense, but he is getting too close to the action. I'm worried that he might make a mistake."

Jack shrugged and said, "Got it." Then he left the office.

Ryan, Corey, Jasper, and Dave returned to the situation room, found a corner, and sat down. All of them were somewhat discouraged by the president's reaction. He obviously didn't want to move yet.

Ryan said, "Well, that didn't turn out to be much. And the administration seems to be stymied on where Jackie and Maria are. Corey, this hasn't turned out to be quite what we expected when I asked you to join us." He looked at his friends. "Anybody got any suggestions?"

All he got was shaking heads.

Wednesday—November 8
Washington, D.C.

Jack Harrison entered the Oval Office for the morning discussion. Mark and Mike were also there this morning, since Jack had mentioned they would be discussing New Persia for a bit.

They all sat down around the center table. The president looked at Jack as Jack was looking at notes. Jack started, "By now you all know from the news that New Persia has struck again. This time they hit three refinery and storage locations. Two in France and one in the UK. Notes from New Persia were received by the governments claiming responsibility for the attacks."

Mike interrupted, "Jack, on the news this morning, New Persia also said that the European nations, as part of the western world, needed to meet the demands. They weren't just after us to reduce oil use; they want the Europeans to meet their demand also."

Jack said, "That's right. We're seeing a broadening of New Persia's efforts. They apparently used the same tactics and methodologies for these attacks that they used in Long Beach."

Mark added, "Yes they did. From our sources they hit at night and it was a ship-based attack. Then they hit with some mortars. The Greenergy storage at Immingham in England, and the Port-Jerome Refinery and Saint-Nazaire complexes in France were all hit within the past forty-eight hours. Lots of damage and several killed."

The president said, "So they are increasing their activities. Is this the same ship we saw in the gulf and on our West Coast?"

Mark nodded. "Yes, it appears so. The unique sailing vessel was seen at all three locations. It has moved on now ... we have it spotted ... and is eastbound through the Mediterranean. Probably heading back to Socotra."

"So now we have, potentially, at least, some more friends in our same boat."

Both Mark and Mike agreed. Jack said, "Okay. That was all we have so far." And he moved on to other issues. The U.S. now had serious company against this terrorist organization.

Friday—November 10
Washington, D.C.

Through diplomatic channels, a request came from the Iranian government. The Iranians were functioning as the go-between for the ayatollah, and he wanted to have a discussion with President Martinez on a face-to-face basis. But it would have to be in a neutral area, and New Persia suggested the country of Bahrain. Would the president consider a private one-on-one with the ayatollah?

Because it was a request through diplomatic channels, Kenton Marshal was informed of the message. He thought it a bit odd, but forwarded the request on to Jack Harrison for consideration. Jack thought about it and quickly passed it on as part of his informal morning discussion with the president.

The president called an emergency meeting of several of his military leaders. General Newt Foley, Admiral Nelson, General Fairchild, Jack Harrison, and Admiral Watkins were present, along with Miriam Blacock.

The president began, "We have received a note, through State, from the ayatollah requesting a meeting in Bahrain. He says he has knowledge of the whereabouts of Jackie and Maria. So this is really a threat for us." He stopped for a moment. "Show up or else."

The president went on to describe what had been happening, and that both Jackie and Maria had disappeared without a trace. He hoped to get Jackie and Maria back, but had his doubts. The ayatollah wouldn't just roll over with that information. The ayatollah was, from the U.S. perspective, an international criminal who had escaped the U.S. and was thus at large. That was why the ayatollah picked a neutral country for the meeting. The president then outlined what he wanted to do. When they all left, they had a good program outlined and ready to initiate. The meeting was proposed by the ayatollah for next Tuesday, November 14. There was just barely enough time to get resources together to accomplish the president's goals.

Monday—November 13
Bahrain

The ayatollah arrived at Bahrain International Airport with several of his assistants. Khatib and Ramiz were present, along with several other lower-level staff personnel. This would be a very important meeting, and they wanted to take advantage of every opportunity. It had taken a lot of planning to reach this point, and the ayatollah, usually confident and very sure of himself, felt a bit overwhelmed.

They had convinced the U.S. president to attend, but it had to be done with coercion, and that had not gone over very well with the infidel Americans. The capture and retention of two of the president's staff had been the motivating factor for his attendance.

They moved on to the hotel facilities and several staffers made sure they were checked in and comfortable. The ayatollah and his party, after the several-hour airplane trip, were slightly tired, and decided to rest before the evening hours.

After dinner and evening prayers, they gathered in one of the conference rooms of the hotel and went over the agenda for the next day's events. Khatib, who had set up the conference with the assistance of Ramiz, went over some of the details and what they hoped to accomplish. The ayatollah had heard all of this before, and paid polite attention. He was more worried about how the Americans might react and what they might do after the conference was over. He was no fool. They were playing with the big boys of the world, and there could be some surprises.

242

Elusive Quarry

The blue and white VC-25A aircraft, a specially configured Boeing 747-200, code-named Air Force One, came in over the Persian Gulf and landed softly at Bahrain International Airport. President Martinez was irritable and did not really want to be there. But with the recent refinery attacks, the capture of two of his staff, the new situation in Europe, and the threat of more of the same, he felt he had no choice. The FBI, so far, had not been able to track down the location of the safe house that held Jackie and Maria. They had tracked down the van license but had not found the actual van as yet. With the threat on the lives of his people, President Martinez had to play along with this charade until the FBI could come up with something. Once they had their people back, he intended to eliminate this risk to the world economic order—permanently. He looked out at a small crowd of welcoming people at the terminal. He took another sip of coffee and waited as the airplane taxied into position.

As he departed the aircraft for the hotel, he shook hands with well-wishers and moved on quickly to his limousine.

Tuesday—November 14
Bahrain

The next morning, feeling a bit of jet lag, the president, Jack Harrison, and Andy Strasner, who had come along in case something broke that the FBI could work with, had breakfast in the presidential suite and sat down for a few moments of discussion. After they reviewed the agenda again and discussed it briefly, they decided to wait and see what happened in the meeting. Other than to listen to the ayatollah's position again, they weren't sure what to expect.

Chapter Forty-Three

Monday, November 13/Tuesday, November 14
North Carolina—Safe House

Ramiz had been gone for several days. Jackie had now been held captive for twelve days. The only way Jackie and Maria could roughly tell time was when they were let out to go to the bathroom. They could look out windows and see daylight or darkness. The window in the bathroom had also been covered over by plywood so they couldn't escape. For Jackie it was certainly easier now that Maria was there, but they were both worried about how long they would be kept and what would actually happen to them. They both knew that kidnap victims frequently did not survive, especially in high-profile cases like this was turning into. They were both sure that help would not arrive. There just weren't any clues left behind, and they both knew that.

They needed to escape, and even if it was a long way to civilization, as Kasim had said, it would be better than this, and they probably could get some help. But how? They were kept in the locked bedroom all day and night and only let out to go to the bathroom. They had looked around the room multiple times, trying to figure a way out, but hadn't found anything yet. The two men spelled each other for sleep and seemed to be pretty alert when they were let out. They were delivered food twice every day. They could hear the vehicle come and go as Kasim and Carlos made food and supply runs. One of their captors stayed behind all the time to make sure there wasn't an escape. But they were getting tired of hamburgers and chicken.

The men, at Ramiz's emphasized word, were not pleasant, but at least they were attentive. When they asked for something, many times they were given it, especially the food. Although it was fast food.

The days were very boring, and they spent a good portion of them sleeping as best they could. Jackie, really angry about the situation, was racking her brain to figure out how to get out of this mess. She was sure the president and Ryan were doing everything they could to find them. But she also knew that there would be very little to go on. The kidnapping was quite devoid of clues. She had just been grabbed and hauled off. Maria had also been grabbed, with no warning or clues left behind.

Maria was scared and frightened of the situation. She could sleep, but just barely. And she did not have the mental toughness that Jackie had, nor did she have the training Jackie had through her Marine Corps service. Jackie watched her sleep and realized that whatever she did, Maria would have to come along with her. It would be harder that way, but if she could figure out a way to escape, Maria had to come. She couldn't be left behind.

As she was thinking of her various options, most of which wouldn't work, Jackie began to realize that she was thinking like a marine again. Not defeated, not morose, not dejected. She was upbeat and would figure a way out. The realization was a stimulant in its own right. A slight smile formed. It would take some time, perhaps, but her training was kicking in and she would beat the problem.

In the semidarkness of the room, lit only by one small light bulb, Jackie sat on the floor and tried to think it all over again. It wasn't easy, because she kept coming to the same old answers and conclusions, and that led her nowhere. There had to be a way of getting out of there. She ran several scenarios through her mind. There was no way of getting out through the windows; the plywood panels were screwed into the outside walls. The deadbolt lock was on the outside of their door and they couldn't get to it. The door had been modified to swing outward so she couldn't get to the hinges. It was solid. If they tried to get through the drywall on an interior wall, they would make too much noise and their guards would hear it. And even if they got out of the room, then what? Kasim and Carlos would be on them in an instant. And they were armed.

She sat.

Maria slept.

Jackie looked around again and again. No way through the roof. The small closet was empty, and they had even taken the clothes rod out so they couldn't use it for anything.

Her brain began to hurt as she was thinking. Obsessed with escape. She was determined to find a way. The president and Ryan wouldn't be able to help much. There just wasn't any way that they could locate the two of them in this hidden safe house, and, to make it even more difficult, she didn't know where they were.

After days and hours of thinking, slowly, an idea formed in her mind. They could just walk out of there if everything went their way. They would have to time it right. She woke Maria and explained what she had in mind. Maria was ready for anything at that point.

245

She understood and readily agreed to do what Jackie was suggesting.

At the next bathroom break, Jackie asked Carlos for a cup of hot tea for each of them. He agreed but said they would have to wait until they made another food run to get the tea. Jackie murmured, "Okay."

A short while later, they heard the vehicle start and leave. After a half-hour or so, it was back, and Carlos brought them some hot tea in Styrofoam cups. He set them down in the room and backed out, locking the door as he went. Jackie noticed, through the door, that there was daylight in the room. And she noticed the Styrofoam cup. She smiled and thought, *No glass or something that could be used as a weapon.* But they enjoyed the tea. Jackie also enjoyed knowing that there was something nearby. The vehicle had only been gone about a half-hour, and that was a round trip. Information was key.

While they were enjoying their tea, Jackie went over to the bed, lifted the mattress, and looked at the supports. It was a bit old-fashioned and had five wooden slats supporting the mattress. There were no box springs. That explained the sagging they had noticed. She hefted one of the boards. It was solid, about an inch by three inches, and about three feet long—probably pine. And dusty. It hadn't been moved in a long time.

The idea was coming together. Now they had to wait until they heard the vehicle depart again. Several hours later, they heard the van start. Then it stopped and was shut down. They looked at each other and wondered. Nothing happened, and a few minutes later it started up again. They heard it leaving on the gravel driveway. Showtime.

They let just a minute go by and yelled for Carlos. He came to the door and they each asked for another cup of tea, but make it really hot this time. He grunted, but went into the kitchen and made them their tea. Two Styrofoam cups. Through the door he told them to back up from the door. They did, and he opened the door and brought the cups in, setting them on the bed while they watched with feigned mild interest. He rose up and they reached for the tea as he was backing out. They both threw the steaming tea into his face and chest at the same time. He screamed and grabbed at his face. Jackie grabbed one of the slats from where she had placed it behind the door, stepped in front of him, and brought the slat, edgewise, like a baseball bat, across his face at cheek level. There was a loud crack as his cheek fractured. Then she stepped back and brought her foot up hard into his crotch. With that, he was out. He collapsed to the floor, where she gave him another vicious kick in the balls. As she bent over him, she quietly said with a sneer, "That'll teach you to play around with my tits, you bastard." She quickly searched him and grabbed a small pistol and a spare magazine. Jackie left the bedroom, pulled the door shut behind her, slammed the deadbolt home, and trapped Carlos in the room. Maria had run to the main house door and quickly looked out. No one there. Jackie went into the kitchen, grabbed a few snack-type foods, and caught up with Maria. They quickly headed out the front door and down the gravel driveway. It had been, perhaps, ten minutes. After several minutes of walking, and being very alert to the possible return of Kasim, they reached a lonely paved county road. No traffic whatsoever. Which way to go?

Jackie headed into the nearby woods. Maria joined her. And they waited. It was apparently very late afternoon or early evening. The sun was warm and the air moist with the nearby fields. They only had to wait for ten minutes or so before the white van came down the road from the left and turned into the driveway. Help would be that way, where he came from.

They quickly headed down the road, backtracking on where the van had come from. Jackie allowed another ten minutes and then they hit the woods again. A few minutes later, the van came barreling out of the driveway and headed down the road in their direction. They watched it go past and then started to walk in the same direction, but staying in the woods.

After several more minutes, they heard the van coming back, only this time it was going very slowly. The driver was looking at both sides of the road, trying to look into the woods for them. He was alone. They crouched down behind bushes and shrubbery until he had gone past. He didn't see them in all the clutter of the woods. They got up again and continued on. He was determined. They could hear the van coming again. Again, they ducked down.

But Maria wasn't fast enough. Kasim saw her light-colored dress in the shrubbery. Jackie was several paces in front of Maria and behind another group of shrubs and small trees. He screeched to a stop and began the chase. Maria bolted out of her cover crying and yelling. He fired at her but missed. He fired again and she went down. He ran up to her and rolled her over with his foot. He yelled at her, "Where's the other bitch?"

In the now semidarkness of the woods, Jackie came up behind him using all the stealth skills she had and quietly said, "Freeze." Still standing over the unconscious Maria, he didn't move at first. He couldn't believe this was happening. His partner was severely burned and had a broken cheekbone, and now he was at risk. No woman was going to get the best of him. He whipped around and dove as he went, his gun coming around with him and rising as he fell. Jackie, anticipating some form of move, tracked him from five feet away. Her eight years in the Marines and the training she had received came together at this moment. There was no hesitation.

There was a small popping sound and two holes appeared in Kasim's head. One just above his right ear and the other in his forehead as he fell. He was dead before he hit the ground, and Jackie was still alive, unhurt.

She bent down over Maria. Maria was unconscious and bleeding from a bullet wound in the shoulder. Jackie quickly made a small bandage out of the tail of her shirt and bound up the wound as best she could. She got the bleeding stopped, but Maria was still unconscious. She checked on Kasim, just to make sure, and by the time she looked back at Maria, Maria was beginning to come around. They waited a few moments and let Maria recover a bit. Then Jackie went back to the road and found the van still idling at the side of the road. She looked in the back to make sure it was empty and went to gather up Maria. Maria was just able to walk with help, and they headed out to the van.

They got in and Jackie headed in the direction they had been going. After just a few minutes, there was a crossroad and a Conoco station. She pulled in and asked where the nearest hospital was. Given directions to one about ten miles down the same road she had been on, she took off as fast as she dared, figuring that by the time an ambulance could get to her, she could have Maria at the hospital. Maria was getting groggy again and not responding the way she should. Jackie pulled into the emergency entrance and ran for help. Emergency personnel quickly came out and took Maria into the hospital for treatment and eventual surgery.

While Maria was being initially treated, Jackie went into a waiting room and sat down to collect her thoughts. It was now dark outside and, her immediate emergency being tended to, she walked over to a free coffee service and poured herself a cup. Then she sat down again. She realized quickly that they were safe and that she needed to notify the president's office and Ryan. She went to the counter and was directed to a wall phone, where she made a call to the White House switchboard. The president was overseas, so she notified the operator that she and Maria had escaped. She gave the operator a brief rundown on Maria's status and their location, and asked that the information be forwarded to the president.

Then she hung up and dialed Ryan's cell phone.

"Hello," said Ryan.

"Hi."

"Oh my God. Where are you and are you okay?" he asked quickly.

"I'm okay but Maria's in surgery for a shoulder wound. I think she will be all right in a few days."

"She was shot?" he asked incredulously.

"Yes. But the shooter is no longer a threat. I took care of that."

"Holy mackerel. Where are you? We've been turning the Virginia counties upside down looking for you."

"I'm at Vidant Hospital in Greenville, North Carolina."

"It'll take me about five hours or so to get there, but I'm on my way. I'm in Washington and will be driving with Corey and Jasper. You're sure you're okay now?"

"Yes, I'm sure. Hopefully, by the time you get here, Maria will be out of surgery and we'll know more then."

"Whew. I'm still shaking from some of this. You'll have to fill us in when we get there. See you soon."

"Bye. And I love you."

"Love you too. Bye."

Nearly two hours went by, and, as she was sitting there, two police officers came in and walked up to her. She was quite disheveled and badly needed a shower, but didn't care. She was finally free. She looked up as they approached.

"Are you the lady who brought"—he quickly looked at his notes—"Ms. Aragon into the hospital?"

"Yes, sir, I am," she responded.

"We get a call anytime there is a gunshot wound brought in to the hospital. I'm Sergeant Pete Lancaster and this is my partner George Harris. Will you please tell me who you are and what happened?"

"Well, my name is Jackie Conover. And there is a bit to tell."

"Wait a minute," Pete said with a startled look on his face. His partner George had also perked up and was paying a lot of attention to her. "You said Jackie Conover?"

"Yes, sir. Why?"

"Because there is a statewide manhunt for you and has been for over a week now. We've had several FBI bulletins to be on the lookout for you and a white van. Is Ms. Aragon the other person who was kidnapped?"

"Yes, sir. She is."

"Excuse me for a minute." Pete went off to the side to make a short radio call to his dispatch then came back. "Okay. You're safe now. Tell us what happened."

Jackie then related the whole story and how they escaped. She didn't let anything go by, including the shooting of Kasim in the woods. And then getting into the van and finding the hospital.

"I think I know the abandoned house you're referring to," said Pete. He made another radio call and dispatch responded with a "roger." They sent another police cruiser to the scene. Pete then said, "We'll need you to make a statement when you feel up to it. But the sooner the better. Do you still have the gun you took from them?"

"Yes. It's in the van parked under the entrance here."

"We'll get it and have the van gone over by our techs."

They were interrupted by a nurse, dressed in surgical scrubs, who came by and said to Jackie and the officers, "Ms. Aragon is out of surgery and is being moved to the third-floor trauma unit. She is still under sedation. A doctor will be by shortly to see you."

Jackie nodded and said, "Thanks. Will she be all right?"

"I'd prefer the doctor answer your questions," responded the nurse. Jackie nodded as the surgical nurse turned and walked away.

Pete said, "Let's go through all of this one more time so I can be sure I have the story right." George turned back from watching the nurse walk away.

Jackie smiled at his motion then turned back to Pete. "Okay. I know it all sounds incredible, but I'm telling you the truth." And then she proceeded to tell him the story again, from the time she was grabbed in her garage until they got to the hospital. He nodded, made some notes, and asked a few questions as she was relating the story again.

She was nearly finished when Pete received a radio call. He stepped to the side and held his ear to hear better. Dispatch was calling. Even with the late hour, the other cruiser had found the dead man in the woods, and gone to the house and found the badly burned second man, still curled up on the floor. They had found the rooms Jackie had mentioned. The evidence techs were on their way to the house and the burned man was being transported to the hospital under police guard.

Pete stood off to the side for a moment and collected his thoughts. What a time these two women must have had. It was just past midnight and it was now three hours since he had received the initial call of a shooting victim at the hospital. He had a lot of paperwork to fill out at the station. It sounded, at least initially, like Jackie's story would hold up.

Chapter Forty-Four

Tuesday—November 14
Bahrain

The meeting in one of the smaller conference rooms began at 10:00 a.m. with a few handshakes with the Bahrainis and the introduction of everyone in the room. They were cool introductions, since the president and his staff refused to shake hands with the ayatollah and his henchmen. The president began, "Ayatollah Sarhardi, you asked for this meeting, so why don't you start."

"Thank you, Mr. President. I would like to think that we can come to some form of accommodation. I do not wish to continue with things as they have recently occurred. The demands I outlined and spoke of during my address to the UN a little over a year ago have not been met. There have not even been reasonable attempts to meet them. You are the leader of the western world and thus must lead the way in complying with those demands. The world's future is at stake and our children deserve to have a life like our own. I asked for this meeting so I could, once again, but personally this time, ask for your cooperation. Please. Take actions to reduce your use of oil and make the shift to other energy resources. In diplomatic channels we need to work together and not have this constant bitterness and disconnected energy goals." He hesitated a moment to take a measure of what he was saying.

The president and all his advisors were watching him with implacable expressions on their faces. He felt he wasn't making the mark he had hoped for. Khatib leaned over and said, "I don't think they are accepting what you are saying. You may wish to become more energetic in your approach to them." The ayatollah nodded and looked at his hands on the table in front of him. He took a swallow of water from the glass.

He continued, "We need to, across the globe, reduce the use of oil." His voice rising, he continued, "We cannot continue to use it so wastefully when there are other options. Don't you see that? Are you so in the pockets of the oil industry that you can't act?"

The president looked back at the ayatollah. He looked at his various advisors. He held up his hand in front of the ayatollah. The ayatollah stopped his diatribe.

The president said, "Is it necessary to get personal, Abdul?" There was a palpable shock through the room as the president used the ayatollah's name. "You have killed people, including some members of my staff—I'm referring to you shooting down Secretary Billings' plane over the Gulf of Mexico—and attempted to kill others. All to push your agenda of extending oil reserves. As stated, I find your goals are quite unreasonable—however, I would support them if they were reasonable and made sense in our modern world. Your methods of achieving them are contrary to common sense and lead to resistance. Murderous actions cannot he condoned. You are a murderer and a criminal and need to be stopped. You were found guilty of multiple charges and condemned to spend the rest of your life in our prison system. Your breakout killed several people. The only reason I am here is to see what you have to say and to ask for the return of my kidnapped and imprisoned people." He leaned forward on the table and continued, "I do not intend to follow any of your demands and will, in fact, fight you until you are completely ineffective in the world arena. I am sorry to be so blunt in my comments, but you leave little choice. Your unwillingness to negotiate your demands will lead to your ultimate destruction."

The ayatollah, unused to the blunt actions and words of these infidels, could not believe his ears. They had used his first name in disrespect, and were refusing to do as he required. The lesson had still not taken effect. He stared at the president and fought the urge to physically strike out.

The president continued, "Now, I want to know where Jackie Conover and Maria Aragon are. You have taken them captive to get my attention. Well, you got my attention. They are innocent bystanders and I insist they be released and returned to us." Then he stared hard at Ramiz, Khatib, and back to the ayatollah as he said very emphatically, "Unharmed. Now, where are they?"

Jack Harrison watched with intense interest as the question was asked. He noticed that Ramiz looked over at Khatib with a knowing look. It was casual, but there.

The ayatollah responded with venom in his voice, "You have insulted me by speaking to me by my first name. You have accused me of atrocities that I didn't commit and you tried to imprison me in your supermax facilities. Of course I broke away. I wasn't about to spend the rest of my life rotting in your prison. I will never go back there; death would be better than that. And it is regrettable about the loss of human life, but that is the way of the world today." He looked around the room and then back at the president. "As for the people you are looking for, they will remain where they are. They are being well cared for. Until I decide otherwise."

The president looked around also. Then back at the ayatollah. "I don't know what you intend to accomplish by holding these people as hostages—and that's what they are, hostages—but it will not work. Coercion and threats are not the way to get what you want. Peaceful negotiations are the way to do that, and you are obviously not willing to negotiate."

The ayatollah looked at him as if he were studying a stone. Curious but unmoving. "No. We will not negotiate. You will do as we demand or further sanctions of various natures will be forthcoming. It is not an idle threat that we make. There are several other courses we can pursue if you do not comply. And ... we will pursue them."

Knowing what the ayatollah had accomplished in the past, these were, indeed, not idle threats. They needed to be taken seriously. The president leaned back in his chair. He said, "So you are threatening to take more actions against us?"

The ayatollah, taking his cue from the president's posture, also leaned back in his chair and responded, "Oh, that remains to be seen. I am merely saying what could happen, not what will happen. None of us can predict the future and what it may hold."

The president looked back with skepticism as he heard the words. He turned to Jack and Andy and whispered, "Do you see any sense in continuing this nonsense? He's not going to tell us where they are and is just threatening again."

Jack nodded slightly and whispered back, "I think we need to get the FBI to double their efforts and find Jackie and Maria. I think we also should watch our backs as we leave. I don't like the sound of his talk."

Andy looked at Jack and then over to the president. "We have already pulled out all the stops. I'm not sure that there is anything more we can do. I've got all our resources primed and supporting the effort now."

The president shrugged and softly said, "I agree. With both of you."

The president, Jack, and Andy looked back across the table. The ayatollah was conversing quietly with Khatib and Ramiz. It was the first time they had actually seen Ramiz, and the accompanying Secret Service personnel were watching him closely. They were also taking notes to see what they could find out about him. More than one lapel camera was used. Ramiz would not be a puzzle for much longer.

A few moments later, the ayatollah turned back to the table. "I think this meeting has had one positive benefit, that being that we now understand where each stands. I also think that this meeting should now be considered complete. I will take my leave. Have a pleasant journey back to the United States." He stood up abruptly as the president and his staff stood up, and he retreated from the room. No handshakes and no photos. The meeting, from the ayatollah's viewpoint, was a failure and did not need to continue. Interestingly, the president had the same view.

It was now close to noon as the meeting finished. The ayatollah and his party had left. Jack discussed the situation with the hotel manager and arranged to have food prepared for the president and staff only. The ayatollah and his staff would not be present during the meal. The Secret Service checked the kitchen and two agents watched as the food was prepared. Thirty minutes later, the food was served to the U.S. delegation and several senior Bahrainis present for the conference.

The ayatollah called Khatib and Ramiz into a hallway conversation right after he departed the meeting. He looked at Ramiz. "Are we ready to respond?"
"Yes, sir. All is ready."
"Good. Implement the backup plan."
Khatib looked worried. But it was the ayatollah's call.

The president called Jack over during their meal. They were having a glass of ice water. The president asked, "Is Spyglass operating?"
Jack looked around to make sure no one was listening. He moved with the president into a corner of the room and said, "Yes, sir. We have them fully operational and standing by to track."
"Good. Make sure they get the right aircraft when he leaves. He might try some form of sleight of hand. Or, if they take multiple planes, we need to track them all."
"Will do. They'll actually watch as he boards the aircraft for wherever he's going. And we can track multiple aircraft with no problem. It's very similar to our air traffic control system. They leave before we do, so we will know if Spyglass got them before we leave here."

Chapter Forty-Five

Tuesday—November 14
North Carolina

Ryan, Corey, Dave, and Jasper made good time and arrived just after 2:00 a.m., five hours after Ryan had gotten Jackie's call. They pulled into the hospital parking lot and ran for the emergency room. There they were directed to the waiting room, where Jackie was just finishing up her second time through with the police officers. Ryan spotted her, and rushed up and held her tight. His eyes moistened a bit and he could feel the tears on his neck as she wept.

Corey, Dave, and Jasper introduced themselves to Pete and George as they all stepped back for a moment. A man dressed in surgical scrubs approached Jackie and said, "Are you Ms. Conover?"

Jackie broke from Ryan, brushed her eyes, and said, "Yes, I am."

He said, "I'm Dr. Palmer, the surgeon who just worked on Ms. Aragon. She was lucky. The bullet went into her shoulder, missed any major arteries, and tore up her muscles a bit. We kept the bullet for the police, as is standard procedure. Ms. Aragon is resting now and is sedated for about the next two hours. You can see her after she wakes up. She will have a very sore shoulder and some of the damage was to her arm muscles. There will be a period of rehab needed for her to get full use of her arm, but I would expect her to be just fine in a few months. Are there any questions?"

"Where is she now?"

"She's on the third floor sedated and resting. She will be out for several more hours. I'd suggest you get some rest until she wakes up. You look like you could use it." He smiled at her and then excused himself.

Pete said, "Well, I've got to get going. Lots to do. Can I assume you could come to the station later today and give us a formal statement?"

Jackie quickly looked at Ryan and he nodded just slightly. She responded, "Yes. I can do that."

"Fine. We'll see you this afternoon, then."

He said to Ryan, "You fellows need directions to a hotel?"

"Yes, we do."

He told them how to find a Residence Inn, then he folded up his notebook and, with George in tow, left the hospital emergency room. They watched as the two officers went out to the van and looked around it a bit. They made another radio call and sat down to wait for an evidence tech to show up. The van was not to be touched.

Ryan held Jackie for another few moments. Jasper, Dave, and Corey all came over and gave her a hug also. She was so relieved.

Ryan said, "Well, I think the five of us need to find a hotel and make arrangements for the rest of the night." He looked at Jackie and continued, "Let's get you some new clothes and you can get cleaned up. Then we can hear what happened."

Corey hesitated for a moment. "You guys go on ahead. I want to see Maria when she wakes up. Make arrangements for me and I'll catch up."

Jackie cocked her head to the side and said slowly, "Okay. We'll meet you back here in a couple of hours." As she looked at him, it dawned on her what was going on, and she hadn't had a clue.

Corey turned and went up to the third floor, located Maria's room, settled in a chair, and began a quiet vigil at her bedside.

They headed out of the hospital and got into the rental car Ryan was driving. After a few moments they found the hotel and were able to get checked in to four rooms. They went out to a local Walmart, the only large store that was open, and got Jackie some fresh clothing and went back to the hotel. Ryan, Dave, and Jasper had a drink at the bar just as it was closing down. Jackie went to the room to clean herself up and joined them afterward.

After two hours of discussions, they all returned to the hospital and found Maria's room without trouble. She was sitting up in bed, still a little woozy, holding hands with Corey. Corey looked around and said to have a seat. Maria had an IV in her arm and a heavy bandage across her chest and left shoulder. Jackie looked at her appraisingly, walked over, and gave her a very gentle hug. "How're you feeling?"

Maria said, "I've been better. I'll have to remember the next time to wear camouflage clothing. That was kind of foolish."

"Well, if you'll remember, we didn't have a lot of time and the wardrobe was limited to what we had on."

Jackie smiled and then, looking at Corey, said, "So what's going on here? Corey's showing a bit more than casual interest here." And she winked at Maria.

Corey laughed a bit and Maria blushed slightly. She said, "Well, ever since you introduced us several weeks ago, Corey and I have been seeing each other as regularly as we can, considering his job. But we haven't made it obvious." Looking at Corey, she continued, "I guess that part of it is over. It's pretty obvious now." She smiled at Jackie and Ryan. Jasper and Dave just stood and grinned.

"Yup. It's pretty obvious. Does the president know?" Jasper asked.

"Not yet. But I have a feeling he will soon. I think he will approve." And she smiled again. She began closing her eyes. Some of the sedation was still having its effect.

Jackie said, "Well, we'll get out of here and let you rest. We'll come back later today and visit again. I have the police matter to attend to, and we'll come over after that." But Maria had already fallen asleep.

They left after giving Corey instructions on finding the hotel. He thanked them and said he would be along soon.

They stopped at the nurses' station and asked how it was really going for Maria. The nurse said she was progressing well and would probably be able to leave in a few days. She just needed to rest and they were going to begin some rehab on her tomorrow. Jackie thanked the nurse and they left.

Jackie said, "Could we stop somewhere and get some decent food and a drink? I could really use one."

Ryan, Dave, and Jasper all said "sure" at the same time and laughed a bit about it. The tension was letting up and they all felt it. They found a small all-night restaurant, were seated, and all ordered drinks. After a good meal and a second round of drinks, Jackie was looking tired, and they headed back to their rooms.

As they went through the lobby, they ran into Corey. "So, big boy. You've captured the heart of one of my best friends," Jackie commented with a smile as they found the bar. It was closed, but they were still able to get some shooters, wine, and Cokes at the registration desk. Then they briefly sat down in the lobby.

"Yeah," he said. "It works both ways for us. We really just hit it off from the beginning. I asked her out for drinks one evening and it hasn't stopped. She's actually quite a gal."

"Well. Best of luck to you both. That was quite a surprise, but I'm glad for you. And I'm sure the president will be pleased also."

Then they took their drinks and headed up to their rooms.

Ryan got undressed while Jackie continued sipping her wine. He took a drink of his bourbon and Coke. She stood up and removed her shirt and slacks. He came up behind her and reached around and turned her shoulders around to face him. She had tears in her eyes. She held on to him for several moments and then backed off slightly, still holding his arms and one hand still held her wine. "I thought of you nearly constantly. I knew you wouldn't have any idea where I was so it was up to me to get out. And then when Maria came, it got slightly more complicated. But we did it. And we're safe."

"Yes," he said, still holding her. "We didn't know for sure, but we were slowly narrowing it down. But I don't think we could ever have found that abandoned house. There just wasn't anything to trace to it."

"You were trying. And they were quite smart about how they did it. Fortunately, they didn't realize there were cameras in the garage. If they had covered the plates, you never would have had a clue." She kissed him softly then turned and put her wine down, and turned back to him. Putting her arms around his neck, she kissed him deeply, tongues exploring each other. He reached around behind her and released her bra, letting it fall to the floor. He cupped her breasts and rubbed gently on her nipples. She arched slightly and inhaled as he lavished his attention on her.

"You don't know how much I need you," she said. He reached for her slacks and pulled them down, leaving them in a pile of the floor. Then her panties. Then his own underwear ended up on the floor. He moaned and they fell to the bed in a mutually pleasurable heap. She was exhausted from the past day's activities, but not that exhausted.

The next half-hour finished her off, though, and she slept curled up against him in a loving embrace. He held her and could not help but quietly weep for her and what they both had gone through. She with the kidnap experience and he with the worry and sheer fright that he might not see her again.

Chapter Forty-Six

Tuesday—November 14
Bahrain—Early Afternoon

The ayatollah, with his immediate staff, left the conference hotel for the airport in an armored limo. Due to the importance of this mission, he had an Iranian Airlines Boeing 767 waiting for him. He, Khatib, Ramiz, and the rest of their staff all boarded the aircraft and were shown to their seats by a flight attendant. They were the only passengers on the aircraft, since it was on a temporary assignment from commercial duties.

Spyglass watched from overhead as the ayatollah's entourage boarded. From its position in orbit, the cameras digitally recorded the boarding and immediately sent the images, encrypted, to the monitoring station at Schriever AFB in Colorado. From there, a communication link had been established for Air Force One and the president could monitor, in real time, the 767 as it began its journey. On board Air Force One, a communication technician recorded the departure so the president, held up at the conference center for a side meeting with the Bahrainis, could later view the ayatollah's departure.

The 767 taxied out to the end of the runway for an immediate departure. The takeoff was smooth and the aircraft turned to a southbound course out over the Northern Arabian Sea. For the Americans, the 767's destination was unknown. Spyglass would track it in real time to see where it was going.

At 4:00 p.m. the president finished up several conversations with the Bahrainis and headed for Air Force One, parked at a secure side terminal at Bahrain International Airport and surrounded by ten armed Secret Service guards. The president, taking advantage of his presence in the Middle East, had two more meetings scheduled for the morning, and then they would begin the long trip home. He settled in, the steward providing him with a margarita as he sat down. They would spend the night on board, with American security on duty. It had been a very long day, and he was both frustrated and tired. Jack sat across from him and enjoyed an extra-strength gin and tonic. He too was tired. And tomorrow would be an early start with a 9:00 a.m. meeting.

A staffer with a wide smile came from the aircraft communication center and walked up to Jack and the president. "We just got word. It's just past four in the morning in North Carolina and both Jackie and Maria have escaped. Maria is in the hospital with a shoulder wound, but will be okay. Jackie is okay and Ryan and his friends are on the way to meet them. Apparently, Jackie killed one of the kidnappers and left the other one in pretty bad shape."

Both Jack and the president broke into broad grins, stood up quickly, and high-fived each other. The president excitedly exclaimed, "Yessss! Isn't that Jackie something? I wouldn't want to get on the wrong side of her." He hesitated, then added with grit in his voice, "The ayatollah just lost his teeth." They sat back down and both of them took a long drink while smiling.

A few hours later, through secure communications links with the Air Force 50th Space Wing at Schriever AFB, they learned that the ayatollah's aircraft had landed in Salalah, Oman. Several people got off, including the ayatollah, while the rest remained on board, and the aircraft then flew on to Socotra. The 50th was continuing to monitor both locations.

Wednesday—November 15
Bahrain

The meetings finished up just after 11:30 a.m. and the president returned to Air Force One. After going through the usual pomp and ceremony given for the departure of a head of state, he finally boarded the aircraft. As he boarded, he stopped and watched as a U.S. Air Force F-22 fighter began its takeoff roll. It would accompany them back to the U.S.

The Air Force One engines were started and all personnel on board were requested to fasten their seatbelts. The pilot spoke with the tower and requested clearance to taxi. They were cleared to the active runway for immediate departure. The huge Boeing rolled onto the active runway and came to a stop aligned with the centerline. A moment later the brakes were released, the copilot slowly advanced the throttles, and the aircraft began its takeoff roll. Smooth. A few bumps in the concrete as the four-hundred-ton aircraft lifted off. The pilot continued on a runway heading, gaining altitude, as the

F-22 came up on the right-hand side to begin the formation flight all the way to the U.S.

Abdul watched from his beater of a car as the blue and white aircraft took off. He saw a small fighter fly right over his position and join up with the president's aircraft. He ignored the fighter. Bringing up an ARPM, he aimed the camera on the right-wing outboard engine, and almost instantly he got a green light as the software identified and locked on the engine. He fired. The rocket blasted out of the launcher on its way to the target. He quickly grabbed another launcher and fired a second ARPM at the climbing aircraft.

Air Force One had all the technology available for countering threats. And its on-board radar immediately picked up the incoming missiles, setting off the cockpit alarm, automatically dispensing metallic chaff, and attempting to confuse the missile's navigation systems. The pilot, recognizing the obvious danger, immediately made a violent move to the left in an attempt to throw off the missile. He had been briefed on what had happened to the secretary of state's aircraft and was trying the same thing. He also quickly monitored the defensive system automated operation. The automated system deployed the 7.62 Minigun from the streamlined pod under the belly of the tail just under the auxiliary power unit. A shield of lead spat out of the Minigun as over two thousand rounds per minute spewed out at the first missile. The missile was tracked by the on-board radar and the Minigun fired in front of the incoming missile so it flew right into the airborne lead wall. The front of the missile was completely destroyed and the remainder fell harmlessly away.

The electronics quickly targeted the second missile, but this time couldn't react before it hit. The violent maneuver also didn't work. The missile, with its explosive warhead, bored into the right inboard engine and exploded. The engine came apart and pieces fell away from the aircraft or were contained by the shielding in the engine pod. The passengers were all jostled about as the flight crew struggled to maintain control of the aircraft. After a few moments of sheer terror, the pilots got the aircraft back under control. The left inboard engine was throttled back slightly to help balance the thrust, and they declared a mayday to the Bahraini control tower.

Abdul watched in fascination as the missiles sped to the target aircraft. One missile suddenly blew up as the aircraft was making a hard climbing turn, and the other missile hit one of the inboard engine pods. Pieces of the engine pod fell off and the aircraft began a roll, but stopped and straightened itself.

Then he noticed the smaller fighter aircraft roaring with afterburners and speeding up. It quickly climbed and rapidly turned around. Time slowed down for him as he watched in horror when the fighter aircraft became a pinpoint in the sky and he realized it was aiming straight at him.

The F-22 pilot, seeing and hearing the situation, turned radically away from Air Force One so there wouldn't be a midair collision, and looked for the launch site to stop any further launches. Major Ken Paulson spotted a lone vehicle with a small dust cloud slowly dissipating. Hours and hours of practice on the gunnery range honed air-to-ground firing capabilities and expertise. Rolling out and accelerating downward at the stationary target, he opened the firing lockout switch, focused on his sights, firmly squeezed the trigger, and fired the 20mm Vulcan Cannon at the lone figure. There was a large cloud of dust as the barrage of cannon shells destroyed the launch vehicle and Abdul. Then he pulled up and turned back to see Air Force One, with its mangled inboard engine, slowly turning back to Bahrain and the safety of the airport. A straight-in approach was performed, and Air Force One landed safely as the F-22 flew by and continued on around for a landing. There was no fire. Security guards and vehicles quickly swarmed over the aircraft as it parked at a distance on the concrete apron.

The president couldn't believe what had just happened. Attacked as they were leaving. He was shaken up a bit, as were all the others on the aircraft, but otherwise he was okay. He departed the aircraft on the truck-mounted stairs that arrived at the side of the parked aircraft. The same U.S. armored limousine that had dropped him off just a short time earlier hadn't been loaded on the U.S. cargo support aircraft. It picked him up and he waited while arrangements were made for the night. He was secure ... but very angry.

While waiting, the president turned to Jack and said, "I think we need to implement our plans."

Jack nodded.

"I think we need to get with General Foley and have him begin preparations for the exercise we outlined earlier this week. By now, the personnel should be in place and ready to go."

Jack just nodded again. He was still apparently in a bit of a shock over the attack.

After arrangements were made, they proceeded to a Marriott Hotel, and security personnel checked it before the president

263

arrived. They would be there for a day or so while another aircraft was flown in to get them. Word was immediately sent back to the Pentagon. Unfortunately, the other VC-25A was in maintenance and wasn't available to pick them up. A presidential support fleet C-32 aircraft, a VIP-configured Boeing 757, was reassigned from a mission to London to pick them up the next day at Bahrain. Out of Lakenheath RAFB in northeastern England, a flight of six U.S. Air Force F-35 fighters immediately deployed to Bahrain with the C-32 aircraft.

The Bahraini ground security forces found the destroyed launch vehicle and the remains of Abdul. In the wreckage they found remains of the launchers, confirming the suspicion that he had been the one attacking the president.

Chapter Forty-Seven

Wednesday—November 15
Oman—Salalah Compound

The ayatollah and his staff had landed in Salalah the previous day and departed the aircraft. Khatib remained on board and they took off for Socotra. Word had reached them that the president had stayed over until this morning and the attempt on President Martinez had been accomplished, but had failed and his attacker had been killed. The president's airplane was on the ground in Bahrain, damaged but not destroyed. Upon hearing this, Ramiz and the ayatollah spent some time together. They both knew the U.S. would make an all-out attempt to stop them and capture, or kill, the ayatollah. It could be grim.

Ramiz thoughtfully commented, "I think it would be best if we found a totally new location for you until this dies down a bit. Socotra and the stronghold are undoubtedly being watched, and they may also know about this place. And we need to move on it. Where would you like to go?"

"Do you really think they can react that fast? After all, it is thousands of miles to their nearest base. They don't know where we are, and to mount an attack would be very difficult under those circumstances."

"What you say is possibly true. But I don't trust them. And with their capabilities, they may know where we are right now. Their satellites have a lot of capability, and tracking people is one of them. Then there is the U.S. Navy task force, with an aircraft carrier, in the Arabian Sea. Their Navy can hit us within a few hours."

"I see what you mean. I hadn't thought of that possibility. Well, I'm not sure where to go. We could also delay them slightly by holding out on the hostages."

"I don't understand."

"We dangle the possibility of their return in exchange for no action on their part to capture us."

"Given the attempt on the president, I doubt that would work. I'll repeat, we need to move, and I mean *now*," he said very emphatically. "Where would you like to go?"

The ayatollah was a bit taken aback by Ramiz's bluntness. He recovered, saw the urgency, and finally said, "Okay. Okay. I guess you're right. Better safe than sorry. Let's go to Char Bahar and have *Persian Quest* pick us up. Then we can go wherever we wish."

Ramiz pursed his lips and nodded. Not bad. "If we can get there without being spotted, that would work quite well." He thought for a moment. "Assuming the Americans know where we are, we could send out several vehicles at once to various locations. You would be in one of them, but the others would be decoys, assuming the Americans are watching, and they probably are. The infidels would not know which one to follow. That would give us a chance to get to the coast, cross over to Char Bahar, and head out on the *Persian Quest* to some other location. A floating command center."

The ayatollah responded, "Yes. And we could pick up Khatib somewhere along the way and no one would be the wiser. He could meet us off Socotra and the Americans wouldn't know he had left."

"Sounds like a plan to me. I'll look into the details and get back to you within the hour."

The ayatollah nodded and Ramiz departed the office to arrange for the detailed travel effort. First he needed to get some identical vans together, along with drivers, and figure out where they could go as decoys out of Salalah. He also needed to find out if *Persian Quest* could support the evacuation. It might not be close enough or available to help out.

After studying the coastline and possible destination of Char Bahar, Ramiz realized that it would make more sense to drive up the coast of Oman to Muscat and be picked up there. Char Bahar was too far away, on the other side of the Gulf of Oman, to be practical. He contacted, through an encrypted phone, the transportation experts in Socotra and found out that *Persian Quest* was currently in the harbor at Socotra. At his request, they could depart in eight hours for the pick-up. Some supplies and fuel needed to be put aboard, since she had just returned from an extensive training mission. It would take them, under turbine power, about eight hours to make the crossing, so Ramiz and the ayatollah could expect to be picked up in about fourteen to sixteen hours. Ramiz gave the order for them to initiate this plan.

Ramiz then went back to the ayatollah and told him of the plans. The vans would arrive in an hour and they would depart in two hours. Ramiz and the ayatollah would take one of the vans to Muscat and wait there for the *Persian Quest*. The other vans would scatter out across Salalah and the nearby countryside and sit for several hours. It was the best he could do in the time available. He did not trust the Americans and wanted to move immediately. He was afraid they might try something very quickly after the conference. And especially after the failed attempt to down President Martinez's plane. The ayatollah readily agreed and began to really sense the urgency radiated by Ramiz.

Wednesday—November 15
Washington, D.C.—The White House

Having returned from North Carolina with Jackie, Dave, and Jasper, Ryan was in the White House talking with Marjorie Hansen. He was sitting there trying to figure out what to do next when she received a phone call. She picked it up and after a few minutes she blanched, all the color going out of her face, and almost dropped the phone. "My God," she said into the phone. "Are you sure about this? Okay. Okay. Thanks for the call."

She looked over at Ryan. "The president's plane has been attacked and seriously damaged. He's okay but they are back on the ground in Bahrain."

Ryan had an expression of shock and dismay on his face. "Marg, what the hell is going on? Two of his close aides are kidnapped, and now this?"

The color started to return to her face. Very slowly, she said, "I don't know. But someone needs to get to the bottom of this."

He nodded and listened as the word spread like wildfire through the entire White House. People were gathered in small clumps throughout the whole complex discussing what little information they had on the attack. He could hear both whispered conversations and some shrieks and moans. The combination of bad news coming so closely on the president's warnings to be careful were really striking home.

After several hours, more information came in from the Pentagon that the president and his entire party were all okay. The aircraft had been damaged by a missile, but had made it back to the airport. Relief was very evident on everyone's faces.

Ryan went down to the White House Situation Room, where the vice president had gathered several crisis management people, and was permitted entry after the VP vouched for him. Approaching the VP, Ryan said, "Sir. Any ideas on who might have done this? Is it who I think it may be?"

Vice President Swanson turned and shook hands with Ryan. "Thanks for being here. We might need your help in this thing."

"You're certainly welcome. Who's behind it?"

Swanson said, "Were not absolutely sure, but it looks like New Persia again. They have found the launchers to the ARPMs and they are the same types used against the secretary of defense last year. And the attacker was known to sympathize with New Persia."

"The ayatollah again."

"Yes. I'm afraid so. Only a lot more dangerous now."

"What next?"

"We've diverted another aircraft, a C-32, along with some F-35 fighters, to get the president and his party out of Bahrain. They should be back here in two days. I mean, it is nearly halfway around the world, you know. And Boeing is sending an emergency repair team to Bahrain. They will temporarily repair Air Force One until it can be flown back to the Boeing plant in Wichita, Kansas, for permanent repairs." He hesitated as he looked at Ryan.

"You've got something on your mind. What is it?"

Swanson looked a bit uncomfortable, but said, "We're going after the ayatollah and his immediate support people."

"Do we know where he is? He left Bahrain and could be anywhere."

Swanson looked at the far wall for a moment. Then he said, "Yes. We think so. He has been tracked to Salalah. We have him on our satellite coverage. He won't get away this time."

Wednesday—November 15
Oman—Salalah Compound

Ramiz, remembering his conversation with Kasim, tried to call Kasim several times, but couldn't get an answer. Kasim was conscientious. He should be answering. Unless? No. Impossible. Two good men. And no answers. He began to worry, and then realized he had significant problems in Salalah that needed immediate attention.

Two hours later, five white vans showed up at the small complex in Salalah. They drove into the warehouse portion of the building and parked. The ayatollah, Ramiz, and three staffers gathered some small supplies and personal effects and loaded up one of the vans. After another two hours, all of the vans departed at the same time for the assigned destinations in various parts of Oman. The ayatollah's van headed inland and north for the nearly six-hundred-mile drive to Muscat.

Spyglass had them. All of them. Since they thought it would confuse the satellite to follow the different vehicles, they were confident of the ruse. They were wrong. At Schriever AFB, in the control station for Spyglass, the young captain saw what was happening and, manipulating software, followed all five of the vehicles simultaneously as they traveled about. Quickly understanding the ruse, he focused an infrared camera on each vehicle. Three of the vehicles only had one person aboard. A fourth one had two people aboard. The fifth vehicle had several people on board. The captain grinned to himself as he leaned forward in his seat, looking at his monitor, and said quietly, "Gotcha." He continued tracking all of the vehicles but concentrated on the one carrying the most people as it headed north.

He, and the shift after him, followed the van through the nighttime Omani desert and towns of Dawkah and Hayma. It stopped in Hayma for two hours and then continued on up to Muscat.

Thursday—November 16
Oman—Muscat

They arrived at the dockside after fourteen hours of rattled driving and pulled into a covered warehouse. They spent an hour waiting. *Persian Quest*, as promised, arrived fifteen hours after Ramiz had made the request. It eased into the dock area, tied up to the pier, and Kadar welcomed them all aboard. Ramiz looked at Kadar with a question in his eyes. Kadar said, "Najid just finished up with some at-sea exercises and we felt it would be best if I pick you and the ayatollah up. And Khatib said he would join us later. He had some other work to do, and also wasn't sure about having all of you together."

Ramiz acknowledged the comment with a nod and began boarding.

Spyglass watched the little parade of people come out of the warehouse and board the large sailing vessel. Through some automated software, the young captain directed the satellite to maintain coverage over the ship at all times, regardless of its motion or destination. That way they wouldn't lose it.

Thursday—November 16
Bahrain

It was the day after the attack. The C-32 and the fighters had arrived in Bahrain a few hours earlier and were being serviced under the watchful eyes of both the crews and the Secret Service. The area off the end of the runway had been cleared by the local police and military. No chances.

The president, and his entire entourage, arrived at the aircraft at 10:00 a.m. and boarded for the long flight back home. The single F-22 and F-35s took off first, did a slow flyby of the area off the end of the runway, climbed to three thousand feet, and circled, waiting for the new Air Force One to take off. The C-32, after everyone was seated and belted in, began to taxi out to the end of the runway. It turned on to the active runway, accelerated, and took off at a steep angle, heading back home to Andrews AFB in Maryland.

After it reached cruise altitude and passengers were able to move about the cabin, the president, on an encrypted satellite communication link, contacted the Pentagon Situation Room and discussed progress with General Foley. The Air Force was tracking the *Persian Quest* and having no trouble doing that. They knew the ayatollah was aboard along with Ramiz, his security head. They were on an easterly course up through the Gulf of Oman, but the Air Force had no idea where they might be heading.

Elusive Quarry

Chapter Forty-Eight

Thursday—November 16
Northern Arabian Sea

Vice Admiral Mack Orcutt, commanding a joint task force from the *USS Harry S. Truman* in the Northern Arabian Sea, was enjoying smooth seas and a beautiful, though hot, day at sea. He was finishing up his breakfast and studying the day's flying schedule and a small internal command exercise schedule. A staff meeting was scheduled in forty-five minutes, and he was preparing for that. He read through several dispatches from the Pentagon on his laptop, with nothing of particular note. It had been exciting the previous day when he was alerted to the attack on the president's plane and the possibility that he might get tasked in some way to support recovery efforts. But nothing came of it as the day moved along.

Ten minutes before the staff meeting, he got a call from the communications room. He was needed there immediately to receive a classified flash message from the Pentagon. Unusual. He got up and proceeded to the comm center and entered the classified receiving booth, and the built-in hardened tablet computer was connected to the message receiving equipment. He read through the message. It was a tasking from the Pentagon to intercept and capture the *Persian Quest*. The message also gave the current coordinates of the *Persian Quest* and her current course of travel. Updates would be provided as the day moved along. Along with the tasking was a short synopsis explaining that the attack of the president was suspected to have originated on the *Persian Quest*, or the people who were on board. Specifically, they were looking for three terrorists: the ayatollah, Khatib, and Ramiz. Approach with caution.

He read through the message several times and then closed the system down. They were on a course in the Northern Arabian Sea and were several hundred miles from the current location of the *Persian Quest*. He headed to the main conference room, where the staff were all gathered for the normal morning activities and reviews of the day's mission requirements. As he entered, they all stood at attention, waited for him to take his seat, and settled down again with slight rustling of papers and sliding chairs.

Admiral Orcutt looked around the room briefly then began. "We have a new tasking today. It will supersede our current scheduled activities."

The room was quiet as the various commanders wondered what the new tasking might be, and what their piece of it might entail.

The admiral continued, "You are all aware that the president narrowly missed being killed in a missile attack on his airplane." Heads were nodding. "The people believed responsible for that attack are in a sophisticated sailing vessel approximately five hundred miles to our northwest. We are to intercept them and capture the leaders. You have all heard of the ayatollah. It's him and some of his crowd." He then outlined course changes for the flotilla and directed each commander to be alert. He tasked the flying wing to send out aircraft on a search to locate the target vessel. Then he dismissed the staff and they went about taking action to comply with his directions.

Two F-18s from Carrier Air Wing 7 stationed on the *USS Truman* took off and headed for the coordinates given in the classified message. They headed northwest of the task force and cruised subsonically for a little over half an hour. They had been told to watch for the oversized sailing vessel that had a unique sail configuration but resembled a large schooner. The weather was clear, with just the usual haze that was regular over the ocean. Visibility was quite good and they found their quarry without too much trouble. They dropped down to just over the waves, made a pass by the *Persian Quest*, and continued on. They radioed back to the *USS Truman* that they had located the vessel, gave the exact coordinates, about one hundred miles south of the Iranian coastline, and were instructed to return to the carrier.

On board the *Persian Quest*, it was very obvious that they had been seen and the fighters that made the low pass were American. Near-panic ensued. If the fighters had found them, an American ship must be nearby and they were in danger. Kadar had the sails furled and the masts taken down, and fired up the twin turbine engines. They would make for the closest landfall and see if the ayatollah and Ramiz could escape overland. They were just about due south of the Iranian coastline and, subtracting the internationally recognized twelve-mile territorial waters, would have to make about eighty-eight miles before the Americans got to them. And since the Iranians were not overly friendly with the Americans, they would be safe in the Iranian territorial waters, safe from the infidels.

As the ship was being reconfigured, he began thinking. They were a trimaran as it stood now. Another option would be to hide the ayatollah among the crew and hope the infidels didn't see him.

Decision time.

Kadar called down to Ramiz and the ayatollah. They came right up and he explained the two options he felt they had. Ramiz thought about it for just a few moments. The risk of hiding in the crew was just too great.

Ramiz asked, "Where are these American ships? How far away are they?"

Kadar responded, "I'm not real sure, but since the fighters went to a high altitude when they left, I don't think the task force is real close. It could be just over the horizon, but I think it may be some distance away."

"So we really don't know when the American ships might show up, then?"

"No. Not for sure."

"And if we make a run for the coast, how long will it take to get there?"

"With the masts down and the turbines at full power, we can do just over fifty knots. We can make it to the coast in just under two hours at that rate."

Ramiz looked back at Kadar. Then he looked over at the ayatollah and said, "The ships are probably, and this is just a guess, a few hundred miles off. If we make a run for the coast, they couldn't catch us even at full steam for their ships. The only things they might do would be try and stop us with a fighter or, if they are closer, use helicopters to bring in a marine force. Either way, the fighters just left and there probably won't be a follow-up for a little while. I think we ought to get moving right away. Head for the coast."

The ayatollah just looked back, barely comprehending what Ramiz was saying. He asked Kadar. "What do you think? Which is the best option?"

Kadar responded, "Ramiz is right. We can do either option, but I agree with him. Let's head for the Iranian coastline and do it immediately. I don't want to lose you or take a chance with the Americans. We are on the high seas, and they could do anything if we wait for them."

The ayatollah looked out over the water for just a moment. Then back at his two main support personnel. They were both very competent men and knew what they were doing. He made up his mind. "Go."

Thursday—November 16
Schriever AFB, Colorado

Lieutenant Lucy Johnson was on duty, and continued to monitor the movements of the *Persian Quest* via their satellite connection. It had been somewhat boring watching a ship at sea move around. Something more interesting occurred as the two F-18 fighters made their pass by the sailing vessel. Her voice communications with the task force had been set up on the previous shift, and she was in constant voice communications with the aircraft carrier command center.

Shortly after the fighters confirmed the ship identity and departed for the carrier, she noticed a significant amount of activity on the *Persian Quest*. The sails basically disappeared and the ship turned toward the north, picking up speed at a very high rate. It was obvious that they were going somewhere fast and not letting anything get in their way.

She keyed her mike and said, "Truman, Schriever. Your bogey just turned north and lit a fire. It's moving fast toward the Iranian coastline."

Thursday—November 16
Northern Arabian Sea

"Damn, roger that," came the reply. It was a calm voice, and it belied what was really happening on board the *Truman.*

Two alert-ready armed F-18 aircraft were quickly moved out onto the catapults and immediately launched into the blue Arabian Sea sky. They joined up and headed to the northwest on full afterburner.

Ramiz and Kadar, both on the bridge of the *Persian Quest*, were concentrating on maintaining their course and progress. The ayatollah had retired to his stateroom to wait out the run. The twin turbines were putting out a maximum effort as they headed for the Iranian coastline in the distance. They were doing an indicated fifty knots and hanging on. No personnel were allowed on deck due to the winds and the speed. There had been no indication of any further activity by the Americans, but they were not taking any chances.

The navigation tech on the bridge suddenly stiffened up as he was watching the on-board radar. Two airborne blips had shown up on his radar, coming in fast from the southeast. He looked at the GPS location indicator for the *Persian Quest* and it showed that they were still about thirty miles from the coast. But the aircraft were closing very fast. He leaned over the scope again and then turned and told Ramiz and Kadar of the fast-approaching aircraft. It had to be the Americans returning, and they had not reached the territorial waters of Iran yet. They needed another twenty minutes to get there and might not make it.

It got tense as the bridge crew watched for the American fighters. Finally, after just a few minutes, they spotted the fighters coming in fast and low, just above the waves.

Returning to his scope, the tech was surprised to see two more blips, but this time they were coming in from the north. What was going on?

Ramiz looked at Kadar as the captain told the helm to maintain course and speed no matter what happened. They were not to slow down or alter their course despite the American aircraft presence.

They watched. But did not know which way to look. Two aircraft coming from the south on the deck and two aircraft coming from the north at a slightly higher altitude. They kept glancing back and forth. They were now within twelve miles of Iranian territorial waters and still moving full out. The two F-18s from the south went by them, one on each side, at wave-top level as two Iranian F-14 interceptors from the north went by at a slightly higher altitude. The aircraft all began circling and doing a frantic dance in the sky.

The *Persian Quest* continued for the coast, only a few miles away now. It looked like the four aircraft were jostling for position with each other. Kadar and Ramiz could not tell what was going on, but Ramiz, thinking about it very quickly, began to realize that the Iranian aircraft had intercepted the Americans and were probably telling them to not get into Iranian airspace without proper authority. He was sure communications were burning up between the fighters and their respective headquarters units. He would love to be able to listen in.

In the meantime, they were really running for the twelve-mile point that marked Iranian territorial waters. The aircraft continued to circle each other as the *Persian Quest* ran. The helmsman on the bridge, looking at the GPS equipment, quickly turned to Kadar and

275

said, "We just crossed the twelve-mile marker. We are in Iranian waters now."

Ramiz began to just slightly relax, not knowing whether the Americans would do anything. He continued to watch the aircraft, and after a few minutes of observing the dance in the sky, he watched as the two American F-18s climbed to altitude and broke off to the southeast. It looked like the Iranian Air Force had won the day. The F-14s came overhead, wagged their wings slightly, and headed back north. Their airspace was intact.

Kadar looked at the coastline through his binoculars and thought about the last few minutes. They had managed to escape the eagle's talons, but just barely. Now they needed to get the ayatollah to safety. He looked at the charts and realized that the only reasonably close place that could handle a ship the size of the *Persian Quest* was just to the east in Pakistan. The city of Gwadar was large enough, and with a major pipeline to China, would be suitable—and Pakistan was on bare terms with the Americans. Even though in Iranian waters, he decided to set a course to the east, staying inside the twelve-mile limit, for the city. Once there, they could figure out the next step. But at least there, the ayatollah would be safe from the infidel Americans.

Ramiz watched as Kadar adjusted the course. They discussed it briefly and Ramiz agreed with what Kadar was doing. Ramiz then went down to the ayatollah's quarters and gave him a quick review of what had happened and what they were doing in the immediate future. The ayatollah agreed, and would be happy to be on solid ground again. And he had a friend, a mullah in Gwadar, who might be able to help out. It was a reasonable plan.

Chapter Forty-Nine

Thursday—November 16
Washington, D.C.—The White House

Air Force One, the C-32 aircraft carrying the president, after a stop for fuel at Lakenheath RAFB in England, came in on approach to Andrews AFB in Maryland. It carried a very upset president and staff. After landing, the president and staff were met by the usual contingent of Secret Service men and women and immediately rushed back to the White House. The president was in no mood for niceties and formalities, and the normal welcoming committee was conspicuously absent.

He was tired and just wanted to get some rest, but that was not meant to be. At least not immediately. Mark Allison and General Foley were at the White House waiting outside the Oval Office. They had some disturbing news.

They were all seated in the Oval Office. The president looked expectantly at General Foley.

General Foley said, "The task force in the Northern Arabian Sea attempted to intercept the *Persian Quest.* They ran into Iranian Air Force F-14s as the carrier-based F-18s approached the sailing vessel just off the southern coast of Iran. This happened while you were heading home yesterday. While they are ancient and barely flyable, the F-14s are still a credible threat, and the F-18s broke off the chase. From satellite coverage, the *Persian Quest* continued in and docked in the Pakistani port of Gwadar. Apparently the F-18s were picked up by the Iranian southern radar net and interceptors were dispatched. It was a bust, and we think the ayatollah departed for Iran a little while later."

"So he got away again and by now would be somewhere in Southern Iran."

"Yes, sir. That's our take on it."

"Okay. What's next?"

Mark said, "We're tracking the vehicle we think he is in, and they are crossing the Southern Iranian deserts. Probably heading for Char Bahar or some other small area for a retreat."

"The vehicle you *think* he is in? So you're not absolutely sure?"

"No, sir. When they got to the port, several vehicles were there, and we couldn't be absolutely sure which one he took. But this is the only one that went into Iran and the safety of his friends there."

"Sounds plausible. And where did the *Persian Quest* go?"

"It's still at the dock and it looks like it's being restocked and refueled."

The president looked at General Foley and said, "I'd like a meeting with you and several others tomorrow. I want your thoughts on what we do next. This simply cannot be left alone. I gave some instructions before I left, and I'd like to review the progress on those."

"Who would you like there?"

"You, General Abe, Mike, Kenton, Miriam, Admiral Nelson, and I'll have Jack and Admiral Watkins involved." He thought for a moment and then added, "And since Ryan is here, let him listen in also."

"We'll get it set up in the situation room. I'll have Marjorie set it up, since Maria isn't back yet."

The president said, "Thanks. I appreciate that. I'm tired. I'll see you tomorrow."

With that, they both left and the president retired to his upstairs quarters for some well-deserved rest.

Friday—November 17
Washington, D.C.—The White House Situation Room

After a night of rest, the president came down to the Oval Office and was surprised to see Jackie Conover sitting at Maria's desk. Before he could say anything, she said, "Your meeting in the situation room is set to go at 9:00 a.m., and all the people you asked to be there will be present with one exception. Kenton is out of the country and won't make it."

The president said, "Okay. Thanks. Now, why are you here? You should be resting after that ordeal you went through. And how's Maria doing?"

Jackie gave as winning a smile as she could muster and said, "Maria is doing fine. She'll be out of the hospital later today and Corey is bringing her back to Washington. She's a bit sore, but that is to be expected. She said she planned to be back in on Monday." She stopped for a moment and then said, "I'm here because I should be here. I wasn't hurt during those days in the so-called 'safe house' and can continue to support you for now. And there is some work to be done to reshuffle your schedule since you took your vacation in Bahrain." She was still smiling. So was he.

She added, "Ryan will also be there, along with Jasper and Dave. The three of them, along with me, are going to go back to Texas later today for a few days. I'll manage your schedule from there and work with Maria once she's back."

"Can you handle all that?"

"I think so. Anything that Maria can't do, or if she gets too tired, I'll work with Marjorie on. Should be doable."

"Okay." He looked at his watch and said, "So it's all set for 9:00 a.m. Then I've got about an hour to get ready."

She was relieved. He'd just accepted her and the planning they had all done in the administrative section.

It was 9:00 a.m. and the requested staff had gathered in the White House Situation Room. The president walked in and sat down after getting his customary cup of coffee.

Ryan, Dave, and Jasper looked over the small crowd. It was notable in that it appeared to be a sort of war council. They watched as the president had the room staff bring up a map of the Northern Arabian Sea, which included both Socotra and the area north of the Gulf of Oman.

"Ladies and gentlemen," he began. "This is the area we are concerned with today. It is where many of our New Persia problems are centered and where we need to take positive action to remove a very real threat."

The general feeling in the room was one of concurrence. Everyone there understood that it had just been a couple of days since the president had been fired on and narrowly missed dying.

The president turned to General Foley and said, "Just before I left on the wasted mission to Bahrain, I left instructions that we were to prepare to take these folks out. That SEALs were to join the task force in the Indian Ocean and that we needed to prepare for another strike in Iran."

The general just nodded as he watched the president. Ryan and Jasper perked up at this news. They weren't aware of the plan.

The president continued, "Where do we stand with the preparations at this point?"

General Foley leaned forward slightly, put his folded hands on the edge of the table, and said, "The SEALs are in place and on the aircraft carrier *Truman* in the Arabian Sea. That carrier also carries the F-18 aircraft we are planning to use to strike the stronghold."

279

The president had a questioning look. "How can the carrier do both? Socotra and the stronghold are a fair distance from each other."

"Yes, sir. That's correct. And normally she would have to do the strikes sequentially with a move between them. However, we have had the nuclear submarine *SSN Jimmy Carter* join the task force. The current plan is to have the SEALs board the sub and deploy underwater to Socotra. They will complete their mission there at the New Persia compound and rejoin the sub just off the New Persia harbor."

Ryan and Jasper looked at each other. They were certainly hearing what they had come to hear. Strike planning was well underway.

The president said, "Okay. That will take care of the two centers that we are sure of. How about his place in Salalah, and, now that I think about it, do we know where the three of them are?"

"I can't speak for Salalah," said the general. "We still don't know where his compound is actually located. Just some warehouses. And even if we did, we can't go in to a foreign civilian town willy-nilly and shoot it up. As for his current location and that of his two buddies, we aren't completely sure. It appears that this guy Khatib is on Socotra, and we think Ramiz is with the ayatollah somewhere in the Southern Iranian desert. Exactly where, we still don't know. We do know that one of the mullahs in Gwadar has helped them, but their current location is not known."

"So, we take out his main center but don't get him or his top aides?"

"Unless we wait for a period until we can absolutely identify where he is, you got it, sir." The general leaned back slightly.

The president looked around the room. Everyone there looked back as he scanned. He had just been told that the ayatollah was not in their crosshairs and they didn't know when he might be.

The president said, "One of the key targets is the main compound on Socotra. If we take it out, we take out much of his support, and it would be a real crippling blow. When can we hit it?"

Admiral Nelson then spoke up. "The SEALs are still on board the *Truman.* To transfer to the sub with their gear will take about half a day, and then the sub, moving at a reasonable speed underwater, could be off Socotra in another day. I would say we could hit it in about three days after they receive the execute message."

The president said, "Have them hold up a bit. I want to think this through a bit more and then get back to you. I'm afraid that not getting them all at once could be a mistake. And if we get one and the other two take off, we could be in for a much tougher situation."

The general said, "Yes, sir. But keep in mind, we may never get the perfect situation. One or two of them, at any point in time, may be unavailable to us."

"I can't disagree, but I want better odds of getting them. When we actually locate the ayatollah, and can get to him, then we'll move. He's the major key. However, that doesn't mean we can't hit the stronghold again and take out whatever is there. When can we hit it?"

Admiral Nelson said, "We are primed to go on that one. We can execute the attack anytime on your word. It is completely separate from the Socotra Island action, and the *Truman* is ready with her F-18s."

The president nodded while looking at the table in front of him. He thought about the refineries, about the loss of life, about the attack on Air Force One. He looked up at the admiral and said, "We'll hold up for a little while. I want to make sure we can really hit them hard and get the ayatollah before we actually move. I understand the frustration, but I don't want to miss again."

The president then stood up, nodded at Ryan, Dave, and Jasper, and left the room. He knew people were frustrated, but so was he.

Chapter Fifty

Tuesday—November 21
Gulf of Oman

They had succeeded in getting into the territorial waters of Iran and avoiding the American F-18 fighters. The Iranian F-14s had delayed the Americans until they could get close enough to the shore to be protected by the twelve-mile international limits. After putting in at Gwadar, Pakistan, they had been able to contact the mullah at a local mosque. A friend of the ayatollah, he agreed to help them. They were able to get an old van, and headed along an old coast road toward Char Bahar in Iran. They did not make very good time, since the van had a questionable engine, but they did eventually make it after traveling for four days. The ayatollah, dressed in traditional Arabic clothes, fit in well with the local people who helped them along the way. And while they knew who he was, they did not have the same reverence for him that his own followers had. Thus they did not pay him a lot of attention.

Ramiz tried again to reach Kasim or Carlos but failed. He called Alim in Arlington, explained the situation, and asked if he could check on the two men. It was just an hour later that Alim called him back and told him that, according to some sources he had in Greensboro, Kasim was dead and Carlos was under arrest and in the hospital with burns to his face.

Startled, Ramiz said, "Thank you," and very slowly hung up. He stood there completely surprised. His men were obviously outdone by the two women. He couldn't believe it. And the leverage of the hostages was gone.

Once they reached Char Bahar, Ramiz was able to get quarters for a few days, and finally arranged for a fishing boat to take them across the Gulf of Oman to Muscat. Again, they were in disguise, so the American satellites would only see some poor fishing people crossing the waters. To accentuate this ruse, the ayatollah placed a rope around his neck and shoulders under his clothing and ran it down through his crotch. This forced him to bend over and shuffle around. The rope kept him from forgetting and straightening up. It was a good ruse ... and it worked.

Elusive Quarry

In Muscat, Ramiz was really getting anxious. They had succeeded in getting the ayatollah back to Muscat, but he wasn't really safe there. He was sure the Americans were watching Salalah, hoping to find the ayatollah and capture him. The ayatollah needed to be moved to somewhere safe, at least for a few weeks, until they could make further plans. He thought about it, and finally came to the conclusion that China would be the best option. They had been the silent partners in the New Persia effort and would shield the ayatollah for a period of time. They could also have some high-level meetings to continue with future planning efforts.

Ramiz was sure the Chinese would welcome that opportunity. It would put some additional emphasis on the cooperative efforts at getting additional energy covertly transferred to the China government. It would also permit Ramiz to make a few special additional requests regarding equipment capabilities for future use. He had several equipment enhancement ideas and wanted to put them into effect. He had, almost a year ago, already put in some special specification changes to the mini-submarines.

He looked around his small office in the compound in Muscat and walked up to a small whiteboard that was attached to the wall. He began to define what he wanted and a timeframe for its accomplishment. By writing the information down, he was able to ponder it better and increase the visual perception. A habit he began in his engineering studies several years earlier at the University of Wisconsin—Madison, he depended on it to clarify his thinking.

He contacted the travel support section in Socotra via encrypted message over the undersea cable and requested travel information for he and the ayatollah from Muscat to the primary Chinese naval port of Zhanjiang. The Chinese naval personnel at the South Sea Fleet based in Zhanjiang, Guangdong, were familiar with their needs, having supported them already for the past three years, and would be the correct organization to respond to his requests. He could kill two birds with one flight, so to speak. He would get the ayatollah into hiding and get his equipment requirements met in one trip. It was a plan. And totally hidden from the infidel Americans and their snooping satellites.

He sat and smiled. It should work, and would solve several problems. And the Americans would be stymied. The thought of it was very pleasant to him. They might actually be able to win this war of nerves.

As he sat there, it suddenly occurred to him that if the Americans were after the ayatollah, they were probably after his immediate staff also, to include Khatib and himself. It would only

R.W. Barton

make sense. And they know where the stronghold was located, along with Socotra. He and Khatib would be at risk.

The ayatollah had remained in a small compound in Muscat for a few days, but that was only a stopgap measure to protect him. When arrangements could be made, they would proceed with the China trip and, hopefully, in the confusion that would cause for the satellite monitors at Schriever AFB, the infidels would lose track of him, if they hadn't already. Then he could continue to lead the movement with less thought to being captured.

Ramiz told the ayatollah of his plans for a visit to China and the safety that would provide … at least temporarily.

"Sir, I think it would be very advisable to visit China. I believe that for several reasons, but two really stand out to me."

The ayatollah motioned with his hands for Ramiz to continue.

"Number one is the opportunity to escape the ever-watchful eyes of the American satellites. You could, in so many words, disappear into the Chinese environment and not be located. The second reason would be for us to be able to meet and discuss our requirements for future support. And those meetings would be with the Chinese men who control that support. It would benefit both of us and clarify several issues that we both have with each other."

The ayatollah responded, "It would probably be a good thing for both of the reasons you mentioned. I have met with Vice Admiral Chang of the People's Liberation Army Navy, but it was some years ago when we were just getting set up. I concur that we could certainly use a good face-to-face review. What did you have in mind for a timing of this proposed visit?"

"As soon as possible," Ramiz said. "I don't want to let the Americans have any more opportunity to catch you than is absolutely necessary. I will contact Zhang Qiang, our Chinese representative, to arrange the visit. It is possible that if Admiral Chang cannot meet right away, we could still go there, remain hidden, and work out some details with their lower-level people."

The ayatollah looked out the window at the sea, then turned back to Ramiz, and said, "Let's carry out that plan. It makes sense to me, and it will also force us to think through some of our future needs. But add Khatib to the trip. He is familiar with many of our needs and would contribute greatly."

Ramiz nodded and said, "Yes, sir. I have already contacted our travel people, and, after they respond, I will further our plans. I will also contact Zhang Qiang to arrange for the visit and discussion."

The ayatollah nodded and turned back to the view of the sea. Ramiz bowed at the ayatollah's back and departed the room. The ayatollah was tired from the running and would like the peace and quiet of China.

Wednesday—November 22
Socotra Island—New Persia Compound

Ramiz, feeling fairly secure about the current location of the ayatollah in Muscat, flew to Socotra the next morning. Both Khatib and Zhang were there, and he wanted to discuss the planned visit with them.

But first he headed to Khatib's office, knocked, and entered. He said, "Khatib, I want you to know that the ayatollah wants to visit China as soon as we can arrange it."

Khatib, surprised at this, said, "Why? He hasn't said anything to me about it."

"No. He and I discussed it and, from a security viewpoint, it makes a lot of sense."

"So it is really your idea and you convinced him."

"Yes. But hear me out."

Khatib, obviously slightly irritated and looking at the floor, pursed his lips and then said, "Okay. I'm listening."

Ramiz then laid out what he had in mind. After just a few moments, Khatib had to agree that it made a lot of sense. "You make a good case for the visit, especially from your security perspective. And we could define what we will need in the future. It would be good to address those issues directly with Admiral Chang."

Shortly after the discussion, they all met in the main conference room. Ramiz turned to Zhang and said, "The ayatollah, Khatib, and I would like to visit with our benefactors in Zhanjiang as soon as possible." He hesitated for a moment to let the request sink in. Ramiz then continued, "In addition to meeting Vice Admiral Chang and conversing about our future requirements, it would have the added benefit of confusing the Americans, possibly to the point they would lose the surveillance over the ayatollah."

Zhang said, "That is a tall order and on very short notice. I understand what you are doing and cannot disagree with it. But I have no idea how fast I can arrange it. It will take me several days to see what the availability of the various players are and when we might meet with them. However, if you're anxious to get there and hide, that may be arranged a little bit quicker. I shall see how that might be done."

Ramiz said, "I understand. We will meet whatever schedule you can arrange for us. However, if we cannot meet right away with Admiral Chang, then we would like to arrive as soon as possible and stay until he is available. My primary concern is the U.S. satellite coverage, and to avoid them tracing our every move."

Zhang nodded. "I understand your motivation and agree with it. I will see what I can do and get back to you within a couple of days."

In the meantime, the ayatollah rested and prayed in Muscat. He made a few minor visits with some of his supporters and the mosques, receiving assurances of their continued support.

Chapter Fifty-One

Thursday—November 23—Thanksgiving
Freeport, Texas—Ryan's Marina

Ryan and Jackie had enjoyed a short sail on the gulf in the morning and were now busy fixing a nice Thanksgiving dinner in their newly finished apartment. Corey, Maria, Jasper, and Dave were all coming over to spend the afternoon watching football and enjoying the company. It would be a good respite from their recent adventures.

Friday—November 24
Freeport, Texas—Ryan's Marina

It was now a little over a week since the president returned from the disastrous meeting in Bahrain. The ayatollah had disappeared into the deserts of Iran, and local authorities were blocking any attempt at finding him. The CIA and FBI really didn't know where he was, and the satellite coverage hadn't been able to locate him. Ryan, Jackie, and Jasper had returned on the twenty-first to Freeport, since there wasn't much they could do in Washington and Thanksgiving was coming up.

Ryan, disgusted with the turn of events—the death of Betty and Orrin, the injury to Jackie, the attack on him, and the destruction of his home—was sitting on the stern of his Hunter sailboat at the marina slip. He was drinking his second martini and listening as Jackie moved about inside the cabin. After having leftovers from Thanksgiving in their new apartment, he had called to her and she joined him on the boat with her glass of wine. They sat there together looking out beyond the breakwater to the Brazos River. He had his arm around her shoulders as she sat there, and he looked at her, thinking.

He said, "I think it may be time to ask the president for another mission assignment to get these guys. Ramiz is going wild with his attacks and needs to be stopped. I can't tolerate any more of his thumbing his nose at us, and we need to get the ayatollah back behind permanent bars. And finally we need to capture this fellow Khatib, who seems to be in the thick of it also. There are some

287

military plans afoot now, but I think the president is too hesitant … this needs to get done."

She stuck out her lower lip and said, "I think you are right. I'm not sure what his reaction might be, but I would think he would certainly want to get this whole adventure over with. He has enough on his plate to deal with and doesn't need this distraction. What do you really have in mind?"

"I'm not sure yet. The last information Jack sent me indicated that they had lost sight of all three of them and didn't know where they were. And that was making the president, and all the others, a bit nervous. They were trying to locate them and not having much success. It has to be very frustrating."

Jackie nodded. "So, again, what do you have in mind?"

"Until we know where they are, we can't do much. But what I'd like to do is track them down while they are out of the operations center and either capture or kill them. I'm mad and upset. They have simply gone too far and made it really personal for me. I think once we can locate them, I need to get Corey and Jasper together, and maybe Dave, and make a good effort at putting them away—one way or another."

"If you do that, I want to be a part of it. After all, I'm the one who has been hurt, and I have the skills to help out. And I'd really like to get revenge for Betty. She was completely innocent and they killed her. Orrin too."

Ryan looked at her. His eyes were full of wonder and he really loved this woman. Could he put her in danger again? It was obvious she was serious, and he couldn't really blame her. Between being injured in the explosion that leveled his home and killed Betty, being kidnapped, captured, and escaping, if he were in her shoes, he would be out for revenge too. But …

Ryan looked back over at the new office and apartment. He took another sip of his drink and just sat there. No more thoughts. Just some regrets that he had let it go this far. It needed to be fixed.

Saturday—November 25
Socotra Island—New Persia Compound

They met in the conference center. Zhang said, "I cannot get a meeting with Admiral Chang until three weeks from now. However, given the problem you are facing, he agreed to your visiting the Chinese Army Naval center, using the quarters they have available, as soon as you can make travel arrangements. I will see to your transportation needs upon your arrival and ensure your quarters are available for you. During the period when you are in the country, and before your meeting with Admiral Chang, lower-level meetings will take place to work the details of your future needs. I think that is what you wanted, and have arranged for it."

Ramiz and Khatib both nodded. Ramiz said, "Yes. That is what we thought would happen, and I appreciate your expediting it for us. I'm sure the meetings will be very fruitful for both of us."

Khatib said, "Thank you for arranging this series of meetings. I'm sure it will benefit both of us a great deal. I am truly looking forward to meeting some of the people I have only heard of in documents and conversations."

Zhang nodded. "Just let me know when the travel arrangements have been made and I will take care of the needs at the other end of the trip."

Ramiz, coordinating with the travel organization, arranged for both he and Khatib to travel back to Muscat. They would leave Socotra, travel to Muscat, pick up the ayatollah, and then fly to Zhanjiang in South China. He called Zhang and passed on the travel arrangements. They would leave the next day. Ramiz did not want to take any more chances on the U.S. finding the ayatollah.

Zhang made the necessary arrangements, along with the travel documentation they would need to arrive in China, and set up a small reception group for their scheduled arrival in Zhanjiang. Zhang passed the information on to Ramiz and Khatib and they began preparations to leave. In both cases, they donned more common clothing to help deceive the satellites.

Monday—November 27
Washington, D.C.—The White House

The president was in the Oval Office as Maria escorted Ryan in for a few minutes of discussion. They shook hands and sat down on the couches across from each other. The president eyed Ryan and said, "Maria said you wanted to talk with me about the New Persia situation. You know we don't know where the ayatollah is at this point, or any of the others, for that matter. So what have you got in mind?"

Ryan took a sip of his Pepsi and said, "I want to go after them. All of them. As you know, my place was destroyed, Betty and Orrin were killed, Jackie injured and then kidnapped, and they have tried three times now to kill me. I want to bring it home to them. Enough pussyfootin' around."

The president's eyebrows went up and he relaxed back onto the couch. He sat and looked at Ryan. It was obvious from the intensity in Ryan's voice that he was serious and really out to respond to the New Persia attacks.

Ryan, seeing some hesitancy in the president, added, "They have made it personal for me and need to be stopped. You have the larger picture of their demands; I have a personal threat to me and a destroyed home. Given their failures at taking me out, I expect they haven't stopped looking for me. I need to take this undeclared war back to them and stop them before they succeed in getting me. But I need your help. And support. I need to know where they are so I can take them out."

The president continued to listen. He said nothing, letting Ryan continue with his statements. After a few moments, he got up and got a ginger ale from his small bar refrigerator. He popped the top and turned to face Ryan again.

"Ryan, I can certainly appreciate what you are saying and how you are feeling." His eyes went directly to Ryan's. "But I cannot support this vigilante concept you are taking. This is a civilized world we live in, and I cannot support you taking on the same attitude that we are fighting against in New Persia." He stopped for a moment and then continued, "And we have some actions underway, which you saw a week ago, that I don't want you involved in. I want those to play out. Your injured leg, even if it has healed, and the concussion could cause a real problem if you were in some form of a serious action. We'll get them, but it will take a little time. And, as I said, we still don't know for sure where they are. The answer is no. I'm sorry."

Ryan couldn't believe what he was hearing. The president had supported the efforts to get rid of New Persia, even to the point of using B-52 bombers to get rid of them. And now he was turning down Ryan's plea for help. Something had turned the president around, and Ryan couldn't accept what he was saying.

Ryan interrupted, "Wait a minute, Al. You won't even help me with information? I'll take on the rest of the effort, the costs for travel and so forth, but I have to have the information." Ryan, since they were in a private conversation, had slipped into the casual mode of calling the president by his first name. It was something that he didn't do very often but that the president said he would prefer in private.

"No. I can't give you any help."

"I see," said Ryan. But he didn't really ... what else was he going to say? The president was pretty plain in his statement.

"Well," said Ryan, "I guess that's all I came for. I appreciate your time but must confess that you surprised me with that reaction. It was certainly nothing like I expected. I'm sorry to have bothered you." Ryan stood, turned, and left the room without shaking hands or saying goodbye.

The president watched him leave and had a heavy heart. There simply was no choice.

The president called Mark Allison and Miriam over for a discussion. They both arrived shortly, came into the Oval Office, shook hands, and sat down. They looked questioningly at the president.

The president asked Mark, "How is Operation New Persia Stop coming along?"

Mark responded, "Well, we still haven't located the ayatollah for sure, but feel he and his immediates are heading for China or are already there. Our analysts, looking at all the info we had available, think that is where he might be. Probably working out their next requirements for support. But we can't be absolutely sure yet."

Miriam was quiet. She had not heard of this information, but thought it was noteworthy.

The president put his hand on his chin. "Hmm. It may be a little while before we can find that out for sure. Once we have it, then we can turn the specialists on to take them out. That's after we find them somewhere we can hit."

"Yes, sir. That's the plan. A covert action to get rid of these criminals."

"Mark. I have another slight problem here. I need you to get with Andy Strasner over at the FBI and keep track of Ryan McKenzie's activities. I hate to say it, but he is, I think, going to take things into his own hands and try to eliminate the ayatollah and his crowd. And I don't want him interfering in what we are doing. We need to monitor him."

Mark looked surprised at the request. Miriam mirrored his surprise. They had supported Ryan in the past. Mark responded, "Okay. Will do. But why not just bring him in on it? He's been heavily involved in the past."

"Yes. But now he is personally chasing this thing and turning it into a vendetta. And that's when mistakes get made. His recent concussion could also come back and haunt him. He has been a big help in the past, but I think it would be better if he stay out of it and we take care of it our own way."

"Okay. I'll get with Andy and we'll figure out a something."

The president then turned to Miriam. "Thought you might like to know what I'm asking Mark to do. About a month ago, I asked you to kind of monitor what these guys were doing and what, if anything, we needed to do to keep moving. Has there been anything I need to know about?"

Miriam looked over at Mark and then back to the president. She said, "Not really. I've met with Mark, Mike, and the others a couple of times over the past couple of weeks, but there hasn't been any sign of problems. We are all just tracking as best we can. Hopefully this will resolve soon."

"Okay. Just wondering." He stood up. The meeting was over.

And with that, Mark and Miriam left the Oval Office.

Monday—November 27
Pakistan—Gwadar

Persian Quest remained in the harbor at Gwadar for the week restocking and refueling. Kadar was in no hurry to head out into the waters occupied by the American task force. While there was no one on board, except him, wanted by the Americans, he did not want to take any chances. He also did not want to see the inside of an American prison again.

However, he couldn't stay there forever. *Persian Quest* departed and made way north toward Char Bahar, inside territorial waters and out of the American task force's area, crossed to Muscat, and headed south for Socotra. He had another mission to prepare for.

Chapter Fifty-Two

Monday—November 27
Freeport, Texas—Ryan's Marina

Ryan flew home to Texas later that day, his mind whirling as he flew and disappointment very much on his mind. He would have to find another way. Looking out the aircraft windows, he determined that he would indeed find another way. He wouldn't be stopped. It didn't make any sense to him. In the past, the president had supported everything he had suggested, and then some. But now, when he really wanted to go after them, he was rebuffed.

It was not expected, and he would have to figure out a way around it. It was actually his own self-defense that he was concerned with, along with Jackie's. They had been targeted by this terrorist group and he needed to stop it. He used the time in the air to think through what he might be able to do.

Arriving back at the marina, he greeted Jackie and sat down in the apartment to figure out the details of his next moves. He needed help and he knew it. Jasper and Corey would be able to help, assuming Corey would be able to get away from work for a few weeks. Dave wouldn't be available due to a distant underwater commitment with his company.

He continued his thinking started in the air. It would be expensive, and he would need to get at least some minimal intel, but if he could just locate the quarry, he could take them out. He knew he needed, as he had suggested in the past, to get the ayatollah while he was moving between locations. That would negate all the security structures at the Socotra Island New Persia Operations Center and the distance limitations of the stronghold. The ideal would be to catch him in Salalah ... but that would be difficult to accomplish.

After he explained to Jackie what had happened in Washington, she was also surprised and disappointed. But she was supportive of his efforts to plan some form of action against New Persia.

Ryan decided to wait a few days and think it through. He had found, in the past, that sometimes if he waited a few days, his way forward would be clearer. Maybe there was something that his subconscious could come up with. And anyway, he had a few things to take care of in finishing the rebuilding process.

Tuesday—November 28
Hadibo Airport

Two days later Khatib and Ramiz were driven down to the Taj, where they changed vehicles and drivers to further the ploy for the satellites. Then they were driven to the airport, exited the vehicles under umbrella cover, and entered the airport terminal. The Felix Airlines 737 was arriving as they entered the terminal, and they passed through security with no problems. Boarding the aircraft, they merged in with other passengers walking out to the aircraft.

A couple of hours later, they arrived at the very modern Muscat airport. After passing through the large terminal and exiting out the covered arriving passenger area, they took a local taxi to the ayatollah's residence. They were quite indistinguishable from the rest of the small throngs of people traveling. Any satellite coverage to locate them would be very difficult, if not impossible.

At Schriever AFB, the satellite monitoring continued coverage of the three locations: the stronghold, Salalah, and Socotra. But nothing of any note was spotted. They recognized that commercial traffic in and out of the locations presented a problem. They could not determine who was traveling with any degree of accuracy. Mixed in with the various tourists and business travelers, any of the New Persia people would not be detectable. It was a vulnerability that had to be recognized, and other methods of surveillance were needed to watch their very elusive quarry.

And they weren't watching Muscat.

The ayatollah, Khatib, and Ramiz gathered their documents, provided by Zhang when they left Socotra, and departed for the airport early in the morning. It would be a very long flight. They would overfly the Arabian Sea, all of India, the Bay of Bengal, Myanmar, Vietnam, and other parts of Southeast Asia before entering Chinese airspace over the South China Sea. Total time was a little over thirty-six hours, with stops in Doha, Qatar, and Guangzhou, China, and would be tiring. But necessary. And the result would be a disappearance of the ayatollah into friendly hands and his safety in the China countryside. It would be a safe retreat, and one that would double as a series of planning meetings for future support. A win-win.

Wednesday—November 29
Socotra Island—New Persia Harbor

Persian Quest pulled into her home harbor on Socotra and began an immediate loading action to ready herself for another mission. She had escaped from the American task force and sailed over to Muscat and then back to Socotra. She pulled into the harbor and tied up, and men began replenishing her and loading mission supplies in her cargo holds and on deck.

Thursday—November 30
Zhanjiang, China

Arrival in Zhanjiang was uneventful, and they were taken to the officers' quarters in the PLAN facility nearby. Zhang met them in their quarters and welcomed them to the South Sea Fleet.

As promised, Zhang had made arrangements for their visit, and the quarters were very satisfactory. They were also given an itinerary for their five-week stay that included multiple meetings with various levels of support personnel from both the PLAN Submarine Force and the PLAN Surface Force. At the end of their third week, they would meet with Vice Admiral Chang and finalize their planning activities, to include schedules for delivery of various systems and the associated training. The final two weeks were for any revisits required due to changed support availabilities.

The ayatollah said, "Thank you for the arrangements and the hospitality. Please pass on my appreciation to Admiral Chang for his assistance. I look forward to the next few weeks and meeting him during the latter part of our stay."

Zhang responded, "He is aware that you have arrived and is pleased that your trip was uneventful. I would suggest, due to the length of your journey and the attendant time difference, that you take the rest of today to rest and regain your strength. I have only one meeting scheduled for you tomorrow, and the purpose of that meeting is to set a firm agenda of meetings and discussions for the rest of your stay." Zhang stopped for a moment, noticing the slightly puzzled look on Khatib's face.

Zhang continued, "The agenda I provided to you before you left Muscat was a proposed agenda and is subject to change. We need to discuss it and I need to make sure the right individuals are available for that schedule to take effect. And your concerns need to be considered, since you may wish some changes or different degrees of emphasis in certain areas. I wish to make this trip as beneficial and mission-supporting as possible. I'm sure you feel the same way." He stopped again for a moment then said, "Are there any questions I might be able to answer?"

Khatib looked at Ramiz and the ayatollah. He looked back at Zhang and said, "Not right now. I think we need to get our heads together and compare what you had proposed with what we have listed as our expectations and then get together with you. We can either do that before the meeting tomorrow or during the meeting. That would be your option."

Zhang said, "You need to get some rest and think things over. Let's just discuss it all during the meeting tomorrow. After all, that is the purpose of that meeting. Then we can resolve any differences in our expectations."

Khatib looked at both the ayatollah and Ramiz, got a slight nod of acceptance from both of them, and said to Zhang, "Until tomorrow, then."

Zhang bowed and left the room.

American satellite coverage over the Zhanjiang area was periodic and not constant. The Chinese, very aware of the satellite capabilities and viewing schedules, made sure the ayatollah and his party were not in view when periodic surveillance was being conducted by the Americans. Thus, the search for the ayatollah in China failed. And the Chinese knew that.

After obtaining some dinner and saying their prayers, the ayatollah, Khatib, and Ramiz sat down with the proposed agenda, compared it to what Khatib and Ramiz had defined as their interests, made a few changes, and discussed it until they were satisfied at the result. The ayatollah was fairly quiet and let the two of them develop the changes. After a short time, they separated to their own assigned rooms. It had been tiring and they needed rest.

The ayatollah looked out at the scene before him. He could see warehouses in the distance and several large naval fighting ships in the harbor. There were vehicles moving about on various assignments in the large complex. It was impressive, and he was uncomfortable being there. Allah had been good to him and had led him to the international recognition he now possessed in the Middle East. He felt safe and knew the Americans were not aware of his location ... yet he wasn't with his own people. He was with a major benefactor and in their debt for the significant support they provided. He really had no option other than to accept their support, because without it, his movement could not exist. But it truly made him feel ... awkward ... and small. He didn't like it.

He wondered what Allah's plan was ... but it was hidden to him, and he had to just deal with it. He shook his head, sat down, and opened his Koran. He wanted some form of guidance, but it didn't come to him ... he was just blank.

The following morning, Khatib was taken to the airport and flew back to Socotra. The three of them had agreed that one of them should be in the operations center monitoring the Americans.

Friday—December 1
Freeport, Texas—Ryan's Marina

Ryan was doing a little tax paperwork when it suddenly occurred to him that if he was going to take on the New Persia leadership, he probably ought to get with it. He was concerned. He had been attacked in the past, and they were always surprises. He didn't want that to happen again. He needed to move before New Persia struck again.

He went to the phone. After dialing Jasper and the visiting Corey, he arranged to meet at the Dolphin restaurant the next morning. He wanted to discuss his thoughts and see what they might think. Bouncing the ideas off his friends could be useful and might be both encouraging and resourceful.

They met in the morning at the Dolphin Restaurant just down the beach from Ryan's marina. Corey and Jasper were both in good shape and seemed like they were looking forward to seeing what Ryan had in mind. After some preliminary discussions over the weather and Ryan's progress on his marina office and apartment complex, they ordered a large breakfast of eggs, ham, hash browns, toast, and coffee. While they were having their second cups of coffee, Ryan began to discuss what he had in mind.

"I had an interesting conversation with the president a few days ago and got turned down for any help in getting the New Persia thugs behind bars."

Jasper hesitated a bit, then put his coffee cup down in surprise and looked back at Ryan with a questioning look in his eyes. Corey just watched carefully. Ryan responded, "Yeah. It surprised me too, but he wouldn't support me, or us, going after these guys. Called it a vendetta and he wouldn't allow it. So I'm on my own on this one."

Jasper said, "Wow. That's quite a turnaround. I woulda thought he'd support anything we could do to get these guys."

Corey just shook his head and didn't say anything.

Ryan said, "Yeah. Me too. Maybe he has something else in the wind that he didn't want to talk about, more than what we already know, but it was not a pleasant experience. But I have to deal with it."

Jasper looked over his coffee cup. "You mean *we* have to deal with it. You aren't in this alone. That's what friends are for, and you need as much help as you can get."

Corey just smiled and nodded, lifting his coffee in agreement.

Ryan responded, "Thanks. I was hoping you both would say that."

Jasper smiled. "Yup. Now, what have you got it mind?"

Ryan laid out a plan for Jasper that included Corey and Jackie in active roles. It would take a few weeks to get started, but they were anxious to get underway.

Friday—December 1
Zhanjiang, China

Ramiz met with the ayatollah the day after they arrived. They had been able to refresh themselves and get rested after the long trip. There was some jet/time lag for them, but they were ready to begin the meeting sessions. Ramiz was pleased to be part of the request committee within the ayatollah's organization. After almost two months of work, the Socotra New Persia compound facility modifications and construction had moved right along and were now well underway. The helicopter operational area was complete and several of the security system upgrades were now operational. Progress was very apparent.

They met in the ayatollah's room for a brief conversation before the meeting with Zhang and others. Ramiz sat down with the ayatollah and reviewed the list of needs they felt the Chinese could satisfy.

Ramiz said, "Sir. Khatib and I both feel we need to have the Chinese continue with their current level of support, with some additions. Zhang has told us that they are quite willing to continue the past efforts in ships, communications, and other logistics areas, and to continue monitoring the U.S. activities in the Indian Ocean. So, the existing support would continue. However, I would propose some additional support, and some of it, we believe, would fit into their strategic planning."

The ayatollah looked questioningly at Ramiz. Ramiz then explained what they had in mind. The ayatollah was surprised at the suggestion, stood up, and walked over to the window as Ramiz maintained a respectful silence. He stood there for a few minutes then turned around and said, "What you are proposing is not for us to give. The government of Yemen would have to concur with this idea. And it would open the area, and us, to very close scrutiny of our activities."

Ramiz said, "Yes. That is true. But the security that we would obtain would be significant, and I think the Yemeni government would welcome the idea. I think the security that you, and New Persia, would obtain is important enough to override any fears of surveillance of our activities."

The ayatollah, still standing by the window, slowly nodded. "I will have to think about this for a short time. You make a good argument, but there are some drawbacks."

Ramiz then said, "We need to resolve this soon. The first meeting is today, and I am sure the Chinese would like to see some form of overview of our thoughts and desires." The comment was intended to push the ayatollah in his decision process, hopefully in the direction they wanted.

"I understand your concern, Ramiz. But I also do not want to make a serious blunder in the interests of speed."

Ramiz said, "The main thing we are after, for your security and our own, is to get the Chinese to provide a couple of helicopters and their crews so we can patrol the waters off our harbor area. We do not want the American Navy to bring their submarines in close again. It would be too risky for them if they knew we had helicopter capabilities to use against them."

The ayatollah nodded. "Let us see how the meeting goes today. After all, it is just to set an agenda for the next week or so. I think we can tell Hai Jun Zhong Xiao Wang, who administers the foreign support organization within the South Seas Fleet PLAN, that we have a list but are considering some other additional items that we would like to approach in a few days. Given the support they have provided so far, I think that will be satisfactory to them. In the meantime, I will consider your suggestion further."

Ramiz looked back and nodded his assent. After all, the ayatollah was the boss. He felt it would be better to be more up-front and ask for what they needed right away. But he wasn't in charge.

That afternoon, the first meeting was held in a sparsely decorated conference room. They filed in for the 2:00 p.m. meeting and took their seats at a long table. Multiple Chinese Navy personnel of lower rank than the captain filed in and filled the chairs along the wall. Zhang met them, shook hands, and bowed, then had a seat next to Ramiz and farther along the table from the captain's seat at the head. A small flurry of action, coming to attention for the Navy personnel, occurred in the room as the captain entered and took his seat. The ayatollah and Ramiz also rose in respect, then sat down after the captain was seated.

Captain Wang looked at the three visitors and said, "We welcome you to our facility. Hai Jun Zhong Jiang (Vice Admiral) Chang, our South Sea Fleet commander, also welcomes you and will be seeing you in a few weeks. The next few days or weeks should be very productive for both of our organizations. I anticipate that there will be some changes to our current arrangements and it will be good to get that information, support, and processes clarified. In turn, you will need to know our expectations for you, and that needs to be well understood on both sides."

He stopped for a moment and then spoke directly to the ayatollah as he continued, "We have a mutually beneficial relationship at this point, and I do not want to alter it in a significant manner. We understand your troubles with the American government and can only hope that they will recede in the near future. But despite those troubles, I have been given direction to continue our support and make sure we do what we can to make your mission and efforts a success."

He hesitated for a moment, and the ayatollah took advantage of it. "Thank you for your comments, and I can assure you that we are of the same mind. As you undoubtedly are aware, we are moving around a bit to avoid the infidels' satellite monitoring capability." He stopped, as the captain had raised his hand.

"Yes, ayatollah. We are aware of this problem, and, since the U.S. periodically focuses their cameras on us, we know when they are viewing us and avoid anything we don't want them to see. You are part of that and, if necessary, we will warn you of any possible coverage that you should avoid. We do know that, at least for now, they are not aware of your presence here. And we want to keep it that way. I think our meeting's productivity will be enhanced through this awareness."

The ayatollah said, "I agree, and thank you for your support. I think we are all in agreement and need to move on to the agenda we are here to develop."

The captain nodded. "I have several subordinates who will be assisting in the discussions. I would like to introduce them to you. Once we have done that, I think we can develop an agenda of sub-meetings and get on with the detailed discussions. Would you agree to this process?"

The ayatollah nodded and said, "Yes. That is exactly what we had in mind."

The meeting then proceeded with Captain Wang introducing people in finance, security, logistics, operations, facilities, weapons, and engineering. A series of meetings were agreed to over the next two weeks, and the ayatollah assigned some of his staff to represent New Persia at the discussions.

Saturday—December 2
Freeport, Texas—Ryan's Marina

Ryan, Corey, Jasper, and Jackie all met to discuss more details of their plan. They would need tourist visas to visit Oman. Corey thought he could handle that fairly quickly, since they all had passports that were current. They already had equipment for outback trekking and could rent scuba gear from outfitters in Salalah. They could not get any weapons due to the airline restrictions, but thought they might be able to get something once they got to Salalah.

Jackie had to, on several occasions during the day, call back to Washington on scheduling problems. She was talking with Marjorie, since Maria wasn't due to fly back until tomorrow with Corey.

It looked like it might all fall into place. Corey would fly back to Washington with their passports and get the visas processed, and return as soon as he could. Jackie would continue to work the president's schedule as long as she could and put in for a couple of weeks of "vacation" toward the middle of the month.

Looking at the calendar, they all agreed that they thought they could get underway, flying to Salalah, on December 16. That would give them almost two weeks to get everything. Ryan would contact an outfitter and get a boat and scuba equipment lined up.

Saturday—December 16
Freeport, Texas—Ryan's Marina

It had all worked out and they were ready to leave. Juan would manage the marina while Ryan was gone and Corey had forwarded their passports and tourist visas. Corey went back to the American embassy in Turkey and would join them in Salalah. Ryan,

Jackie, and Jasper drove to Hobby Airport for their long flight to Salalah. It would be quite an adventure, and they hoped it would put an end to this difficult situation.

Ryan had some second thoughts about going against the president's desires, but he had to think about Jackie and his own possible survival. He still didn't have any fresh intel, and they were going to have to pretty much wing it. But he suspected that one of the three New Persia leaders would be on Socotra. So they were going to try there after they tried to find the compound in Salalah. New Persia was not going to quit until they got him, and he needed to make sure he got to them first. It would be tense.

Monday—December 18
Salalah, Oman

Ryan, Jackie, and Jasper arrived at the commercial airport in Salalah, retrieved their luggage, and walked outside into the Omani desert heat. It was hot even in December. They took a taxi to the oceanfront Hilton hotel where they had made reservations. Expensive but very nice. Not somewhere that an assassination team would gather ... but there they were.

It had been a tiring trip, with well over twenty-four hours of flying to Salalah's modern and very impressive airport. With a population exceeding two hundred thousand, Salalah was a large and modern city, and the second largest in Oman. There was even a large cruise ship in the harbor, and tourists were very evident. Ryan looked out the hotel window at the oceanfront and marveled at the view. He could certainly understand why the ayatollah had taken refuge in this city. But he had no idea where in the city he might be found. They would have to do some searching, and Corey's presence was critical.

Ryan, Jackie, and Jasper unpacked their few items in the two connected rooms, since they were traveling light, and called their point of contact, Namir. They had made arrangements to rent a small forty-foot sailing boat, along with various pieces of scuba gear. After they had looked over the warehouse with the disappearing antenna and seen whatever they could see there, Ryan's plan was to sail the boat over the Gulf of Aden to the Socotran coastline and go from there.

Ryan looked at Jackie and shook his head with a slight smile. She was really something, and very determined to participate in their little raid and adventure. He had tried to convince her otherwise, but she would have nothing to do with staying behind. So he had relented.

The next morning they were having breakfast in the hotel when Corey Gaskins, as planned, showed up in the dining room. He had flown in the previous night and was a very welcome sight. He had been critical in capturing the ayatollah the last time and would be very important to their efforts on this unofficial mission.

After finishing breakfast, they obtained a rental car and went searching through the city. Corey, because he spoke fluent Arabic, drove as they looked around. They stopped and parked outside the warehouse that contained the antenna, but the intel they had from previous visits by U.S. State Department people proved to be correct. There was nothing really to see. But they did observe that the big overhead door on the side was where the ayatollah had come and gone, in a multicar motorcade, as he was moving around the city. They also noticed that the small marina near the warehouse was where they had been told the yacht had tied up. It made a lot more sense to them now that they could actually visualize what the environment looked like.

Corey commented, "It looks to me like this warehouse is just used once in a while. There aren't any signs of it being used a lot. Since it is fairly new, even the roads around it aren't heavily used."

"I have to agree," said Jasper. "Usually there is more wear on the roads from trucks going in and out. I think it is just a seldom-used transfer point. He probably doesn't use it very often. And that's not good for us. We can't wait around here for him. It could be months."

Ryan and Jackie both nodded. They had been thinking the same thing. Ryan said, "Okay. I think we can all agree on that. But anybody got any ideas on how we might find where he normally stays when he's in the city? That's what we really need to find."

Everybody shook their heads. It was the real problem they had to deal with, and none of them had a solution. Since the president had declined to help them out, his information channel was closed and they had no way to tell where the ayatollah and his people were located.

They drove around for a short while but had no real purpose. The city was a myriad of streets and there was no way to determine the ayatollah's normal location. They were at a loss. After an hour of aimless driving, they went back to the hotel ... wasted time. They did anticipate that one of their three targets would be on Socotra in the operations center, and that was where they decided to concentrate their efforts.

Namir had the sailboat ready and would pick them up the next morning. He would escort them to the marina and finalize the rental agreement. It had not been as difficult as Ryan had first thought ... his U.S. Coast Guard-issued license and sailing papers had been adequate for the rental, and the cost was reasonable.

Then they had to load the boat, take it out on a trial run, and finish with supplies. They planned to leave on Saturday.

Saturday—December 23
Oman—Salalah

On Saturday they were all looking forward to getting underway. They had made the excuse that they were just going out for a few days of scuba diving and enjoying parts of the gulf and some of the myriad offshore islands. They were playing tourists and, given their sailing expertise and obvious diving capabilities, fit the image of being semi-rich. There were no real questions asked, and the marina personnel were helpful in explaining where good diving locations could be found. The ruse appeared to be working well.

After loading up supplies for several days, and checking out the navigation and support equipment on the boat, they checked out of the hotel and put their personal things away on the boat. Looking at the GPS and the local maps, Ryan then started the small motor and backed away from the pier. They worked their way through several other anchored boats and headed out to the south after clearing the breakwaters. In the outer harbor they went past several commercial ships at anchor and continued on their southerly route.

It was slightly over three hundred miles to Socotra and would take a day and a half to make the journey. Ryan anticipated having to avoid several large commercial carriers, since this route was a major shipping lane leading into and out of the Suez Canal. But he did not anticipate any problems with the journey. Namir had even provided some small-caliber rifles and a pistol, should they have a problem with pirates. But they hoped they wouldn't have to use them.

Several hours later, out of sight of land to the north, the four of them were enjoying the cruise. The water was relatively calm and they were making good progress. The warm sun felt good to them, and Ryan was able to steer clear of several ships as they made their way south. Jackie was busy in the small galley and came up with some refreshments and drinks. Corey was stretched out on the foredeck and Jasper was lounging next to Ryan in the cockpit. They gratefully accepted the drinks.

Now that they were outside of landfall, Ryan said, "You know, I think we may be able to find either Ramiz or Khatib on Socotra. But I doubt the ayatollah will be there. It would be quite risky for him to be spotted on the island. Our satellite folks would have him very quickly, and the U.S. Navy could raid the place in a heartbeat."

Jasper, looking at the frosty drink, nodded and added, "Yes, they would. Since the task force is not very far away, and they have marines on board for anti-pirate action, it wouldn't be hard to picture that happening."

Ryan looked off in the distance and thought for a moment. "I wonder if that's the reason the president wasn't willing to support us? I mean, maybe he's already got something underway that, for some reason, he didn't want to reveal to us. We were in the briefing, when General Foley discussed a raid, but maybe there's more to it."

Corey shrugged. "Could be. Maybe he didn't want you to interfere in what they had planned. I can't believe he just dropped the whole thing. There's been too much action already and he would not just ignore it."

Jackie remained thoughtful. She wasn't sure. She knew the president well and knew he wouldn't just let this situation drop. There had been too many issues and too many people had already died. She was sure he was going to take some form of action but just didn't know what. Her sudden request for a two-week leave of absence had taken the president by surprise, but he relented. She thought, from the look on his face, that he had figured out she wasn't actually going on a vacation.

The three men kept up their speculating for close to half an hour, and then quieted down in individual contemplation. Their conversation just sort of drifted off and they settled into quiet thoughts. Jackie listened for a bit and then went below to rest a bit. Nighttime was coming, and they needed someone to be alert through the night.

Saturday—December 23
Washington, D.C.—The White House

The president received the report with misgivings. The CIA was tracing Ryan and his people and reported that they were in Salalah and had rented a small sailing boat. They had just departed to the south for an unknown destination and had supplies for several days.

The president looked at a map and quickly determined what that destination must be. Socotra. He looked out the window and pinched his brow. He had hoped that Ryan would drop the effort. But he obviously had not. From surveillance, he knew Khatib was in the operations center, but didn't know where Ramiz or the ayatollah were located. Ryan didn't have that information, so must be working on a best-guess assumption. The president took a deep breath of misgiving and turned back to his desk. He wasn't sure what to do about the situation.

He thought about the current planning. The U.S. Navy had a submarine just off the coast of Socotra in relatively deep water to avoid any chance of detection. As soon as intelligence confirmed Khatib's presence, the SEALs would enter the blocked harbor at night, set off several distracting explosives in the harbor and residential areas, and wait for the inevitable action by Khatib to escape the apparent invasion. Then they would get him. Both the roads and the helicopter areas were going to be covered so he couldn't possibly escape. He would be the first.

It would strike more fear into the ayatollah and, hopefully, Ramiz. Though Ramiz might be calm and collected enough to manage to avoid the fear. He certainly had been a cool customer so far. And very clever.

The president called Maria. "Please get Admiral Nelson on the phone for me. We have a slight problem and I need to get his help."

Chapter Fifty-Three

Sunday/Monday—December 24/25
Gulf of Aden

It was nighttime as they continued across the Gulf of Aden toward the coast of Socotra. They planned to anchor outside the twelve-mile international boundary, scope out the defenses in a series of nighttime incursions, and regroup to figure out how they might capture Khatib or at least some senior members of New Persia's staff. Given the past capture of the ayatollah, they were sure the defenses had been built up significantly. It was maddening to Ryan that he had absolutely no intelligence. And he knew their risk factors went out of sight because of that lack. But he was determined.

As the night began to fade into daylight, Ryan took over the helm from Corey, who had spelled off Jackie much earlier that morning. They were still too far out to see the Socotra Island shoreline, but their GPS indicated they were right on course and about seventy-five miles away. They had made reasonable time, moving at a little over ten knots, and Ryan's planning was, so far, right on schedule. He was anxious to get the actual effort underway.

He was concentrating on the course and his morning coffee. The water off to his portside started to churn about fifty yards away and he looked over, thinking it might be a large whale or even a shark making the disturbance. It wasn't. A large American nuclear submarine was surfacing and matching his relatively slow pace and course direction. He wasn't sure what to make of it. Jasper, Corey, and Jackie all came up and watched. They too were puzzled.

Corey screwed up his face and said, "I wonder what this is all about. American submarines at sea don't usually surface without good reason. And it is obvious they are here because we are here."

Ryan nodded. "I think so too."

They watched as the conning tower hatch opened up and several people scurried about. The submarine eased over toward the sailing boat until it was just ten feet or so away and continued to match speeds. One person, obviously an officer, cupped his hands over his mouth and yelled, "Please heave to. We need to have a discussion with you."

Ryan waved back in acknowledgement and modified the rigging, and the boat began to slow down. After a few minutes, he had stopped and they were wallowing in the slight waves. The submarine had also stopped, and lines were thrown from the submarine to tie the two vessels together. Jasper caught the lines and made them tight on two portside gunwale fittings.

Ryan stood up at the stern with a questioning attitude in his posture. He didn't know what to expect. He didn't have long to wait.

Commander Allen Miller came down to the forward part of his submarine and was just a few feet from Ryan. He said, "Are you Ryan McKenzie?"

"Yes, sir. I must say, this is very unusual. What can I do for you?"

"Leave, and go back to Salalah," he said curtly. "I have orders from the Pentagon, and they originated higher than that, to make sure you return. Now please turn around and return to Oman without delay. We will monitor you as you leave."

Ryan didn't know what to make of the situation. He turned to Corey, Jackie, and Jasper. They shrugged at him. Corey spread his hands slightly and shrugged again, tilting his head and nodding slowly. Jackie, studying the deck at her feet, began to slowly shake her head. She knew where this was coming from. And they had been right. The president wasn't leaving this alone after all.

Ryan looked back at the commander. He said, "I'm sorry, but we are here on our own to accomplish a task we feel is important. Why are you asking us to return?"

"I can't get into specifics. We have a classified mission to perform and you are possibly interfering with it."

Ryan nodded. It confirmed what they had all thought. Now he had a decision to make. He stood there for a moment looking back at the U.S. Navy commander. He said, "Excuse me for a minute. I want to discuss this with my crew." The commander nodded but was obviously annoyed.

Ryan turned back to the three others and they moved down into the cabin.

"What do you think?" Ryan said.

They all just looked back at him. Finally Jasper said, "Well, I think it's pretty obvious what they are up to. We don't know any of the real details, but I'll bet there's a bunch of SEALs on that submarine and they have a nighttime mission to perform. Maybe our being here triggered the president to act. Or maybe they've figured out where all three of them are." Then he shrugged slightly.

Corey nodded and said, "Makes sense to me. And they don't want us mucking it up for them."

Jackie looked down at the deck then back up at all of them. "I think that we may have started this when you asked the president for help. I'll bet he figured he better get on with it before we got into a lot of trouble. I also think that we don't want to be messin' with these guys." And she let the thought hang.

Ryan listened. And thought for a minute. He looked at the deck then over to the massive submarine tied to their port side. The commander was impatiently waiting.

Ryan walked over, climbed up on the gunwale, and hopped over to the submarine. The commander was startled, and two of his deck crew started toward Ryan. The commander put up his hand to the crew and they stopped.

He looked closely at Ryan and said, "What are you doing?"

"Without shouting, I want to know what this mysterious mission is. I'm sure you know who we are and that I have the required clearances. Or at least I did have them, unless the president cancelled them."

The commander looked back, especially at the reference to the president, then pursed his lips slightly, and stood back a step. Then he stepped forward again and got into Ryan's personal space. "I don't have the authority to explain that to you nor do I have the need. You are to leave this area—"

He was interrupted by a shout from the conning tower. "Commander McKenzie! What the devil are you doing out here?"

They both looked over and up at the conning tower. Master Chief Colin Spieth was standing looking down at them both. He added, looking at Commander Miller, "Sorry, sir. My surprise got the best of me." The master chief was dressed in nearly full SEAL attire and was obviously getting ready for a mission. Looking back at Ryan, he continued, "I thought you had retired a couple of years ago."

Ryan waved back and said to Commander Miller, "Master Chief Spieth and I go back a long ways. I'm sorry for the interruption, but he's always been a bit abrupt in his behavior. Very good man, though. And if he's aboard and dressed that way ... well, it tells me something."

Commander Miller, recovering from his surprise, just nodded. He said with a slightly modified tone in his voice, "Commander," and his eyebrows and voice went up slightly, "I still have my orders. Please leave the area."

Ryan stuck out his hand and they shook. "I'll compromise with you. We won't do anything for the next seventy-two hours. That will give you time to complete your assignment. We will move in closer so that we can see the action, but stay out beyond the twelve-mile limit. No interference. From what we already know, we know why you are here and what you are doing. And it is basically the same thing we were going to do."

Commander Miller stood there for a minute. "I'm asking you to leave and return to Salalah. I cannot complete my mission with you here. But at the same time"—he hesitated for just a moment, looking Ryan squarely in the eyes—"if you leave, wait a while, and then come back, I can't control that. Nor would I be watching for you. In forty-eight hours we will be wrapped up in our ... activities, and hopefully finished in seventy-two hours." He continued to gaze at Ryan with an unspoken message.

Ryan looked back with understanding. He waved at the master chief and gave him a thumbs up. Looking back at Commander Miller, he stuck out his hand and they shook again. He turned to his crew as he jumped back on board the boat and said, "We're leaving the area. Prepare to come about."

Ryan then turned as the lines were untied, looked at the commander, and gave him a salute. It was returned and the commander headed back to the conning tower. He disappeared into the submarine along with the rest of the crew. Shortly, the submarine moved away and slowly began to sink out of sight.

Ryan breathed a sigh of relief. He explained what had happened and that they would depart the area on a course back to Salalah. They would then wait for "a while" and return to twelve miles off the harbor area of the Socotra New Persia Operations Center. Corey, Jackie, and Jasper all nodded.

Ryan sat there for several minutes. The others were all in their own thoughts. Finally he said, "I don't think this changes anything we were doing. The SEALs may be hitting them, but I want to make sure they get what they came after. Whoever is on Socotra cannot be allowed to get away."

Corey added, "I feel the same way. We are familiar with the layout and the thinking of these people. We need to stick around and make sure this mission is successful."

Jasper and Jackie just nodded in agreement.

Ryan continued, "So here's what I have in mind." He then laid out his plan for the next two days.

Corey said, "So really, we are just going to continue with what we had planned, except let the SEALs do the invading."

"Yep. I think we need to provide the SEALs with some backup near the airport just in case there is an escape attempt by air."

Jackie added, "Makes sense to me also. If I were in New Persia's shoes, I'd make a break that way. Let's do it."

Jasper just nodded. He was all for it.

It wasn't over yet.

Sunday—December 24
Northern Arabian Sea

The American task force moved slowly up the Gulf of Oman. They knew exactly where the stronghold was located, and very recent satellite images of it were available. The F-18s were armed and ready. They only needed a final go-ahead for the mission from the Pentagon. They were in a holding action until then. But they did have several aircraft on constant alert. The Iranian F-14s that had shown up when they were chasing the *Persian Quest* indicated some offensive capability, and they didn't want to be caught unawares. There would be no contest between the F-14s and the much newer and more sophisticated F-18s.

The message came in from the Pentagon. The CNO had given the approval after a meeting with the president. The mission was a go. Execute when ready.

The most recent satellite photos were called up on computers, plots to the stronghold were developed, crews briefed, munitions loaded in addition to what were already loaded, and electronic countermeasures developed for any known threat radars. Given the reception the B-52s got the last time, nothing would be left to chance.

Two flights of three F-18s fighters each were ready for launch at 2300 hours. One EA-18H Growler was in the flight for electronic countermeasures should they need them. Two additional F-18s with air-to-air capability would accompany the strike aircraft to the target area. Should F-14s show up, the two F-18s would quickly dispatch them.

The catapults were readied, and one after another of the strike aircraft were launched along with their fighter escorts. They formed up to the north of the task force and proceeded to the coast of Iran. Nine aircraft in all. A formidable force. And coming in at night.

311

The stronghold had few defenses, but they had managed to bring back some early warning radars and they were on constant alert. Especially after the strikes on the American refineries. They expected to be attacked, since their location was known to the Americans. For several days, families and relatives had been dispersed throughout the countryside and back into the small towns and cities in the area. It was a rough life, but necessary to the overall New Persia mission.

Their expectations were realized as their radars, quickly countered by the inbound EA-18H aircraft, gave them slight warning. Those that still remained in the stronghold, and it amounted to just twenty-two fighters, prepared to intercept the American fighters with ARPMs and some RPGs, along with whatever ground fire they could muster.

After slightly less than thirty minutes of flying, and no resistance from the Iranian Air Force, the F-18s arrived in the area of the stronghold. The ARPMs proved to be almost useless against this fighter group. The fighters came in with all lights out and, using air-to-ground missiles and bombs, obliterated the stronghold area completely on the first pass. Those New Persia fighters that had the ARPMs could not, at the speed the fighters were flying, get a lock on any of the aircraft. The darkness combined with the speed just did not allow enough reaction time for the humans to move the ARPMs into position for lock-on. Not a single missile round from the ground was fired. And the ground fire, mostly AK-74 rounds, did only minor sheet-metal damage to three of the F-18s.

The F-18s made two passes each over the stronghold and departed. No loses and only minor damage to some of the fighters. As they departed the site of destruction, the flight lead, looking back at the obliterated targets, said over the radios, "Merry Christmas to all, and to all a good night." There were multiple clicks as the other flight pilots responded.

Mission accomplished.

Chapter Fifty-Four

Tuesday—December 26—Very Early Morning
Socotra Island—Off the Coast

Ryan and Jasper very quietly slipped into the water. It was just after midnight, and they were off the shore of Socotra Island with the New Persia Operations Center harbor in sight. It was partially lit up from the breakwater lights. They had moved the boat in the darkness and were now just two miles off shore. No sails and no lights to give them away. Still not visible from the shore but a lot closer in than the twelve-mile limit they had been observing during the day after the discussion with the submarine commander. Through their binoculars, they could periodically see guards pacing back and forth on the breakwater rocks. It would be a touch-and-go operation to get in, get what they were after, and get back out again ... without being detected.

Their silent scuba gear was a backup, and they swam slowly on the surface. If someone did see them, they would probably be mistaken for marine life. It was dark and difficult to see, and they knew most of the time guards would be bored and not very attentive to their chores. They moved in close to the harbor entrance and silently went below water. They approached the in-water gates and found what they were looking for. Maintenance was not a strong suit for most Middle Eastern organizations, and this proved to be true here. There were several small holes in the underwater fencing due to corrosion and careless operations. Enlarging one hole slightly, they were able to slip through and were in the murky waters of the harbor. Their luck had held.

Ryan, familiar with the harbor surrounds from his previous visits, led them both to the pier with the large warehouse on it. The armory. He eased up in the water and saw both the guards, together, a good distance away, smoking and talking. He was in the shadows of the pier and could not be seen. Jasper was right next to him, a very large presence.

They waited a few moments watching the guards. The guards just casually looked around a few times but did not move from their location. Ryan and Jasper slipped to the other side of the pier and slowly emerged from the water. They removed their flippers and scuba gear but left on the sock-like soft shoes. They were absolutely silent. Ryan led them to the entrance of the warehouse where they had found the munitions store on their previous trip. He tried the door. Locked. He quickly looked around. Nothing there, and they were around the corner of the building from the guards, out of sight. What now?

Jasper touched his arm and held up a small piece of what looked like string. Ryan nodded, took the "string," and shoved a small portion of it into the keyhole. It might work—then again, it might jam up the whole lock and they'd never get in. It was a small amount of plastic explosive and should disable the lock. Ryan put a small detonator in the keyhole, covered the whole thing with a glove, and set it off. A small popping sound occurred that he barely heard. He moved the glove and the door gave way. They were in.

They looked around and found that not much had changed. The warehouse was full of mines, rifles, ARPMs, RPGs, and other munitions. A veritable war supply.

They quietly eased over to the stored munitions and found three of what they were looking for in tubes inside coffin-like boxes. They wrapped them in expansive plastic bags and tape to keep out the water, and strapped them on their backs for the return. A few additional munitions were added and they headed out of the building.

They retraced their steps, found the guards hadn't moved, put on their scuba gear, and slid back into the water. Back out the hole in the underwater fence and then out into the dark ocean. After several minutes of lazy and quiet swimming, Ryan set off a high-frequency sonic signal and received one in return from Jackie. He homed in on the response and, after several minutes of additional swimming, they re-boarded the sailboat. Corey came over and helped them with their packages and stowed them below decks. Then he came up and helped them with the rest of their gear. After shedding his scuba gear, Ryan took the helm, and they quietly moved back out to sea and the twelve-mile limit. The night had been a real success.

As they moved out to sea, Jackie brought Ryan a small martini and they gathered in the cockpit. They all looked around at the nearly absolute darkness with one thought in mind. They could not see any sign of the submarine. They had no idea where it might be.

"Okay," said Ryan. "We succeeded tonight. And that was great. We got what we were after. I think our suspicion that an aircraft is the way Khatib, or possibly Ramiz if he's there, would escape is still correct. He certainly won't come toward the harbor with the SEALs coming from that direction. Now we need to keep on going and head into the Hadibo harbor and wait in case we can help out with the SEAL raid. I think what we got will come in handy if things develop the way we think they might."

Jasper, after taking a sip of some precious beer they had obtained, added, "Yes. And I think we have a very good chance of, as the commander said, 'interfering' with their mission. In fact, we might even be able to save it."

Corey smiled at the thought, but kept quiet. Jackie did the same.

Ryan said, "Yes. We might. If what happens is what I think might happen, we have a chance of getting Khatib or Ramiz ourselves. That would be quite an accomplishment. And it's the reason we came all this way. In spite of the obstacles we have run into, we may yet come out on top." He lifted his glass. "At least, let's hope so." And they all matched his toast.

Ryan headed out to a set of coordinates and then headed toward the main harbor in Hadibo. They planned to get to the harbor by midmorning, and register with the Socotra authorities as just some tourists out enjoying some diving and in need of some minor supplies and overnight anchorage. They were actually going to wait in the harbor for the action to start. It would be interesting.

They entered the harbor after clearing with the Hadibo harbormaster for an anchorage. Looking off to the left from their position, they could see the Socotra airport a half-mile off the harbor. They then took the small skiff and headed in to the pier and the small shops that had some of the supplies they needed. All in order to keep up the guise of just being tourists on a diving vacation.

Not the reality of their mission, though.

Chapter Fifty-Five

Wednesday—December 27—Very Early Morning
On Board SSN *Jimmy Carter*

During the previous day, the submarine had returned to its station just off the island and still in deep water. The commander had verified that Ryan's boat was no longer in the area. They had seen it briefly the previous evening as they loitered off the coast, but it was gone now. They would continue their mission as planned.

Master Chief Spieth had been truly surprised when he saw Ryan out in the middle of the Northern Arabian Sea, and right near where their mission was to occur. After overhearing some of the discussion with the commander, he put two and two together and figured out what was happening. They were all on the same mission, but Ryan was a civilian now.

Commander Miller was satisfied that they had convinced Ryan and his crew to depart the area. There was no sign of them. They had seen Ryan head out then head back in, spend some time near the harbor, looking innocent enough, and then head back out to sea. After that, they did not know where they had gone, but they were not in the immediate area. Therefore, as he had requested, they couldn't interfere with their mission needs that night.

Master Chief Spieth looked over his forty men as they prepared for the mission in Socotra. The ultra-quiet nuclear submarine had slipped slowly into the area outside the harbor entrance. The submarine had gotten them in to just under a mile from the shore, and they were preparing to invade the island, capture or kill whatever New Persia leadership they could find, and then return to the submarine. It was dark, just after midnight local time. Nerves were on edge, as they always were just before a mission. It was a nervous energy and put people on hyper-alert.

The New Persia Operations Center personnel did not recognize the danger they were in. They were unaware of the presence of the American submarine just off their coast.

The submarine eased to the surface and the crew, in near silence, launched four small inflatable boats. The grey of the submarine blended in well with the nighttime seas, and it was nearly invisible. The forty SEALs departed the submarine on their mission shortly after midnight. The men boarded their assigned inflatables. Master Chief Spieth took the lead and they headed to shore using small electric drive motors instead of outboards. They maintained as low a profile as they could and approached the harbor gates. They were to take out the harbor and work their way up to the operations center and take it out too. They were to capture Khatib and/or Ramiz and return them to custody on the submarine ... or kill them. It was a staged attack meant to confuse and complicate any attempted escape.

The first boat of SEALs moved in and split into two groups. A diversion was needed so they could get through the fencing without delay and any resistance. Three SEALs moved to the underwater harbor gate and set explosives.

The remaining three boats headed for the shoreline and beached in silence. All was quiet. The men scattered to preplanned positions as the timers on the explosives worked their way to zero. The cameras at the guard shack were lasered and the guards quickly disabled. Then charges were set on the automated gate at the gatehouse. They sat back to wait. Two other teams approached other sites on the fence line and set charges. All of the charges going off at the same time would cause both confusion and diversions. The main force of thirty men would approach from two directions: through the gate and further up the hill through the fence. It would be sudden, and coming from several directions at once—very confusing, and that was the intent.

The first charges at the underwater harbor gates went off and the two surprised guards at the pier were eliminated immediately. The main road gate blew up and the fence holes were set off. Quietly and expertly, the teams of men ran through the access points and headed for the operations center building.

Inside the operations center, chaos reigned. From a quiet evening of no action, suddenly they were overwhelmed with sensors going off, cameras burning out, and guards non-responsive to calls. Aban, the operations center supervisor, immediately called Marin, Ghanim, and Khatib. They came running into the operations center and saw the confusion and fear. Looking at what few cameras were still operating, it was obvious that they had been invaded. The eight-man response force had been deployed at the first explosion by the operations center personnel, but they were not responding to calls.

In the center, Khatib was watching the action on the various cameras and sensors. The SEALs were coming up the road and doing away quickly with the minor resistance of the guards and response force. It was a full assault on New Persia. They were just too good. He looked at the situation. They had actually arrived and would soon be in the operations center itself. He had to move and get out of there.

They could see shadowy figures every once in a while on the remaining cameras. Gunfire could be heard, and more explosions in various parts of the compound. It was too confusing. Khatib called Marin and Ghanim. They headed for the emergency escape tunnel in the lower level, where a small truck waited. Moving through a side door in the lower part of the operations center, Khatib headed for the truck sitting idle at an overhead door. They were underground.

As Khatib and party headed out of the main part of the operations center, they could hear gunfire coming from the hallway as some of their guard force was defending the center from the intruders. Gunfire that suddenly stopped as a grenade was set off. The intruders came rapidly through the doors of the center with guns ready to fire. The three men at the control consoles immediately lay on the floor. They were controllers, not warriors.

The SEALs heard the truck start up, quickly followed the sound to the lower level, and got to the room just as the truck disappeared through a large overhead door. The door was rapidly closing.

The driver headed down the tunnel, closing the door behind using a remote, as three SEALs came through the room door. The SEALs fired but did no damage as the overhead door came down, blocking them. Bouncing down the tunnel, Khatib, Marin, Ghanim, and the driver came out into a rougher section and finally came out of a cave in the mountains on the outskirts of Hadibo. They headed down the rough road and continued on to the airport.

The five SEALs, after blasting through the door, followed a few minutes later out of the tunnel and headed to the airport also.

Along the runway at the airport was a small berm built from construction debris and a small, shallow drainage ditch. Ryan and Corey hopped the fence on the airport perimeter and headed for the berm. In the dark, they were nearly invisible. They could look down the runway to the aircraft ramp, which was well lit and nearly empty of people. It was just after midnight and they could hear some explosions in the distance. The raid had started. Ryan focused his binoculars on a hangar as he saw the doors being rapidly opened. A small four-passenger Honda jet was pushed out and two men ran up to it, opened the side door, and quickly climbed in. Chocks were not even put in place. Shortly, one engine could be heard as it started.

Ryan smiled. They had been right. He tapped Corey on the shoulder and pointed at the small jet. Corey nodded once and set up the advanced rocket-propelled missile they had stolen. Ryan focused on a small, rapidly moving truck that came around the corner of the operations building and ran up to the jet. Three men quickly got out of the truck and ran. Ryan recognized Khatib immediately and looked at the other two men. He didn't know them, but guessed they were part of the New Persia senior management team. They quickly boarded as the other engine began to spool up. The door was shut and the aircraft started to move rapidly down the taxiway. It didn't hesitate at the end of the runway and continued to turn and line up for takeoff without stopping. The engines went to full power and the aircraft quickly picked up speed. They were obviously in a hurry.

As the aircraft passed Ryan and Corey, it rotated and began to lift off the ground. Corey wheeled around with the ARPM, took careful aim, got a right engine lock-on, waited until the aircraft was airborne over the water, and fired. The wheels of the aircraft were just retracting. The missile leaped out of the launch tube and, like an arrow, bored into the right engine of the fleeing jet. After just a few moments the missile found its target and blew up the right engine, along with part of the fuselage. The mortally wounded airplane rolled to the left at several thousand feet and plunged into the dark ocean waters. No survivors. Just an oil slick that caught on fire and some miscellaneous pieces floating on the surface of the warm tropical ocean. Khatib and company were no more.

Ryan looked at Corey and they high-fived. As they clapped hands, another truck came careening around the operations building and screeched to a stop on the runway. Ryan quickly looked over and realized he was looking at members of the SEAL team. Five of them in the truck looking at the oil slick and small fire in the water. They got out of the truck and were watching when yet another larger truck came around the building and began firing on the SEALs. A small group of eight or nine of the New Persia response team was engaging the SEALs, thinking they'd downed the aircraft. The SEALs were caught out in the open and surprised. One went down under the fire. Four of them returned fire but were obviously outmanned and outgunned. The four managed to take shelter behind their small truck, but it would only be a matter of time before they were cut down.

Ryan and Corey, quickly sizing up the situation and only two hundred yards from the action, decided the SEALs needed help. And they were on the flank of the New Persia response team. Corey quickly brought his second ARPM around, raised it slightly to sight it in on the response team truck, got a lock, and fired. When the rocket hit, the entire truck exploded in flame and debris. Only two members of the response team survived, and they ran for the operations building, one of them limping badly.

The SEAL team, watching with complete surprise, didn't know who had helped them out. Ryan slowly climbed up on the berm and, with a flashlight, signaled to the SEAL team. He told Corey to stay put just in case there was more action coming. Ryan then ran the short distance to the SEAL team, slowed down as he got closer, and yelled out. The SEAL team leader had a bead on Ryan but then the two recognized each other. It was Master Chief Spieth and some of his team. The chief dropped his weapon so it was aiming at the ground. Ryan ran up, grabbed him by the shirt, and clapped him on the shoulder.

They hugged briefly and the chief said, "Commander, you don't know how glad I am to see you."

"Actually, chief, I think I do. Now let's get you and the rest of the team out of here. What's your situation?"

"One dead and two wounded. One is superficial and the other is pretty serious. We need help."

Ryan said, "Got it." Then he turned and waved to Corey. Corey immediately headed their way and, after loading the dead SEAL, they all loaded into the small truck. They got off the airport as the local police were coming. They raced for the Hadibo harbor, placed everyone in the small skiff, and beat it for their sailing boat.

Jackie and Jasper helped unload everyone and Corey started attending to the most seriously wounded man. Jackie patched up the superficial wounds on the other. Ryan pulled anchor and motored out of the small harbor as fast as he could and headed for open sea.

"Chief, have you got communications with the rest of your team?"

"Yes, sir. Sure do."

"I'd suggest they hold their positions at the center, then once it is secure, they gather at the New Persia harbor for return to the ship."

"Close. They'll return to the beach and head out that way. But first they are going to destroy the ops center and the harbor warehouse and its close neighbors." As the chief was talking, they heard a very loud series of explosions and the sky lit up over the island. It was obvious the chief wasn't kidding.

Ryan said, "Contact them and tell them to head back to the sub. Then"—he stopped for a moment and looked at a sea chart of the area—"tell the sub to meet us at these coordinates. We should be there in about three hours." Ryan gave the chief a set of coordinates.

The chief got on his radio and passed on the information from Ryan. Then he went below, where Corey was tending to the injured SEAL. Corey's Special Forces medical background was coming in handy, and he thought the SEAL would make it until they could get proper attention on the sub. But it wasn't easy.

Several hours later, in the very early morning hours, and to the north and west of Socotra Island, they were cruising slowly in a calm sea. Again the water churned and the submarine appeared off their portside. After it surfaced and slowed to a stop, Commander Miller appeared on the conning tower. He hailed them and they pulled over next to the submarine and, after a few minutes, were tied fast. With the help of several submariners, the two wounded SEALs and the deceased SEAL were transferred to the submarine and sent below for treatment by a medic. Master Chief Spieth also transferred over as Commander Miller came down to speak with Ryan and crew.

Ryan said, "Thanks for picking these guys up. Hopefully Sam Mason, the seriously wounded SEAL, will recover. We did what we could for him. And sorry about Curt Logan. The chief said he was really a good man and just got caught in the fire."

Commander Miller responded, "We'll take care of them from here." He looked over at Jasper, Corey, and Jackie, and then back to Ryan. "I heard what you did, and thank you for it. You saved the mission for us with the downing of Khatib's plane and getting the SEALs out of a tough spot. I'm irritated that you didn't follow our directions to the letter, but, given what happened, we appreciate what you did. As far as Sam is concerned, there is a large task force about sixty miles north of here headed up by the *USS Truman*. They have a surgeon and proper medical capabilities. We are going to head up there as soon as we are finished here."

Ryan nodded. "What's the status on Socotra?"

"The operations center and all the facilities except the residences are no more. Our guys destroyed all of it, including the small patrol boats on the harbor. The thirty-meter satellite communications antennas are also in pieces, and the harbor is useless. The underwater gates have now blocked the entrance. If New Persia wants to continue here, it will be very difficult and expensive. We had two other SEALs wounded, but the rest are okay. Oh, and from a very brief discussion with the New Persia ops crews, Marin, their logistics guy, and Ghanim, their chief ops planner, were with Khatib. Looks like we got three of their top staff people."

"Sounds pretty complete. If that's all, we will head back to Salalah and on to the next phase of our effort."

"Sounds good to me. By the way, while I'm not supposed to talk with you beyond this interface"—he hesitated, took a piece of paper out of his pocket, and handed it over to Ryan—"this might be of help to you in your work."

Ryan took the paper, stuck it in his pocket, then reached over, shook hands, and said, "Thanks."

The commander started to leave but turned back to Ryan. "In case you haven't heard, we also hit the stronghold. It is no more."

Ryan looked back with raised eyebrows. They hadn't heard that news. "Thanks for the info. Maybe that'll put a final nail in New Persia's coffin."

The commander turned and headed back up the conning tower and disappeared down the hatch. The lines were released and the two vessels drifted apart. Ryan stood there for several seconds, glanced over at his crew, and then back at the submarine as the rest of the Navy crew disappeared into the sub. A few moments later, the submarine moved slowly off, picked up speed, and disappeared beneath the waves.

Ryan and crew were left alone on the Indian Ocean. Their mission here was complete.

Chapter Fifty-Six

Wednesday—December 27
Arabian Sea

Ryan stood watching the place where the SSN *Jimmy Carter* disappeared under the waves of the vast ocean. He was quite thoughtful for a few moments and then turned to see his crew all watching him.

He said, "Well, let's get going. It's a good distance back to Salalah and we might as well get underway."

Corey said, "Okay, boss. What was in the note he passed to you?"

Ryan had forgotten the note, and quickly reached in his pocket. He took out the note and, in the dim light of early morning, read it. He began to grin. "Well, I'll be damned," he exclaimed.

Corey, Jasper, and Jackie all waited impatiently. "Well," said Jackie, "what's it say?"

"He says, 'You might check out this address in Salalah. Our intel guys think there might be something of interest for you there.' And he listed a street address in Salalah."

Jasper said, "You mean he just gave us the ayatollah's address in the city?"

"Seems like it. We'll have to check it out when we get back there."

All four looked at each other. They actually had a chance to get this job done. Corey and Jasper high-fived each other, and Ryan went to the rigging and adjusted the sails, and they began to move to the north and Salalah. A few minutes later, they all gathered up on the deck near the cockpit and enjoyed the wind and sea breeze. Jackie brought up some mimosas—after all, it was early morning— and they were all lost in their own thoughts for some time. They relished their success on Socotra and the news of the destruction of the stronghold.

Sobering.

Wednesday—December 27
Washington, D.C.—The White House

"They did *what?*" exclaimed the president as he was talking in the Oval Office. He was being briefed by Admiral Nelson on the results of the raid on Socotra. General Foley, Jack, and Mark Allison were also there.

"Yes, sir. Ryan and his friends shot down the aircraft carrying Khatib and two others of the ayatollah's senior staffers. They also saved a small SEAL group from getting annihilated. The group was caught out on the runway and being fired on. Ryan and Corey took out the New Persia guards with an RPG ... or at least that's what we think they did. It's still a bit confusing."

The president looked at his two top military people and just shook his head. Unbelievable.

He looked at Admiral Nelson and said, "Well, they're there and obviously determined to act." He looked over at Mark. "What do you think?"

"We ought to help them," said Mark. "It doesn't matter how this plays out. We just need to get the New Persia senior leadership dead."

The president looked back at the admiral and said, "Okay. Stop them again and give them the info we have on the Salalah compound. At least then they will have some information they can work with."

The admiral looked a bit embarrassed. "Ahh, sir. Commander Miller, the *SSN Jimmy Carter* commander, did that when they picked up the SEALs from Ryan's boat. They already have the information."

The president looked a bit dismayed and then began to grin. "A step ahead of me, again. One of these days I'm going to learn." He turned to Mark and said, "Get with Kenton and see what help you guys might be able to provide when they get back to Salalah."

Mark smiled and nodded. He thought, *Back on track.*

Wednesday—December 27
Zhanjiang, China

It was early morning and they were having breakfast in the small conference room that had been given to them for small meetings. Ramiz was handed two notes from one of the junior enlisted Chinese Navy men who were functioning as the gofers for the various meetings.

Ramiz opened the first note and could not believe his eyes. It was from Socotra. The note was from Humam, one of the operations center controllers. He had sent the email from his home. Ramiz read:

The Socotra Operations Center was attacked last night by Americans. It has been destroyed, including the building, our normal communications, and the harbor. Khatib, Ghanin, and Marin have all been killed in an aircraft as they were escaping. Nothing was left except the residences. The response force tried, but seven of them were killed and another six were wounded. Personnel are in hiding at various places on the island. Use my home email to reach me.

Ramiz couldn't believe it. His mind went blank for several moments as he absorbed the message. They had been attacked, and the primary New Persia Operations Center and most of the facilities were destroyed. He sat down for several minutes to think and try and figure what to do next.

Then he opened the second note. It was from Omar Al Habash, their training manager at the stronghold. The Americans had destroyed the stronghold again this past early Monday morning. Most of the men who were there were okay, since their radars had picked up the raid in time to get them away from the facilities, but several had been killed as they were firing back at the American fighters. The facilities were all rubble ... again.

Ramiz sat with both messages and was nearly overwhelmed. It was difficult to absorb. The ayatollah had to be told, and he did not relish that at all. Here, they were in the safety of the Chinese, but they needed to go back and see what could be salvaged. But if they did, they might be targeted also.

He moved out of the conference room into the hall to think about the options. If they actually went back to Socotra, they might be hunted down. Salalah was an unknown. The infidels might know of it, but he wasn't sure. It might be the best bet until they could figure out what to do. Or they could stay right where they were, which was safe, and the Americans didn't know where they were.

Or Muscat? Or maybe something in between.

He went back into the conference room and sat down across from the ayatollah. Six members of the New Persia staff were also in the room. They were in the process of figuring out who was going to support the various meetings that had been set up. Ramiz looked across the table at the ayatollah and caught his eye. There was immediate recognition. They stepped outside into the corridor and Ramiz passed the notes to the ayatollah. They ayatollah read them, stopped for a moment, and then read them again. He leaned on the doorframe for support, held on to it for a moment, then slowly walked into the conference room again and sat down.

He sat there for several minutes as Ramiz quietly asked the people in the conference room to go elsewhere. The staff had not heard and wondered about the problem, but did not question the request for solitude. Ramiz came back after a few moments. The ayatollah was in deep concentration.

Finally the ayatollah said, "We must be strong in the face of this, yet another disaster, to our movement. Allah is testing us and we must remain steadfast in our mission."

Ramiz nodded, but said nothing.

Finally, after several more minutes of silence, the ayatollah turned to Ramiz and asked, "What do you think we should do next?"

Ramiz replied, "I have given that some thought and feel that I should go back and see what can be done. You are too important to our movement to be discovered. I suggest that you stay here and continue with the meetings. When I get back, we will plan what the next effort will be."

"I think that would be wise. I would like to go back and support our people, but understand your concern and rationale. We shall do as you suggest. When and where will you go?"

"Salalah for now, then we shall see."

"I will await your return here and continue with our Chinese discussions."

Thursday—December 28
Oman—Salalah

Two days later, Ryan and crew pulled in to the harbor in Salalah and tied up to their assigned berth. It had been an eventful few days, and very successful. Khatib was no more and they had a lead on the ayatollah … and probably Ramiz. They were chipping away at New Persia.

They unloaded their gear and took care of the rental paperwork, and a taxi took them back to the Hilton. They had a good chance to relax. That evening they had a good meal and retired for a night of rest.

After breakfast the next morning, they met in Jasper's room, since it had a view out over the city, got out a map of the city they had gotten from the concierge, and looked for the address the commander had given them. Over some hot coffee, they had to make some plans. They found it and realized that this was no guarantee. Just an intel guess, so they had to make sure it was right and then figure out what to do about it. It was a bit of a quandary.

A knock on the door took them out of their thoughts. They looked at each other and Jasper asked, "Did someone order something from room service?" His question was answered with blank stares and head shakes. He went to the door, looked through the peephole, and saw a thin, clean-cut Arabic man in a nice western-style golf shirt and slacks. He wore a turban and had a well-trimmed full beard. Jasper opened the door and the man, in excellent English, said, "Are you Jack Charleston?"

Jasper responded, "Yes. What can I do for you?"

"My name is Tarik Marike." He held out an identification wallet. "I'm from the American embassy in Muscat and have been requested to assist you and your party."

Jasper looked at the ID and then opened the door further so Tarik could come in. Ryan, Corey, and Jackie stood up, not knowing what was going on, and looked questioningly at Jasper.

Jasper said, "It looks like we have some help here. His ID looks good. If I had to guess, I'd say some high-level communications from the past couple of days activities led to this."

Nodding and looking at the group, Tarik said, "We received a message from State two days ago to find you and see if we can be of any assistance. Since the message came from Mr. Kenton Marshal, the secretary of state, we obviously took it seriously, and here I am. The bottom line is to help you with your search and, hopefully, conclude this matter soon."

Ryan shook his head. First the president turned them down and didn't help at all, and now this. He must have had a change of heart after they began to take some action against New Persia. The U.S. Navy and now the State Department. But it certainly would help to have someone from inside Oman to help them out.

Corey stood and in Arabic said, "Thank you for your offer. We can certainly use it." Then he turned to the crew and explained what he had said.

Tarik was surprised at the comment in the native language. He responded in English, "You speak our language. That is very good. And you will need it here. While many here speak some English, not all, and it will come in handy in our investigations." It was obvious that Tarik was considering himself as part of the group.

Ryan looked at all of them and nodded. It, perhaps, would be better. They invited Tarik to sit down.

Ryan turned to Tarik and asked, "What do you think you can do to help us out?"

"I believe I've found this address that you are looking for, and it didn't take long. I arrived last night and took a look. It isn't hard to find, but there isn't much there. It looks deserted except for a lone groundskeeper I saw working on the small grounds. It is a small compound surrounded by a high adobe-type fence. The gate is substantial, and that is where I saw the man working. But inside, the house looks quiet."

Ryan said, "So you don't think anyone's there?"

"No."

Corey said, "It's quite possible that he isn't there. I mean, he has been moving around quite a bit and may be somewhere that we don't know about."

Jackie said, "Makes sense to me. And by now he knows what happened in Socotra and the stronghold and would really be lying low. He could be anywhere and we wouldn't know how to locate him. If it were me, I wouldn't go back to any of my old haunts. We know about them and he knows we know. I think he's somewhere totally out of our reach."

Ryan said, "Good synopsis, Jackie. I have to agree." He turned to Tarik and asked, "Do you have access to any intel that might help us locate him?"

"Not off hand. But I can check at the embassy and see if they have any idea. It would be unusual for them to have that type of information unless they were specifically asked."

"We need to cover every possibility. Please check and see."

Tarik nodded. "I'll see what I can find out. What's your next step?"

"I think it would be a good idea for us to see this place and kind of get a feel for the area. There may be some action in the future and it would be good to be prepared," responded Ryan.

"If you have a car, I'll run you over there right now. It isn't far and won't take long."

Jackie said, "You guys go along. I have a few things to do, given our days at sea and the excessive sun drying I had. I don't need to see the compound anyway."

Ryan looked a little puzzled but went along with her. It wasn't like her to back away from action like this. "Okay. We'll check it out and be back soon. Enjoy the spa."

The four men then left for the address.

Jackie went to their room, booted up her computer, accessed the internet through the Hilton Wi-Fi, drafted a message, and sent it off to the White House. This situation just seemed to be too pat for her. It was possible that Kenton had done this, but she wanted verification. Then she did as she said she would do: she booked time in the spa.

An hour later, she came back and the men still hadn't returned. She checked her computer and found a response from Maria. Mark Allison had asked the State Department to locate them and help out. That was all Maria knew. Maria also wished her well and offered congratulations on the successful mission. The president was both angered and pleased over the situation. But more pleased.

Jackie went to their luggage, took out a bottle of gin, and made herself a martini. She was relieved that, apparently, Tarik was legit. She hadn't been sure, and for some unknown reason felt he was a dark horse, not to be trusted. Maybe she was getting too suspicious?

Ramiz, standing well back from the window to avoid being seen, briefly looked out the window. While the gate was still intact, he was dismayed to see four men stop, get out of a car, and stare at the compound. He was sure he couldn't be seen. It had been a couple of traumatic days for he and the ayatollah when they realized they were being actively hunted. The news from Socotra and the stronghold was devastating to them, and the death of Khatib, Marin, and Ghanim was a real blow. It would take time to recover emotionally for the ayatollah. Ramiz was colder and wanted to escape first and then exact revenge when he could.

But for now, he was really surprised because he recognized Ryan in the group of men. They had found the compound. Fortunately, he had thought this might happen and made sure the compound looked vacant. No vehicles, no trash, windows blocked up, and no guards or other people around. He wanted it to look like no one was there. He hoped the ruse would work. If it didn't, he realized he was in real trouble.

Ramiz watched as the group milled about outside the fence and finally left. It only took a few moments for him to realize that the compound had been compromised and the location known to the Americans. He couldn't stay. He immediately gathered his things and walked out the back and down an alley, where he had a rental car parked. He headed out for the airport. He decided to go to Socotra and see what had really happened, and then on back to China.

After two hours of looking around, all of the men arrived back in the Hilton. They had resigned looks on their faces. They had found the place, and Tarik was right. It definitely did not look occupied right now. No sign of anyone except the groundskeeper. While they thought they had a lead, it looked like it was a dead end. They didn't realize how close they had come to one of their primary targets.

Ryan gave Jackie a quick rundown in their room, and Jackie told him about her message back to Washington and the result. He thought about it a little and decided it was a good thing she had done it. After all, Tarik had just shown up, unexpected, and they didn't really know who he was.

They all gathered in Ryan and Jackie's room to figure out the next step. Tarik was included, since he said he was staying at the Hilton also, one floor up. They needed to strategize over their next move. If the ayatollah and Ramiz were not at the Salalah address, where were they and how could the group find out? Earlier, Tarik had called the embassy and left a message for security to get whatever they could on the ayatollah's current location. But so far, he had not heard back. It could be a little while.

Ryan said, "Well, hopefully the embassy will have an idea on this. If he's not here and not in Socotra, which I doubt, then where is he? Could be at the stronghold, but that would be stretching it a bit."

Corey said, "You know, you just said something that could be a clue to his whereabouts."

"What's that?"

"Well, if it were me, what would I do? I'd think of the least likely place to look. And to me, I'd think of either a vacant-looking house or the destroyed operations center on Socotra."

Ryan pursed his lips and nodded. "Either that or someplace completely different from what we know." He thought for a few moments and then added, "And that could be China. After all, they have been the hidden partner in all this, even though the Chinese deny any part in it."

Jasper and Jackie both nodded.

Corey said, "Maybe. But China is a long haul from here. And they may not want him to show up on their doorstep and point at them as the silent one. They've denied everything so far, and him showing up there would be quite embarrassing."

"Okay," said Ryan. "Maybe we ought to take a closer look at that compound here. Perhaps they are there and we just don't know it. We could watch it for a couple of days in shifts and see what happens."

Tarik added, "That would work if they are there. But do you really want to occupy your time here with that kind of surveillance? I'd suggest that I get some help and let a local do that. Also, a local wouldn't be as obvious as you would be."

Ryan nodded in thought. Tarik had a point. Of course, he and the crew weren't doing anything else either, but a local would be less obvious. Then again, could a local be trusted?

They decided to wait for a couple of hours and get some dinner, since it was now late in the afternoon. Then they would get together again and develop a plan to watch the address. All of them were still a little tired from the past few days of activity, and Ryan wanted them all to be in top shape mentally as they made their plans. Ryan asked each of them to get two hours' rest and they would meet in the hotel restaurant. Then, after dinner, they would meet in Ryan's room to discuss planning. Everyone agreed, and they broke to return to their rooms for rest.

After an hour, Tarik called Ryan on the hotel phone and asked if they could meet privately for a few minutes. Ryan, puzzled, but willing to see what Tarik wanted, agreed. He told Jackie what was going on and she decided to continue her rest. Ryan could see what the issue was. Ryan and Tarik met downstairs in the hotel business center, which, fortunately, was not occupied.

"Ryan, I have been on the phone with our people in Muscat and have the name of a person who can watch the compound. I wasn't sure how open you wanted to be about this information, so that's why I asked for the private conversation. In this country, nearly everything is considered private."

Ryan thought for a moment and then said, "I understand. However, in our case, we are completely open among ourselves. But thank you for the concern. This person you are talking about, is he trustworthy and is he available?"

"Yes. I took the liberty of contacting him and he is very willing to watch the compound, and he is not very expensive. The embassy in Muscat has also agreed to cover his expense for you."

"Good. Thank you. When can he start?"

"They can start—oh, it is actually two people, he and his wife—anytime we want."

"So they would run in shifts?"

"Yes. And I will meet with them each day and see if there has been any sign of New Persia. And if they do see anything, they will contact me immediately."

Ryan thought for a moment and then said, "Okay. You're sure about these people?"

"Yes. They have helped us before and have always been reliable."

"Okay. Have them start immediately. We will tell the others later so everyone is aware of what is going on."

Later that afternoon, Ryan contacted each of his people and they met in Ryan and Jackie's room for a few minutes. Ryan explained what they were doing for compound surveillance and they all agreed to it. Following that short meeting, they all gathered in the hotel lobby and then went in to the restaurant for a fresh fish dinner.

The surveillance went on as planned, but nothing resulted from it. They were not aware that Ramiz had seen them the first day and immediately left. The compound was empty.

After three days of boredom and no results, Ryan called them all together. "I see no sense in continuing this effort. It's obvious they are not here and we are just wasting our time. What do the rest of you think?"

Corey spoke up first. "I have to agree. We don't know where they might be, but it isn't here, and I'm sure they aren't on Socotra or at the stronghold. I think we ought to go home and see if something else turns up."

Jasper nodded and said, "I have to agree. We're wasting our time here."

Tarik said, "I have to agree also. Tell you what. Why don't I continue with the surveillance for a few more days? You can all head home and I will keep you informed. I don't think anything will happen, but I'd like to cover it a little longer. Plus the surveillance couple can use the money. Just good for us for the future if we need them again."

Ryan agreed.

After several minutes of more conversation, airline reservations were made to begin the journey back home. At least they had managed to get Khatib and a couple of his men. The trip was successful.

Chapter Fifty-Seven

Monday—January 1
Northern Pacific/Washington, D.C.

Ryan, Jackie, Corey, and Jasper were all on their way back to Washington after their non-event in Salalah. After they left Salalah for the West Coast of the U.S., Corey had been paged while they were airborne and been sent a message that they were to go directly to Washington at the personal request of the president. A change of plans.

After making changes to their reservations in Los Angeles, they spent the night and continued on to the east coast. Just before leaving LAX, Ryan made a quick phone call to Juan and found that all was well at the marina. He was relieved, because he thought there just might be some retaliation by New Persia. But all was quiet and normal.

All four of them arrived at Dulles. Jackie and Ryan went to Jackie's apartment and Jasper and Corey headed downtown to the Ritz. They agreed to all meet at the Ritz for breakfast and then go over to the White House for whatever awaited them there. Jackie was quite upbeat, but Ryan wasn't so sure. He had gone against the president's wishes and didn't know how a meeting with Martinez might go. Corey was just glad to be able to see Maria again, and the normally cheerful Jasper was … just cheerful. He felt they had done an extraordinary job and was looking forward to presidential kudos. He wasn't worried.

Tuesday—January 2
Washington, D.C.

The following morning, they all met at the Ritz. After a good, solid American breakfast, and several Bloody Marys or mimosas, they departed via a Secret Service limousine for the White House. All had their clearances verified at security and they proceeded, with escorts, to the outer office near the Oval Office. Maria was waiting for them. She greeted each with a hug and, for Corey, a very demure kiss. She said, "The president will see you in fifteen minutes. He's getting a final CIA briefing on the current status and assessment of New Persia. Mark Allison wants to be present for this meeting also."

Ryan said, "Thank you. And thank you for making the arrangements at the Ritz and transportation this morning. It was very helpful." He hesitated a moment and then, looking at her shoulder, asked, "How's the shoulder now? Pretty well healed up?"

She was standing with her arm around Corey's waist. "It's much better, thank you. Still a bit sore, but some physical training has helped quite a bit. I'm not one hundred percent yet, but I'll get there."

"Good. I'm pleased to hear that."

Jackie came over and said, "Well, I'm glad too. Now all that would make it good in the world would be to find out where the remaining New Persia leadership is located and get them. We succeeded with Khatib and two others, but we still have Ramiz and the ayatollah to contend with."

Maria nodded and said, "I think that is one of the subjects the president wants to discuss with you. I don't know what he has in mind, but this whole New Persia thing really bothers him. And I don't blame him ... I mean, they almost got him personally."

Jasper commented, "Yeah, I suppose that would get my attention too. It will be interesting to see what they might have on their location."

Maria's intercom buzzed. She led them to the door to the Oval Office and opened it for all of them to file in. The president, with Mark and Jack Harrison, was standing in the rear center of the room and watched as they came in. They all circled the small coffee table that was in the center of the chairs. It was silent for a moment as they heard Maria quietly close the door.

Ryan and the president locked eyes. The president motioned for all of them to sit down. After they were comfortable, the president, looking at Ryan, said, "You will need to submit travel expenses for your little escapade to Oman and Socotra. Since you succeeded with at least one of our quarry, I'll make an exception in this case and cover you." Then he began to grin, looked around the room, and continued, "Now, I want to know how you succeeded. Our other efforts only partially got there."

There was a palpable air of relief in the room as they all realized the president was taking the situation easy and was just glad New Persia was now on the run.

Ryan relaxed, as did everyone else, and related what they had done. When he got to the Honda jet, the president stopped him. "How did you know they would try to escape that way?"

"When we were thinking about it after the meeting with the submarine, and realizing the SEALS were going to come in from the harbor area, there wasn't much else we could think of for Khatib to do. He could stay, but that would play into our hands; he couldn't go toward the harbor, because that was where the SEALS were coming from; so that just left the harbor at Hadibo ... and the obvious airport there. We assumed that they would have some form of aircraft available in case there was an invasion. So after thinking about it some more ... I knew about the munitions warehouse from our last trip, and the answer was obvious. We got the ARPMs and an RPG along with some smaller weapons, got back to the boat, and headed for the Hadibo harbor. It all just lined up for us."

The president, Jack, and Mark just nodded. Incredible story.

Corey added, "We were quite surprised when the *Jimmy Carter* showed up. But their 'request' to us to leave, and our basic understanding of the situation ... well, we knew what was about to happen and decided to put ourselves in a position to stop any escape by that route. And it all worked. The SEALS did a great job, but no one knew about that tunnel, the truck, and the escape road to the airport. Then when the SEALS got caught out in the open—and I can't fault that, they were in hot pursuit—we were ready to help out. It really paid off."

Jasper turned to the president and asked, "So, at this point, do we know where the other two are? Ramiz and the ayatollah?"

Mark said, "We are not a hundred percent certain, but we think they are both in China."

Jasper closed his eyes and thought a moment. "That would make a lot of sense. It would certainly explain why we haven't been able to locate them. Even with good satellite coverage, they could hide quite easily."

Mark just nodded.

The president added, "We are trying to verify that information and have been for some time now. But the Chinese are very familiar with our capabilities, much to our dismay, and can hide a person quite readily. And they are very difficult to crack with any on-site resources—spies, that is. They are just very tight."

Ryan said, "So, essentially, until they leave wherever they're at, we won't be able to get to them."

The president said, "I'm afraid you're quite right on that one. We have no choice." And with a pointed finger at Ryan, and a very large grin on his face, he added, "And don't you go getting any ideas on invading the Chinese naval port. This time I do want you to stay out of it ... got it?"

Ryan and the others shrugged as Ryan, also grinning, said, "Yes, sir. Got it. We'll stay out of it. I wouldn't know where to start with it anyway. At least on Socotra, we had some familiarity with the territory. But China? No way."

"Good. If we get any good info, I'll see to it that you are in on it. But no action without our say-so."

Ryan and the others nodded.

Maria interrupted: "Sir, you next appointment is waiting."

The president responded, "Another five minutes, Maria."

Then he turned to the group and said, "When I heard you were off on your little adventure, I was, to say the least, a bit upset. I kinda figured you might try something, especially when Jackie asked for the time off. But given the sequence of events, I cannot argue with the way things turned out. Especially that action on the Hadibo airport runway. Spectacular. So, the end justifies the means, or something like that. Thanks for the help and we'll be in touch. Oh, by the way, this fellow Tarik has been pulled off the Salalah compound. Nothing happening."

Then he turned to Corey and said with a smile, "Maria is quite a catch. But I would hope you leave her here with me for a while longer. She's too valuable to me."

Corey, with a surprised look, got slightly embarrassed and said, "Yes, sir. No plans for a move ... at least yet."

The president stood up, and they shook hands all around and left the Oval Office.

Chapter Fifty-Eight

Thursday—January 4
Zhanjiang, China

Ramiz arrived back in Zhanjiang after a long flight and immediately was transported to his quarters. He met that evening with the ayatollah in their small conference room. After some minor pleasantries, he began. He told the ayatollah about his experiences seeing Ryan's group around their small compound in Salalah. The ayatollah's shoulders slumped a bit at that news, for it meant he could not go back there, since the Americans had located it. Ramiz then continued.

"Ayatollah. I have been to Socotra and spent the weekend there. We still have people there. The Americans did not take any of our support people. They destroyed most of the facilities except for the residential buildings. The harbor is currently unusable, the hangars were destroyed, and the main operations center buildings are rubble. And finally, the two thirty-meter antennas are in pieces scattered around their bases. They cannot be repaired. Fortunately, *Persian Quest* was out on a training effort. She used Hadibo harbor to anchor, since our harbor was destroyed.

"And the information I have on the stronghold is not much better. The facilities were all destroyed and it will take some time to rebuild. But we only lost seven men in the attack and some of the training can continue."

The ayatollah just looked impassively at Ramiz as he explained the situation.

Ramiz continued, "Several of our people, the ones who worked directly for Marin and Ghanim, have continued their support and the food, and other services continue. I directed that they keep up with that effort until we can determine a future course of action. Until we can assess what we want to do, any effort at rebuilding right now may be a waste of time and resources."

Still no response from the ayatollah. Ramiz could tell he was listening because he was moving around a bit and watching Ramiz intently. Finally, the ayatollah said, "Thank you for what you have done. I'm sure we can rebuild, but it will take some time and a lot of support from our allies. Allah is really testing us. The loss of

337

Khatib, Marin, and Ghanim is very difficult to accept. I take it that you did not cause any actions that might draw the attention of the Americans."

"No. I purposely told our people there to not do anything special for me so my presence would not be noticed, and they didn't."

The ayatollah nodded slightly. "It is what it is." He hesitated for a moment. "Let me absorb the information for the rest of the day and we can talk some more later. I need to be in silence and prayer."

Ramiz nodded and said, "Certainly. I will spend the rest of today and tomorrow checking the status of meetings here." Ramiz then left the conference room and closed the door for the ayatollah.

Friday—January 12
Zhanjiang, China

The series of meetings were held and support changes, though mostly minor, were agreed to. An executive session was held between the ayatollah, Ramiz, and Captain Wang as the meetings wound down after two weeks. During the executive session, Ramiz requested a side meeting to include the operations ship's personnel and the submarine personnel. He also asked for a meeting to discuss potential future helicopter support. The ayatollah had considered suggestions by Ramiz on reconstruction and had agreed to their revised plan for rebuilding. Now Ramiz needed to discuss it with the Chinese Navy support personnel.

It might be a tough sell.

Ramiz briefed Captain Wang on the position New Persia wished the Chinese to take on support. He had already determined the need for helicopter patrols over the harbor area of the Socotra Operations Center. He wanted the Chinese to provide two helicopters and armed Z-20 utility patrol helicopters, along with maintenance and flight personnel. They would be stationed in the rebuilt helicopter facilities near the harbor and would set their own schedule of patrols. The exact schedule would depend on when the facilities could be activated after rebuilding was complete.

Captain Wang was a bit taken aback by the suggestion, since there had been no discussions of this helicopter support in the past. He looked at Ramiz and then over to the ayatollah. The ayatollah just looked back at him with a slight nod.

The ayatollah said, "Since the Americans have opted to use submarines for their incursion into our waters, and your satellites can't track them, we need some form of active defense against them striking again. We're going to rebuild and need to make sure this kind of attack cannot happen again. Especially without warning of any kind. We feel this type of support would help with that warning capability."

The captain, with an inscrutable look on his face, simply looked back at the ayatollah. He motioned for the ayatollah to continue. "And, from your perspective, it would provide you with a forward operating location very close to major shipping lanes. Everything that goes into, or out of, the Gulf of Aden, to include Suez Canal traffic, has to go past the Socotra Island chain. A modern version of the old desert forts controlling passes. While you may not need that type of control right now, you might want to have it if a world situation presents itself. And such a location would help counter the U.S. presence in Diego Garcia."

The captain nodded in thought. He waited a few moments and then said, "Yes. But that right is not yours to give. The Yemeni government would have to approve of such an arrangement, and both we and you do not have that right now."

"True. But I would think that your influence would be fairly substantial with the Yemenis, and they might be interested in such a proposal. After all, right now, those islands are considered worthless. Your operating location there would enhance their value considerably. And the world would quickly notice the strategic value of your presence."

Captain Wang's eyebrows went up at that suggestion. He hadn't thought of the position the ayatollah was proposing. His government had been concentrating for many years now on making the South China Sea a Chinese lake. This would be a change in strategic focus. He walked over to a map of the Southeast Asia subcontinent and moved it slightly to expose the Horn of Africa area. He saw the point. Even a small group of Chinese military personnel would have a disproportional impact on the area. And with the proper in-place facilities and capabilities, reinforcements could be expedited very quickly should the need arise. The ayatollah had a good point.

The captain said, "I see your point. And you, in turn, get the pre-attack warning you are looking for."

The ayatollah just nodded solemnly. He didn't say anything.

The captain, looking at Ramiz, said, "And your organization gets open Chinese support. The Americans would significantly hesitate to take any action against you if we were on the island. They would not wish to take a chance of a confrontation with us over such a minor, in their mind, criminal action."

Ramiz glanced at the map. "And that's the main reason it makes sense for us to rebuild there. Your forces, even though they would be relatively small, could patrol the entire entranceway to the Gulf of Aden. It would be a very noticeable presence. And you could also claim it was an effort to continue with the anti-pirate activities you already pursue." He stopped and looked back at the captain. "And yes. We would get the security we desire. It becomes a win-win situation, to use that western world idiom."

Captain Wang said, "This is too big for me to decide on my own. It will involve several other PLAN organizations, and, as you pointed out, would be a strategic shift for us. I will have to brief the idea to my superiors and see what happens. I do thank you for the thought. It is not something I have considered."

Ramiz nodded. "I expected as much. We are prepared to assist you in those briefings if you desire. While our facilities are rubble right now, I think we can have some minimal capability, including helicopter operating areas, in about six months."

The captain was deep in thought. He heard Ramiz and turned to him. "No. This is an internal briefing effort. The only request would be to have a copy of your slides so I can steal information"—he smiled slightly—"and combine it with some of our own internal information. Then we'll develop our own version for up-channel reviews." He stopped for a minute as he continued to think. "We have built several of the ports around the Arabian Sea but none that far down on the African Coast. This might just be another justification for expanding that effort."

He eyed Ramiz and said, "When can we get a copy of those slides?" He nodded at the screen in front of him.

Ramiz responded, "In a few minutes, if you have a copier that can accept our Microsoft software and a flash drive."

The captain looked over at a staffer. The young man jumped up, took the flash drive from Ramiz, and disappeared through a side door. Ramiz followed him with his eyes as he disappeared, then turned back to the captain.

"How long would it take to get a decision on our proposal?"

The captain said, "That depends. It has some serious political ramifications and could take some time to see it through all the bureaucracies. It certainly won't be this month or even the next."

Ramiz said, "Then would it be possible to have an exercise in our area involving helicopters using temporary or field quarters? That way you could test the various patrol routes. If there are problems with either the facilities or the routes, we could be resolving them while the reviews are progressing."

"Yes. We could do that. But only with the permission of the Yemeni government. We would be conducting those activities on their territory and they would need to approve it. But it certainly could be pursued."

The ayatollah interrupted, "I think that would be a good interim solution and should be pursued. Can you do that? Get permission, I mean."

"Again, we can try, and I will process a request up our command channel." The captain stopped for a moment, put his finger in the air, and said, "But there may be a better way to get the immediate coverage you are looking for. You want to be aware of any American submarine activity in your harbor area, right?" Both men nodded. "Then I would suggest you have hydrophones installed in an arc around the harbor at some suitable distance."

The ayatollah asked, "What are hydrophones?"

"They are underwater listening devices and can pick up very faint sounds from ships and even submerged vessels. They also pick up marine animal life, called biologics, but that can be sorted out. And they have the advantage of being installable without the Americans knowing about it. They could be monitored inside your control center and then you would be able to detect any submarine coming into your immediate harbor area. If you did that, along with a helicopter exercise, you would really be sending a message to the Americans. That message would be 'stay away.'"

Ramiz began smiling. They had taken note of the captain's comment about not getting a decision soon. The hydrophones and an exercise could solve that scheduling problem. The hydrophones, especially, since they did not require any permission from the Yemenis.

Ramiz said, "I think that would be a splendid idea. It would alleviate our concerns for the ayatollah's safety. And, I might add, our own also."

The captain looked at both men, nodded, and folded his hands on the table in front of himself. He looked down at his hands briefly and said, "The rest of the support issues are, as I understand it, pretty much resolved given the schedule changes driven by the American ... intrusion. There is one more issue I need to address with you."

The ayatollah and Ramiz were both paying close attention. They had no idea what he was about to say.

341

"You have requested a replacement for the sailing vessel, *Persian Desert*, which was captured in Alaskan waters. We cannot do that. Those sailing vessels were an experiment and there are no more planned to be built. However, understanding your need for a replacement, and the fact that you are pulling the Americans' tail, so to speak, we have retrofitted the *Persian Wind* for your use. It is one of the so-called yachts that you had before and was replaced by the now captured *Persian Desert* in Alaska. Its capabilities are not diminished—in fact, we have added slightly more powerful turbines in it—and it should serve you well."

Ramiz sat there for a moment, taking in what the captain had said. He had thought about the sailing vessels before and that they had some limitations he didn't care for. They weren't as fast nor were they as maneuverable as the yachts. And they did stand out in people's memories, since they were so unique. Not necessarily a good thing when you were trying to maintain a low profile with the ayatollah's location.

Ramiz's thoughts returned to the present. He asked, "I don't think that would be a problem. We have crews trained, and a little refresher would be all that we would need to go operational with them again." Out of the corner of his eye he could see the ayatollah nodding in agreement. He continued, "But I have a question on the hydrophones. How long would it take to get them operational?"

The captain looked pleased with Ramiz's comments. He said, "Good. The yacht will be fine. As for the hydrophones, it will take a few weeks. I have to task my engineering people to survey the harbor and the outlying subsurface to determine the best placement of the hydrophones. Then, after we determine the optimal placement, it will take several weeks to install them. And there is some monitoring equipment that has to be installed in your center. While that is all going on, we could be training your operations center personnel."

Ramiz, looking at the captain, nodded in agreement. It would be an ideal answer to their problem and could be done fairly quickly. "I think that would be a very smart thing to do. What you are telling us is that it would probably be four to six weeks before we could be operational ... and that would be if your people could jump on it right away. But, in the meantime, we have the problem of securing the ayatollah's safety. It has now been almost three weeks since we got here, and our stay was planned for three weeks. Can that be extended, at least for the ayatollah? I can head back on my own, since I have a lot of other tasks to perform, especially with the death of Khatib."

Elusive Quarry

The captain rapidly looked at both men, then back at his hands on the table, then back at the ayatollah. He said, "I will put in a request to extend your stay for another three weeks. Since"—he looked knowingly at the ayatollah—"we have some additional, unforeseen, discussions to finish our business, especially in light of the destruction you have suffered. I will bring this effort up in our list of priorities. That should move things along well. After the three weeks are finished, we can re-evaluate where we are and make a decision at that point. Would that be satisfactory to you?"

The ayatollah and Ramiz both said, "Yes."

The captain then turned in his chair slightly, looking at both of them from a slight angle, and said with great seriousness, "We have been at this for the past three weeks and have, I think, met the goals of our meeting. Before you arrived, I received direction to make sure you have the support you need so we, as a country, will have an energy source in the future. I am not at a level where I am aware of what arrangements exist for future support of our economy, but I am convinced that our support will meet your needs both now and in the future."

The ayatollah took the lead in answering. "Yes. I concur with your assessment and thank you, again, for the support. The three weeks you referred to would work out well for us. I would like, as the time goes by, to monitor the implementation of our plans, and it would be good to do that here. Plus the Americans cannot track my progress, and that is, from my perspective, very positive."

The captain then stood up, bowed slightly, and said, "Then I bid you a good day and wish you a pleasant evening." He turned and left the room with several of his staff people following.

Monday—January 15
Schriever AFB, Colorado

Lieutenant Thompson, sitting at her monitoring console in the 50th Space Wing complex at Schriever AFB, was puzzled. She had read through the various reports covering the past full month of activities in their tracking of the ayatollah and his immediate staff. It had been several weeks now since they had seen any of them. The coverage over the stronghold, Salalah, and Socotra had been constant, but there was no indication of their location. After the SEAL raid and the destruction of the operations center, that they were able to watch, and the death of Khatib, there had been very little activity on Socotra. There wasn't any sign of support people showing deference to anything or anyone. The wing commander was

343

concerned and had been for a while. They both had the same question. Where had they gone?

Colonel McMichaels called for a discussion in his office. Lieutenant Thompson and Captain Carver hiked down the hallway to the commander's office and waited as the secretary checked with Colonel McMichaels. They were shortly admitted into the inner sanctum of a wing commander's office. They were informally invited to sit down by a motion of the colonel's hands.

Colonel McMichaels began, "We haven't seen any sign of these two characters in close to three weeks now since the raid where Khatib was killed. What can we do to track them down? I'm getting quite concerned that they are up to no good and we need to find them."

Captain Carver said, "It's like looking for the proverbial needle in a haystack. We lost him somewhere along the line and haven't been able to pick him up ... or the other one with him. I don't think they are at any of the three locations. I suspect he's out drumming up support somewhere, but there's no way to tell where. It's quite frustrating."

Lieutenant Thompson added, "The last we actually saw of the ayatollah was leaving the stronghold in a supply vehicle. And that was several weeks ago. There just haven't been any indications of his location since then."

The colonel said, "Okay. We have full satellite coverage over the three sites and can't locate any of them. So they've disappeared somewhere."

Both the captain and lieutenant just nodded in agreement.

"So," continued the colonel, "how do we locate him? Do you have any suggestions?"

The captain looked at Lieutenant Thompson for a moment and then back to the colonel. "Yes, sir. I do have a suggestion, but I don't know how viable it might be."

"Go ahead and suggest. We don't have any answers yet."

Captain Carver hesitated for a moment and then said, "I think we need to bring in the CIA and see if they can figure anything out. They have all these assets in foreign countries and may be able to tell where he is and what he's doing. But I don't know how to go about doing that." He looked questioningly at Colonel McMichaels.

The colonel just looked thoughtfully back. He finally said, "I don't know either, but I think you may have a good point. It sounds like we need some help." He looked out the window at the eastern Colorado plains stretching into the distance toward Kansas. He looked back and continued, "I'm going to request, through Space

Command, that CIA assistance be obtained to find this ayatollah. I'm not sure how it might all turn out, but the bigwigs have been asking about him. Now let's see how they react to this type of request. The CIA is outside the military and we can't control the outcome. But I think the benefits outweigh any negatives. We can at least try."

The colonel got up from behind his desk and the two young officers departed the office. He walked over to the window and looked out at the cold, wintery landscape. The snow covering the ground was blowing around in the constant wind that was a trademark feature on the western plains. It was pretty in its own way, but really cold. He thought for a few more minutes, went back to his desk, and composed a message to forward to Space Command suggesting that the CIA be contacted for assistance in locating the ayatollah. He didn't know what kind of response he might get, but felt that some action would be better than sitting on his hands.

Tuesday—January 16
Zhanjiang, China

Ramiz made an additional request to visit with the submarine development people in the PLAN. During several meetings and explanations of his previously requested sub actions close to a year ago, he met with several of the design engineers. Changes to the mini-submarine design had resulted from his request, and he finished his tasks and reviews with them. While it had delayed the final construction details of the next mini, it was now ninety-eight percent complete, only needing a final internal fitting, and Ramiz felt it was worth the time and effort.

Ramiz, a few days later, left the ayatollah behind and flew back to Muscat. Ramiz did some additional minor engineering work in Muscat and forwarded the information back to the mini-sub designers. Then he had other matters to attend to working on the rebuilding of Socotra and the stronghold.

Tuesday—January 16
Schriever AFB, Colorado

Colonel McMichaels was concerned. They hadn't been able to track down the whereabouts of the ayatollah. All three of the usual haunts were quiet. He thought about it for several minutes, trying to place himself in the ayatollah's shoes. What would he do and where would he go? After a few minutes, he gave up. He just didn't have enough information to even guess at it.

He walked back to his desk and began reading some reports turned in by the various satellite monitoring units in the 50th Space Wing. His attention was really piqued when he came across a short note. Their weekly surveillance of the Chinese naval complex at Zhanjiang had revealed the presence of a large yacht-like vessel. While it had been moved into a hangar-like facility over the water, the satellite had still been able to get photos of it as it was being moved. While he couldn't be certain, Colonel McMichaels, looking at the photos, thought he had seen one of these vessels before. But he couldn't place it.

After thinking about it for a few minutes, he called in his vice commander, Colonel Mason and showed him the photos. Colonel Mason said, "Yes, sir. That looks just like the ship we covered that was captured by our Coast Guard last year in Alaskan waters. It was a New Persia asset at the time."

"You're right. That where I remember it from. The New Persia group had set bombs on the Alaskan pipeline from that type of yacht."

Colonel Mason just nodded.

Colonel McMichaels added, "I wonder what they are up to now?" He looked at the photos again and finally came to a conclusion. He winked at Colonel Mason, smiled, and said, "You know what? We may have just discovered something. Since those yacht-like boats were used by New Persia in Alaska and down in the Gulf of Mexico, I'll just bet the Chinese are getting ready to turn another one over to the ayatollah. And if I were the ayatollah, with the two recent strikes on my facilities, the stronghold and the operations center on Socotra, I'd be hiding out where we can't see much. And that could very well be the Chinese port where they're fixing up a boat for him."

Colonel Mason added, "That would certainly make a lot of sense. The Chinese have been helping him all along, and they would be an excellent hiding location for him. It would certainly explain why we haven't been able to find him."

Colonel McMichaels said, "Let's spend some monitoring time over that port and see if we can find anything of interest ... like this fellow Ramiz or the ayatollah."

Colonel Mason nodded. "Can do. I'll set it up and we'll see what we can see. It will take a day or two to move an asset, but in a few days we should begin coverage." He departed the office and headed down the hall to one of the satellite control offices.

Colonel McMichaels sat down and drafted up a message to forward to Space Command headquarters, detailing what they had found and what their suspicious were. He was sure it would draw quite a bit of attention, given the recent New Persia European activities and the attempt on the president's life in Bahrain.

He was correct. When his note reached Space Command headquarters, it was immediately forwarded to the Pentagon and briefed to General Foley and General Fairchild. They, in turn, passed the information on to Jack Harrison who told the president. They, hopefully, would be able to confirm the ayatollah's whereabouts in China in a few days.

Colonel McMichaels realized that if they were correct, they might not need to ask for CIA assistance. He called the commander's office at Space Command and spoke with the general's aide. It turned out that they had not taken action yet on his CIA request. They agreed to table the request and see what happened with the potential Chinese connection.

Friday—January 19
Zhanjiang, China

Ramiz met with several of the naval support personnel and received familiarization briefs from them on the capabilities and changes that had been incorporated in the *Persian Wind*. The New Persia crew had arrived and were also getting training on the changes. Kadar was buried up to his neck in the details. He was very much a detail-oriented person and knew every aspect of the ship's operation. The current plans called for them to take her out on a shakedown cruise for several days, and then, after any problems were resolved, to head back to Socotra. Since the New Persia harbor was still not useable, they would anchor off shore at the capital of Socotra, Hadibo, until the harbor was cleared and able to support *Persian Wind*.

The ayatollah would stay in China until the following month, when the new mini-sub would be ready for pick-up. Then the *Persian Wind* would return and be fitted out for the mini and then leave again for Socotra. This time, the ayatollah and Ramiz would both be on board for the trip.

Chapter Fifty-Nine

Thursday—February 1
Freeport, Texas—Ryan's Marina

Ryan had been periodically in touch with Jack, and received short briefing notes as time went by. But not much was happening. He knew from personal visits and discussions with Jackie that it appeared they had located the ayatollah in China. But that meant they couldn't get to the ayatollah. He was frustrated with that development, because he wanted to stop looking over his shoulder waiting for the next shoe to drop on him. Uncomfortable.

Thursday—February 15
Zhanjiang, China

Persian Wind had docked and been modified slightly to accept the new mini-sub. The various sea trials were over and New Persia was taking the mini-sub and returning to Socotra. Ramiz and the ayatollah were now aboard and Kadar was making final checks before departing the safe Chinese harbor. The ayatollah had been in Zhanjiang for several months now, and was anxious to get back to Socotra and his Allah-given mission requirements.

As they gathered on the dock, Admiral Chang came down and visited them for their send-off. He wished them well with their mission and hoped the new support program would meet their needs.

The ayatollah was very uncomfortable with all the attention. He knew that the Americans might catch him in the open, or have their suspicions based on the admiral's presence. But he could do little about it. Ramiz saw the concern but they were at the mercy of the Chinese and, politically, had to go along.

After receiving the well-wishers, they waited until the Chinese military and staff left the *Persian Wind*, and Kadar then started to back away from the dock. As usual, it was a slow process, and they began to make their way out of the harbor. A pleasant day was before them and they hoped to be back in Socotra within a week or so. All was going according to plan.

Elusive Quarry

Thursday—February 15
Schriever AFB, Colorado

In the distant sky overhead, the constantly staring satellite recorded the activity and sent it back to the monitoring station in Colorado. At the 50th Space Wing, the human military monitors were watching with interest. They had waited for some time for this event and now their suspicions had been confirmed. It was the ayatollah and he was getting a lot of attention. Reports were forwarded to the Pentagon and over to the White House. They had finally found the man they had been looking for. And he was going to sea. He could be intercepted once his ship got into open international waters.

Thursday—February 22
Northern Indian Ocean

The *Persian Wind* was westbound in the Northern Indian Ocean on her way back to the partially rebuilt operations center on Socotra. The ayatollah and Ramiz were aboard after a trip to the Chinese port, where they had picked up the latest version of a newly built mini-submarine. As before, it was fitted to the internal moon bay structure and was not visible when they were underway. After watching and, in some manner, participating in the sea trials of the mini, they had departed the previous week and were anticipating a smooth voyage back home. Ramiz was pleased with the modifications he had insisted on for the new mini and was happy with the trial results. It was a very capable machine.

The *Persian Wind* was running very well with her twin turbines whining smoothly in concert. It was proving to be a quiet and uneventful crossing of the Northern Indian Ocean. The large yacht-appearing *Persian Wind* was to be home-berthed in the partially restored harbor at the New Persian center headquarters on Socotra, and was a marvel of Chinese nautical engineering. Over two hundred and fifty feet long, she was capable of close to ninety knots with her hydrofoils deployed. Extremely fast for a ship of her size. Intentionally painted a medium dark grey, she was also very difficult to see.

The ayatollah and Ramiz were in the conference room discussing the next series of moves against the western powers who had been ignoring the New Persia list of demands for reducing oil usage. The ayatollah was still adamant that the west reduce their use of oil, and was using various forceful methods to get compliance.

349

So far, their attempts had not worked, and he was getting quite frustrated with the lack of progress.

They were in deep discussion over planned attacks on U.S. and European oil infrastructure and political targets. Kadar came into the room suddenly and said, "We must get you to the mini-sub right away."

The ayatollah looked startled and asked, "Why? What has happened?"

Kadar responded, "An American submarine has just surfaced nearby and is insisting on boarding us. They say we have an international criminal on board and will be arresting him. They identified you as that individual. They mean to take you off the ship and return you to prison in the U.S. The only way to get away from them is on the mini. At least you will have some chance that way. To stay aboard is to give up. And I don't think you want to do that."

The ayatollah looked at Ramiz and asked, "Do you concur? Is there any other course of action we could take? Can we outrun them?"

Ramiz looked at Kadar and then over to the ayatollah. "No, sir. I see no other course but to try and flee in the mini-sub. We can outrun them. Their submarine can do close to fifty knots underwater and we can do, maximum, nearly ninety knots on the surface. And that's maximum, using the turbines full out. They couldn't overtake us, but, if they wished, they could sink us with torpedoes or an anti-ship missile."

The ayatollah nodded. He obviously did not want to take the action to flee his vessel. But he also did not want to go to the supermax facility in Colorado.

Ramiz knew what he was thinking. "Let's go. We have no option."

The ayatollah stood up. Looking around the room, he said, "Ramiz, I want you to come with me. You are too valuable to fall into the hands of the Americans. You know the engineering details of that sub, how to run it, and there is room, as I understand it, for four to six people. Kadar is very capable and can handle the Americans."

"Yes, sir," said Ramiz. "There is room for both of us."

"Fine. Then we'd better get going."

They headed down to the moon pool where the mini-sub was located. The ayatollah climbed through the top hatch and took a place in one of the rear positions. He had no idea how it operated or what else to do. Ramiz and the mini-sub operator followed. The mini-sub operator did some quick routine checks as the *Persian*

Wind slowed down to comply with the U.S. submarine's demands to stop. Captain Kadar, using the turbines, turned the *Persian Wind* slightly so it was parallel to the submarine. He hoped the maneuver would cause enough noise and turbulence to partially or completely hide the mini-sub's departure. Ramiz took the controls and launched into the water as the U.S. submarine began sending a party of boarders over to the *Persian Wind*. To create a further diversion, as the U.S. boarding party approached, several New Persia crewmen fired small weapons in the air in the direction of the boarding craft. Initially the boarding craft broke off and backed off for several minutes, during which the mini-sub departed almost straight down into the waters of the Indian Ocean. Then the boarding craft headed back in toward the yacht with weapons in plain sight and ready to fire. But the diversion had been accomplished.

On board the *SSN North Carolina*, Commander Rich Luce was anxiously watching the action unfold. Through a recent highly classified message, he had been told to look out for this particular yacht or warship, whatever it was, because it might have an international criminal, the Ayatollah Sarhardi, aboard.

On a routine patrol in the Northern Indian Ocean, he had not expected this turn of events. But they had come across an unusual sound as they patrolled. A sound they did not recognize and one that was not in their sonic database of vessels. They rose near the surface and observed, through the photonics systems aboard, a vessel that was quite remarkable and making very good time. Probably close to forty knots. Following it for a short time, while maintaining a submerged presence, they realized that its current course would probably take it to the islands of Socotra. They knew who it was. Commander Luce's instructions had been quite clear. If he came across the vessel, he was to stop it, board it, and arrest the ayatollah. And he could use any force, including deadly force, necessary to achieve that end.

They would worry about the international consequences of their actions later through the State Department. The man they were after had escaped, with significant loss of life, as he was being transported to the supermax prison in Florence, Colorado. He had been the inspiration for the near downing of Air Force One in Bahrain. He was dangerous and to be apprehended and returned to federal authorities. If he could not be apprehended, he was to be eliminated. Very clear instructions. The bottom line was: get him or kill him.

Continuing to follow the vessel for over an hour, they sent off a message to COMSUBPAC in Hawaii of their discovery. As they waited for a reply, they began to prepare for surfacing and boarding of the yacht. Marines, carried on board for just this purpose, began to ready themselves and their equipment for the potential dangerous seaborne assault. After just a few minutes, they were surprised to get a response back from COMSUBPAC directing the immediate boarding and arrest action.

With that direction, Commander Luce directed the exec to prepare to surface and conduct a stop-and-board action. The marine commander, the young Captain Janis, listened as the commands were given for surfacing. After they were on the surface and the commander was communicating with the vessel, the captain headed to his men in the forward part of the submarine.

As they waited, they saw the yacht, men busy on the large deck, begin to slow down. She was responding to the communications sent by Commander Luce to either stop and prepare to be boarded, or be sunk. He further explained that they had orders to capture the ayatollah and return him to the U.S. The yacht had stopped and the marines headed out for the port side. They had already deployed a small skiff, and ten fully armed and combat-capable men were ready to go. They were doing what they had practiced many times over in the recent past. This was for real and they were really keyed up. As they approached the vessel, they could see several of the crewmen suddenly appear on the side, weapons raised, and threatening. Several shots had been fired.

Captain Kadar, on the *Persian Wind,* radioed back to the *North Carolina* that he had instructions to resist any boarding and for the armed party to return to the submarine or they would come under fire from his men. The *North Carolina* notified Captain Janis of the situation and he backed off for several minutes as the *North Carolina* considered her options.

As they were considering their next action, they watched as the yacht slowly turned in the water. She became broadside to the submarine and the marines still in the skiff in the water. Several crew members were visible on the deck still brandishing their weapons.

The moon-pool doors had closed as they left the *Persian Wind*. Ramiz headed for deeper water and quickly passed two hundred feet and was still heading down. He turned to the ayatollah and said, "We are going down a little farther and then wait to see what happens to the *Persian Wind*. If we can, we will stay in the area until the infidels have left. If not, we will continue to escape to the west. Fortunately, we are only a few hundred miles from Socotra and can be there in a few days."

The ayatollah just nodded. He didn't know much about what was really going on or what might result from their departure.

The *SSN North Carolina's* sonics operator, listening closely to the action on the yacht, heard the turbulence caused by the churning turbine-driven shafts and propellers as the vessel turned slightly. The noise, and their relative closeness to the sailing vessel, masked the slight sound of the diving mini-sub. He didn't hear the departure of the ayatollah and party.

Commander Luce was in a quandary. If he tried to board, there could be a firefight, with possible loss of some of his men. If he didn't board, the criminal could escape and his mission would fail. COMSUBPAC had directed the boarding action and would expect him to succeed. He looked at his exec. Both were puzzled over the next action to take. He turned to the weapons officer and said, "Prepare a Mark 48 Torpedo in tube one, run at just three feet, open outer doors, and be prepared to fire. Solution on the yacht." Weaps looked back for just a moment then gave the directions over the intercom to the forward torpedo room. After a short period, the forward torpedo doors were open and ready to fire.

Commander Luce then notified Captain Kadar that he was about to open fire with a torpedo unless he stood down his forces and prepared for boarding. Commander Luce had made the decision to either sink the vessel or board her. One or the other. He had his orders and he would carry them out. The decision was now in the yacht captain's court. The captain had two minutes to decide.

Captain Kadar turned red when informed of the American ultimatum. He considered this to be a form of piracy on the high seas. He looked at his first mate. He said, "Has the sub departed yet?"

"Yes, sir. It is gone and clear of our hull. Should be a mile or two away by now, moving ultra-quietly and with some recorded biologics being used."

Kadar thought for a moment. "Good. Good. They got away. Now we can be very insulted and angry about this act of piracy. Communicate back to the Americans that we will cooperate. Have the men stand down and put their weapons away. Use the turbines to turn ninety degrees. I want some noise in the water to continue to hide the mini's movements. Lower a boarding ladder for the

American infidels, and don't be quiet about it. We have accomplished our mission. They have failed in theirs. They just don't know it yet."

The first mate hurried off to pass the word to his men.

Commander Luce breathed a sigh of relief. The yacht, after that threat, was cooperating. He notified Captain Janis to go ahead with the boarding process, capture the ayatollah, and return him to the *North Carolina*.

The sonics operator was still monitoring the action from his station. Passive sonar was not picking up any information other than known biologics (from a recording on the mini), the noises from the boarding party, and turbine and shaft sounds as the yacht maneuvered slightly. Nothing unusual.

Captain Janis approached the side of the yacht where a boarding ladder had been dropped. With weapons ready to fire in case of an ambush, he and his ten men quickly boarded the large vessel. Each of the *Persian Wind* crewmen made a show of being unarmed, and cooperated with the directions from the Americans. Captain Kadar waited on the bridge as the U.S. marine approached.

Captain Kadar said, "Why have you stopped and boarded us? This is an act of piracy and we object in the strongest possible terms."

Captain Janis responded, "We have reason to believe that you have a criminal on board. We already told you that when we first stopped you. Now, where is he?"

"We have no such person on board. Search if you must, but whoever you are looking for is not here. It is just me and my men on board."

Captain Janis looked around and directed his men to search the entire ship to look for the ayatollah. They had a picture of him transmitted from COMSUBPAC, taken during his trial in the U.S., and began an intensive search. They finished the quick look at the ship's crew and did not find the ayatollah or any of his immediate staff. Just the sailing crew was on board. The marines had found the moon pool where the mini had been located, and some information on launch and recovery procedures for the mini. The stanchion that held it in place was empty. The mini was gone. The doors were closed. Captain Janis turned to Captain Kadar, looked at him briefly, then looked up at the ceiling in disgust. "Where's the rest of your equipment? There is obviously something missing from there." And he pointed at the empty mini support structure.

Captain Kadar just shrugged. "I don't know what you're talking about. It is as it was."

Captain Janis keyed his shoulder mike and said, "Mother, chick. No ayatollah. Suspect a mini-sub departed while we were occupied. There's an empty moon pool here."

Commander Luce said, "Roger. Complete your investigation and return to ship."

Commander Luce turned to the exec and said, "Have weaps stand down the forward torpedo station and close the outer doors. See if sonics has anything. Play back the last two hours of recordings and see if we missed something. And check our video when we were tracking the yacht."

The exec nodded in response and went off to accomplish the tasking.

In the semidarkness of the mini-sub, lit up only by some of the sub's instrumentation, Ramiz turned to the ayatollah. "We are cruising at three hundred feet and running very quietly right now. I think we need to stay within ten miles or so of the *Persian Wind*, wait for an hour or so, and then sneak back toward them. Then determine what we want to do."

The ayatollah nodded in agreement. "What if they discover us? What do we do then? At this point, hopefully, they don't know where we are."

"We have a very small profile and I don't think that will be a problem. If they do find us, we will move slowly away, with junk and debris clogging their sensors."

Twenty minutes later, the exec came back. She said, "We found it. Very faint; we had to do some computer enhancements to it, but we found it. As they turned with their turbines and prop shafts churning, there was a very faint thruster sound. We did a cross-check of known submersibles and found it matched a Chinese-built mini-sub launched several months ago. It's actually a fairly shallow mini. Our data indicates that it runs at five hundred feet with a crush depth of just over seven hundred. After launch, it disappeared. It's out there."

The commander nodded. "Any idea which way it went?"

"Working on it, but nothing so far. They can't have gotten too far yet. Running super quiet like that means you don't move fast. We're thinking of going active with a ping and see if anything turns up."

"Okay. Do it and let me know when you get something."

A few moments later, a loud ping resounded around the submarine as the active sonar was initiated.

They were still cruising at three hundred feet and moving slowly away from the *Persian Wind,* still a good five miles away. All had been quiet and they were all absorbed in their own thoughts. In the darkness of that depth, contemplation came easily.

Once they got out of this particular situation, mused the ayatollah, he would have to make sure the infidels began to toe the line. So far there had been relatively small incidents around the world where they had created problems for the western nations. He needed to increase the intensity and broaden the impacts of his actions. His increasing population of fighters, centered in his Iranian stronghold training area, could be used much more effectively. Even though the stronghold had been destroyed again, his personnel there had managed to continue with their training. More recruits were coming in all the time, but he now had a good-sized cadre of trained fighters available. He would strike back in terms the infidels could readily understand.

The quiet was suddenly interrupted by an earsplitting sound that reverberated off the mini-sub hull. All three of them covered their ears in a hasty move to deaden the sound. Dhakwan, the mini-sub operator, did a quick check of his instruments and found nothing wrong. The mini was equipped with a sonar-deadening coating as part of its defenses, but they weren't sure it would be effective. Ramiz looked at Dhakwan and shook his head rapidly. They began an immediate dive and increased speed as they tried to escape what they knew had just happened. Ramiz increased the dive angle and quickly went through five hundred feet.

"Commander, we've got him!" exclaimed the sonar supervisor. "He's only about nine thousand yards out and making a sudden move diving."

Commander Luce came over to the sonar station and began watching. "Keep on top of him. I don't want to lose him."

The supervisor nodded his understanding and continued to watch the sonar operator track the running mini. He said, "Hit him again and focus the beam right at him. Let him know we have him."

The sonar operator triggered another ping and watched as the mini continued its dive. The commander called the exec over. "What did you say about that mini's crush depth?"

"Sir, our data indicates that she can't go below about seven hundred feet. Below that, the pressure is just too great, and that can will implode." She stopped for just a second as she watched the sonar display. "And ... that's ... usually ... fatal."

Ramiz continued the dive. The operator was getting nervous as they went through six hundred feet. But Ramiz didn't hesitate. He reached back into a small case he carried and pulled out a flash drive. He inserted it into the external communications port and began to power up the small external communications computer. After several moments, the computer indicated the system was ready and available. He continued the dive. They went through seven hundred feet. He executed a program on the computer.

The sonar operator, overhearing the discussion on the crush depth, couldn't believe what he was seeing on the display. The mini had gone through seven hundred feet and was still going down!

As he watched, over his headset he heard a tremendous *whump* sound, and his display suddenly showed several different returns where the mini had been. Some parts were going up and some were going further down, some fairly fast. All signs of a breakup. The mini had imploded as they watched. The commander, the exec, and the supervisor all looked in dismay and awe at the display. They had just seen the mini destroyed. And whoever was in that mini-submarine had just died.

The commander turned to the exec and said, "Make a copy of that recording so we can send it off to COMSUBPAC. I don't want to take a chance that someone there doesn't believe us. We just witnessed a multiple murder/suicide and need to be able to prove it. What a tragedy."

Commander Luce then, after pausing for a moment, turned to the helm and gave directions. He turned to his exec and said, "Let's take a quick look and see if there is anything that we can see." The exec nodded, gave directions to the helm and they closed in on the remains of the mini-sub. After a few moments, using their sensors and ultra-strong LED lights, they could see that the mini had fatal cracks in the view ports and was just barely moving, rocking really, in the slight current. It was on its side on a seafloor mount, and basically stationary surrounded by disturbed sediment. There was no sign of life aboard. They cruised over the site several times, taking video of the wreckage for their reporting.

Realizing that there was nothing they could do at the one thousand foot depth, Commander Luce directed the helm and a few moments later the submarine banked slightly in the water, changed course, and came up to normal patrol cruise speed back to the location of the *Persian Wind.*

The exec turned away from the commander and worked with the sonics supervisor to make sure the recording, that was made routinely, was copied to a flash drive along with the digital video of the sunken mini-sub. She then composed a message for COMSUBPAC telling them what had happened and attached a digital file of the recording for their analysis and confirmation.

An international criminal and a couple of his staff had just been eliminated.

Listening in to their own sonar, the *Persian Wind* technical operators heard the unmistakable sound of the breakup of the mini-sub. They were on the bridge and Kadar was listening. He understood the meaning of the sounds. Dreadful sounds of screeching metal and loosened air rapidly floating to the surface. The breakup was unmistakable. And the people on board the mini-submarine were no longer alive. Death would have been instant at that depth and pressure.

Kadar looked off in the distance as a silence permeated the bridge. They were alone now on the Indian Ocean. It appeared the infidels had just had a major victory, and he had not been prepared for it. He was worn and disheartened.

The *North Carolina* surfaced near the *Persian Wind* and raised the yacht on guard channel. Commander Luce said to Kadar, "It would appear that your mini-sub has imploded and sunk. We're sorry about this outcome. We had hoped for a different ending for your ayatollah."

Kadar, both incensed and discouraged, responded, "It was not what we thought would happen. The ayatollah and Ramiz will be missed greatly, and the future generations of New Persia will suffer their loss. Now, please leave us to our grief."

Commander Luce acknowledged their request over the radio, reviewed the message to COMSUBPAC, modified it slightly to add Ramiz's name, and directed it be sent off.

Thursday—February 22
COMSUBPAC Headquarters, Pearl Harbor, Hawaii

COMSUBPAC received the message from the *SSN North Carolina* and, after reviewing the message and recordings with some disbelief, forwarded it to the CNO office in the Pentagon. Admiral Nelson then sent a quick note over to the White House informing Jack Harrison and the president of the apparent demise of the ayatollah and a person named Ramiz.

Friday—February 23
Washington, D.C.

The president, hearing the news, looked out his window in thought. They had killed five of the senior New Persia leaders. He shook his head in wonder at what had transpired. There was just no way to predict what people might do. The ayatollah had said he wouldn't go back to the American prison. He obviously meant it.

Word spread quickly through the White House staff. Jackie heard it within a few minutes, asked the president if it was true, and he confirmed it. The ayatollah was apparently dead, along with Ramiz.

Jackie quickly called Ryan with the news. "Ryan, the ayatollah and Ramiz are dead! They were in a mini-sub that imploded in the ocean."

Ryan stood there ... stunned. The long problem was over. A feeling of relief and peace washed over him. "Thank you for the call. I think we can all breathe easier now. Love you, and I expect to see you this evening."

"On my way in another hour. Love you too, and I'll see you later."

A chapter in American history was thus closed.

Friday—February 23
Zhanjiang, China

Admiral Chang read the transcripts from the intercepts of the American satellite transmissions from the submarine to its headquarters in Hawaii. He thought it over and called in his top marine engineer, Liu.

A few moments later Liu showed up and respectfully enter the admiral's office, bowed, and sat down as the admiral came around his desk to join him at the small table.

Admiral Chang said, "We have intercepted a message from an American submarine that states they have witnessed the destruction of our latest mini-submarine that was provided to the New Persia movement. The message states that the submarine went to such a depth, beyond the seven-hundred-foot crush depth, that it imploded. Were the modifications requested by Ramiz implemented?"

Liu responded, "Yes, Admiral Chang. All of the modifications he requested were made a part of the design." Liu stopped for a moment, then added, "The actual crush depth was increased significantly and was tested to four hundred meters, or over twelve hundred feet. And Ramiz knew that. He was there for the testing. However, the configuration documentation was kept highly classified and, as far as the rest of the world knows, the crush depth was still seven hundred feet. The Americans do not know the real crush depth. The data they have is not accurate."

"Hmmm. Okay. Thank you, Liu." With the apparent dismissal, Liu left the office in a puzzled state of mind.

Admiral Chang stood up and walked to his window overlooking the naval shipyard. His mind had taken in all the information. He processed it several times ... and he came to an inescapable conclusion.

He smiled slightly.

The author, Richard W. Barton, lives in Colorado with his family. A retired member of the US Air Force, and also retired from a major aerospace company, he spends his time on the golf course and climbing the trails and mountains of his adopted state. He can be reached via email at bartonrw1@gmail.com

Other Books by Richard W. Barton

- o **DiVersion**

- o **Relentless Target**